THE SWORD
IS FORGED

OTHER BOOKS BY EVANGELINE WALTON

THE SWORD IS FORGED

by
Evangeline Walton

———— TIMESCAPE BOOKS
Distributed by Simon and Schuster
New York

Copyright © 1983 by Evangeline Walton

All rights reserved
including the right of reproduction
in whole or in part in any form
A Timescape Book
Published by Pocket Books, a Simon & Schuster
Division of Gulf & Western Corporation
Simon & Schuster Building
Rockefeller Center
1230 Avenue of the Americas
New York, New York 10020
Use of the trademark TIMESCAPE is by exclusive license from Gregory Benford, the trademark owner
SIMON AND SCHUSTER and colophon are registered trademarks of Simon & Schuster.

Designed by Irving Perkins Associates
Manufactured in the United States of America

10 9 8 7 6 5 4 3 2 1

Library of Congress Cataloging in Publication Data
Walton, Evangeline.
  The sword is forged.

  1. Theseus (Greek mythology)—Fiction. I. Title.
PS3545.A6296S9 1983   813'.52   82-19653

ISBN 0-671-46490-6

TO MY GRANDMOTHER, BOTH A QUAKERESS
AND A PIONEER, OF WHOSE MIXTURE OF
TENDERNESS AND TOUGHNESS ANTIOPE
SOMETIMES REMINDS ME

CONTENTS

———— *We could not live with your women—our ways are different from their ways. To draw the bow, to hurl the javelin, to ride horses, these are our arts. . . . But your women do none of these things, they stay at home . . . and never go out to hunt, or to do anything. Never could we and they get along together.*

WORDS OF THE AMAZONS IN HERODOTUS, BOOK IV

Book I

THE
BLADE

CHAPTER 1.
___THE DEATHSINGER DREAMS

MOLPADIA, WAR-QUEEN of the Amazons, woke with both hands clutching at her weapons; they were always near her, even in sleep. But to her straining ears came only the web of small sounds that night always weaves, only the quiet breathing of the girls who slept beside her, her dead sister Otrere's children. They were safe! The moon was full, and in the light that poured through the slitlike windows under the eaves everything looked as it ought to look. Save for her cup, made from the skull of the first man she had killed in battle. For a breath's space it laughed in her face, yellowed teeth gnashing, inlaid black obsidian eyes gleaming as if triumphing over her at last.

Then it was still again, still as the enshrined, painted face of Lysippe, Mother of Amazons, above her. But the old pain was back where her right breast had been—the breast that she had burned off years ago, when she had given up all hope of bearing more children. Women so mutilated could handle the bow better. Only mothers needed two breasts. . . .

Child, was it you? Come to torment me because I weaned you too soon? Because you died on the way to your Hittite father, crying for my milk?

They had warned her, Otrere her sister and the older women. "Wait. Send him when the other mothers send their boys. The journey is long and hard for a little one." But she had known herself and what she must do. She had kept the Law of her people: *No Amazon may rear a son.* Nothing else mattered, though never anywhere now would there be living flesh of her flesh. . . .

Better, far better, if that dream had come from a lying, embittered little ghost. Not from the Goddess, as all true dreams of warning came. Then no danger was coming.

13

None had as yet; that was sure. She looked across at the two sleeping girls. At dark Melanippe, her co-queen, who would be the Childbearer, and at young Antiope, her fosterling. In her sleep Antiope had thrown off the covering bearskin. How sweetly the bare young thigh was shaping toward womanhood! Daintiness and smoothly muscled strength together, exquisitely mated. *May your children be many, and all of them daughters, O my heart's joy!*

She rose to cover that bare leg, or thought she did, but then the horror came. Black night swooped down and covered her eyes; when her sight came back blood was pouring in a scarlet flood over the white bearskin—fresh, pulsing blood. Both girls' faces looked white and oddly still; like the emptied faces of the dead. Then with an awful crash the walls split asunder, and the surging sea poured in. The painted head of Foremother Lysippe fell from above the altar; it was rolled over and swept away. So was Antiope, though the waves covered Melanippe.

Shrieking, the War-Queen woke. Both girls' hands were clutching her, their young eyes wide with fright. "Mother's sister, what is it?"

For a breath's space it seemed to Molpadia that blood still covered Melanippe. Then she heard cries and running feet outside; her shrieks must have wakened all in the nearby House of the Maidens. She steadied herself. "Go out to your age-mates, Antiope. Tell them to go back to bed, and seek a bed among them yourself. I must speak with your sister alone."

With great dignity Antiope picked up her bearskin and stalked out. She herself had killed that huge white bear. High in the mountains and all alone she had done it—a deed for a full-grown warrior to be proud of. Yet now she was being sent away like a child.

Alone the two queens faced each other, the Deathsinger and the Childbearer. Melanippe spoke first; quietly, although her face was pale. "Did the Goddess come, Aunt?"

"Child, I dreamed twice, yet know this only: Evil threatens you and your sister, and so the whole race of the Amazons. For only through those of her own blood can Foremother Lysippe guide and guard us, and you two are the last who can carry on that blood."

"What did you dream, Aunt?"

"I stood outside beneath the moon. I saw three great birds come flying over Themiskyra. Their wings flapped, and our walls shook like leaves in a mighty wind. Our people came rushing out. Feathers fell upon them like hail—turned in falling to spears and fire. The spears pierced us, the flames kindled our roofs. Amazons died in blood and flame."

She stopped. Both women shuddered, warriors though they were. Outside a wind was rising; it moaned thinly through the night, like the voices of a horde of homeless dead trying to get back inside the warmth of human flesh.

"And the second dream, Aunt?" Melanippe's voice was toneless.

"I woke, or seemed to wake, and saw that skull yonder. He laughed—laughed as if he still had a mouth, instead of that piece of painted bone that long ago Areia the smith made fast behind his teeth. He mocked me—that Kaska dog whose head has been my cup these many years. He whose life I took, whose blood I drank."

Again Molpadia paused. She could not bear to tell the rest—of the blood and ruin she had seen in this very room. Above all, of how she had seen Antiope swept away. . . . And Melanippe did not notice the omission. She stood pondering, her brows knit in thought.

"Can the Kaska have joined with the men of Azzi, Aunt? With those dogs whose accursed forefathers were once our kin? How else could foes come in force enough to attack our walls?"

Molpadia laughed fiercely, herself again. "Let them try it! We have made those walls strong. No king lives who would be willing to spare the army that must die in storming Themiskyra. Not even the gold-covered, cruel kings of Babylon and Assyria. Not even Subbiluliuma, Sun of the Hittites—him your mother thought her friend!"

Melanippe's eyes flashed. "He is our friend! For more years than I have lived he has kept faith with us. Even as the Goddess told Mother he would. You know that, Aunt—and well."

"Child, to trust any man is the road to slavery. Our foremothers learned that, and sad will be the day when any Amazon forgets it. But this is no time for wrangling. Soon the moon will set, and before the sun is high I must be out of here with my warriors."

"Which way will you ride?"

"Up into the mountains. Where else? The Kaska must have grown clever at last—have spied out our watchwomen's camps. They think to kill them all, and take us by surprise."

"Truly they would have to be clever, Aunt, to kill all the watchers without one sounding her great war-horn in time to give warning. Are you sure the foe will come from the mountains?"

"From where else? No shore king is strong enough to attack us now—not since baleful-hearted Aietes fell, the Lord of Kolchis in the east."

"But you saw birds, and wings could mean sails—"

"Symbol is the language of dreams, girl, but it is not always easy to read. No, they who come creep through the mountains like snakes."

Melanippe said no more; war was the War-Queen's business. Yet she felt uneasy. On the north, west, and southeast the sea surrounded the lovely green plain of Themiskyra; but to the south mountains guarded it. Sky-piercing, pine-clad walls, formidable yet also full of hiding places, and therefore treacherous. They were the usual path of all enemies, and yet—

Together the queens left the small, half-temple dwelling that was called the House of Lysippe. The Amazons were divided into three groups: maidens, mothers, and grandmothers. Each had its own house: a fortress in which, at need, desperate women could make a last stand. Huge, ring-round, and windowless, the fortresses could be entered only by ladders let down from dark holes. If any foes could have reached those entrances, they would have had to crawl through them snakewise, on their bellies, one at a time, and then fall down in the midst of women whose long belt knives or short swords never left them, and would have cut each trespasser down before he could rise. Light and air came from central courts whose own centers held stairways leading down into the black depths where lay the well that gave the city water. The House of the Mothers was the largest, three stories high, with a long narrow room for each mother and her children. In the House of the Grandmothers, each of the one-breasted women past child-bearing had her own cubicle. In the House of the Maidens, those who paid their blood dues to the moon but had not yet borne children, each girl had only her own bed, built against the wall; yet usually there was much giggling there. Now it was very silent:

a waiting silence. But Molpadia strode on past it, to ward the two more distant houses.

Curtly she answered Melanippe's look of wonder. "I want only veterans. No green girls to waste arrows shooting at shadows. No pregnant ones either, spewing when their minds should be on their horses, or on keeping watch."

"May the Goddess send all those pregnant ones daughters!" Melanippe spoke piously, but with a pang. Had her birthday come half a moon sooner she too could have made the spring pilgrimages to the Isle of the Black Stone and to the Gardens of the Sun Goddess of Arinna. She did not regret the Isle of the Black Stone; there begettings were done as of old, by gray-faced captives who knew they must die cruel deaths as soon as their power to beget was exhausted. But the Gardens of the Hittite Sun Goddess—there would have been the Mystery, the unknown thing, heady as wine. *What would it have been like, lying with a Hittite under the green trees in the Holy Groves? Would I have liked him? And I so need to have a daughter. . . .*

Molpadia read her heart. Long generations of hardship, suffering, and shared effort had welded the Amazons into a closeness unknown to all other races. They worked together, felt together, like fingers on one hand.

She sighed wearily. "Child, child, if only you young girls could understand! Better to lie with the Kaska, whose vileness we know. Not with grinning strangers, who spin and spin, like spiders, to entrap us—"

"How? We come home safely. We give them nothing but our sons, who otherwise must die."

"And one day those same sons may ride against us! It is sweet, this sea-washed land at the feet of the mountains. Some day, when the Hittites have tamed all other men, they will want it."

Melanippe stared. "Aunt, are you mad? The Goddess Herself bade Mother make treaty with the Hittites."

"Then the Hittites were about to be crushed—they who had turned from their Goddess Halmasuitta, ancient Throne-Guardian, and banished Her to a far-off mountain. So that he who was king then might hold the land by his own strength—or so he said, the fool! Rightly have his descendants paid for his sacrilegious folly. Yet had they fallen utterly, the accursed men of Azzi, who were already gaining strength from their weakness, would have joined with the Kaska to crush us. Never otherwise would the Goddess have sanctioned any treaty with men. She must have meant it to be broken as soon as he who then was King of Azzi was broken. Him your mother helped Subbiluliuma to defeat." In her heart she added, *Subbiluliuma, who bewitched her.*

"Had the treaty been meant to be broken, Mother would have broken it. She lived for many years after that victory." Melanippe's eyes were ice-cold. "You are the elder queen, and I owe you respect, but you have no right to doubt that she was the Goddess' faithful servant—you, her own sister."

For a breath's space then she did not know what would happen. Never might Amazon strike Amazon—they loved each other well, who for long had had nothing else to love. Also, though prudent, the peace they kept among themselves had become sacred, part of their weird half-oneness. Yet though Melanippe had been in battle, never before had she seen eyes blaze as Molpadia's blazed then. Slowly the flame faded; the War-Queen's face became like stone.

"You put words into my mouth, niece."

"You spoke enough. Too many."

"Child, loyalty is good, but fancies are not. All spring you have been restless, dissatisfied. As a maiden often is when she should be conceiving and cannot. And that is partly my fault"—the hard face softened—"for in council I spoke against letting you lie with a man before you had reached the lawful age, and they followed my lead. I was afraid—afraid, in these days of many changes, to allow any change I could prevent."

"I have never held it against you, Mother's sister. Also this is, as you have said, no time for wrangling."

"Yet the time involved was little—so very little. I should have remembered how important it is to carry on the blood of Lysippe. The War-Queen need not be of that blood—she is barren—though usually she is the Childbearer's ageing mother. But the Childbearer must be, and her first duty is to bear—as soon as she can."

"I will lose only one year, Aunt. I am young yet."

"Maybe I can still make it up to you. Bring home a captive to father your babe."

Melanippe thought bitterly, *I should thank her,* but could not.

Another doomed captive, after all—sweating with fear, stinking, miserable, and loathsome. . . .

In the fire-gold of morning the royal sisters stood with other Amazons—mostly maidens and the mothers of young children—atop the walls of Themiskyra. They watched the War-Queen ride out with her warriors, they cried the ancient cry: "Bring home the heads of the foe!" Those who lived probably would bring back heads enough, but their own smiling faces, safe on heads that still grew from their own necks, would be the sight that would truly gladden mothers and sisters and daughters. They who died would come back too, in time; be born again of the wombs of those they had loved. Not even death could make an Amazon desert her people.

But even before the host was gone, swallowed up by the hills, the watchers hurried out to round up the best of the remaining horses. Laughing for joy of this last outing they might have for many days—they who must now live like besieged folk—they rode the swift, beloved beasts into the long crevicelike pit that long ago had been dug a few yards inside the city walls. The city gates opened into it, for there was no break in those walls themselves, and above it reared another wall of logs. Incoming and outgoing Amazons always had to use rope ladders held by those within. If invaders broke in, the merciless Amazon arrows would hail down on them through slits in the log walls above.

"But if we have to do that we will hurt the horses," said young Antiope suddenly. Melanippe put an arm around her. "Such a thing has not been done since our grandmother's time, little sister. And since then both walls and gates have been strengthened."

Yet as she spoke she tried to make her mind blank, lest the child read her feelings. She had seen many raids, had fought and killed more than her share of savage raiders, but never in her lifetime had Themiskyra been besieged. If Molpadia and her army were lost, utter darkness might come, and the end of all Amazons. *For we who are left inside these walls are too few to drive away a strong besieging force, and in the end hunger would defeat us.* But surely the Goddess would not let that happen! What hurt her most was to think of the green plain outside. Some horses were still there, and all the cattle; far back, in a fold of the hills, sheep were penned. There were trees too; their lovely intricate splendor of branches and green leaves did the eye good, but were far from being their only virtue. The Amazons, who had long known hunger, never planted a tree that would not bear either fruit or nuts. To see all that wealth and beauty destroyed would be hard indeed.

But this was war, and the War-Queen had said: "None must go outside the walls save those watchwomen who watch the sea—none." To those who had dared to protest—"Must we see our fields and trees burned? Our herds butchered?"—her answer had been implacable: "Only life and freedom matter. Have you forgotten those first words of our Law? And as for your precious cows and sheep, when I was a girl Amazons still weaned their babies on mares' milk, and wore the hides of beasts. Harder stuff to stitch than fine soft wool, but you young women nowadays grow soft. Lysippe kept no beasts but horses—they that speed flight, never slow it!"

Sour words, but with some grim truth in them. Freedom did matter above all; it never must be risked for mere possessions.

Snail-slow, the day dragged on. The Amazons were restless, like birds unused to being caged. Young mothers fared best; they had their children to see to. Others fell back on their usual war games. They set up marks and shot arrows. They tried to run races—Amazons, like their horses, must be fleet, since they might be unhorsed in battle. But continually dodging around obstacles was not like the clean wild joy a runner had in the open. Wrestling and swordplay they could do and did—until they ached, and sweat soaked them. Sweat that now could not be washed off in the river Thermodon outside, or in the sea into which that river emptied.

And always one thought grinned coldly, evilly, over every shoulder: *When warriors go forth to war, not all of them come back. Will those you love come?*

Another shadow lay heavy on them too. Amazons, who once had been hunted like wild beasts, and still fought against great odds, used poisoned arrows, whose least scratch meant death. War always meant that more poison must be brewed. And before she left Molpadia had laid that task upon Xanthippe, the oldest living Amazon. Uncomplaining, old Xanthippe had left her snug nook in the House of the Grandmothers and gone, as many old women before her had gone, to a grim little hut set as far as might be from the houses of the living. For two days and two nights she must stand over the huge caldron within, stirring, always stirring, while the deadly fumes soaked into her lungs. She would die, and if she died before her work was done another grandmother, already chosen, would take her place.

Always old Xanthippe had been well beloved. Many could remember how when they were little she had treated them to bowls of hot porridge sweetened with fruit and honey—the Amazons had no cake or bread; they used the once-wild, mountain-grown einkorn that is more nutritious than ordinary wheat, but bad for baking. Antiope could still see her smiling face above those sweet, steaming bowls—steam so different from that which rose in the old face now. . . . As the day wore, and the shadows of many walls grew longer and blacker, shrinking the sunlight into miserable streaks and patches, Antiope drew nearer and nearer to that hut. To speak to the one within was not actually forbidden, but only the other grandmothers who brought her food and drink usually did so, and they did not linger. *We treat her as one already dead, yet she is not—she is still there!*

The young girl came at last to the doorway, which had no door —air was badly needed inside. She saw the old woman standing there, stirring. Sweat poured down the wrinkled face; dripped down, through the hot smoke, into that death-filled, bubbling brew that already was dealing death. . . .

Antiope spoke quickly, her voice seeming to break out of her: "Grandmother, please come out! You look so tired. Rest just long enough to get your breath—I can stir for you that long." Xanthippe was not her grandmother, but any dweller in the Three Houses had a right to be called by the name of her House.

Smiling, old Xanthippe shook her head. "No, child. Go away. You know you should not come near these fumes, you who carry the blood of Lysippe."

"Breathing them a little while will not hurt me. Please, Grandmother!"

"Child, this is a good way to die: making something for my people. A proud way for me, who can no longer fight for them. I have borne and reared my daughters; I have seen my granddaughters grow up. My life has—been—good." She coughed; talking had let too much steam into her already irritated throat. "Go now

—quickly, child—" She coughed again and again, coughs that racked her thin old body. Antiope ran into the hut and snatched the spoon from her.

"Get out! Until you do, I will breathe in the fumes as hard as I can." She did, opening her mouth wide and bending as far over the boiling brew as she could force herself to do.

The old woman tottered out and called for help. Inside, Antiope straightened up and stirred vigorously. Amazons came running. Melanippe came to the doorway and said quietly: "I will count to one hundred, Antiope; then you must come out, who have already breathed in many fumes. And I will go in and stir while you count to one thousand. Xanthippe once fed me sweet things too."

Many cried out in protest, Xanthippe most loudly of all, until the queen bade her be quiet. "Do not waste what we do for you, Grandmother. It is little."

Later, in the House of Lysippe, she said firmly: "Never do that again. To let one so doomed alone is wisest."

"But if we all took turns stirring, maybe nobody need die—"

"You know better. Too many young women might sicken— maybe bear weakly babes. We cannot take that risk."

"It is wrong—wrong! I know she was too old and stiff to ride to war, but she was still happy, there in her little room, talking to old friends and puttering around. Feeding other children as she used to feed us—"

"She could not have been happy much longer."

"But that little while—she should have had it!"

"Better for an old woman to lose two or three years than for a young woman to lose many. And her death might have been slow and hard. Without pride; she has that now."

"It is still wrong!"

"It is. But in the old hard days as soon as an Amazon grew too old to ride she had to leap from a cliff."

That night Melanippe lay down in Molpadia's place before the altar, beneath that painted mask of Lysippe that had been modeled over Lysippe's own skull. That face seemed to watch as every night some queen of her blood must watch, sleeping yet sleepless, for danger to her people. . . .

She slept. She saw woods and fields and mountains. Moonlit places that lay still as sleeping children. Wild places, where birds and beasts preyed on each other. She saw Molpadia and her warriors camped uncomfortably upon a mountainside, with no fire to cook over or to warm them, since fire might bring down upon them the foes they sought. She saw the watchwomen in their tiny, lonely camps. But nowhere was there any sign of man.

She woke, wondering: *Could Molpadia have been wrong? Are no foes coming?* Once before Molpadia had been mistaken; she had said then: "What I saw must have been in some enemy chieftain's mind. His evil hope." If only that were true now too! But it was too soon to tell.

Another day dragged on. The younger Amazons spent much of it in cleaning out the pit and grooming the horses. Melanippe was glad that Antiope's mind now seemed to be focused altogether on her young golden mare, Chrysippe. Or was the child only trying to forget what she could not change?

Night came again. Antiope slept soundly beneath her treasured bearskin, but Melanippe prayed: *Let me see the foe tonight, O Lady, Mother of all things! If they are real, let me see them, let me know, be sure.*

But she saw only beasts and green lonely places, and the Deathsinger vainly hunting for men to deal death to. . . .

Antiope rose early next morning to groom Chrysippe again. She took the filly one of the few apples left from last year. She talked to her and petted her. *Soon now, my golden one! Soon the War-Queen will come home, maybe with many heads, and you and I will go out, and run and run! Until the birds look down from heaven, and wonder how we can go so fast or move so beautifully, we who have no wings.*

The golden morning sang in her blood, and she ached to get outside the walls. The young often easily forget what respected elders have often told them it is no use to worry about, but only her fierce desire for freedom could have made Antiope forget Xanthippe's slow dying.

But when she went back up into the city she found that that was over. The grandmothers who had taken Xanthippe her morning food and drink had found her dead beside the caldron. But the poison was brewed; she could go with pride to her place among the shadows who waited for rebirth. Many mourned for her, but with little noise. Loud lamentation was never the way of the Amazons. But Antiope sat long with her back to the others, tears running down her face. Melanippe found herself thinking, *And if there is no enemy to make us need that poison, Xanthippe has died for nothing.*

That day she walked on the archers' platform inside the highest, thinnest part of the city walls. Slits were there through which the archers could fire their deadly arrows. They also let in the sweet west wind, and Melanippe, breathing deeply of it, suddenly remembered what it meant. Any day now the Trojan traders would come. She would have preferred a splendid, chariot-riding Hittite captain, but a trader would do. Then Molpadia's words came back to smite her: "Let only the watchwomen go out." Had Molpadia had the traders in mind? She did not like them. She was always saying, "Amazons need only what they can make or grow with their own hands." When reminded how little danger of attack there was since the Trojans sent only one ship at a time, with the usual thirty-man crew, she would say, "Girls, few men are needed to seize a foolish, unwary woman and carry her off to slavery. That is all women ever are to men—goods to be used, or goods to be sold."

The last time she had said that Melanippe had grinned. "They are businessmen, Aunt. To them no one woman would be worth the loss of their trade with us. But we are careful." And so they were. No Amazon ever lay with a trader unless he and his comrades had disarmed themselves and stacked their weapons up in a pile over which the girls with her kept guard. Yet at such times there was usually plenty of fun and giggling. She herself had always been a watcher, too young to join in, also thinking with proud distaste: *I would not want to do it this way. Before so many people.*

But now—! She knew Molpadia. If the War-Queen could find no foes to capture, she would rake up some miserable shepherd or goatherd somewhere and drag him back to Themiskyra. All the way he would be kept trotting after the horses, many times both fear and necessity would make him befoul his sheepskin pants, yet Molpadia would laugh at the idea of his having a bath before the begetting. "Why soil our clean river with such trash, girl? You want to get a daughter from him. Not pleasure." Though even if he did not stink it would be a loathsome, sickening business, lying with a man who was so afraid. . . .

But she herself is always afraid—afraid we young women will get pleasure from men, not only their seed. Why? Mother was not like that.

Why, too, could she not see that the treaty with the Hittites had

done the Amazons great good? Never until the night before her
going had she spoken out frankly—such dreams often left the
dreamer cruelly shaken—but always it had been there, her suspi-
cious hatred of the Hittites. Contact with it had been like wearing
a tunic that scratched the wearer's skin. Her objections to some
results of the treaty were clear enough. Subbiluliuma's frontier
forts bought all the grain, dried meat, and dried fruit that the
Amazons could spare. They had some comforts now, those women
whose foremothers had been hunted like beasts until they finally
won lovely Themiskyra. Who for long, even then, had had to fight
and work too hard to have much time to enjoy it. Now they wore
wool and linen, they bought pretty things—unnecessary, yes, but
pleasant and harmless—from the traders. But Molpadia saw all
such comforts as weakness, softness, corruption.

Yet one advantage she should be able to see. The Amazons
always had been a small people, but already the spring meetings
with the Hittites—laughing, lusty men, great begetters—had doubled their numbers. Taking men captive never had been easy;
poisoned arrows had been no help there. Often, before the Black
Stone, there had been seven or eight Amazons to one man—or to
what was left of him. Melanippe shivered, thinking of the deep,
well-covered pits beneath the sea cliffs, where captives sometimes
waited all winter long before being taken to the Black Stone. They
never gave any trouble; the right hand of each was always twisted
out of its socket, and the left foot too was maimed. Enemies
charged the Amazons with a depraved taste for such cripples. But
they were the only men Melanippe had ever feared. Never would
she forget the first time she had seen them hobbling, blinking,
after they had been hauled up out of those pits by ropes. . . . After
making treaty with the Hittites, Mother had stopped taking prisoners, but as soon as she was dead Molpadia had begun it again.
And when asked why, she had had an answer.

"Remember Foremother Lysippe. How she had to crawl through
what had been her own house, a crippled slave. By day a drudge,
by night a rug for many masters."

Through how many lifetimes had Amazon blood boiled at tales
of the wrongs done Foremother Lysippe? Of the Great Betrayal,
of the massacre and the raping and the maiming? Lysippe had been
a great woman, truly worthy to be honored like a Goddess. Crip-

pled, doomed never to stand again, her indomitable will yet had
freed her people from bondage, shaped the pattern of their future.
It still ruled them, drove them, made them all parts of one whole.

Yet was there still need for so much hate? Melanippe remembered her mother saying, years ago: "For long it helped us to keep
free; in some ways it still does. But we can no longer let it keep
us shut into our grim past, as into a tight, iron-hard box. To the
living any box is a coffin." And coffins were the sterile resting
places of proud, dead kings. Amazons were buried naked in their
own fields, both to enrich the soil and to ensure a quick return to
Earth the Mother. Melanippe would have died sooner than put
herself into a man's power; nobody ought ever to live that way—
in another's power. For men and women to live together would not
do; it always meant the woman's taking second place. But they
could meet without being enemies; Mother and Subbiluliuma had
proved that. Surely a child ought to be begotten in friendliness and
joy . . .

*Am I free and a queen, to let myself be made to open my legs for a dirty,
stinking dog?*

That day too dragged to an end. Night came, and in her sleep
again Melanippe saw only the high quiet mountains, no war but
the everlasting war for food, it that the birds and the beasts wage
against each other forever. The Deathsinger and her host still
wandered aimlessly. . . .

*Are there any two-legged foes for them to find? Is too much hate warping the
War-Queen's judgment? She should be able to tell a* teshas, *a true dream, from
the visions sent by the demons of the night.*

Rebellious thoughts came. *I will do whatever I must do for my people's
sake, but I will not wallow in filth only because Molpadia wills it. If the traders
come, I will go out to meet them.*

Morning came, golden and good, and also a sudden cry from
outside. The Amazons sprang to their feet, scattering their breakfast bowls upon the floor. The watchwomen who always patrolled
the archers' platforms on the city walls had sounded no alarm. The
watchwomen by the sea had not used their great war-horns to give
warning of any approaching fleet. Yet something was happening.
What?

Bird-swift, Antiope ran to find out. For a breath's space Melanippe stood still. Lysippe's face, above the altar, seemed to be

looking at her. Its painted mouth seemed to be trying to speak to her, yet she could hear no sound.

Then she too was off, joining Antiope as one bird joins another in flight. They met a watchwoman coming down from the walls. "Queen, two of the watchwomen who watch the sea are below! We have spoken with them."

"They have seen traders?" Melanippe's eyes shone, her voice was eager.

"They do not know. They cried, 'Ships! Ships are coming! Three of them!' Only one has ever come before."

CHAPTER 2.
_____THE ADVENTURERS

T HEY HAD come far, the men of Hellas. Up through the blue southern sea they knew, on into the fierce currents that seethed in the straits named for drowned Helle, she who was said to have fallen from the back of the Golden Ram. By night they had sneaked past Troy, that city whose fall will be a song forever. To them it was only a town of fat traders, jealously barring all others from the unknown riches of the northern sea. In a shore skirmish they had killed a few Trojans, so later tales were to make their captain, strong Herakles, Troy's first conqueror and sacker. But in truth no handful of adventurers—three ships with thirty men aboard each—ever could have gone up against the God-built walls of mighty Troy.

On they sailed, out of Helle's straits and into the Straits of the Cow, that opened into the sea they sought. Into the dark Unfriendly Sea that was said to lead to the World's End. There fog and night came upon them. They had to row as cautiously as blind men, through a narrow way that they knew must be growing ever narrower. Fearing the awful jolt and crash that must come if their ships hit the rocks. Fearing also, with a more terrible fear, that which might hear and come. They rowed softly and spoke in whispers. For the Argonauts, the only mainland Greeks who had sailed this sea before them, had claimed to have been chased by monstrous rocks that did not stand still as rocks should. Wandering cliffs that floated upon water and clashed together with a noise like thunder, they could have crushed the ships into splinters and the crews into bloody pulp. Once, when an oar slapped sharply against the unseen water, a man cried out, and another hissed: "Fool! Would you bring black death upon us?"

Big Herakles heard them both and laughed. "The Argonauts got away. And before Jason, their fool of a captain, got his pretty witch Medea to take care of him. Where other men have gone, Herakles can go."

That made them all feel better, yet many still peered over their shoulders, trying hard to see through the cold black mist. Cliffs that could move across water would be terrible foes even for Herakles, whose strength made men believe him the son of a mighty God, of Thundering Zeus. Shivering, they rowed on, though their bodies cried for rest; at least work kept off some of the damp, bone-piercing chill.

Morning came at last, and the fog was gone. They could see! All around them the dark sea rolled, bleak and sunless, the sea they had sought. But nothing save their own craft moved on the face of the waters.

"Now you see the worth of sailors' yarns!" Big Herakles' laughter boomed out again, and this time all the rest laughed with him. Even grim Telamon, the brooding son of Aiakos, who never before had been known to laugh with other men, only at them. But the redheaded boy who was Herakles' kinsman and by far the youngest there soon frowned thoughtfully. "Poets say those wandering cliffs are blue, and shine like ice. In hard winters at home the mountain pools freeze over. And then, when the ice breaks up, pieces of it float. What if—"

"You think a whole sea could freeze over? That is fools' talk, boy." Telamon laughed again, his ugly, cutting laugh, and many laughed with him. Men just relieved from needless fear enjoy finding foolishness in others. The Redhead flushed but said stubbornly: "A sea that freezes over is no queerer than rocks that can float."

"It is not, at that," said Herakles, grinning. "But now let us go ashore and eat."

The wooded shores to the south looked gray and grim, but they were shores. The men landed and found no sign of man, but they did find game. They killed and cooked their kill, then ate the first hot meal they had had in days. Never had anything tasted so good. They drank hot wine too. Night found them still lolling happily around their fires. Even crusty Telamon grinned, patting his full belly. "This will make us strong to smite Amazons!"

Herakles said shortly: "Trading is better than smiting, this far from home. We will try it first."

"Trade with those mad bitches!" Telamon's jaw dropped. "The savage Skythians, their own kin, call them *Oiorpata,* 'Slayers of Men.' If once you turn your back on them—man, it would take Father Zeus Himself to keep their knives out of it!"

"Yet King Eurystheus sent me to get their queen's golden girdle, not her head, and women like gewgaws. She will probably be like the rest." Herakles shrugged. "When we go among the Amazons we will keep our eyes open, and our hands at our sides. Remember that, all of you."

"Smiting has not done us too much good lately, brother." Peleus drawled that, the other son of Aiakos. Both had been exiled by their father for killing a half brother, perhaps not quite by accident, in a game of quoits. Since Telamon had thrown the fatal quoit, the Redhead was sure there had been no accident, but he did not believe that Peleus had known what was going to happen; he liked merry Peleus. He said quickly, eager to comfort, and also too young and too warmed by unaccustomed wine-drinking to realize his tactlessness: "It is too bad about your brother, the noble Phokos. Yet except for that mishap you might not be here, Peleus. And it is a great honor to sail with Herakles—"

"Phokos was not noble—that bondswoman's brat!" growled Telamon. "He was a bastard. Like too many others."

His eyes made his meaning plain. The Redhead flushed scarlet, to the roots of his hair. Then his tawny eyes flashed as red as that hair. "You call me bastard, murdering son of Aiakos?"

"He has not, and he will not." Before Herakles' eyes Telamon's fell, as the eyes of other men always did before the son of Zeus.

"Lad"—Herakles swung to the boy—"he is sore because of a mishap that has happened among our kin also. Atreus and Thyestes were exiled by their father, Pelops—our great-grandfather—for the slaying of a brother."

"I know." The Redhead, sober now, had sense enough not to add, *Those other two vultures who now roost beside our kinsman Eurystheus in golden Mycenae.* He only thought it.

"Such troubles are best not spoken of. They will always plague great houses unless kings learn to sleep only in their own wives' beds. And that is not likely. How many other men do?"

All chuckled then, and soon lay down to sleep. But the Redhead could not sleep. He tossed until finally, as he had hoped, he woke Herakles. The big man came wide awake at once, as fighting men often do when suddenly roused from sleep.

"Boy, what is it?"

"You heard him—that foul-mouthed, barking dog!"

"He will not bark at you again, boy."

"No, but he will whisper; so will others. Behind my back. They already have—and he is worst of all, that sour cur. Why did you bring him along?"

"Because he is good company, lad."

The boy stared. "When?"

"In a fight," Herakles said simply. "Nowhere else. But I will speak with Peleus about these whispers. If there are any—which I doubt, for your pride is tender—he can settle them quietly. While I might knock a few men's heads together, and that would be too likely to break their skulls. And we are not many; I do not want to lose men."

"They do whisper! Because—my mother is not married." The boy swallowed once, then words poured out of him like a long pent-up torrent, suddenly released. "Until I left Troizen I did not know—I did not dream—that any other king's daughter on our shores would have been slain or maimed for bearing a child out of wedlock. And the child exposed—thrown out to die!"

Herakles said slowly: "Boy, there has to be a man—loins for the God's seed to be poured through. Those tales of swans and sunbeams getting women pregnant are for children. Surely you knew that; you are old enough. You must have talked with other boys—"

"In Troizen none speaks of what happens on holy Sphairia! We know that it is holy—a Mystery."

"And so it is. Your grandfather, wise King Pittheus, respects the old ways. At the destined time your mother went to the temple of the Goddess on holy Sphairia. There Sea Lord Poseidon's crown and mantle are kept, and when the destined man puts them on the God enters into him—"

"But why? Why must there be a man—why cannot the God wear His own cloak and crown?"

"Child, I cannot tell you why; I do not know. It is the way the Gods arrange things."

"And why should the man be the woman's husband? What difference does that make?"

The boy was shivering. The man put a great arm around him and held him close. He groped for words; they were not the usual weapons of Herakles.

"Lad, we Zeus-worshipers are latecomers in Hellas. Ours are the new ways. Among us men own the land, and every man wants to leave it to his own son—not to his sisters or his daughter's. So the Holy Marriage must take place between husband and wife. Many people say that Zeus came to my mother in my fath—in her husband's shape. Even as in Egypt the God is said to don Pharaoh's shape when He comes to beget the heir upon Pharaoh's queen. Such things are hard for common folk to understand. But there is no shape-changing—the God enters into the man and then the man enters the woman."

The boy lay still awhile, thinking. He said at last, very slowly: "I see—partly. Of old the land used to pass through women. Now in all the great cities the kingship passes from father to son, but in smaller towns it often goes to a son-in-law. And in small, out-of-the-way places sometimes kings are still glad to let a God-like guest sleep with his daughter—or so I have heard—"

"They are that!" Herakles chuckled. "Old King Thespios asked me to sleep with all fifty of his daughters."

"And got fifty fine grandsons out of you."

"Forty-nine, boy. The last girl refused me."

"Refused *you?*" The Redhead stared.

"She did, and some men say I cursed her for it. But the fools lie. I never was so thankful to anybody in my life. Never visit a king with fifty daughters, boy—not if he is old-fashioned, and you are in a hurry, and cannot stay but one night."

"But she was discourteous, disobedient!" The Redhead swallowed hard; his voice sank very low, and he had to fight to keep it steady. "My mother was not like that, was she?"

Herakles said quietly: "I am not your father, lad. If I were, nothing could make me keep my mouth shut about it. Whoever wore that crown and cloak, he did a good job. But now go back to sleep, and let me sleep."

He fell asleep promptly, glad to get out of a situation that had been worse than most fights. But the boy still lay awake. Much still puzzled him, but he was sure of one thing now. It had happened on little Sphairia—that tiny isle to which you could wade out when the water was low—just as he had always been told. Yet Earth-holding Poseidon had not risen up out of the blue sea Himself in His own shape of splendor—there had been a real man. One who had not been Herakles. . . .

Let him have been Godlike who lay with my lovely mother—let him! Yet surely he had been; the God's seed could not have poured through a mean man's loins. And it had been the God's seed—it had! *I too am God-begotten, and one day I will be great.*

Meanwhile he was where he had always wanted to be—he was with Herakles, and on a great adventure.

He had been seven years old when he had first seen Herakles. What a joy it had been to know that the great hero was coming, the mighty man of all the stories! With three other boys—Euneos, Thoas, and Hermos, his dearest friends among his age-mates—he had sneaked out onto the steep mountain path that led up to high Troizen. Herakles would have to come that way—they would be the first to see him! All day long they had waited, baked by the summer sun, among crumbling rocks that were too treacherous underfoot to be played on, too hot to be sat on. They had grown sleepy, and to one side of them a great black patch of shadow had been growing, a refuge almost cool. They had taken turns dozing in it, three precariously rolled up, while the fourth kept watch. Or was supposed to keep it. . . . Suddenly they woke to see the sky all red and gold with sunset, and the Redhead, having been the sleeping sentry, said sturdily, "He cannot have come! I would have waked up then!" But they dared wait no longer. Tired, hungry, and disappointed, they trudged homeward, not anxious to meet their mothers, who must long have been wondering where they were.

The way up was a hard climb, though the way down had been easy. They finally reached the great gates and found them wide open, with no gatekeeper there. That would not have been strange on any other day. Small ancient Troizen of the Mysteries did not have the kind of wealth men can steal. But the old gatekeeper too had wanted to see Herakles; what could have happened to him?

The streets were empty and very still. The sun was gone now, but the sky was still bright and clear, a pale, shining vastness. Only in the deep porch of the king's house had Night, the most ancient Goddess, already found a dwelling, woven Her black web of mystery and fear. The boys had just come abreast of that darkness when they saw the Thing that lurked in it. The red glaring eyes, the huge, fang-filled mouth snarling at them . . .

Like one boy they shrieked and fled. The Redhead yelled the loudest and ran the fastest, but he was the first to stop. He dodged round the corner of another house and stood there panting. Would the lion turn where he had turned—seize him? But no great tawny shape came; not even a roar pursued him. Yet he had heard Grandfather say that a charging lion could outrun the swiftest of men.

In him the desire to know would always outweigh fear. He crept back, and from behind a corner he peered into the awful black depths of the porch.

The lion sat there unmoving.

He had not chased the boys. Why? Because he was—full? Had he already eaten everybody up? Even wise Grandfather? Even—*Mother?*

Mad with grief and rage, the child ran sobbing round the house; found the ax he had often seen a servant chop wood with, and ran back. . . .

Fear poured through him, cold as new-melted ice, when he saw them again—the red gleaming eyes, the terrible gleaming teeth. But rage kept him going; he set his own teeth and charged. Again and again the ax crashed down upon the great head. Yet still the lion never moved. There were no sounds but the child's gasping breath, and the thudding of the heavy ax that soon wobbled in the small hands.

Until suddenly there were cries and rushing feet. Mother herself came running—unhurt. She seized both child and ax.

"He meant no harm, kinsman! He must have thought—"

"That it was alive. I know, Aithra. Once I had boys of my own." The big stranger was smiling down at both of them, yet as he ended for a breath's space his face grew grave, looked hurt. Then he grinned at the Redhead. "You will kill your own monster someday, little kinsman. But I have already killed the Lion of Nemea."

He stooped and picked the great lion up, and it hung limply

from his hands—an enormous empty hide! The terrible eyes—one of them somewhat chipped now—were only shiny stones.

He was Herakles, and this was the cloak he had had made from the skin of the famous Lion of Nemea! Everybody had been so quiet only to let him sleep after his long, hot journey.

At first the child felt afraid and ashamed, but that soon passed. At the feast that night he sat on Herakles' knee, he ate from Herakles' plate, and drank—though he was not allowed to drink much—from Herakles' own winecup. Never in his life had he been so proud and happy.

Later, when his great kinsman was gone, Aithra told him what had happened to Herakles' own sons. Once, for a little while, the great hero had gone mad; not knowing them, he had killed his own wife and children. Then, at holy Delphi, the bright young God from Crete had bidden him cleanse himself by performing the now famous Twelve Labors for his cousin Eurystheus. For golden Mycenae's king, whose father had driven the rightful sovereigns, Herakles' own father and mother into exile.

"But that was not fair!" The child was indignant. "Herakles didn't mean to do wrong. Didn't the God know that?"

"Child, it is not the Labors that grieve Herakles. They are only whips to drive off memory. Also, mortals may not question the wisdom of the immortal Gods. Men everywhere honor the God of Delphi even as we of Troizen honor Poseidon Earthholder. We will speak of this no more."

Words that left her boy angry and unsatisfied. No God ought to be honored like Poseidon Earthholder. His blood had boiled when he had first heard that many men now called Zeus Rain-Giver and All-Highest, but for love of Herakles he had forgiven Zeus the folly of His worshipers. But who was this God of Delphi, to dare to be unkind to Herakles? No use asking wise Grandfather; what Mother would not speak of he probably would not either. Maybe the servants would.

Their answer surprised him. "Of old we of Troizen worshiped only the Mother Who came from Egypt and Her Son. But ages before Troizen was, Earth the Mother answered the questions of all who came to Delphi. She gave good counsel always, and finally Father Poseidon joined her there, as He now has joined the Mother and Son here in Troizen. But after the woeful time of the Great

Darkness and the Great Sound the young God came—the son of the God of Crete. He alone speaks now in Delphi, but in exchange He gave Poseidon lovely Kalaureia, just off our shores, it that was once the place of the Son whose Mother came from Egypt. Him that folk now say is one with the Son who came from Crete."

"And where does She speak now? Earth the Mother?"

But they grew uneasy then; they shuffled and looked down. To his horror the boy realized at last that they believed neither Poseidon nor Earth had left Delphi willingly—that both had been driven out. He did go to his grandfather then, outraged and afraid.

Pittheus said gravely: "Child, Gods do not strive together. But the Mother and the Son are worshiped in many lands, in different tongues and so under different names. So now in Delphi men call the Son by His Cretan name, and believe that Poseidon was driven out. But the Gods are everywhere, and laugh at these foolish tales told by men."

Words that comforted the boy; after all, what God could have a holy place lovelier than Kalaureia? He went back to the servants, who were glad to talk of Herakles' other enemy, Eurystheus. Mycenae was the greatest city in all Apia—in all the land south of the craggy Isthmus. She sat like a golden spider amid a web of roads so skillfully planned that no trader could trade without using them. So all traders paid her tribute; she was fat and rich, like Eurystheus himself, whose big bottom filled her golden throne. He sat there racking his brains to think of a Labor that would be a sure mankiller, but so far Herakles had always returned triumphant. To be cheered by the men of Mycenae, who knew him for their rightful king.

"And someday he shall be king!" the small Redhead exulted. "He will kill fat Eurystheus and feed him to his own dogs—his true kin!"

He was nearing fourteen when strong Herakles came again. On a day of dismal autumn rains when both sky and cliffs looked gray with misery. Herakles gulped down hot wine, then said: "I bring you greetings from your brothers, Uncle. From Atreus and Thyestes."

"They are with Eurystheus?" The old king's face grew troubled.

"Yes. Thick as thieves, all three of them. I think they helped him to think up my Ninth Labor. . . . Uncle, you alone of all our kin can now teach me the royal tongue of Kanesh, that our forefathers used of old in the Hittite lands."

"Surely Eurystheus does not mean to send you against Sub-biluliuma, Sun of the Hittites?" Pittheus' face grew yet more troubled. The Hittite lands lay far off, in the Lands of the Sunrise. Long had their famed fighting men been torn by strife, both within their realm and without, but now at last a warrior king strong enough to make all men follow him had risen among them. Subbiluliuma, Pharaoh's equal in might, though not in wealth.

"No, Uncle. I go yet farther. To get the Golden Girdle of Hippolyte, Queen of the Amazons. It that their first queen wore when she crossed the mountains at the World's End."

Aithra shuddered; her old nurse cried: "And be eaten when you have satisfied their lust? Like mother spiders those hags feed on their lovers—on the flesh of men!"

Tales of the fierce Amazons had spread from sea to sea. Of those warrior women who had ridden past the World's End—that sheer drop into black nothingness—and were more terrible than even that unthinkable abyss.

But the Redhead's eyes shone round and bright as twin suns. "Is it true that no man has ever set foot inside their city of Themiskyra?"

"If any has, he has not come out again." Herakles shrugged his great shoulders.

"But you cannot get there! Fishing boats could not sail so far—or carry the warriors you will need!" Aithra's face shone with relief, but her son felt a sudden angry stir of resentment. Why should mainland men be forbidden to build ships?

"I will have ships." Herakles laughed grimly, then spoke words that to most ears would have seemed blasphemous. "Eurystheus will not even have to make the priests rich gifts to get the God of Delphi to lift His ban, as Jason's rich, usurping uncle did when he wanted to get rid of Jason. He will buy them from Messene."

Pittheus nodded. Messene was the queen city of western Apia, as Mycenae was in the east. A few even dared to say, under their breath, that she was as rich as—Mycenae. He said: "But those ships cannot sail until spring. I will have all winter to teach you in, grandson of my sister."

"And you will need it. You know me." Herakles grinned.

But the Redhead's heart swelled within him: *Father Poseidon, Earth-keeper and Earthshaker, hear me! Let me sail with Herakles!*

None ever knew how long the old king sat wakeful by his fire that night. He had seen his grandson's eyes; had accepted what he had long known must come. But he grieved for Aithra; to her the boy's red head was the sun. He sighed once; how different men were! For him little Troizen had always been the right place; but it would never hold the boy. A woman versed in the Mysteries had built it: the foremother of Aithra's mother. An Egyptian priestess, she had fled with her folk from the invading Hyksos, from "them who knew not Ra." Egyptian Ra, like other eastern Sun Gods, was also seen as all-seeing Justice. In a dream the fugitive had seen this sweet plain beyond the sea, and the safety-giving heights above it, and when she had found them she had built well. Here too invaders had come, but none with the crushing might of the Hyksos. Within two or three lifetimes the alien blood and ideas had always been absorbed, the old pattern rewoven. Poseidon was the only newcomer who had ever stayed on. Troizen was one of the few places in which He had not yet been challenged by Zeus, the later Father God. Yet Zeus and Poseidon—there was little to choose between them, these new warrior Gods. Both accepted blood offerings. Neither could lead men where they should be led. He smiled, thinking how that thought would shock the boy.

You alone will endure, Lady, Queen of Heaven, Mistress of Earth and Sea. You who bring forth all things, Gods and men, beasts and the green life we all feed on. You will be here always, no matter how men glorify Your many-named Son or the Fathers they create for Him. You give all life, and yet Earth that is Your womb we must all return to at last.

His grandfather, Tantalos, had been one of the last kings to call Her the highest. And now strange white eagles flew over the blue waters of Lake Saloe beyond the sea, those waters that hid the fallen walls of Tantalos. Flood and earthquake had swallowed up both king and city, and since most men believed such disasters God-sent, Tantalos, once honored like a God, was now called accursed. Poets were still inventing crimes for him, and probably some of the mud would stick to him forever.

"At least you will be luckier than your grandfather, fool—you will only be forgotten!" So Pelops, Pittheus' own father, had said

bitterly when his firstborn had chosen to wed the heiress of little
Troizen and settle there. Pelops had spent his own life in trying
to regain lost greatness, then in seeking new greatness overseas.
And his half-Greek younger sons were what he had made them.
Yet Eurystheus had taken them in, foolish enough to fear only
Herakles.

A sudden horror took Pittheus. He groaned, his hands clenched
so tightly on the arms of his chair that the ivory-inlaid wood
cracked beneath them. Blood dripping from the eaves of every
roof in Mycenae, shadows blacker than night writhing beneath
them! The vision passed; Pittheus rose. He went for water, not
wine, drank, and then dashed what was left in his face.

*Truly you will not be forgotten, my brothers! You who have been taught only
war and greed and cunning will end by warring on each other. The seed you
sow will be sharper than serpents' teeth, and more poisonous. Blackness and ruin
will cover all.*

He had long known that ruin must come to Hellas. The small
dark folk of the land had been crushed too long, beneath too many
different waves of invaders. Yet more invaders might help them,
perhaps led by exiles of the old conquering stock. But he had not
known that men of his own blood would speed the darkness that
must come. An age-long darkness, for men mad for vengeance,
men long crushed, find it easier to destroy than to rebuild. . . .

Yet soon his tired old shoulders straightened; his mouth smiled.
*Seership is a hard burden to bear; it always tells a man both too much and too
little. Yet this much I am sure of. In spite of you, my poor mad dogs of brothers,
new freedom, new kinds of beauty and greatness, shall be born in these lands of
the West. Let golden Mycenae fall, as she herself will make Troy fall—let
Messene and Korinth and Tiryns fall, and even Troizen's wisdom be spilled—
one city shall stand. Do the work that is fated, and bring forth what is to be.*

Human pride shone in his eyes then, and joy curiously mixed
with pain. "For whatever else he does or fails to do—whatever
death he dies—the son of my daughter shall give that city the
strength and the dreams needed for that birthing. Lady, Mother
of all, I thank You!"

CHAPTER 3.
STILL THE ADVENTURERS

ALL WINTER long, Herakles worked hard to learn the royal tongue of Kanesh, without much success, for the strength of great Herakles had never lain in his head.

"This is harder than all my Labors," he groaned once. "Worse than anything I have ever tried to do since poor old Linos set out to teach me how to play the flute."

"That was worse for Linos than for you," said Aithra, somewhat sternly.

"He was a fool. He hit me, and how was I to know that his skull would break when I hit him back?" Herakles groaned again. "I was already big then, and a big man's lot is hard. All his life he must be so very careful, so very gentle."

He was silent then, perhaps remembering that other time that, blessedly, he could not remember. That night when his wife and children had died.

But in the calm of Troizen no fits of madness came upon him, those frenzies that some said were the real secret of his strength, more important even than his bigness, for in times of stress they always came upon him, made him terrible as a God.

But neither did he learn much. At last, one day when they were alone, the Redhead dared to whisper—he well knew the keenness of his mother's ears—"Let me go with you, kinsman. I can tell you what those barbarian strangers say, and also tell them what you say." For he had shared Herakles' studies, and had learned many times as much.

Herakles stared aghast. "Child, are you mad? Your mother and grandfather never would let you go."

"Mother may make a fuss at first, but every boy must grow into

40

a man. And where could I learn men's ways and deeds better than
with you? Or as safely?"

"I am not going to be safe myself," said Herakles. "Also, your
time for manhood is not yet."

But in the end the plan was told, and Herakles made no protests.
He counted on Pittheus and Aithra to do that. Aithra did, but
when at last she stopped and looked expectantly to her father, old
Pittheus said quietly: "Daughter, the time must come for the
young birds to leave the nest. The sky is their home. Because I
knew that, I taught the boy too the tongue used by our fathers."

She went white; both men flinched before the pain and fear in
her face. But the boy did not see it; he was soaring high on the
bright wings of triumph and dream.

"Child"—Pittheus spoke as gently as if Aithra were still a little
girl—"remember what I told you the night before this boy was
conceived. He has a destiny to fulfill, and I think now that this
journey may be a part of it."

"He will come back? Whole? You are sure of that?" Her voice
clutched at him like hands.

"Of that much. More I cannot tell. The web the Fates weave for
him may be more vast than I foresaw."

"And Zeus Himself dare not alter the will of the white-robed
Fates," Herakles said, half-pious, half-awed.

"No. The Goddess is older than all Gods, and the Fates are not
only born of Her wisdom, they are Herself."

Aithra drew a deep, ragged breath. "So be it. I am not greater
than the Gods."

But later, alone with her father, she said: "I fear for more than
his body. Always war and adventure have held far too much
glamour for him. All these *ptoliporthes,* these city-sackers, who will
follow Herakles may corrupt him. Make him forget what we have
tried to teach him—kindness to all, the fact that even the least of
men has a right to keep what he has built or grown with his own
sweat and toil—"

Pittheus said, rather sadly: "No. Not understanding our ways,
they will mock him, and later, in his day of power, he will be too
proud to be one of them. He will always be the friend of the poor
and the small."

But the Redhead thought only, *I will go with Herakles!* And his mind flamed with dreams. He would see them—all the strange places, all the strange peoples. He would fight the Amazons—the terrible, fierce warrior women of Themiskyra. He burned to show them that he could fight better than they could—what business had women to fight, anyway? And after that, perhaps—perhaps—

His mind churned with questions, the greatest of which was: *Are they good-looking?*

If one was young and pretty, it would be a shame to kill her. Better to get her down on the ground and then do something else with her . . . the thing that older boys were always bragging about doing. Girls were a mystery to him now; when he had been little many of them had been as good playmates as boys. But now they wore long, Cretan-style skirts in which nobody could run or jump. They could not look a boy straight in the eye, but giggled and gave him silly, sidelong glances. They disgusted him; yet of late he had begun to feel a queer, shamed curiosity about them. . . .

People said the savage Amazons must be hideous, but outdoor life did not make a boy ugly. And what of the Goddess Artemis, Whose priest he would be until he lay with his first woman? All princes born in Troizen were Her priests, as all princesses, until fit for childbearing, were priestesses of Poseidon on Kalaureia, as his own mother had been. Like the Amazons, Artemis took no husband; She roamed the wildwood, bow in hand. A huntress, yet fierce in wrath against the greatest king if he slew the least of furred mothers, even the pregnant hare. She could fight, too—when the Giants of old had risen against the Gods and tried to bring back primeval chaos, Her arrows had slain the hill-high pair who would have raped Her. And She was beautiful. . . .

Sometimes, standing before Her secret shrine in the marshes, the boy had tried to picture that beauty. Slender and fine, hard yet soft. She would look you in the eye and laugh. Her short hunter's tunic would leave Her legs bare . . . no! Impious for a mortal to wonder about a Goddess' legs, and what must lie just above them, with its saucy little tuft of hair. But there was nothing holy about the Amazons; he could think about every part of them, and he did.

The scarlet winter anemones began to die. The inner side of Troizen's great salt lagoon soon glowed golden with spring iris. Soon too word must come that the ships were ready. Surely he who would sail on them was a man—old enough to ask any questions. On a balmy night, when the king and his family sat outside on the deep porch, the Redhead asked one that long had troubled him.

"Grandfather, why are mainland men forbidden to build ships?"

Aithra spoke before her father could. "To keep wild boys and men from turning pirate. Child, you know that."

"I know that the God of Delphi forbade us to have ships. Not long after the time of the Great Darkness and the Great Sound. That time that people are still afraid to talk about. What did happen then? Did night really come at noon? Last through what should have been many days and many nights?"

Aithra said nothing; even great Herakles was silent. But wise Pittheus answered quietly: "First came the Great Sound. Louder than any sound that ever had been heard in this world. It seemed as if it must topple the mountains into the valleys, and bring down the sky upon that ruin. It pierced men's ears like the sharpest spear. Maybe many who heard it never heard again.

"And then night fell. Not a night without moon or stars, but such blackness as blind men walk in forever. None could see his hand before his face. People cowered indoors beside their lamps and fires, and thought of that blackness as of a great, world-filling beast, crouching outside their doors. What if their little lights went out before the sun came back? What if it never came back? If they must starve and die, there in the dark?

"None knows how long the blackness lasted. None has any way of knowing. In it the length of half a day could have seemed weeks long, moons long. Maybe it passed before the roaring sea rushed in upon the land—some say one thing, some another. Maybe many who heard that roaring rushed out, shrieking, into the blackness they had feared. Into the waves. But when at last the sea fell and the light came back, all who dwelt near the sea saw only ruin. Houses torn down, fields flooded, goods and beasts swept away. So it was even where no searing rain of hot ash had fallen."

The boy leaned forward, tense. "I know—that is why so many men now call Poseidon Earthshaker instead of Earthholder. They say He raised up the sea and with His trident knocked the sun out of heaven. Because He was fighting His brother Zeus for the king-ship of the Gods. But they lie! Never would Poseidon have so butchered us! He is good—"

Herakles stirred uneasily. "Sometimes the best of brothers fight, boy. In their younger days. I sometimes fought my brother, but although my twin, he was so much weaker than I, not being Zeus' son, that I had to put up with a great deal from him."

But Pittheus said, still quietly: "No God smites another, child; I have told you that before. No God smites a man, either. They seek to guide us, to steer us as the Cretans steer their ships. Not to drive us like cattle."

"Then what did happen?"

"Who knows, child? There are Powers who have no names and are not aware of men. And when messengers were sent to holy Delphi they came back in fear. 'The shrines are overturned, the walls have fallen! Earth the Mother speaks to Her children no more.' Then all wept like children who have lost their mother. But soon some began to look seaward. 'Maybe the good teacher-queens will help us, they who of old sent messengers from Crete the Morning Land to teach us how to sow and reap, how to build houses. Crete was mother to all the arts of men.' But no ships came. Hunger did, and lawlessness, always the child of hunger. For fishermen had no boats, traders no trading ships; all had been broken or swept away. And the farmers found that no crops would grow in their sea-soaked fields; Earth Herself had been poisoned. Even those who still looked seaward shivered. Had the many islands of the sea sunk beneath those fearful waves? Even glorious Crete?"

"But why didn't they build more ships, Grandfather? We must still have had forests."

"Child, men feared those vast, haunted waters from which the Great Sound had come. Soon ships were built, but only to prey, hawklike, upon our own coasts, manned by hungry men who wanted what little their neighbors had left. In time piracy became a game, the joy of all young men, and of many not so young. Even when Earth the Mother had healed Herself, no man ever knew whether he could keep the crops he had raised, or when fire and sword would break his sleep.

"Then at last Cretan ships did come. Their captains said: 'We are the men of Minos the Just.' Some asked: 'Where are the teacher-queens?' But the Cretans answered: 'Dead. They were women— too weak to drive away the Great Darkness. Minos did, he saved the sun. He saved all of us—Minos the Son and Friend of God.'

"His ships swept the sea clean of pirates. Men could live and work in peace again, and all who wished to do that praised Minos. More ships came, and one bore a new kind of cargo. Priests, who climbed up to ruined Delphi."

Herakles spoke, uneasy again. "Some say that one old priestess met them there. Came out of hiding with the great Snake beside her, Delphi's guardian from of old."

"That is true." Pittheus' face was as cold as carved stone. "The Cretans slew the Snake. To the woman they said: 'The Goddess has grown old. She slept and did not warn Her people. Let Her sleep again now. Her young grandson comes, the bright Son of our Cretan Zeus. He will care well for His own.' Then they seized the woman, and slew the snake. At first some murmured, but the land still prospered, and soon all said: 'Again Minos has done us good, sending us this Bright One, his own half brother. The world needs man's strength now; the time for woman's rule has passed.' Then a king went to ask whether he should build new ships, and the God answered: 'Let mainland men never again build ships. Only boats that can carry no more than five men at a time. So only can they keep the peace won for them by Minos the Just.' So He bade, and so we did, and ever since the ships of Crete have guarded our shores well."

He stopped, and for a breath's space the silence seemed as deep as a well. Then big Herakles stretched and yawned. "Well, I am glad I did not live in that time. There is much that I would like to change about my own, but at least the sun is safe in the sky. I will go to bed now."

He went. Soon Aithra too went to her chamber. But still the Redhead sat there, his thoughts crackling within him, fiery as his hair. At last he lifted his head and looked straight into the eyes of wise Pittheus.

"Grandfather, since Gods do not smite men it must be safe— safe and easy—for men to put words into their mouths."

"Such words are unsafe, child of my daughter."

"I know it." The boy's fists clenched, his face darkened. "Oh, truly Minos the Just is Minos the Clever! Maybe those queens were good, but they never invented sowing or reaping or house-building. Lies! All lies, like the tales nurses frighten children with! And I would have swallowed them all, if I had not heard you say that the oldest cities in the world are in Egypt and the eastern lands!"

"Crete has taught the lands of the West much. She is nearer us than is the East."

"And we have paid her back many times over!" The boy spat.

"Tell me how, child of my daughter."

"Because no man dare disobey the word of holy Delphi. We have a great bay here in Troizen—I think it would hold all the ships of Minos. But we have no ships—we are poor, like all towns on this shore! We must take whatever Minos or Mycenae chooses to give us for our goods. Even great Mycenae, when she sends goods overseas, must take whatever Minos chooses to give her. Minos has conquered the mainland without a blow! Made fools of us all—dogs to jump at his bidding!"

He stopped, panting. For a breath's space Pittheus made no answer; maybe for all his wisdom the old king's heart swelled with ordinary human pride. He had taught the lad much that others on that shore did not know; much that he had learned from his own father, that schemer bred in the older, more wily East. And the boy had not only remembered, he was using his knowledge. Fitting facts and suspicions together as a skilled weaver fits his threads.

Then he said: "Child, you reason well. You forgot only one thing. The holy heights of Delphi also command the way to the inland plains of the North. A trader's key to wealth; Minos did not overlook that."

The boy laughed with delight; his face glowed. "You see then, Grandfather? But you could not help seeing, you wisest of men!"

"Child, I have known all this long, and kept silent. For now, one must. You know that Minos has come to be honored, not only as the son of a God, but as a God himself. His earthly self sits in Crete, but His greater self sits in Hades, as Judge of the Dead. There is no escape from Him, in heaven or earth. It is not easy to rouse men against such a one."

"I see." The Redhead ground his teeth. "Well, one day I will rouse them! I too will have ships—and show proud Minos who is master!"

"Better to show him only that he is not master. That all men have rights. The world has known many conquerors; must you be only one more?"

"I will give men their rights. I will make them free! Our people, and all the people of this coast!" The boy's jaw was set man-hard, for all his bluster. But then wrath faded; wonder came back. "What did really happen, all those years ago? Did the sun really fall out of the sky? If those nameless Powers threw it down, why did not our Gods stop them?"

"Child, all Powers, including our Gods, have Their own work, Their own realms; none may interfere with another's. The order of the universe is beyond our understanding. Even as the ways of men are beyond the understanding of an ant."

"But did the sun really fall?" The Redhead's mind clung stubbornly to what he could hope to understand.

"No. Huge clouds of ash covered it. Ash spat up by the mountain that crowned the island then called moon-round Kalliste, fairest of isles. That was the Great Darkness. The fires within that mountain split open the breast of Earth, Mother of us all. That was the Great Sound. Now waters roll where that mountain once towered."

The Redhead's jaw dropped. "You mean the whole island sank beneath the sea?"

"No. But what is left of once moon-fair Kalliste is fair no more. Not even sea birds nest on the cliffs of her burned and dismembered corpse. Even they cannot drink from the sea."

The boy went to bed then, glad, for all his boasts, to be sure that Poseidon, his own divine Father, had been guiltless. But the old king still sat there in his Godlike loneliness, he whose full thought no other man might share. Once he smiled, quietly and without pride, as within his own mind he spoke to another who was not there.

"You have knowledge, Pterelas, priest of Delphi. Too much, for a man who uses knowledge as you do, yet not enough. Many years ago you held a lock of hair in your hand—the tribute that nowadays all young men make to Delphi, not knowing that their shorn locks put them in the power of magician priests. Or that that would not be so if they too had knowledge. . . . You looked at that lock, which was bright red—and it seemed to burst into flame before your eyes. Flame that burned up the great city of Cretan Knossos. The city of Minos, the only master you truly served. But you comforted yourself, thinking, 'His son, not he, is the fated destroyer, and so long as we of Delphi hold this hair, no son can be born to him.' You put your trust in old dark magic that has nothing to do with any God. Yet a power more pure has defeated you, the power long stored up in little Troizen of the Mysteries, waiting for its time to come."

His face changed then. Suddenly it grew old and tired and troubled; older even than his years, which were many. "Maybe I do not know enough, either. Have I taught the boy too much or too little? But it seems unlikely that on this turn of the Wheel he could learn what I would like to teach him. Also he was born for fighting and for doing, not for the quiet life I understand and love."

Before the Redhead's going, attention was drawn to his hair, and in a way that many would have thought ill-omened. The women of Troizen were making their yearly lament for long-dead King Saron, for their murdered lord, so young and beautiful and good. He had died while still the priest of Artemis, lured out to drown in the little sea beside the Isthmus, it that now was named for him: the Sea of Saron. When the wailing was loudest Herakles and the Redhead walked beside the Mere of Artemis, and came upon a very old woman, one of the few in whom the blood of Egypt still ran strong. Wild-eyed, she shrank from the boy, screaming: "He is here! He is here! Red Set the Destroyer!" Others came running, strove to silence her. "No, no, old mother! This is our young lord himself, he whom Queen Aithra bore in the Holy Birthplace!" But she cried again: "He too was born of Mother Sky, that Red One who slew His brother! Let the queen beware, for she has borne the Wrong Son—the Kinslayer! His hair will be a fire to burn up her House!" The boy went home sick and scared, glad for the first time that he had no brother. In vain Aithra strove to comfort him; he could see that she herself was afraid.

Herakles laughed and said, "They are true Egyptians, your old folk here. I remember when Eurystheus sent me to Busiris in Egypt; there they sacrifice all redheaded men, even all reddish-coated donkeys, to Asar, whom we call Osiris, because Set, who slew Him, had red hair. They would have sacrificed me, but my strength came upon me, and I broke my bonds, and slew the high priest at his own altar."

The boy laughed dutifully, but felt no better until old Pittheus came and said: "Child, we are all children of Earth and Starry Heaven. No man may kill another without slaying his own brother."

If so, it might often be necessary to kill your own brothers, when they were strangers and came to slay you and those you knew, yet somehow the boy was comforted.

On the ships of Herakles sailed, their prows cleaving the dark Unfriendly Sea. Round the cape called the Black, and those rocky Acherusian heights where the wind wails always, it is said to rise up ice-cold out of caves that lead down to the Kingdom of the Dead. Past the mouths of many-storied rivers: of the Sangarios and the Wolf, and of the flower-bordered Parthenios, the River of the Virgin, in whose sweet waters Bow-bearing Artemis was said to bathe after the day's hunting, before She rose again to heaven. They came to the mighty Halys, roaring like a lion as it plunged into the sea, and beyond that to the Iris, that has a valley lovely as a flower.

They came at last to the Thermodon, the river like no other, said to lack but four of having a hundred streams. They saw the plain of Themiskyra, lovely with deep grass and noble trees. But even when they saw fat cattle grazing, they saw no sign of man, or rather, of woman.

A boatful of them landed, reconnoitered, constantly expecting the sweet silence to be split by the sound of war-cries. But still all was unbroken calm.

Herakles stood frowning. "This is queer. Some of those women must be somewhere around."

"Maybe they are," growled Telamon, leaning on his great ashen spear. "Hiding and waiting to ambush us."

Nobody liked that speech; it put into words everybody's secret
fear. The emptiness of the green plain suddenly seemed to be as
full of eyes as a peacock's tail. Hidden, hostile eyes. Some men
reminded Herakles of the Amazons' poisoned arrows, begged him
to go back to the ships and wait for night. "Then we can creep
ashore unseen."

"Then they would be sure we came to attack them," rumbled
Herakles. "Peaceful traders do not sneak ashore after dark."

The Redhead had an idea. "Let us do what many traders do
when they do not speak the same tongue as those they would deal
with. Lay our goods out on the shore, then go aboard ship again
and keep watch."

"Leave the stuff for them to steal?" Telamon snorted.

"Only fools steal traders' goods, for then the traders do not
come back. Besides, I will stay here with the goods."

"Idiot, do you think you could stop a whole pack of Amazons?"
Telamon snorted again.

"No man could," said Herakles grimly. "Not even Herakles. No
flesh is poison-proof."

"But I will be living proof that we mean peace—sitting here
alone and unarmed! And I am the only one who can talk with
them. We must get at them somehow."

That last was true, and Herakles knew it. If he had to storm the
grim walls that rose to the south, his men would fall like flies.
Those walls seemed to be of unbaked brick, not stone, but he
guessed that they had a hard core of iron-hard logs. And there
would be the venomous hail of arrows. In the end, though most
reluctantly, he gave way.

"But be careful, lad; be very careful."

They laid out their goods as near the water as they could, so that
if need be the Redhead could jump in and swim, though thought
of those arrows made it seem very unlikely that he could reach the
sea. They set out cloth of gay colors, tall, beautifully decorated
pots such as the Cretans had once taught mainland men how to
make, and many shiny beads and gilded things.

Left alone, the boy sat and waited. The sun grew hot; he began
to sweat; also he grew very tired of sitting still. All his life sitting
still had been the thing that had tired him most. But to fidget
would be undignified, if unseen eyes were truly watching him.

Eyes somewhere in those cool-looking green inland places where
he could not go.

Eyes . . .

Maybe presently a few smiling Amazons would come and lay
down goods beside the Greek goods. Their first bid, a mute offer
of exchange. That was the way such trading was done. Inside their
walls the Amazons might be talking now, debating what to offer
and how much.

The sun grew hotter and hotter. Not to fidget became harder and
harder. His sweat tickled like small, teasing fingers. Once, twice,
he got up and added some water of his own to the sea. Doing that
was not undignified; a man had to relieve himself.

Noon came, that bright, strange time when shadows stand still
and evil Powers are supposed to be as strong as at midnight. He felt
hungry; why had he not asked the others to leave him something to
eat? Would those women never make up their minds? never come?

And then they came! Black as a storm cloud against the bright
still light, a host of thundering hooves, of shrill yet thunderous
war-cries: "Hip-POL-y-te! HIP-pol-y-TE! HIP-pol-y-TE-E!"

They had no chariots. They bestrode their horses as no male
warrior ever yet had done in battle, one heel of each rider digging
into one side of each horse. In their hands were bows and arrows
—and to each bow an arrow was fitted!

He sprang to his feet to face them. If he must die, he would die.
But he would not please them by showing fear.

Arrows whizzed and flew. Over his head, and around him,
between his arms and his body. When one flew between his legs,
a hair's breath below his as yet untested manhood, he could not
keep from jerking, and they laughed. Gloating laughter, that made
their white teeth shine like those of beasts. Suddenly all those
faces seemed to become one Face, vast, gaunt, and terrible, old
beyond imagining and as strong as it was old, ablaze with triumphant hate. . . .

It was gone. They were gone. They had wheeled their horses and
sped away. His heart leaped—he wanted to shout with relief and
joy. But then, wind-swift, they spun around and came at him
again, still laughing. Again arrows were fitted to their bows. Was
this the end?

He strained his eyes to see their faces, only their faces. Not their bows, or that other Face. They were all young, and none was ugly. One was magnificent; the golden circlet on her helm did not outshine her flying black hair. The younger girl beside her had the same face, but her hair was less dark; in it the sun found the gold of autumn leaves.

His eyes met hers, they leaped together. She seemed somehow to be close to him, as close as if their bodies were actually touching, breast to breast. Her mouth was not laughing, her eyes were warm and kind, troubled. . . .

Again the arrows whistled, but this time he stood firm, though their weird whine filled his head like the roaring of the sea. This time his legs were too close together for there to be any danger to his manhood; they could only kill him.

Again the riders wheeled and fled, then wheeled again, laughing. But this time their bows did not rise. They galloped back and surrounded him, gay and friendly now. The gold-crowned one, she who he thought must be the queen, stopped beside him, smiling.

"Boy, you are brave. But your comrades did wrong to leave you here. We cannot buy you. We are the Amazons, among whom no man may dwell."

He stiffened, his pride pricked. "Lady, I am not for sale. I am a freeborn man, the kinsman and herald of my captain, great Herakles, son of Zeus."

"Hera-kles?" She frowned. "I have never heard of him. And he has brought nothing worth buying except you and those pots. We weave much better cloth ourselves; and the jewelry is fit only for children to play with."

She was not bargaining; she meant it. The Redhead bit his lip, then said: "Lady, all this stuff belongs to King Eurystheus, who is a fool. But a God bade my cousin do his will and bring it here. Mortals may not fathom the purposes of the immortal Gods. Let Herakles himself come ashore, Lady, and speak with you."

"And bring his men with him? How many of them are there? And what do they look like?" She shot her questions at him as she had shot her arrows, but again his heart leaped. She did not want gewgaws, but maybe she wanted something else.

"We are ninety men, Lady. Most of us are young, and all of us are tall and straight and well shaped everywhere." He grinned.

"Well, we will see. Let all your men come ashore, bearing no arms but their short swords, if they have any—or else big knives to cut meat with. Ninety of us will come back with food—and armed only with our short swords."

CHAPTER 4.
___THE FEASTING

B IG HERAKLES gave thanks to all the Gods for his young kinsman's safety and cleverness. He also gave the Redhead a bear hug that all but cracked the boy's ribs. All were joyful but Telamon, who said grimly: "This is a trap. Will all of you be fools enough to stick your heads into the jaws of those accursed she-wolves?"

Herakles shrugged. "Stay aboard, if you are afraid. We will leave one ship afloat for you." Then Telamon said no more, only helped his comrades to beach all three ships. In the sea men bathed, washing off the sweat of weeks. There was much laughing and splashing, and later much combing of hair and beards. Finery long stored in sea chests was unpacked. To each man it seemed long since he had had a woman.

At last the Amazons came riding back, driving before them oxen laden with honey and meal and fruit. They had laid aside their leather war tunics. When the queen came forward to greet the strangers the thin fine Egyptian linen of her tunic showed every line of her splendid body. The luscious curves of hip and thigh, the rounded sweetness of her right breast, rippled as if through water. Her left breast, bared as an Amazon's always was in weather fit for battle, was a marvelous upstanding globe of ivory and rose. Herakles stared at her, and she at him. He thought: *This is a woman. Have I ever known one before?* And her heart sang: *O Lady, I thank You who have rewarded my waiting and sent me this man to be my man!*

He was made like a God. His bronzed arms and legs, even his face, bore the scars of many battles, but these were only proofs of his valor, of his humanness. All doubt and suspicion fell from her; truly this meeting had been meant to be. . . .

54

The Redhead soon saw that they needed no interpreter. To talk of the Golden Girdle so soon would not have been good manners anyhow. He slipped away and wandered among the fires over which the now slaughtered oxen were being roasted. He looked into the face of every Amazon he saw, but none was the right face. His heart sank.

But then at last he found her—the chestnut-haired girl he had seen among the arrows. She was helping others to put up a rude trestle table, to pile fruit on platters. At sight of him she stopped and they stared at each other, neither quite sure what to do. Then she smiled at him, frank and friendly, as another boy might have been.

"I am Antiope, sister of Melanippe the Queen. Who are you?"

"I am the Red One, and someday I will be King of Troizen." He was glad that he could match her, rank for rank; his pride was still sensitive. "But I thought your sister's name was Hippolyte."

"All our queens are called Hippolyte, 'She of the Galloping Horses.' Just as all Egypt's kings are called Pharaoh, and all Cretan ones Minos. Would you like to see our horses?"

"I would."

She led him to a green grove near the sea. For once he was not interested in horses, all he really wanted was to be with her. But he gasped when he saw them—he had not seen them well before, when they were coming at him beneath bows and arrows. They were all beautiful, all proud and graceful and sleekly glossy, built for both speed and strength. Never had he dreamed that there could be such horses anywhere.

"This is my own Chrysippe." With pride Antiope showed him a slender filly whose coat shone brownish gold. "Her color is rare —a true gift from the Goddess."

"It must be. She is beautiful. All your horses are; they make me proud to be akin to horses. Like me, the first horse sprang from Poseidon's own loins."

"You are the son of a God then?" She spoke without surprise or wonder. Many kings and kings' sons made that claim.

"Yes. But I see only mares here. Is it true, then, that in some lands the wind can get mares with foal?"

"No. We keep a few stallions to breed from, but not to ride. For every Amazon hopes her horse will be her comrade for many years, perhaps all her life, and as stallions age, their tempers grow uncertain. The grandmothers say they are too much like men—" She broke off, flushing. "I am sorry! I forgot you were a man!"

That last unmeant insult was far worse than the first one. His eyes flashed, but he kept his temper; he must not endanger Herakles' mission. He did say, hoping it would annoy her to be reminded of such carelessness: "All you women seem to have forgotten to tether your horses. I will help you do it now. It would be a shame for any of them to run away."

"They will not run away!" Now Antiope's eyes flashed. "Amazons do not lay bonds on those they love. Our horses know our feelings, as often we know each other's, without speech. They would never desert us, any more than an Amazon would desert a comrade in battle."

"But they could be stolen."

"The thieves would die beneath their hoofs and teeth! Also they have been taught to neigh their loudest whenever strangers draw near. We would come swiftly." She smiled again. "But let us not quarrel. You were brave today. I am glad now that our peoples did not fight; at first I hoped they would, for I have never been in battle."

That smile disarmed him; he grinned back at her. They sat down beneath a tree, and she stretched out her long, lovely legs. He started then, for he had never been so close to a girl's legs before.

"You were brave," she said again, "but you were never really in danger. We do not hit what we do not intend to hit. We were using only our hunting arrows too. The poisoned ones"—her voice saddened briefly—"are precious."

"I was never afraid." He tossed his head and laughed.

"You were," said Antiope coolly. "Anybody with any sense would have been. I do not like such jokes myself. I would never enjoy scaring people unless I really wanted to hurt them. But many do. . . . Have an apple"—she took two from a pocket inside her light summer cloak—"and stop pretending."

"I am not pretending! I was not afraid!" He nearly said, "of women."

"That is silly. I was afraid when I killed my bear."

"*You* killed a bear?" He stared at her, dumbfounded.

"Last summer. My first arrow did not bring him down, although it hit him squarely—Amazons never miss their mark, but bears are very strong—and he charged me. I was terribly afraid then."

"What happened?" Thought of her danger made him feel sick.

"Oh, I dodged back and forth among the pines, and my third arrow did get him. But he nearly got me. I have a great scar where he scratched my side. But a queer thing"—she hesitated, her voice lowering—"happened after he fell. His eyes—while I watched him dying they made me feel his pain."

The Redhead suddenly remembered the first deer he had killed. How he had looked down and seen the long legs twitching in helpless pain, all their power and fleetness gone. But he could not bring himself to match her, confession for confession. Only girls could admit to such softness . . . though never had he expected to know a girl who could kill a bear.

Antiope sat and wondered why she had told him what she had never told anyone before. Not even Marpe, her best friend among her age-mates. He was beautiful and brave, but only a stranger. Only a man. She began to munch her apple and he munched his.

But he looked at her. Her breasts were just beginning; they sat boldly upright, round as small apples, upon her young chest. Her tunic, like all Amazon tunics, left one bare. It was loose enough to let him see the soft path between the two, tender and rosy as apple blossoms, though all the rest of her that showed—especially those legs—was tanned to a smooth golden bronze. It was beautiful, that soft, sheltered place . . . Unknowingly, his hand reached toward her. They were old enough—surely they were old enough. . . .

"Princess, will you lie with me?" For all his longed-for manhood, his voice shook.

"I would like to very much," said Antiope politely, "but I cannot. It would be against our Law."

"Why? All the rest of you will sleep with my shipmates tonight. Your sister will sleep with Herakles—" He broke off sharply, remembering the ancient unwritten law of Troizen, that forbade a man to outrage a girl-child. "But you must be a woman! You are husband-high, and more. Tall and fine—"

"It is not that." Antiope understood, and her own pride rose. "Three moons ago the Moon-Bull came to me in my sleep, and thrust one of His horns into me—He who alone can enter a maid without breaking her maidenhead! I am able to bear a child. But I have not yet served my warrior years, or killed my man."

"You have not done *what?*"

"No Amazon may lie with a man until she has killed a man. So we make sure that weaklings will not bear children. Even then we must wait until we are twenty. Long ago, when we were fighting our way across the Great Mountains, Foremother Lysippe laid down that Law for us. So only can we keep a good-sized fighting force fit and ready for battle. Women with child too soon grow heavy and slow-moving."

"But to wait until you are twenty—by then you are almost old! To make you waste your youth without love—that is cruel!" He was shocked and aghast.

"Only an uncontrolled bitch would hate to do that much for her people." Again Antiope's eyes flashed. "We are not like your women, who sit in the dark all day, in smelly houses, while you men are outside in the wind and the sun. Maybe they need plenty of bed sport, who get so little of any other kind."

"Our women do not have to ride around shooting at other people. We protect them. They tend our houses and our children, they cook and weave. And the poor man's wife, who has to help her husband in the field—she gets plenty of your sun and wind." The Redhead's tawny eyes blazed.

"We too have houses and children to tend—and we protect ourselves. We work our fields. We too cook and weave, and also we dig and build and do smith's work. We train both ourselves and our horses for war. We run, leap, wrestle, hurl darts, and practice with the bow. It is good work—joyous work—all of it that can be done outdoors, anyhow. But when night comes we are ready to sleep—we need no men to wind our legs around!"

She stopped, panting. He said, appalled: "You work like slaves. You need men to take care of you—"

Antiope laughed. The sound did not seem to come from her own throat. "Men! Once we had men! We know their care. Never again will we bear that—better to die on the battlefield, even in defeat, raped and eyeless, mauled by men we fought as long as we could ride or stand. To some of us that has happened. But however we die we will live free!"

Her face had ceased to be her face. It was an old woman's, worn out by savage cruelties and long pain. Battered, scarred, and withered, yet still burning with a hate that would last as long as she did. For a breath's space the boy had a strange feeling that he had seen it before—that it was the same Face that had seemed to swallow up the faces of all those women whose arrows had whizzed around him. Then it was gone. Antiope's face was young again, her eyes were her own eyes, and bewildered.

"Stranger, what have I said?"

"Terrible things. What kind of low-bred dog would gouge a woman's eyes out?" His voice was sick with disgust.

"Some of the Kaska. Many of the men of Azzi." Antiope shrugged, then grew grave again. "Maybe I should explain to you. For long we Amazons have had to live like bees in a hive, and the Hive-Spirit grows within us. In battle it can make us terrible, give us strength beyond our own strength. Some say it is the spirit of Foremother Lysippe, that Molpadia, the War-Queen, says we must keep alive forever, but most think that we have all helped to build it—all of us, through all the generations."

"It can come and possess any of you—this Spirit?"

"Most of the time each of us is herself only, a sister to all the rest. But in times of danger we do work and fight like one woman. And—yes, sometimes that Spirit does seize one of us. For a little while." Within herself she added: *But my mouth is my mouth. Never again shall it speak any words but my words.* For Antiope could not bear not to be mistress of herself.

The Redhead said in wonder: "But what did your own men do? How could they have been worse than the enemies you have?"

For a breath's space Antiope hesitated again, then said: "They did evil—such evil as befouls the tongue that speaks of it. But since it is not a secret on which our safety turns, and you already know so much, maybe it would be unfair not to tell you the rest." Antiope also always prided herself on being fair.

She thought too: *If I can tell this tale without the Hive-Spirit's coming upon me I think I need never fear that it will come again.*

She said: "North of this sea is a little sea called the Maiotis. We Amazons dwelt beside it of old. Then women and men still fought side by side in war, as was the way of the First Folk. But only we women tended the fields and houses. For we alone owned them, we who had first thought of them. A woman needs a settled home to raise her children in.

"The men still hunted and fished and roamed, but they did not roam as far as of old. Each brought his catch home to be cooked by his mother or sister, or by the woman he wished to sleep with that night. None laid bonds upon another. None thought, "I was born better than certain others,' though any who was skilled in anything took pride in that skill.

"But times changed. We had new neighbors, with new ways. Men heard that elsewhere men were greater than women—their masters. Some of our young men grew restless and presumptuous; a few did evil. The old Wise Women grew angry; great sicknesses of the belly came upon those evildoers, and the worst of them died. Women said, 'It was the wrath of the Goddess,' but men began to mutter, 'Witchcraft.' "

They were not so easy to fool, thought the Redhead complacently. "But they should have said, 'poison.' " His sympathies had swung to the men.

"Yet still most men and women were friends. Tanais, son of Lysippe, was a leader among the young men, and he sought peace, for he loved his mother well. Every night he went home to sleep in her house, never in any other woman's. But Lysippe had been only thirteen when she had borne him; she was still the most beautiful of women, and one night she woke to find Tanais in bed with her, seeking to do that which no son should do with his mother."

The boy's breath caught in a sharp gasp. Antiope went on as if she had not heard. "He was driven out with curses, but many young men followed him. Deep in the forest they built themselves a house, and set up an idol, such a Man-God as our evil neighbors had. To Him they made bloody offerings. Soon no woman dared work alone in the fields; some were raped, others were carried off and never seen again.

"And then one night some of the men we still had left were caught trying to open the gates to those exiled and accursed ones. We drove them all out then—we who dared no longer trust any men. Mothers and sisters wept, but the Wise Women said, 'The Goddess wills it. The small sons we have left must be better reared.' And for a while all was quiet. When the Harvest Feast came women danced naked beneath the moon as of old, before the image of the Goddess. And there the men fell upon them. Brother slew sister, son slew mother—yes, many ripped open the bellies out of which they had come. They laughed, those murderers; they cried, 'We are free now from witchcraft forever!' Oh, Tanais had taught them well."

"Had he—killed Lysippe?" The Redhead's hands were clenched fists. He feared her answer.

"No. He struck her down. He stood over her and cried: 'Let us break her legs! Cripple her so that she cannot run away, or plot against us, but must always do as we bid. Work for us, and also lie with us, who for long can have no wives!' "

Antiope spoke slowly then, as if she hated to go on. "Evil was that time; of it I will say little. By day Lysippe crawled, who could not walk, a toiling drudge. By night for part of each moon she was all men's bed mate, and always she was Tanais'. The men made the little girls work hard too, for they had spared those too young to know the use of herbs. They said: 'These shall grow up knowing their place. Be what women ought to be, and henceforth always shall be. We will make good wives of them!' They beat them with sticks—never before had our children been beaten. Many little girls learned to fawn upon them, as dogs do upon cruel masters. But Lysippe watched well; she found a few she could trust, her own sister's child among them, and taught them what herbs they must gather. . . .

"Another Harvest Feast came, and in a fine new hall they had built the men gave thanks to their Man-God. But in the midst of their merriment agony came upon them. They spewed, they writhed and groaned, weak as little children. And Lysippe called upon all girls who had not become dogs to seize weapons and slay them. Tanais lived longest; they set him up in the fine, carved chair that he had called his throne, and Lysippe laughed in his face. 'Burn now with a new fire, son, you who have burned with such unhallowed fires!' She drove arrows through his arms and legs, pinned him to that chair. She and her girls fired the hall; they stood outside and watched it burn, laughing at his howls. When these were over they took horses and fled, those avengers, being too few to hold their land against those evil neighbors who had corrupted their men. But they had to ford a great river, and there the birth pangs seized Lysippe. She bore a boy. She looked once into his face, then cried, 'Go seek your father, Tanais, son of Tanais!' and hurled him into the flood. That river still bears his name."

Antiope's voice, that had faltered, grew steady again. "For many years Lysippe rode on, she who never walked again. Hard, hungry years; we were always in flight, we whom all men sought to slay or enslave. Anybody who was too weak to sit her horse we killed; her fate would have been worse had our foes found her alive. Oh, it was long and hard, that journey over the Great Mountains! But we finally reached these shores, we turned westward, and presently we saw a great flaming star fall from heaven—it that is now the Black Stone. Lysippe died that same night, first bidding us seek the place where it had fallen. 'For not too far from there will be your new home. And there you who have been hunted shall turn huntresses. Find and catch men, but lie with them before you kill them. So our race may live.' And as she said, so have we done. Her niece, the foremother of Melanippe and of me, led us here to lovely Themiskyra."

She was silent then, thinking uneasily of the murdered baby; she never had liked that part, and if anything it sounded even worse when you told it to a man. The Redhead too sat silent; never had he thought to hear a tale worse than that of the Great Darkness and the Great Sound.

He is a wanderer. Perhaps that was not always so, but something has hurt him —hurt him as deeply and as much, I think, as a man can be hurt—and he can never find true peace again. Never be quiet, content to stay long in any one place. And that is best, since he cannot stay here. Yet for this little while I have him, to hold and comfort and cherish, as one day I will the daughter he must have already planted in my womb. So thought Melanippe, where she lay with Herakles in her arms, in the black shadow of a beached ship. The sun had set, for now its fires were spent, like those of the lovers. But the west still bloomed softly, every cloud the color of a rose; its fading brightness seemed like both blessing and farewell. Herakles, drowsing, knew only that Melanippe was with him, and how good her nearness was. But Melanippe's heart ached for him. Had she not been Queen of the Amazons she would have been glad to go away with him forever, doing what she could to stanch that deep wound of which she knew only through her brief oneness with him. But she knew her duty to her people. How foolish it all seemed now, that morning-long wrangling with the mothers and the grand- mothers, and also her own secret, stabbing fears! Yet because she was a queen and knew her business, watchwomen still watched on the cliffs; no fleet for which these three ships were spying could steal up unseen in the night, find sleeping Amazons locked in the arms of their betrayers. Inland too, under the green cover of trees and bushes, more watchers waited. Three times between moonset and moonrise those sentries would be changed, but first certain chosen girls would creep out of this camp of lovers to reassure the watchers that all was well. That word would be carried back to sleepless, waiting Themiskyra. She had agreed to all that, and it was right, and yet what nonsense! Her arms tightened around dozing Herakles; she laid her cheek against his bearded one. She too drowsed a little....

The good smells coming from the campfires woke them both: the smells of roasting beef and lamb, and of grain puddings. They smiled at each other, knowing that dinner would soon be ready, and that then the black gentleness of the summer night would come. Night, and the pale, shining moonrise, and more love. ... Melanippe smiled, and laid her brown hand on his bigger one. Once again they needed no interpreter. Together they rose, and went toward the campfires.

Antiope and the Redhead had dozed a little while too; the grass beneath their tree was soft. She had let him hold her hand, and he had wondered what she would do if he tried to do more, but once again had been cautious for Herakles' sake. When they did wake, he suddenly shot another of his always numerous questions at her.

"You say your foremothers crossed the mountains at the World's End. That must have been a sight to see, the Black Noth- ingness on the other side of them! Did any of you fall off?"

Antiope stared in bewilderment, then threw back her head and laughed. "What tales people will tell about a place if it is far enough off!" Then, seeing him flinch, hurt, she sobered swiftly. "I did not mean to mock you; that would be no way to treat a guest. But I do not know where the world ends, and I do not know anybody who does. Beyond the Great Mountains called Kaukasos lies another sea, and then more mountains. Peaks higher than even the grim peaks of Kaukasos."

The Redhead felt astonished and also a little dizzy, wondering how far the earth did extend. But it was good to think how far off it must be, that black gulf of Nothingness. Then he remembered something else. "Folk say too that there are huge floating rocks near the mouth of this sea—stone islands that chase ships. Is that another lie?"

"It is! But"—the girl laughed merrily—"I know how that one got started. In winter parts of the sea sometimes freeze over, and then in spring great masses of ice float around for a while."

So he had been right! That thought gave him great satisfaction. He stretched and looked upward through the leaves. Where it showed between them the sky was rosy, all abloom with colors as tender as dawn.

Antiope looked up at that rosy brightness too and said, "Soon dinner will be ready. Maybe we had better go back to the others."

The Redhead wanted to go on being alone with her, but the mention of food made another desire stir in his belly. Since early morning he had had nothing but a little cheese hastily crammed down before he and the other men bathed. He went back with her to the shore, and from the cooking fires a delicious wave of smells rolled out to greet them. They saw Herakles and dark-haired Melanippe coming out, somewhat sandy, from under one of the ships, and Herakles, grinning, waved to his young kinsman. The Redhead felt wonder and a swift stab of envy. Then he and Antiope got their shares of steaming hot meat and pudding, piled on crude wooden platters, and she set hers down beside his on the sand. "Try to keep the ants off them while I get us a cup of wine."

One cup! Then they would share it. Across the brim their mouths might come close together, might even meet—no, should meet! But when she came back he gave a jump that nearly jerked him out of his smooth, sun-tanned skin. For she carried the whitened skull of a man!

She saw his startled look, and smiled matter-of-factly, without derision. "We drink from the skulls of the savage Kaska. Just as they drink from ours—when they can get them."

"Well, that sounds fair enough." She must not think him squeamish. He took a hearty swig from the skull, and warmth poured back into him, though his head swam a little. How red the wine seemed to glow where once the brains had been! Was that the last red light of the sunset? Then he thought of another question.

"These Kaska—do they father your babes? Somebody must." What a grisly business that would be—drinking from the skulls of your own fathers!

"For long they did. They were all we could get—except now and then a man of Azzi. The chiefs of Azzi claim to be our far-off kin, sprung from those few of our men who escaped the Great Kinslaying. It may well be true, for they are treacherous snakes. Even the Kaska are better, though they do not wash often enough." She made a face.

"Then you have somebody else now?"

"When my mother became queen the Hittites were in great trouble. They were being attacked on four fronts; their great city of Hattusas itself had been partly burned down. Subbiluliuma— he who is now the Sun, the Great King—was then a young prince fighting the Kaska, here in the north. He held them back while his father lay ill and his brother, the royal heir, let the other foes keep coming. Also the weak brother feared the strong one—he did not send him needed supplies. That forsaken prince seemed doomed; his lot was hard, and to my mother it seemed that no Amazon could have borne it more bravely."

"She helped him, then?"

"In a dream the Goddess bade her do so if he would swear to respect the Law of the Amazons—never to cross our borders and to be our friend against all other foes. And he has kept that oath always. When his father died and the generals slew his wicked brother he laid it upon all the kings who will come after him. And now, every spring, when the Hittites hold the feast of their Sun Goddess of Arinna—She that is truly the same as our Goddess— our young women go to meet his men in Her holy groves and gardens at Arinna. The daughters born afterward are ours; we send them the sons."

"You mate with the Hittites? Those mighty warriors!"

"Only their mightiest lie with us. The Rabutti, the Great Ones, and the most valiant captains. Only the Great King ever lay with my mother, Queen Otrere."

"Then he—Subbiluliuma—is your father!" The Redhead stared. Subbiluliuma—the man mighty as Pharaoh. Arrow-swift, a thought darted through his head: What a father-in-law for a man to have!

"Mine and Melanippe's. But he has no rights over us." Antiope's young chin rose proudly. "Most Amazons do not know who their fathers are, and it does not matter. Not that Melanippe and I do not like the Great King—we do. But we are freeborn Amazons; our own mistresses."

"But he could marry you to kings! You would never have to work again or to risk your beautiful bodies in battle. And your husbands would never dare ill use you—I have heard my grandfather say that when a Hittite princess is given in marriage she must always be the first wife, honored like a Goddess!"

"And how would we—or he—know that he would choose us men we would like to sleep with?" Antiope's lip curled. "And if we did not like them we could not leave them. No. We are free women, and freedom is worth work and wounds and death."

Argument was useless; she would never understand, she had been too badly brought up for that. The Redhead swung to another matter, one she had not made clear.

"You say that most of you do not know who your fathers are. But your mothers must—or how could they send your brothers to them?"

Antiope shrugged. "Amazons bear fine sons. Any Hittite is glad to get one."

"But how is it worked?"

"My brothers—Telepinu and Sharra-Kushukh and little Zannanza, the youngest of us all—were sent straight to the royal palace. The others are sent to the Temple of the Sun Goddess, where men come to claim them."

"Men who think they may be the fathers?"

"Those who meet by night in the Holy Groves are not supposed to see or speak to each other. The grandmothers insisted on that. But"—hers was the sudden, mischievous grin of a boy planning to steal apples—"the moonlight does fall through the leaves. I think the same couples often do meet more than once. Even tell each other their names."

She would go to those unholy Holy Groves—she! Lay down that straight, splendid young body beneath the Gods knew how many men! Sick rage boiled within the Redhead. If only he could save her—carry her off! In Troizen he could marry her, teach her civilized ways; she would soon be glad that she had only him. But if her sister gave Herakles the Girdle, would he think woman-stealing a breach of hospitality?

Then Herakles' own great voice came booming through the merriment of the feast. "Boy!" The Redhead rose, and Antiope with him; together they went to Herakles and her sister.

Herakles said: "Boy, tell the queen that King Eurystheus wants her Golden Girdle. That if she will give it to me I will fight any foe of hers she names. Bring her his head."

The Redhead translated, and when Melanippe looked blank he explained: "The Golden Girdle that your foremother wore when she crossed the Great Mountains."

For a breath's space both girls looked blank, then Antiope laughed. "They think we have some kind of sacred girdle!"

Slowly and carefully the queen explained: "Foremother Lysippe had no golden girdle. We were poor and few when we crossed the Great Mountains, glad to get enough skins and blankets to cover us on winter nights. And since all men we met on that journey sought to rape us, in a dream the Goddess showed Lysippe how to make a girdle of knotted hide that would hold off ravishers awhile—give a girl's comrades a chance to come to her help."

When Herakles understood his jaw dropped. "Then what on earth am I to take back to Eurystheus?"

The queen smiled. "You have heard of that night-black stuff, the hardest of all metals, called iron? Of old even the cunning Egyptians believed it could be found only in stones that fell from heaven. But here in the north it can be dug from the ground. From that we Amazons now make our girdles. Treasures more precious than gold, and with locks so cunningly wrought that even if smashed they cannot be forced. I will get you one tomorrow. You can have it goldwashed on your way home if Eurystheus does not know the value of iron."

Antiope laughed. "He can have mine now. I alone of all here tonight am wearing such a girdle."

After a breath's space Melanippe laughed too. "Well thought of. Areia the smith can soon make you a new one."

Both sisters went into the shadow beneath the ship. When they came back and put the blackly gleaming thing into his hand—then indeed did the laughter of great Herakles boom through the graying twilight.

CHAPTER 5.
WAR AT THE WORLD'S END

NIGHT FELL. The moon rose. Amazons and Greeks began pairing off, walking farther down the pale, shining shore, or turning inland, to lie down in the sweet-scented grasses. Melanippe and Herakles rose to go back into that blackness beneath his ship, but first Melanippe said to Antiope: "Go home now, little sister. And the Goddess be with you."

"And with you." Antiope rose.

"I will go with you as far as the horses." The Redhead rose too.

He had no plan; he only wanted to be with her a little longer. But as they walked inland, smelling the sweet live smells of growing things in the darkness, he thought of what those other couples must be doing, and warmth rose in him. He caught her hand. "Princess, must you go so soon?"

Antiope knew then that she had been wanting him to touch her. Knew too the unwisdom of that, now that her girdle was gone. She wondered whether to pull her hand away or to try merely saying no and shaking her head. Then suddenly something made her look back over her shoulder at the curving beach that stretched, weird and silvery, toward the southern mountains. Like the coils of a white, waiting snake. . . .

"I must go." She pulled her hand away. "Molpadia has been searching the mountains for foes of whom a dream warned her. If she came home to find both Melanippe and me gone, she might think your people those foes. For you do have three ships, and she dreamed of three birds."

"Molpadia? Her you called the War-Queen?"

"Yes. My mother's sister, who reared me. She does not like men, but if I am there to tell her that Melanippe's pledged word protects you strangers, she will do you no harm."

But she will not be there. She is not likely to come back for two or three more nights. Folly, folly, to be afraid! And yet—what might happen if Molpadia and her war band were to come riding furiously down that white beach. . . .

The Redhead said no more. They had nearly reached the horses when suddenly a shadow blackened the moonlight. Telamon sprang out of the darkness, breathing hard, blood dripping from his knife.

"Boy, has Herakles already gone to bed with that—?" He called Melanippe a foul name.

Antiope saw the blood, heard his rage, although she could not understand his words. She leaped away, but not fast enough. Telamon caught her by the arm, "Be still, girl—if you would live!"

Lightning-swift, her free hand became a fist that drove into his belly. One knee drove as hard for his groin; it did not hit its mark squarely, but Telamon doubled up, gasping. Then she was gone; the night had swallowed her up.

The Redhead sprang after her, but Telamon's hand grasped him. "Back! Back to the ships! The Gods curse that bitch pup—now she will warn her pack."

"Of course she will, you fool! You have made her think us all traitors!" The Redhead cried out again, now in the royal tongue of Kanesh, trying to reassure Antiope, begging her to come back. But there was no answer; the night was as still as death.

But not for long. Bewildered Greeks and Amazons came running. Melanippe, doe-swift, was ahead of even Herakles.

"Dogs, where is my sister?" Her eyes blazed at both Telamon and the boy, but only for a breath's space. Telamon's knife pierced her throat. Between his teeth he growled one word, "Traitress!" Bubbling blood choked her death-cry. So, in the words of Hesiod, died blameless Melanippe.

Herakles' roar was the roar of a wounded bull. His great fist shot up. The Redhead thought in swift joy: *He will kill Telamon with one blow!* But before that dreadful fist could fall the Amazons were upon all three of them, men and boy. Their war-cry seemed to split the heavens: "HIP-POL-Y-TE! HIP-POL-Y-TE-E-E!" Their prey went down beneath a mass of knives and teeth and kicking feet. But Herakles was still Herakles. As a volcanic mountain rises up through boiling waves, so he rose up. Bruised and cut in many places, bitten in as many, he shook off the maddened women and pulled his bleeding comrades free. His voice rang through even that battle cry: "Back! Back to the ships!"

The Redhead never clearly remembered that battle, his first. The flight, the blows, nothing was real save that terrible battle cry that beat at them like a sword of flame: "HIP-PO-OL-Y-TE! HIP-POL-Y-TE-E-E!" He knew that, shamefully, he worked while others fought; with a few comrades he drove his stinging, mauled body to get a ship upright and back into the sea. Greek short sword clashed against Amazon short sword, made a wall of death to shield the workers. Yet again and again a few Amazons broke through. One the Redhead knew: a girl who had spoken to him and Antiope at the feast; she had smiled and been friendly then. He knew her name and cried it aloud, absurdly trying to make her change back and be friendly again. But he had to kill her even as he cried it, driving his knife deep between her young breasts. He was never able to remember that name again.

The Greeks had only their knives; all their other weapons had been stored in locked chests in one ship, and Herakles had given Melanippe the keys. Where she had put them no man knew. Men died trying to reach those chests; shrieking Amazons guarded that ship so that none could try to right it. But at last the other two were upright, slowly sliding down into the sea. Raging Amazons sprang at them and were knocked off with oars, yet most sprang back again. One man fell with the woman he had struck, fast in her arms; many knives pierced him before he hit the sand. A girl fell, and screamed horribly as she was ground beneath the hull. Yet finally the ships floated free. Herakles, savagely beset from two sides, was fighting fiercely for the third ship when a great new war-cry tore through the night.

"HIP-PO-OL-Y-TE! HIP-POL-Y-TE-E-E!"

A fresh horde of Amazons, mounted and fully armed, was charging down upon the Greeks!

Herakles turned to cover his men's retreat. Like the Hittite Storm God he stood, or like his own Father Zeus, the flailing oar in his right hand mighty as a thunderbolt. The Redhead thought in horror: *They are not using their poisoned arrows because they want to take him alive! And they can ride him down!* Somehow he tore himself from the men who were dragging him to the sea, ran back to join the few who still fought beside Herakles. But a sweep of the great left arm hurled him back; two of those badly needed men seized him again, to carry him seaward. In anguish he squirmed and screamed. For a breath's space it seemed to him that that whole oncoming horde had only one Face: that terrible old woman's face that briefly had blotted out Antiope's.

Then he saw her. Antiope herself was charging Herakles!

Ax in hand she came, standing upright upon the back of golden Chrysippe. Her face was her own face, but it blazed with fury such as he never would have dreamed that it could hold. A man leaped from one side, trying to stab her horse, and the Redhead's heart came into his mouth. But she swerved, arrow-swift, and her ax came down, splitting the man's skull. Antiope had killed her man.

Again she swung toward Herakles. Could she dodge that terrible oar? And if she did—if she did . . . The Redhead bit his lips until the blood ran down them. But now the Amazons behind her were rushing up. A tall woman, her helm gold-encircled, caught her round the body. Antiope's cry rang over shore and sea: "Let me go! Let me at him! He has murdered my sister!"

Big Herakles did not wait to see which Amazon won. He waded out into the sea, what men he had left around him. Arrows whizzed after them, then stopped when a wave of mounted Amazons poured into the sea. With joyous shouts the men in the nearer ship pulled Herakles and his comrades aboard, but the screaming women were close behind. Battle still raged; the oars struck down woman after woman, smote the chests of rearing horses; but men died too. At last the ships pulled free and sailed away. A great cry followed them: a cry that to all aboard seemed like the howl of one gigantic balked and savage beast.

But the Redhead, looking back toward the moonlit shore, saw a sight that made his heart sing. Antiope was still there. Still fast in her aunt's grip—if that tall, gold-crowned woman was indeed Molpadia the War-Queen, as he guessed. Then the black waters widened between them, and he saw Antiope no more.

· · ·

In the dawn that was breaking gray and comfortless, bleak as the face of Death Himself, Telamon faced Herakles. "I saved you from those treacherous bitches, O son of Zeus."

"Saved us!" Herakles' harsh laughter was like a bellow of pain. "You raised them against us! She is dead—dead! And many of our people with her. You did it all—you killed her! Oh, dog and fool —dog and fool!"

His head lowered like that of a bull about to charge. Men held their breath, and again the Redhead thought gladly, *This time he will kill him!* But the sea was choppy, and the ship rolled beneath their feet. Once-merry Peleus, ashen now, had time to spring to his brother's side.

"Hear him, Herakles! We are all your men here, all Greeks together, and we two brothers stood beside you on the beach till the last. He has a right to be heard!"

Herakles' great chest heaved, his fingers worked. All men looked to see him seize the two and crack their heads together, smashing both like eggs. But he was hurt and weary, also his lifelong training held, his warrior's code. These were his men. . . .

He said heavily, his voice hoarse and still savage: "Speak."

Telamon's voice rose high and almost shrill; he clung to his anger, warming himself at its sinking fires to keep out the cold of fear. "They meant treachery, those murdering bitches—I knew it from the beginning! So at moonrise, when my bitch pretended she had to go into the bushes to relieve herself, I knew better. I crept after her, I saw her meet another woman—one helmeted and fully armed! They whispered together, there in the dark."

"Of course they did!" The Redhead cried angrily. "Your girl was only telling the other that everything was all right! The women in the city were bound to be anxious, so they arranged to get news of those by the shore."

Telamon laughed. "Without doubt that one bore a message, but I did not let her deliver it—halfway back to the city I caught and killed her! Then when I came back to camp I grinned at my own bitch and made signs that I wanted to be alone with her. And once I was I took her by the throat and strangled her!"

"And what does all that prove except that you are a truce-breaking murderer?" The Redhead's tawny eyes blazed.

Peleus said, his voice tired: "You could have told Herakles about the meeting between the women. Have let him speak to the queen. She had shown us great hospitality."

"She would have lied!" Telamon's voice became a howl. "They all lied, those bastard mothers of bastards! What else would any of them use their mouths for? Except maybe to eat our flesh with, after they had worn us out with their whoring, and then butchered us in our sleep. With their whole pack to help them! But at least I slowed its coming!"

"You brought it down upon us!" the Redhead cried out again.

Telamon was silent then. All men were silent, holding their breath. Until at last great Herakles said drearily: "This is the curse that has followed me always. The wrath of jealous Hera, my Father Zeus' Goddess-wife. She drove me mad and made me murder my own wife and children—and now, under some shape of illusion, She has done this. The queen was true—she put herself into my hands, hostage as well as hostess. She gave me the girdle as a gift. Never again let me hear any man speak evil of her!"

Men breathed easily again then, satisfied. After all, the Amazons were outlanders—women with strange, unnatural ways—and Telamon was a man and a Greek, one of themselves. Better to lay all blame upon a jealous Goddess, about whose misdeeds nothing could be done.

But dreary was that homeward voyage. Herakles had won the Girdle (some girdle, at least), but at the cost of many Greek lives. Of a Greek ship, too, and much gear. Losses that mattered far more to most men than the shameful murder of a friendly queen. Yet poets of a later age were to manage to turn all this into glory, giving Herakles nine ships (far more than Eurystheus ever would have trusted him with), and letting him lose none. Only Hesiod, the earliest, even remembered who had slain Melanippe. Most gave Herakles himself the credit, for he, being the greatest man there, should have done the greatest deed. So, through the ages, the murder of the Amazon has stained his name, and always will. Perhaps not altogether unjustly; he had always known that Telamon was a murderer.

Only once on the long way home did he ever speak of her again. Then, alone with the Redhead, he said simply and sadly: "It was a pity—a great pity. I never had a woman a man could have had better sons by." That was the greatest praise Herakles could give a woman, he who had no skill to say what was in his heart. How far Melanippe herself had been from wanting a son never entered his head.

But Telamon sulked all the way home. He had saved everybody, and nobody had praised him. So it had been always—in his father's house, when he was young, all the smiles and petting had always been for that gay, grinning young bastard Phokos, who had had no right even to be born. But nobody noticed Telamon's sulks; all were too used to them. In afteryears, according to great Sophocles, his own son was to say of him: "He never smiles more for good luck than for bad." His unjust exile of that same son—suspected by nobody but him of having plotted to kill a brother —seems like a kind of twisted confession. He could believe no other guiltless of his own crime.

But the Redhead thought often, with sick anger, of that lovely queen lying in her blood. Thought oftener of lovely, living Antiope. She too would make a glorious mother for sons—his sons! And though she must hate him now, she would not, when she understood. When storm winds beat about the returning ships they were never louder than his inward cry to her: "I will come back!"

He would get her. There was plenty of time. Not for a long while yet would she be twenty.

Of old, beside the little Sea of Maiotis, the Amazons would have built a great mound over their slain queen, and have impaled the stuffed bodies of her enemies on stakes all around it. Now they could spare no food-raising land for mounds, no lives to defend such eye-drawing targets from desecrating raiders.

Yet inside the city of Themiskyra they did build her a kind of couchlike earthen mound, house-high, with dead Greeks piled all about it. For three days and three nights she lay there, fine furs and mantles shielding her from the birds of the air, and for three days and nights they wept and wailed for her. Sometimes some stopped to kick and curse or further mutilate the bodies of those they thought her slayers. Whenever they could, they also urinated or defecated on that stinking flesh.

But on the morning of the fourth day they burned the Greek corpses, so cleansing the city of much of the foul stench, then put what was left in great wide-mouthed jars. Later those charred fragments would be sprinkled on the fields to give the earth something of the dead men's strength and life. Though treacherous and evil, the dead had been good fighters. At nightfall the Amazons took down the young queen herself; they cut off her head so that later, as a skull, it might be given obsidian eyes and a plaster mask and sit, like those of her foremothers, upon the shelf that ran around the little room behind the Goddess' altar. Only Lysippe's own head hung above that altar, though all shared her guardianship, faithful even in death to Themiskyra.

The queen's body they bore reverently to one of the log-terraced fields that lined the lower mountainsides. There, when the moon had set and the night was at its blackest, they buried her. No sound was made save by cloth-muffled spades; no Kaska spy, if any, by fantastic ill luck, should have reached the heights above, must know what befell below. For that same reason they carefully replanted and watered the tender young grain that had just been sprouting. Amazons were thrifty; they always buried their dead where that emptied flesh could enrich the fields that fed their people. But any other body so unseasonably dead, even a War-Queen's, would have had to wait in the deep cellars beneath the Three Houses of Themiskyra, until the now-tender young grain grew tall and was reaped. But this was the queen who would have been the Childbearer; her body would enrich the earth enough to repay any loss.

Molpadia spoke the words of old ritual: "Sleep well, Child and Queen, in the womb of Earth your Mother. Help Her to make the grain grow; then rise again when the time comes for you to return to us, your people."

Antiope spoke the last words, her voice trembling: "May your new body be born of me, O my sister! May it be flesh of my flesh, blood and bone of me who love you!"

She waited, hoping, longing for some sign, some answer. A bird flying across the dark heavens, some tiny thing scuttering through the field beside her. But none came; there was nothing, nothing save the silence and the blackness. . . .

She wept then, her face buried in her hands to hide the tears that she forgot none could see. For the time of mourning was over; now

life and work must go on. Then she threw back her head and cried
fiercely: "If only I had gone back to her!"

Molpadia's voice, cold as snow, was yet soft as snow. "You did
what was best, saving yourself. You who now are the last Childbearer of the blood of Lysippe."

"Yet I might have saved her! Side by side we might have fought
and lived! Many others did."

"Side by side you might have fought and died, as too many
others did. Now we have you, and therefore hope. Enough of ifs
and what-might-have-beens. They cannot change what is. I too
could wail aloud because the dream that brought me home came
a night too late. Because my eagerness to search out foes who were
not there shut out even the Goddess—twisted Her warning."

Antiope thought bitterly: *Melanippe too tried to tell you that the foe
might come from the sea.* She said tonelessly: "Yet you did come
back."

"Even then I wasted time. I was cautious, I waited. When you
rode into the city we had not yet sent out scouts to search for that
murdered messenger. Though I had not let my warriors take their
arms off—I who know the ways of men."

"We did not know them—we did not!" Antiope moaned.

"Now you do, and you will listen to no more smiling traitors.
Nor will you outride your friends when charging the foe, you who
have neither sister nor daughter. If saving you had not been my
first care, we might have got them all, the dogs—have had all their
vile heads to drink from!"

Antiope stiffened. "You saved *him*—their leader, the guiltiest of
all! He that had looked at her as if he loved her!" Her voice broke;
that other agony she never could confess to any stabbed her. *He
too looked at me as if he loved me, that boy I thought my friend. And all the
time he must have known—have shared his comrades' cruel cunning plot!* Yet
for half a breath's space, when she had seen him fighting to get
back to his kinsman, she had been proud—proud of his courage.
Of that murdering traitor's! She fought that horror back; remembered only Herakles and Melanippe. "I would have killed him if
you had not stopped me, seized me. I was so close to him—so
close!" Again her voice broke, this time in grief and rage of which
she was not ashamed.

"And then his comrade might well have slain you." Again Molpadia's voice was snow-cold, but not snow-soft.

"Maybe—maybe not. But it was not I—nor any of those green girls, my fellow maidens, whom you did not think fit to ride with you into battle—who rode into the sea that night and so kept us from using our arrows on the fugitives for fear of hitting them too —and those arrows were our only hope!" To her shame she wept aloud then, unable to strangle her sobs.

"That too happened after you had drawn my eyes from the fools. They should have known better, but not only maidens go mad with grief." Suddenly the older woman's arms went around her. "Oh, child, child, all this is folly! Only one thing matters now. The Amazons have no treasure so precious as your life! Remember that."

After a breath's space Antiope said soberly: "You are right, Mother's sister. I will remember."

The parched, hotly golden days of late summer were already ending when Herakles brought the Redhead back to Troizen. He turned back swiftly to golden Mycenae to deliver the girdle and also to give Eurystheus the chance to set him another Labor. Truly Herakles would never again know rest. His ships went with him. All ships were making for their home ports now—or so men thought. Not even Minos' captains cared to brave the season of cold and storms.

At night, approaching winter soon made the gray cliffs above Troizen's salt mere white with frost. The trees on the lower mountain slopes turned red and gold, as if on fire. And then, when all ships should have been in their home ports, a great fleet came sailing up from the south. Unnatural was that coming, as if the birds had come back to build their nests in winter instead of spring. Grim-faced fishermen bore the news to Troizen—"Only Cretan Minos could have so many ships." Like frightened birds the women fluttered around Aithra. Calm and queenlike she comforted them: "We have done no wrong, my dears. We have nothing to fear from Minos the Just." And they were comforted; by ancient custom she was their ruler, as her father was their men's. Only the Redhead saw that his mother too was afraid.

Sadly, wise Pittheus spoke, out of his serenity that seemed as unbreakable as that of Troizen's great gray rocks. "We of the south are safe. But I fear that Minos comes to avenge his son's death upon him who has always been our friend. Upon Aegeus, King of Athens."

Many sighed with relief; some nodded in understanding. Athens was the greatest of the so-called Twelve Cities of Attica, the first land north of the Isthmus. Athens was but a poor, mean place beside the great cities of the south, beside Messene and Mycenae rich in gold. Yet last summer Androgeos, son of Minos, had died there, in the great bull games given in his honor.

Aithra cried out sharply: "But how could Aegeus have expected the Prince of Crete to fall before any bull? Are not the Cretans famed for their skill with bulls? We of the mainland only ape them."

Pittheus said heavily: "Our young men and maidens play with young bulls; the skilled keep the game bloodless. But even the Cretans never let their own children face mighty, full-grown bulls like the Bull of Marathon—him that Aegeus sent against Androgeos. Not unless the huge beasts have first been well dosed with poppy juice to make them slow-moving. Such risks are taken only by trained slaves from the Sunrise Lands."

Aithra cried out again: "Then this is her doing—the vile witch Medea's! Never of himself would Aegeus have thought of planning harm to a guest. Ill has she repaid his pity—she whom he took in when Jason the Argonaut deserted her! May the Gods help him in his trouble—and may the Furies tear the flesh from her bones!"

The Redhead felt the anger, dull as yet, that he would always feel whenever the great Cretan moved against any mainland man. But he also felt a little wonder. *By sea, Athens is not far away. Why, if Aegeus is an old friend of ours, has he never visited us here in Troizen? He could have, so easily, before this trouble came upon him.*

CHAPTER 6.

WAR BETWEEN KINGS

AEGEUS WAS indeed in trouble. He may have found it hard to remember when he had ever been out of it. As boys he and his brothers had plotted joyously against great odds to restore their father, exiled King Pandion of Athens, to his throne. As sturdy redheaded young men they had done it, killing their usurping kinsman Metion and all but one of his sons; Pandion had died a king again, but his death had ended the unity between the brothers. Nisos, the second-born, had gone back peaceably to be king in Nisa on the Isthmus, the little city-state that had been their mother's heritage, and the home of their childhood. But the two youngest brothers, big Pallas and young Lykos, "the Wolf," had been dissatisfied with their portions. Soon they had begun to whisper against Aegeus, the firstborn:

Our mother's belly was already big with him when our father first saw her. But who can blame an exile for wanting to climb into the warm comfortable bed of a king's daughter? Of an heiress princess?

The whispers grieved Aegeus; he had loved his dead mother, and would have liked to keep on loving his brothers. But what grieved him more was that he had no son; he was a big fine man, as lusty a lover as any of his brothers, but he never got any results and they did. The Wolf's wife whelped in due time, and all men marveled at the prodigious stream of sons that poured from Pallas' mighty loins. It lent added force to the whispers: _The true-born is fruitful, but the bastard a barren stock._ And the common people still believed that the land's fertility depended upon that of the king's loins. Aegeus must have lived in fear of the weather; a prolonged drought or unseasonable rains such as might rot the crops in the fields—either could have finished him.

One day his wife, Melite, came to him. "Lord, we have been married many years, yet I am barren. None will blame you if you send me back to my father's house." But Aegeus answered heavily: "Woman, be still. Which of our slave women has had a child by me?" Within a moon Melite was dead—of a witch's brew that she and her old nurse had been told was sure to get any woman with child.

He had no better luck with his next wife, buxom young Chalkiope. In her time witches came openly to the palace, and the night she died the eldest of them faced Aegeus over her body.

"Seek no more help of us, King. Once the Mother was mighty, but now Her power wanes. One stronger than we fears him you might beget—" But on that word she choked, her face turned purple as if unseen hands grasped her throat, and she fell to the floor and died.

Only the foolish words of a crazy, dying old woman. Yet they haunted Aegeus; he thought, *I will kill no more good women,* and took no more wives. Presently Lykos grew bold and plotted against his brother, who caught him at it and exiled him. Then Pallas, though secretly glad to be rid of a rival, came before Aegeus, his eyes tear-filled, and said, where many men could hear him: "Brother, how could you believe such cruel lies? Drive out the youngest son of our mother?" The whispers grew louder; they buzzed and hissed.

Daidalos became Aegeus' one comfort. He, the sole surviving son of Metion, the man whose father had exiled Aegeus', walked free and unafraid in Athens—living proof that the king was no cruel and jealous man, hating his own kin. Daidalos was no warrior (one reason for his survival), but a great artist. He made both beautiful things and strange ones, such as no man had ever heard of; some of his quaint contraptions, like folding chairs, were even useful. But he took an apprentice, the son of his sister Perdix, who alone had cherished him during his bullied boyhood, when both father and brothers had despised him who was unlike them. Maybe the pupil showed signs of equaling or excelling the master, maybe his doting mother only thought he did, but in a fit of jealous rage Daidalos struck the boy down. He was caught trying to bury the body; Aegeus had to exile him too.

Then again rage took Daidalos. He said: "Gladly will I go—to great Crete, where artists are honored, where a man can get justice, even if he is not exactly like all other men."

Rage took Aegeus too. "Go then! But if ever you rouse the wrath of Minos the Just, you will find mine feather-light beside it."

So Daidalos went away across the wine-dark sea, and no mainland man thought ever to see his face again. But Aegeus went home, to be greeted with the news that Pallas had another son. The boy may have been Pallas' twentieth or thirtieth; he was surely one more than Aegeus could bear.

He called for his chariot and horses and set out for holy Delphi to ask the question he long had both feared and ached to ask: *How shall I get a son?* Once long ago he had gone there, like other noble youths, to have his hair cut and the shorn locks given to the God. But the power and sanctity of Delphi, out of which Poseidon had been driven, were not yet altogether sweet to Poseidon-worshipers, and the Athenians loved Poseidon. Aegeus had foolishly hated leaving his hair there; a man's hair was one of the things that could give witches and sorcerers power over him. Yet they were honored men, the priests of Delphi; they served a God. *Do not be a fool, son of Pandion—for son of Pandion you are! Go humbly and in reverence to Delphi, for there is your last hope.*

He came to those bare, awesome crags called the Phaidriades, the Shining Ones, that will keep watch over Delphi forever. To Pterelas, whose name meant "the Feathered," that same high priest he had met in his youth. Lean, hawk-eyed Pterelas had been in his prime then; he was old now, yet that aged, changed face startled Aegeus. He seemed to have seen it many times, in many unremembered dreams. While the heat of flames rose around him, and the smell of scorching hair; while over and over those beaklike lips spoke one terrible, half-remembered sentence: *You will never—* Never what? Then the hawk eyes met his squarely, and both question and grim dreams were forgotten as if they never had been.

Pterelas led him to that dark place where the God entered the Pythia, making her writhe like a beast in heat. Of old the oracular priestesses of Earth the Mother had been proud, noble women; now they were but drugged, mumbling things. This one's words, even when interpreted by the priests—as all messages now were —made no sense to Aegeus.

"Loose not the bulging wineskin's mouth, O King of men, until you come again to high Athens."

In vain Aegeus offered Pterelas all the gold he had or could hope to raise. "The God has spoken, man of Athens. Who are you to be discontented with His word?" The hawk eyes gloated; for a weird breath's space Aegeus had a vision of a long sharp beak sprouting from the hard mouth beneath them, tearing at his testicles. He almost fled.

Outside, in the clean sunlight, he suddenly thought of Pittheus. Of the wise first-born of Pelops, who yet had cut himself off from the fierce and cunning race of Pelops, and now reigned peacefully in little Troizen. If any man on earth could tell him what that oracle meant, Pittheus could.

But on his way south he stopped at Korinth, where Jason of the Argonauts had just repudiated Medea, daughter of sun-born Aietes. She could not go home; she had incurred her terrible father's wrath by helping Jason to win the Golden Fleece; plenty of men said under their breath that she had really won it by herself. Now she sat alone in her darkened house while all made merry at Jason's wedding to the King of Korinth's daughter. On the morrow she must go into banishment.

"And Jason allows that? Lets you be cast out homeless after all you have done for him?" Aegeus asked, aghast.

"Jason says he owes no thanks to me." The wry twist of her lips was too bitter to be a smile. "Only to the terrible bright Love Goddess who made me serve him. Well, so be it. The Gods know what I have done for Jason, and what he has done to me."

Aegeus was outraged. How could any man abandon a faithful wife—especially one who had borne him two fine sons? He looked at the boys—whom Jason would keep—and then at her again. Long ago he had admired her, when Jason had been a guest in Athens. With some color on her cheeks, some flesh on her bones, she might still be beautiful. . . . And she said softly, "Lord, if you take me in, if you give a home to me who am homeless, you too shall have a son. By all my powers, I swear it!"

He swore by Earth the Mother and by the all-seeing Sun to take her into his own house, never to turn her out or give her up to any foe. Then he gave her gold and left her. "For to carry you off with me now might mean trouble between Athens and Korinth, where you are called a banished witch. But come to me in my own land, where I am lord, and none may question my doings."

But he did not wholly believe in her powers; he still went on to Troizen. And before he reached there all the roads of Apia were buzzing with tales of horror. Medea had sent her two boys to Jason's new bride armed unknowingly with deadly gifts—with golden robes that burst into flame on the flesh of the wearer. The princess had died in agony, as had the old king her father—he had tried to help her, a risk her strong, still-young bridegroom had not taken. Then, because she could not bear to leave the little boys to mob vengeance in Korinth, yet feared they might slow her flight, she had murdered them with her own hands. Hearing that, Aegeus longed to murder her with his. But his oath was sworn.

"Truly she made me word it well," he said to Pittheus, when at last they sat together in the blue evening. "Never to turn her out, or to give her up to any foe! Oh, she is clever, that sow who has eaten her own litter—that mother who has made herself child-less!"

"She has suffered much," said Pittheus, "and will suffer far more."

"With what?" Aegeus laughed grimly. "She has no heart—only lust and pride and hate! And yet"—he laughed again, a harsh, bitter sound—"if I find her in my house when I get there, I have little doubt we will soon be in bed together. For I know myself, and what her voice and look and touch can do to a man. May all the Gods make that bed fruitless! Never did I think to speak such words, I who for many years have never taken a woman without praying, 'Let this be the time!' But *her* son—sooner would I beget a leper!"

"I doubt that she can give life again," said Pittheus, "she who has sinned so sorely against life. Yet tell me over again those words you heard in Delphi."

When he had heard them he sat long in silence. At last he said: "I will make no promises to you who have heard too many. But off these shores is another, far smaller isle than lovely Kalaureia. Tiny, ring-round Sphaeria, the place of the Holy Marriage. Go there, and you will find the ancient sanctuary of the Goddess: a hut of reeds such as Egyptian marsh dwellers build. In it is a chest of stone that holds a mantle and crown more splendid than any king's. Treasures of Poseidon, the God you worship. Put them on, and you will be the Holy Bridegroom. And if a woman comes to you there, I think you will get your heart's desire."

Aegeus went to that isle, and a woman did come to him there, and she was Pittheus' own young daughter Aithra, lovely as the shining sky for which she was named. In the morning, when he knew who the woman had been, Aegeus spoke again with his host, "Truly is it said, Lord, that you give generously to a friend. Yet you should not have staked your own child's maidenhead on my power to get sons."

Wise Pittheus smiled and said: "You might well blame me for having made you open the bulging wineskin's mouth here, not in Athens. But I had your own word for it that you did not want Medea to be the mother of your only son."

Aegeus thought it was not likely to make much difference where he had or had not opened his wineskin's mouth, yet for days he lingered on. He hated to leave Aithra; she was like cool water to a man who has wandered long in the desert. She was his lost youth, the brightness and magic that time always takes from earth and sky, and the tender depth of color that it so soon takes from the flowers. She was all he wanted, and she loved him. Even if that love sprang mostly from pity, as he feared, it was a marvel almost as marvelous as herself.

"Would that I could take you home with me to be my queen in Athens!" he said on their last night together. "But however well I guarded you, Medea the accursed would find a way to slay you. And I am oath-bound never to turn her out."

"No Queen of Troizen ever leaves Troizen." Aithra's smile was as sweet as pure water; it shone like moonlit water. "Down by the shore is the Birthplace reared by the Foundress, by her who fled from Egypt. There every king born in Troizen has first seen the light. There our son will see it."

He will be long in coming, thought Aegeus. He opened his mouth to say so, then shut it again. Let the child keep her dream as long as she could. But she smiled again, as if she had heard the unspoken words.

"He will come, Lord. And I think that his coming has been long fated, and that he will bring great good to men."

Dreams, all dreams, thought Aegeus again. And felt ashamed of being glad that he would not be there to see the pain of her waking. But she was young, a young man would soon comfort her. . . . Fiercely he caught her close, buried his head in the sweet ivory swell of her breast. For this one night she still was his.

Morning came, his last morning in Troizen. He delayed his going a little to drive her to the silvery-green olive grove where stood the great rock called the Altar of Strong Zeus. A relic of the last of those successful yet somehow unsuccessful conquerors who had sometimes seized Troizen. Huge indeed was that stone, worthy of the God of the Thunderbolts. Aegeus winced at the sight of it, then set his jaw. Let her see, this girl, that he was as strong as any boy-lover who would ever give her sons!

He bent, he scooped out earth enough to get his hands beneath that massive slab, then his arms. He heaved, and heaved again. He heard his muscles crack, he felt as if his heart must burst within him, but he could not bear the shame of failure before her. He set his teeth, he strained and panted, and somehow heaved again. And then, at last, the great rock stirred! With one last, tremendous effort he raised it up and let it fall to one side. Shaking, his breath coming in hard, painful gasps, he stood and looked down at its brown, ancient bed—upon earth that the sun had never seen before! Aithra ran to him, but he waved her back. As soon as he could he scooped out more earth, made a hollow in which he laid his sandals, the golden sandals of a king. With them, well wrapped, he left his short sword, the shining blade he used both at table and in battle. Once it had belonged to Kekrops the Serpent King, Lord of Athens long ago. *Am I a fool, throwing away an heirloom on a childish gesture? Too late to think of that now. Besides, why should I save it for the sons of Pallas?* Once again he gathered all his strength; the stone must be set back in its ancient place. . . .

That done, he turned to Aithra. "Girl, if ever you bear a son, when he reaches man's strength, bring him here. If he can lift this stone and bring me this sword and these sandals, then I will acknowledge him as my true son and heir of Athens!"

Her shining eyes, full of pride and wonder, were yet grave and steady. "I will send you your own son, Lord. No other man's."

How long ago had that been? Too long. Now he was truly old; his arms could never now budge that mighty stone. Son after son of Pallas had grown to manhood, and many more were nearing it. Pallas had acknowledged a full fifty in all. In fact, every healthy son born to any woman in his household, slave or free. Not all of them looked like him, but enough did. They squabbled among themselves, and some were bullies, arrogant with common folk. Both the squabbles and the bullying were often fanned into flame by Medea's well-trained spies. They made men frown and say, "We have justice now, while the old king lives. But what will happen when he dies?"

Why had Androgeos come, the son of Minos? Had Pallas sent letters to Crete, saying: "My brother is old and jealous; he will not choose one of my sons to succeed him. So when he dies, there may be trouble, and strife"? Minos might be glad of a chance to intervene in Athenian affairs; he never had forgiven earth-born Erechtheus, Aegeus' sturdy ancestor, for refusing an earlier Minos the tribute that Athens had paid Crete under the Serpent King. Now a bastard son of his ruled Kea, a prosperous island north of Attica, and one of the many Cretan bases called Minoa had been openly established near Nisa, on the Isthmus. Athens was well watched, both from the north and from the south. . . . Hemmed in.

My people are not rich. And I cannot pay that tribute again without making them poor. . . .

Had Pallas offered to pay it? The sons of Pallas were making much of Androgeos, holding games and races, feasts and hunts in his honor. The Cretan prince, young himself, liked them. What if he went home and said to his father, "Pallas is the true king, eager to be our friend, and he has many fine sons to uphold him"?

That question tortured Aegeus. One day he sat brooding in his own house, the strong house of Erechtheus, that Homer later was to tell of. And there Medea came to him, the daughter of sun-born Aietes. Her voice was as sweet as honey, as sly as a snake. "Lord, let me help you."

"That would take some doing, woman." His laugh was bitter.

"Lord, it is not hard to kill a foolish boy."

Aegeus said in horror: "Woman, so long as the Cretan is in my land, he is my guest! Speak no more such evil folly."

"He is your enemy, betraying his guesthood. Why not kill him? You have killed many enemies before."

"I killed them in war, woman. In fair fight!"

"Fair? What is fair? Since they died, their arms must have been weaker than yours, or their skill less. So what good did it do them, their being given a chance to fight? Can only strength make killing fair and honorable? Is it not fair for the weak to use guile, their only weapon?"

Aegeus tried to tell her that you had to fight a man to be sure which of you was the stronger, the more skilled. To explain the laws of hospitality. But her eyes held his, and the right words would not come. He floundered like a caught fish in the bottom of a boat.

He said at last, weakly: "Woman, Minos would seek vengeance for his son's death."

"For his murder, yes. But who will murder him? Androgeos likes to play with young bulls. Well, let him play with one that is not so young. Hold a game for him, and bring the Bull of Marathon here secretly. When Androgeos goes into the ring and meets him he may be surprised, but his young man's pride will not let him draw back."

"Set the God-Bull on him? That killer too mighty for any man to face? Woman, what do you call murder?"

"Lord, the Cretans say that a bit of their God dwells in every God-Bull. If so, that bit must recognize the son of Minos—the grandson of its whole vast Self. Then if the God chooses to accept His own flesh in sacrifice, is that your doing? Even Minos must bow to His will."

As a spider weaves, she wove. Tightening the cunning, silken net of her words around him until he was caught, bound as fast as any fly.

Yet Medea, who loved her own cleverness, never seems to have been able to foresee its results. No spider can weave a web strong enough to hold a bull's horns. No logic can stop ruthless power. Like a swarm of devouring locusts Minos and his men fell upon Attica. They burned every house and every fruit tree between Athens and the sea. But the crops had been harvested, and the people, with the best of their beasts, had found refuge within the walled Akropolis, as they were used to doing when the savage northern raiders came.

Like a thunderbolt Minos, undaunted, hurled his host against those walls. The walls of Athens, like those of Troy, were said to have been God-built. Minos was hurled back.

Again and again he charged, like the Bull that was his God, but in vain. Old Aegeus, a man again, fought and planned. Whenever the great main gates—strong gates, though the famous Nine Gates cannot yet have been built—seemed too hard pressed, he led forth sallies from the little postern gate. Men who remembered his youth loved him, and men who did not marveled at him. Whatever he had or had not done, he was a man.

Minos ground his teeth. Never before had he realized the strength of the mainland fortresses; no Minos had ever thought of opposing their building. These mainland dogs were always whining about the wild raiders who swept down from the north to loot and kill, and for his own profit's sake no wise man wants his own goods left unguarded. Was not the mainland Crete's own, her wealth like wool for Cretan shepherds to shear? But now—

Long ago you warned me, Pterelas. You said, "Red as flame is his hair, and he must beget no son. For I have seen the fire of that son's hair spreading across the sea, engulfing even wide-wayed Knossos in smoke and flame. Maybe even your own palace, King." Aegeus should have died then and there, with his hair still in Pterelas' hand, but the old fool had been so sure that his spells could keep the big man childless. Had misread his vision and let disaster come.

For though you have no son, you have killed my son, mainland cur! Oh, Androgeos—Androgeos! Alone in his tent of royal purple Minos bowed his head and wept as ordinary men weep. Like a father, not a king. But not for long. More than vengeance was at stake now. He must punish Athens. Else men would soon begin to doubt his power; awe of Crete, the fabled Island of the Gods, would melt like morning mists. . . .

Father, Bull of Heaven, help me! You cannot let Your own son be shamed!
But he heard no answer, nothing but the coughing of his own men outside in the cold. Here in the north winter was coming far more quickly, would be far colder than in Crete. He never should have sailed before spring. But he had been so sure that he could crush Athens quickly, as a man crushes a beetle beneath his heel. As she still must be crushed. Best for now, though, to fall back to his small Isthmian Minoa, where rough winter shelters could eas-

ily be built for his men. He might even be able to get them something better. . . . He grinned.

Mainland hearts leaped high when the mighty fleet sailed away.
Sank like stones when the black ships turned inland again toward
Minoa, that was so near Nisa, where Nisos lived. Nisos, the one
brother that Aegeus could trust. . . .

But though Nisa was small, her walls too were strong, and
Nisos was an old fox, wise in war. Again the might of Minos
was hurled back. Grimly he settled down to wait. Spring would
bring him a powerful ally—hunger. With their food gone, the
besieged soon would have to hand over their impious kings for
punishment—and that punishment would make the mainland
shudder for generations. He could not fail; his forces were
greater than those of both cities put together, and none would
dare to help them. Not against Minos. . . . But he did not like to
sit and wait. Also he feared to be away from Crete too long. His
one remaining true-born son, Asterion, exiled to Kolchis for trying to murder his brother Androgeos, must know by now that
others had succeeded where he had failed. Minos himself had
sent messages promising to send a fleet next spring to bring his
heir home in glory. But would the boy wait? If he came home
before his father did, could he manage to seize the throne? With
his mother's help or without? In his heart Minos cursed Pasiphae, his sister-wife and queen.

*This is all your doing, witch! Had you made your bed a pleasanter place for
me I would have begotten more lawful sons. This mad dog could have been quietly
poisoned. Women! Always regretting your lost power, that you never should have
had. Always scheming against, resenting, the proper and lawful power of men.
All of you need the whip!*

What was she doing now, alone there in Crete that she had
always thought rightfully hers? She would love to bear another
man's child, one whose father she herself had chosen. That at least
she would not dare—there would not be time enough. But if
Asterion refused to beget lawful children—and he was clever
enough to know they would make his own life needless—then
Pasiphae would have to stomach her disgust and give him, Minos,
another true-born son.

*Oh, Androgeos, my dearest, why must you be dead, and Asterion alive? Well,
at least these mainlanders who slew you shall tell out the price!*

Savagely, ceaselessly, he worried at Nisa. If only Aegeus could be lured out of his own mighty walls to help his brother! The besieged fell by ones and twos, but they fell. Nisa bled slowly, but surely. By midwinter few red hairs were left on Nisos' graying head. Often Skylla, his youngest daughter, helped carry food to the gate towers. One day she lingered and looked down.

She saw the sea-king in his golden arms, with his men about him: all that terrible host that was spread out before her city, hungry, wolflike, waiting . . . and Minos was still lean and sword-straight; he looked young. The terrible Lord of Hosts, the Son and Friend of God, yet beautiful . . . a man. Superstition joined force with other, older strength. With her young body that was ripe for love. *Is it not sin—useless sin—to fight against God?*

She found other chances to look down at him, and the few spies Minos had within Nisa brought him word of those watching, fascinated eyes. He laughed like a wolf when he heard. "Another treacherous snake of Pandion's breed!" But he sent her messages and gifts. The poet Aeschylus speaks of "gold-chased Cretan bracelets." Wonder-work of the smiths of great Knossos; treasures such as the simple mainland girl had never seen.

Bracelets fit for a queen. You can be a queen—his queen! Or else his slave. Spoil of a fallen city, of a burned and bloody city. . . . Why do you hesitate, you who can save both father and city? Minos swears to spare what is his queen's, and Minos the Just does not lie.

Better, far better, to kneel and worship. To throw city, father and self into the arms of God. . . .

She stole her father's keys in the nighttime, she opened the little postern gate. Minos' men swarmed in, they butchered men, women, and children. Minos had the walls of Nisa razed—those strong walls that had defied him—then boarded his flagship, the red-and-gray head of Nisos swinging from his hand. There they brought him the daughter of Nisos. They met at last, those two who had been father and mother to death.

She said like a child: "But you said you would marry me—spare my father. You promised."

Minos turned upon her, his face savage with scorn. "I swore to spare what was my queen's. Never will you be that, you treacherous bitch. If you follow me, it will be as a dog follows—at the end of a rope!"

"But you promised—you said you loved me . . ." She was dazed, and he laughed. "You shall have love enough. I will reward you as you deserve."

He raped her, then threw her to his sailors, and when they tired of her they tied a rope around her, and dragged her from the prow of his flagship. She was dragged through the water until she died.

Many chuckled over Skylla's reward, and praised the cleverness of Minos the Just. He himself may have thought it a good joke all his days. Or most of them. . . . But the body of the drowned girl who had loved him was washed ashore at Cape Skylleion, that still bears her name. The indignant fisherfolk there refused to bury it, saying: "Let her flesh rot and her ghost wander homeless forever." Such homelessness was believed to be the fate of the unburied dead. Ages later men still said that on that rocky coast one bird could be seen pursuing another forever, and that the pursuer was Nisos, and the pursued his traitress daughter. Foolish tales, that denied both her and Nisos rest.

No tale has ever denied Minos rest.

But on a dark spring night one came quietly to Cape Skylleion. He gathered up those bones that birds and crawling things had stripped; put them into a bag to be taken back to Troizen, where he could safely bury them.

"We of your own people had a right to judge you," he told them grimly. "But he had not—he who tempted you, and took the fruits of your crime. I piss on such righteousness. May he too be betrayed one day—this just man, who tricked you into betraying your own father!"

And perhaps, far away in the Palace of Minos, in mighty Crete, the child Ariadne, daughter of Minos, stirred in her sleep. . . .

CHAPTER 7.
___A MAN LEARNS HIS NAME

T HE REDHEAD went home feeling better. At first he too
had felt blazing wrath against Skylla, even while gagging
over the praise showered on Minos the Just, her fellow
traitor. Yet gradually those poor gnawed bones had become pitiful, had come to seem only those of another mainlander done to
death by the proud more-than-man. And if Grandfather was right,
if all men were indeed children of Earth and Starry Heaven, then
what on earth could be greater than a man? Any man? A ragged
beggar too must be the son of God. Briefly, there in the black
night, a golden dawn seemed to glow about him, fill him with
wonder. . . .

It passed. He never bragged about that night's doings—indeed,
he was always half-ashamed of them—yet they may have marked
the birth of that spirit for which men were to remember him in
after-ages, when, in the words of Plutarch, "His tomb was a refuge
for runaway slaves, and for poor men who feared the powerful,
since while Theseus lived he had always championed those who
were poor and in need."

But the boy did not yet know that his name was Theseus.

In triumph and high hope Minos had sailed away from ruined
Nisa. Her fate surely would strike terror into all Attica. But if he
had hoped for help against Athens from any of the other cities, he
was disappointed. Skylla's fate had frightened all men, even the
sons of Pallas. In Minos' place a master of strategy like Subbiluliuma would have cherished traitors as a gardener does the flowers
in his garden. But Minos had never known adversity.

Yet the refugees from Nisa did help him; there were enough of them to pack Athens' already crowded Akropolis to bursting. When the city was besieged again, pestilence soon threatened to run through it as fire runs through dry grass. And the extra food Aegeus had stripped his treasury to buy while the Cretans were away was going fast. When the heads of all the noble houses in Athens begged him to send messengers to seek counsel of holy Delphi, the old king could only bow his head.

The God's answer came back promptly, no riddle this time, but short and simple. "Let Minos the Just name his own terms. Beg for his mercy."

Aegeus may well have expected his own head to roll after his brother's. But Minos had just received word that Asterion had come home to Crete. So before his own ships, splendid in purple and gold, he received the humbled people of Athens. Bearing leafy branches they came, after the ritual fashion of suppliants.

He said: "Truly it is Godlike to show mercy to those who clasp one's knees in supplication. I will ask little: neither cattle nor gold nor silver. The blood of no man."

Like sunrise joy flamed on all faces; died when he spoke again. "Only this: that every Ninth Horai, when I go up into the mountains to talk with the God my father, you of Athens send seven youths and seven maidens—your fairest and finest, your most highborn—to the Great Games that then we hold at Knossos. There they shall play with our great bulls. Even as here Androgeos, my son, played with the greatest of your bulls."

All faces grew blanched as those of corpses; one father groaned aloud. Minos laughed in his heart, but went on: "Only the unwedded shall be chosen; bride shall not be deprived of bridegroom, nor bridegroom of bride. One more mercy I will grant. If any of those chosen slays the Minotauros, the great God-Bull of Knossos, he shall be crowned with the Crown of Lilies. The victor's crown. He shall return home, and no other Athenian need ever follow him to Knossos."

He paused, watching for signs of hope; saw a few, and smiled. "But in a hundred winters no player has won that crown. So be glad, fathers and mothers of Athens, that this year is not that of the Ninth Horai, the Ninth Season. Not until next spring will I—

or my deputies—come to choose and claim the first of those whose blood must be shed as was the blood of Androgeos."

But there was no gladness, only weeping. Some sobbed aloud; tears ran quietly down the faces of many. But the gloating eyes of Minos sought those of Aegeus and held them. *How long do you think you will live now, old dog, who have brought this upon your pack? Well have I armed the sons of Pallas against you—and while you do live, fear must lie down with you every night and rise up with you every morning.*

For one breath's space his manhood flamed again in Aegeus. His eyes replied: *Do you think I fear death, after this?* But then he bowed his head wearily, broken and ashamed.

Summer passed, and another winter. Again the Maid came back to the Mother. Dawn-fresh, She rose from the bed of the dread Lord of the Underworld. Her maidenhead grew again. She walked in the lands of men, and flowers sprang up wherever Her feet trod. The birds came back and sang for joy of her, the Risen One.

That spring the Redhead was man-tall—taller than most men— narrow-hipped yet broad-shouldered. One day Aithra spoke to him, her eyes proud yet sad: "Come, my son. There is that which I must show you. It is time."

Wondering, he followed her through the silvery groves to the altar of Strong Zeus, that forsaken altar where now no man worshiped. And that was good, the Redhead thought, in spite of his love for Herakles. Those high-nosed Zeus-worshipers were too fond of calling other men bastards.

Aithra said: "Lift this stone, my son. The task will be hard, but I have good reason to ask it of you."

Wondering more than ever, he knelt, felt around the great rock with his hands, and scooped out earth, as Aegeus had done. Then he gritted his teeth and braced his back. He heaved, he strained, sweat poured from him, until Aithra's face grew white with fear. *Have I brought him here too soon? If he is hurt—* And still he labored mightily. Then at last, as before, the huge stone trembled, rose, fell to one side. The boy rose too, laughing triumphantly into his mother's eyes. But she did not laugh.

"Look at what lies there, my son. Unwrap it, for it is yours."

He undid the dirty bundle. He stared at the sandals and the

sword, especially at the sword. It was a great prize. And the golden snakes writhing across it looked alive enough to bite a man. Then his eyes narrowed as his head reeled.

"Mother, only one royal house on the mainland bears these golden serpents as its sign. The House of the Earth-born, in Athens."

Aithra laughed, but the laugh twisted into a sob. "I told him I would send him his son. But he was so sure I would not—he had given up all hope—"

"Then"—the boy's voice was very low—"he is Aegeus?"

Shining and steady, her eyes met his. "Child, he is. On the Holy Isle, that water encircles, the dark magic of Pterelas the Cretan could not follow him. There the spell was broken, and you were begotten. And your true name is Theseus, 'Establisher,' for you will be the Establisher of your father's house."

She gave another half-laugh, half-sob. "He was so like a child himself—big man though he was. A child that has been hurt, yet is being brave—" And then she wept in earnest, and Theseus held her in his sweaty arms and comforted her.

He felt dizzy. Once he had been so proud of his high, mysterious begetting—then so sure he never could be proud of any mortal father unless of Herakles. But now his heart went out in loving pity and in a new kind of pride to this man who, old and alone, had held his city against Minos.

He said slowly: "Those are good loins to have sprung from." And then: "But by all the Gods in Heaven, Mother—why did he never come back or send word? Never even try to find out whether I had been born?"

She smiled. "Child, child, have you forgotten Medea? That witch woman who murdered her own sons? How could he risk bringing down her wrath upon you and me?"

That night Theseus talked long with wise Pittheus. "Grandfather, there is so much I do not understand! Why did those sorcerer priests bid my father lie with no woman until he reached Athens? Did they know he would meet Medea? Think she was barren, and could not be my mother?"

"Child, I think that for all their ugly tricks with shorn hair and evil dreams—tricks that never could have prevailed against knowledge, even such as hers—they did at last see truly, know that he would meet Medea, and that the time for your conception had come. But they either thought her barren, or believed any son she could still bear would be too savage-hearted to draw men to him, would be no foe mighty Crete need fear."

"Then they do fear me! But how did they get such sight?"

"From a scanty knowledge of star-reading, that ancient art which wise men still keep secret, knowing how much later men will misuse it. So they foresaw and feared your birth. Even as I foresaw it."

"Then you can read the stars, Grandfather? You saw that I would overthrow Crete? *I?*" The young face flamed, exultant.

"Child, Crete's downfall may be only the beginning. You may have work to do of which you do not yet dream. But the fire that grows on your head too often gets inside it. Remember that and beware, child of my daughter, for even the patterns shaped by the stars can be altered."

"I will remember." But the answer came too quickly, too easily, and old Pittheus sighed.

In the morning Theseus, heir of Athens, set out for Athens. The poet Bakchylides says that two comrades went with him, but does not name them. They were Euneos and Thoas, the friends of his childhood. Solois, their youngest brother, wept for their going, but more for Theseus'. For him, as for Aithra, Theseus' red head was the sun that lit the world.

Hermos said: "Would I were not my parents' only son! Then I too could be with you. We were always four before."

"And will be again. But"—Theseus grinned—"here you will have Solois to comfort. I know well that you love him as much as he thinks he loves me."

"You will not mind? He is so beautiful! I thought surely you must soon turn to him." Hermos' face glowed.

"You may have him. I want a bedmate who can bear me sons."

Long and sadly Hermos looked after his old comrades. But Aithra could not bear to look. Theseus had tried to comfort her, saying: "Mother, I will be back." But she knew that Troizen would never again be his home. It had served its purpose, having produced him . . . even as she had.

She was afraid too. She had begged him to go by sea; Athens

was only a thirty miles' sail from Troizen. But he had said: "I will bring my father more proof than he asked for, Mother. Enough to show all men that I am worthy to be king." *Hubris* that had seemed to her, too much pride. Yet wise Pittheus, her own father, had said only: "Daughter, do not strive with destiny. He must choose his own road."

Terrible, though, was that northern land road. Snakelike it wound across the Isthmus, through crumbly cliffs far above the sea, then up through southern Attica, now as perilous. Aegeus and Nisos between them once had kept that road free of evil men, but now it was a true path to the Kingdom of the Dead in the Underworld. Only strong caravans, armed to the teeth, dared use it. Fierce robber barons roosted there like hawks, mostly men of northern stock, with a crude, cruel sense of humor. If travelers proved poor pickings, ugly games were likely to be played with them. Aithra thought of grim Skiron, who kicked men over a cliff to feed the great turtle he said lived below, in truth but a queerly shaped rock. A hard rock. Of bone-breaking Kerkuon, whose cruelties defiled Eleusis, the Holy city of the Mother and the Maid. Of the two Phaias, the two Bright Ones, once avatars of the Mother and the Maid, but now tormentors of men.

Keep him safe, O my Sky-Goddess, whom only we of Egyptian blood call Mother! Let him be lost to me—that even you cannot help—only keep him safe!

And even if Theseus did reach Athens, another peril would be waiting for him there, painted and bedizened, by his father's side. Medea, her beauty withered, but her cunning and cruelty unabated. . . .

Book II
ANTIOPE

CHAPTER 1.
THE DRAGON ILUYANKES

ANTIOPE, QUEEN of the Amazons, stood on the heights of Buyukkale, the Great King's citadel in Hattusas. Across from her, above a deep, chasmlike slash in the breast of Earth the Mother, reared a huge grim rock shaped like a serpent's head. A true image, she thought, of him the Hittites called Iluyankes, the Dragon of the Beginning. Once he had felled even their Storm God. The God had risen again and felled the Dragon, yet surely the Dragon had risen too. In one shape or another he confronted every Hittite king. To keep open the great eastern trade routes that brought them the metals they must have, those kings must live and die in war.

Yet they had to keep their capital here in the north, far from those trade routes, to face the one enemy they could never crush: the fierce Kaska who loved to raid their rich cornlands, then vanish into wooded hills where the terrible three-man Hittite chariots could not follow, those chariots that mowed down all other men like grain. Even now, in the southwest, they were gobbling up the Syrian cities, Pharaoh's vassals. Preparing to sweep over great Mitanni, Pharaoh's ally. . . .

Antiope thought: _To be an Amazon is good—it is the best thing in all the world to be. We live simply, we fight only when men come to attack us. You need not have feared my coming to Hattusas, Molpadia; it has only shown me how right you are._

Strange how much easier it was to appreciate Molpadia's rightness when she was not there. Close at hand it beat one down, like the great wings of a mother eagle, shutting out light and air. Yet to think that made the girl feel guilty. As she had when she was little and had tagged after her mother and sister until Mother

101

would turn and say, "Go back to Molpadia, child. It is not right that I should have two little girls, and my sister none." Amazons never beat children, but once Mother had made up her mind neither tears nor tantrums could change it. Besides, she had sounded so fair. . . . But the child, turning back, had always felt what then she could neither clearly think nor say: *To be given away was not fair to me.* She had missed so much of Mother—of Melanippe too. . . .

Nor had Molpadia ever been truly satisfied. Once, in a rare outburst, she had said: "You are Otrere's child, not mine. Oh, she tried to give you to me—tried hard, and to her own hurt. But she nursed you; nothing would bring back milk to my one breast. She said: 'Once she is weaned, she will be all yours, sister.' But whenever she saw you she smiled—how could she help it?—and you smiled back, and tried to go to her. . . . Sometimes I hated her— Otrere, my own sister, whom I loved!"

That memory still hurt Antiope. Yet even in her pity she had longed to escape. For a while, after they had railed at each other at Melanippe's burial, they had been close, but that closeness had not lasted. Molpadia's arms could not hold long without clutching. . . .

Then last autumn the Great King's envoys had come, courteously inviting Antiope to Hattusas. "For travel is a good teacher, and the world is changing. Let the young Hippolyte see and learn, before children bind her, the Childbearer, to Themiskyra." Molpadia's scornful eyes had said: *What changes for Amazons? In peace we work, in war we fight.* Those eyes had made very clear what she expected of her niece. But Antiope was young; the unspoken command had made it necessary for her to prove her independence. Also she had suddenly remembered that she had always wanted to see the great world outside Themiskyra: the palaces and temples, with their golden tables and silver images, those wonderful, conquering chariots.

And she had been happy, here in Themiskyra; her time had been full of seeing, of learning. Subbiluliuma had taught her much, both of war and of statecraft. Which was good; she now knew more about the enemies of her people, and what the Amazons must face. But she had also learned much that the king had not meant to teach her. It was too big, this outside world. A few men in it were too great, and everybody else (men as well as women) too small. Amazons had neither slaves nor classes; for the first time she had seen both evils at close quarters and been appalled. Yet set in its ways as it was, boxed in by cruel, stupid customs, this big world was full of feverish gambling. People were forever plotting, planning, scheming to get more than they had. While all Amazons wanted was enough. She marveled at her father's skill in the game, yet could not see how his winnings—or any other man's—could ever be secure. Once she had said to him: "Father" —when they were alone she often called him that—"why do you want so many cities?"

He had grinned, then shrugged. "Child, once I get them, nobody else can use them against me."

"But what if they try to get away again?"

"Few of them will." He shrugged again. "Comfortable men never want change; they do not like to fight. I never set my tribute too high, or send bullies to collect it. To have a little king flogged in his own palace, shamed before his own people—that is for fat fools of Pharaohs."

"Is that why you get the Syrian cities so easily? But I think, Father, that it would be better if there were many little free kings —no great ones. When a Great King is not sensible, like you, he hurts too many people."

Her father had smiled indulgently. "Girl, no power in all the world could keep all those little free kings from fighting each other until the strong had gobbled up the weak."

"But if all the little cities swore to league together to depose the first king who broke the peace—?"

His smile broadened. "Then the peace-breaker would say, 'Blame him who drove me to it,' and the other would say, 'He lies!' And soon the friends of both would be fighting, and then their friends. Your peace would vanish like the smoothness of a sheet of water into which a stone has been dropped."

He said that only a great state could ever be safe, and that only so long as its kings were strong and watchful. *But how long will they stay that way?* Antiope wondered now, where she waited for him here beneath the Dragon's black stare. Must not a Great King's descendants, being too rich, always grow soft and pleasure-loving, and fall before a strong new king? Amazons knew they never could be strong in wealth or in numbers; Amazons must always be strong and watchful and self-controlled. That was the best way to be. And yet—if the day of the one free city-state was really over, if henceforth there were to be but a few great states, made up of many cities, how long could the Amazons hold out? Their lovely little delta-plain, though guarded by mountains, was a tempting morsel. To realize how much Amazons needed Hittite friendship hurt her pride.

Mitanni was the Great King's chief goal now. Mitanni, akin to the Hittites, yet long Egypt's friend and their foe. Of late many messengers had been coming and going between them and Azzi, a small land, yet so placed that its king could harry any army that marched upon Mitanni from the Hittite heartlands. All morning Subbiluliuma had been closeted with its envoys. Antiope hated to think of the treaty he might be making: Azzi was the Amazons' foe from of old.

When he came at last slaves were with him; they bore small golden tables and food, fruit, and wine. When they had poured the wine and gone he took a hearty swig and sighed, "I needed that," then looked quizzically at Antiope. "Well, girl, the treaty is made. Do you still trust me? Your aunt would not."

"She never has. And if this treaty holds I will wish that my own brothers, not my half brothers, were your heirs in Hattusas. But now the one I feel sorry for is my other aunt, Kadussi. Whatever else you do, you will throw her to Hukkana of Azzi, as a man throws a bone to a dog."

He chuckled. "Well, she is a well-fleshed, shapely bone, my little half sister Kadussi. And she will enjoy being a queen."

"I would not call it queenship."

"Kadussi will."

Well, that might be so. Kadussi had been traded like a cow, but she would get the kind of glittering foolishness she liked. And it would take a braver man than Hukkana, King of Azzi, to dare to ill use the Great King's sister. Antiope shrugged, made a face, and took a piece of fruit. "We Amazons would have liked to help you beat this particular dog again, instead of throwing him bones."

"No doubt. No enmity is so bitter as that between kin." His face darkened; she knew he was remembering how enmity between royal kinsmen had plagued the Hittites of old. "But this is your

chance to make peace with Hukkana, girl. I know as well as you
do that his young men have been helping the Kaska to raid Amazon lands."

"He wants no peace." She stared at the king, surprised.

"He will make it. Because I will it." Subbiluliuma's voice had
not risen, but it had grown grim.

"Why bother? He will never keep it. Then, when we Amazons
complain, he will laugh and say, 'Women!' Blame all on the Kaska
—and on our foolish female spite."

"And until I get Mitanni I will laugh with him, pretending to
believe him. After that—well, then he will learn to keep his word."

"Then why make peace yet?"

"Because he is accusing you Amazons of raiding *his* lands. That
is the raiders' way." Again the king chuckled.

She thought that over. She did not like this counsel; Hukkana
was as double-tongued as any snake; he never could be trusted.
Yet fear might well keep him quiet while Subbiluliuma lived. At
least after Mitanni fell . . . and even such a peace would be precious.

She said slowly: "I thank you, Father. It is worth trying. I will
make peace—if he will. But Molpadia is War-Queen; by law I
cannot make it by myself."

"Hukkana will not know that. Nor will Molpadia know that any
peace has been made. Unless you tell her."

"I will tell her. She will not bother to send him a denial. She will
only smile at my folly, and say, 'Girl, you will learn.' "

The Great King smothered yet another chuckle. He thought,
Daughter, you know your aunt well. He said, "Then will you go to Azzi
with Kadussi? The letters I send with you will show how much
I honor and prize you."

She was startled. How horrified Molpadia would be—how certain that both kings meant treachery! Then she smiled dryly. She
was sure that he loved her, but equally sure that he would use her
and her Amazons if he could.

"Then he asked you to send me to him, Father?"

"Yes. He claims to want to bury old hatreds—to make friends
with one who will soon be doubly his kinswoman. I can only guess
what he has in mind, but my letters explain to him carefully how
a Hittite princess' husband must *not* behave toward his wife's

female relations, adding, 'Among the Hittites a man who does such deeds does not continue to live.' He will not defy those words. Yet for good measure Mariyas and two regiments of guards —not one—will go with you."

Mariyas was one of the few captains whom the Great King truly trusted. Whatever Hukkana had been plotting against her, he was not likely to attempt it now. She drew a deep breath and then laughed. "Well, I thank you again for the warning, but I am not afraid to go."

"You are your mother's daughter and mine." He laid his hand on her shoulder, and for a breath's space neither spoke. Then she smiled at him, her eyes twinkling. "You trust that man of Azzi no more than I do, Father."

"Yet sometimes, girl, it is better to leave a snake lying in the sun than to bash his head in."

"Since you do not want to lose men bashing his head in—men you might use against Mitanni. Well, I do not want to lose Amazons either. But I will have to teach the maidens who came here with me how to be good liars. I will have to teach myself the same thing."

"You will do it. I need not tell you to keep good watch—to guard yourself and those girls. You will do that too."

"I will indeed." Then suddenly, to her own surprise, she said: "What will you do after you get Mitanni, Father? Which city comes next?"

He said soberly: "I do not know. I might take Egypt herself— if those jealous priests of Amon do not send Pharaoh Akhnaton to his new God too soon. He is a fool to enrage them so. Certainly Egypt already had Gods enough, without his thinking up another one. Let alone calling Him the only one."

"You Hittites have a thousand Gods, Father."

He grinned. "Because we are shrewd enough to honor the Gods of those we conquer. But I would hate to try to name half of them." He sobered again, frowning. "Your brother Sharra-Kushukh would make a good Pharaoh—and I cannot leave him what I want to leave him. Your mother, Otrere, was a queen, but not in Hattusas. . . . And how long would it take me to get Egypt? It is not wise for a Hittite king to go too far from home. Mursil our forefather did that—he conquered Babylon, and brought home rich spoil—but he was slain by his own kin at his homecoming feast. . . . "

"Well, you will not have to worry about that if you keep out of Egypt. And you have already made my brother Sharra-Kushukh a king."

"Only of Halep. Doubtless it is best to keep out of Egypt. Yet I think we will have to thrash those Pharaohs some day. They are too proud; in Egypt all who are not Egyptians are called Not-People."

"That is bad." The face she made now was one of disgust. "Well, I wish you and my brothers luck."

She kissed him before she left him, as an ordinary daughter would have done. But for long he sat there, twiddling his empty winecup. Why had this journey to Azzi had to come up, to shorten his time with the girl? The precautions he had taken would surely keep her safe, but she would not come back. Azzi was much nearer Themiskyra than Hattusas was. She would go home—to Molpadia. He cursed softly under his breath; what ailed the woman? Most Amazons did not hate the Hittites; they laughed and drank and joked with them like other men. But hate burned ceaselessly inside Molpadia, like a caged, tormented beast. "Woman, what possessed you to give our baby to that cross-grained bitch? After what she did to her own?" Years ago he had said that to Otrere, shocked into forgetting, for the first and last time, that he had no rights over any female child of hers. She had answered quietly, "I hope the child will make her whole again," and he had had just sense enough left not to shout back: "What that sister of yours needs is a man the whole year round—and one with a strong arm!" He still thought that there would have been a good deal of truth in those words; Molpadia did need a man. Self-control, self-denial, had been ground into the Amazons; most of them seemed content with their way of life. Yet maybe those whose fires burned too high for comfortable abstinence had to learn to hate what they could not have. . . . Well, no matter now. After Melanippe's death he had been afraid that the madwoman might be able to grind her hate into Antiope. But if so he had got the girl away from her in time. No need, either, for this queer cold feeling of dread and loss. He would see the girl again, though maybe never again for long at a time. . . .

You have what you bargained for, and no man can have everything. From across the chasm the stone Dragon's eyes spoke, black pits of emptiness, yet grimly eloquent. Or were they the small beady eyes of that man the generals had sent to him long ago? Eyes that had watched him unceasingly. . . .

"If your brother becomes king, you will not live long, Prince. Neither you nor any he believes to be your friends."

That would have included Otrere, who had been carrying their first child. Yet he had said harshly: "Why should I believe you? You who admit you seek my brother's death?"

He could still hear the answer, soft, sly, and calm: "Prince, do you not believe it yourself?"

"Why should I? Why should he be jealous of me? Any victories that a man can win here are small. Here in this wild, mountainous land of the Kaska!"

"Any victory is a slap in the face to him who has never won any. And no other man has ever driven the Kaska back and back, on their home ground, as you have done."

"He is the heir. We Hittites have learned in a hard school to obey the law. If he wills my death, I must die."

"If he who wills your death were dead, there would be no queen's son left. You are the king's; all men would be glad to see you the heir."

For a little while then he had been silent. *We were friends once, Tudhaliyas. As boys we played together and fought together, as boys will.* . . . His lot had not been easy. His father had loved his mother; for her sake he had been named Subbiluliuma, "Son of the Clear Spring." But she had died, and the queen's party had had another name for him. "Bastard! Bastard!" He had grown up with that word ringing in his ears. Knowing Tudhaliyas for his father's true-born son, the heir.

"Man, I will never kill my brother to get his heritage!" His honor had spoken then, everything he had built for himself, everything of which he had been proud.

"Then you will die, Lord. With many, many others. For if his folly goes on unchecked the whole nation of the Hittites will be butchered and enslaved."

Words and more words, all of them guileful, too many of them true. And underneath all the knowledge that he had no time, that the decision was upon him, here and now. Also for many moons —for years—he had dreamed of how, in his brother's place, he would outmarch, outwit, outfight the enemies of their people. Never in any of those dreams had he pictured harm befalling his brother, yet—had not all turned on that? He had to face that fact at last, and also another. If he refused this offer, the generals, to save their own skins, would betray their own plot to Tudhaliyas, and call it his. That threat never had been spoken; it had not had to be. . . .

Yet then, whatever men thought of me, I would die with my honor clean.

Then your people would die too. For you. So many—so many—your own people, whom you could save! That other voice within him had surely been that of pity, of a man's greatest loyalty. But had it also been the voice of his disguised desire?

And then again that voice from without: "Why throw away your life for nothing, Prince? You cannot save your brother's. If he lives long, it will only be because some king of our foes wants to parade him eyeless in his royal robes. As a trophy of victory."

He had decided then. But he had made one condition. "Let the king my father die in peace. He must soon mount the hill—he cannot last much longer." But if he had been wholly honest he would have said: *I do not want to risk his guessing what I have done—having to bear that useless pain. But it is myself too that I would spare—from the knowledge of his knowledge. . . .*

The messenger had not been pleased. "Time is pressing now. To wait even a little longer may be to wait too long." But Subbiluli-uma had won his point; the old man had died in peace. *And with how many lives did I buy both of us that peace?*

You made yourself king. Those black empty pits that were the Dragon's eyes seemed to accuse him again, cold and cruel and full of all evil. Twisting all they saw into evil. . . . *You can fool yourself and all those mist-thin Gods of yours, They that live in the light—in the frail, ever-changing light. But not Me whose true place is in the depths. In the everlasting, changeless dark.*

For a breath's space the king's spirit seemed to whirl over measureless black abysses. Then he pulled himself together, looked back into the eyes of the Dragon: "Yes, I am king, as I chose to be, and though a man can lie to himself, darkness too can lie. Twist all truth."

But he knew now that he would never take Egypt. It would have been a great gift for Sharra-Kushukh, but it would have cost his people too much—too many dead men, too many widows. . . . And what he had done for them was his justification. He had won back all that his strife-torn ancestors had lost, all that his brother had lost. He had made the Hittites greater, safer, than they had ever been before. He had worked tirelessly to that end. He had shed no more blood unlawfully, he had upheld all laws, all treaties, yet never known rest.

What if I had broken my oath to you, Otrere, and carried you off to be my queen, here in Hattusas? She would not have died in battle then, pretty Melanippe would not have been murdered. She and both girls would have been here in his palace, safe. Sharra-Kushukh, his firstborn, would have been his lawful heir. He would have been happy. Or would he? Otrere probably would have settled down. Women usually did, although they made a fuss at first. Yet the man who had known his woman was not quite sure. . . .

Antiope—she too loved her Amazon freedom. Well, her world ought to last as long as she did. Had she half guessed, once today, that it was doomed? The Amazons would make no trouble—they wanted freedom, not power, and would let others alone as long as they were let alone. But they were beautiful wild things, and in the end men hunt all beautiful wild things down. He could only hope that no son or grandson of his would lead that hunt; he could not be sure. A man sired unpredictable strangers. His own father had never dreamed—

He smiled and thought grimly: *Better if I too die in battle. If I live to be old, and my sons take over my work, and let me sit by the fire as an old man should, I will see too many pictures in that fire. . . .*

To the Princess Kadussi and her ladies the road to Azzi seemed hard, though they rode in curtained litters. To the Amazons, who rode horseback, it only seemed good, as always, to get out-doors again, after being cooped up all winter. They laughed, they ran races with each other, they breathed deep of the winds, that smelled of spring. They exchanged merry banter with the Hittite soldiers, and at night the Hittite ladies, shocked, would whisper together, sure that they knew where the other girls were now. "Brazen, bloodstained hussies!" Every one of them would have sworn that none of those so-called maidens had her maidenhead.

They came at last to the walls of Azzi, chief city of Azzi, and the king and his nobles rode out to meet them. He was a fine man, gold-bearded and clad in gold and scarlet. He looked first at Antiope, riding proudly with high-held head among her maidens, then toward the curtained litter. Kadussi had been pulling bits of curtain this way and that, trying to get a look at him, but now suddenly the curtains hung unmoving; she was modestly hidden. He grinned.

"Welcome, king-born ladies! Welcome, my Queen, sister of the sun! And to you too, daughter of the sun, whose beauty no clouds hide. I am proud to have such a kinswoman."

Antiope's eyes hardened; she had not been given her proper title. "I am Queen of the Amazons, man of Azzi. A free ruler, who pays tribute to none."

His grin widened, showing sharp white teeth above the golden beard. "Lady, you warrior women let no man forget that. But surely there will be peace between us now, since your great father wills it?"

"Since peace is always a good thing, I will be glad if we can make it, kinsman." She hated to add that last word, yet courtesy demanded it, and it was the truth.

Then Kadussi, having been greeted, thought it time to make a bid for her share of attention. She opened the curtains and the king saw her and smiled as if in delighted wonder. "Sister of the sun, truly you outshine the sun!"

Kadussi dropped the curtains again, but not until after she had smiled at him with her pretty, painted mouth. He greeted Captain Mariyas, then turned again to Antiope, who was staring in frank admiration. "He has fine horses who rides behind you, man of Azzi."

They were beautiful beasts, that chariot team, slender, sleek, and proud. Antiope thought they must be of the best stock of horse-breeding Mitanni, once famed above all lands for her chariot-driving. Her eyes were all for the horses; she had not yet looked at the man behind them.

"Their master is Asterion, son of Minos, Lady. Of him who is Lord of the Islands of the West, and rich as Pharaoh himself. And he longs to meet you, having heard much of your beauty and bravery." Again the king smiled that broad smile of which Antiope had already had more than enough.

"And I am not disappointed, Lady. If your kinswoman outshines the sun, then you outshine sun, moon, and all the stars!"

He who cried that stood beside the driver. He was dark and slender, not as big as any Amazon, and beautiful as any woman. But the eyes that smiled boldly into Antiope's had the sinister, jewel-like brilliance of a snake's. For a breath's space they two seemed, oddly, to be alone together. Antiope stiffened, as if before a suddenly bared sword. Then understanding came, and with it warming anger. She wanted to shout to King Hukkana: "So this be why you asked me here. Because this proud, puffed-up boy thinks Amazons are whores. And you, a king, are willing to be his pimp!"

To Asterion she said coolly: "We sun-browned, hardy warrior women are not used to such flowery words, king's son. But truly your horses do outshine the stars." Then she swung back to the King of Azzi. "Lord, the queen my kinswoman and her ladies are weary. It would be a kindness to get them within doors."

"So we will. But will you too be kind, Lady, and let the Isle-Prince ride beside you on the way? I value his father's friendship. Especially now that I must lose my trade with Mitanni." Again that eternal smile.

Trapped, she swung back to Asterion, her smile hard and bright, a challenge. "Let us see which of us can reach the gates first, king's son. The way is short; the chariot should not hinder your horses much." Then she was off, like an arrow shot from her own bow. But at a low, savage word from Asterion the charioteer's whip—a thing no Amazon ever would have carried—shot forward too. The chariot sprang abreast of Antiope, and she saw a long red wheal across one shining flank. She winced, and the islander laughed. "You are not so hard after all, Lady!" Asterion cried as he shot past her. She let him win then; she could not bear to see another whiplash on those beautiful, glossy coats.

At the banquet that night she was not surprised to find him seated beside her. He grinned. "So I worry you, Lady."

"The way you treat your horses does."

"It began before that. When your eyes first met mine you were afraid. You wanted to get away."

Had she been half afraid? The unpleasant thought startled her. She said bluntly: "You should not have had the king ask me here, Prince."

For a breath's space he looked startled. Then he grinned again. "Why not? We two should deal well together, Lady. The Star of Crete, and the most beautiful of women."

"My beauty will do you no good." Tersely she explained the Law of the Amazons.

Rage blazed in his face then. Not the red rage she had sometimes seen in men's faces on the battlefield, but something black as night itself. It passed; he smiled ruefully.

"*Ai*, Lady, *ai!* I had heard that in spring you Amazons were friendly—yes, as friendly as spring itself!"

"I have explained all that, Star of Crete." Her voice was cold. She did not like those swift changes; fierce as his passions were, he had strength enough to control them. That could make him dangerous.

He said quietly, suddenly sober again: "Make no mistake, Lady. You may have heard that I came to Kolchis an exile, but now I am going home in pride. Minos has sent ships and treasure to fetch me—me, his true-born son, who will be Minos after him."

"Do you think that what I just told you was a lie? No man can buy an Amazon with gifts."

He smiled lazily. "Lady, you should be kinder. I would not have waited for my father's ships—I would have been in Crete already had I not heard tales of your beauty, and waited to see how much truth there was in them. One does not expect to hear such tales of you sun-browned, hardy Amazons."

He had turned her own words against her neatly. She knew she should have laughed, but thought of the curiosity he had felt sickened her. No doubt he had wanted to see whether she was worth breaking . . . like his unlucky horses.

She said rather grimly: "If I have heard the cause of your exile I do not remember it. But I do remember now another tale I heard in Hattusas. Of how the founder of your house won his throne by slaying the queen he had sworn to serve."

Asterion's smile flashed again. "What matter? He did win it. We who were meant to be kings know our own worth. I knew I was more fit to be king than my brother Androgeos, the so-called heir. I arranged for an accident to befall him, but a bad sword will break in the best of hands. A man I had bribed betrayed me, so my brother triumphed—for a little while."

"Until the friends you had left behind arranged a more successful accident?" Disgust twisted her mouth.

"No. The God of Crete loves me. He judged between us, and now my brother is dead."

"A God loves *you?*" She did not try to keep the scorn out of her voice.

"The God of Crete, woman. He who is greater than all other Gods." Once again Asterion had changed; his voice was deep, his face shone with a terrible pride. "Part of Him lives on earth in each King Minos, but all of Him sits enthroned forever in the Afterworld. Living or dead, the wicked cannot escape His justice."

Antiope wanted to ask him what his ideas of wickedness and justice were. Instead somehow she found herself asking: "Do all the Western Isles bow to Crete? Troizen and Mycenae too?"

He laughed. "They are not isles. Though few of you Sunrise folk realize it, there is a western mainland. Its people are dogs, and we of Crete know how to keep them in their place. We will not let them build ships."

"Herakles of Mycenae has ships. Or had, two winters ago."

"Herakles!" Asterion shrugged. "We wink at his poor little boats. He is a true mainlander—big enough for six, and without enough brains for one."

"Have you ever heard of a young kinsman of his called the Redhead? Not as big, but much brighter."

"No." His eyes suddenly narrowed. "What do you know of these lumpish mainlanders?"

"Too much. Two years ago they landed on our shores, and by treachery slew my sister. Whose death I did not want, though it made me queen. But you would not understand that."

She spoke harshly, angry with both herself and him. What had

made her ask about the Redhead? For one lovely evening he had
seemed to be her friend, close to her in a warm closeness she had
never quite understood. Yet all the time he had been a traitor, and
if ever they met again she would kill him.

But suddenly Asterion's eyes kindled. "If men here in the north
had had hot blood like us of the south, you mad imitators of men
would have been conquered long ago. All this shameful waste of
beauty ended. Lady, you do not know what joys you are missing!
Or how much else I could give you. Gold and silver, jewels and
ivory—"

Snake-quick his hand leaped for hers, but Antiope jerked away
in time. Her eyes met his squarely. "Amazons imitate nobody. Nor
does talk of war befit the guests of one's host. Speak better words,
Prince, or leave me."

For another breath's space that black rage burned in his eyes
again. Then he laughed, rose, and left her. Nearby the King of Azzi
sat in black gloom. One glance at his face brought trouble to his
new queen's. But Antiope ate with satisfaction, for the first time
having a chance to enjoy her food.

"When I get her alone! By the Bull, when!" Asterion, the Star
of Crete, wailed that, his slim, savage hands ripping out great
pieces of the fine embroidered stuffs that covered his bed. The
Cretans around him shrank in fear. Tamos, his servant from boyhood, dared to say: "Lord, she is no common Amazon. She is the
Great King's daughter—"

"What great King's? An upstart barbarian's! He should feel
honored to have his true-born daughter wash my feet, let alone
his she-bastard—"

He threw back his head and howled like a wolf. Froth stood on
his lips. "She scorned me—*me*, Asterion, who will be Minos! This
harlot, born of a long line of harlots—she dares to withhold her
body from me. She dares! I will humble her—I will break her. By
the Bull, I swear it!"

He writhed this way and that, teeth as well as nails now rending
the rich coverlet. The graybearded old admiral whom Minos had
sent to bring his son home—who at first had been blissfully glad
not to find that the prince had not already stolen away as Minos

feared—groaned within himself. He said uneasily, "Lord, we are far from Crete. To carry off a woman with great kin here would be dangerous—"

Asterion struck him; the blow filled the old man's mouth with blood. Then of a sudden the prince grew calm; he said softly, gloatingly: "She has sinned against the Bull. Against the God of Crete Himself, and for that she shall pay. I will bring her pride low —low. . . ."

CHAPTER 2.
_____TREACHERY

I N THE morning his herald bore Antiope a challenge. "My lord is the greatest of Cretan wrestlers, and he has heard that the Amazons also claim great skill. Let the Queen of the Amazons wrestle with him tomorrow, that all the guests at her kinswoman's wedding feast may marvel."

With something like relief Antiope accepted that challenge. Amazons avoided fisticuffs, at which they knew some men would always excel them—and why be ashamed of that, since a great healthy bull or stallion was always stronger than anything human? But they had made an art of wrestling, had invented several tricks of their own. . . . When Marpe, her playmate of old, said, ashen-faced, "Queen, he means treachery!" Antiope only smiled. "Of course. But he will not dare it openly—the Hittites will be there, not only the men of Azzi. His ships are what we must fear. We must be very careful always to keep together—no Amazons must go out of sight or sound of other Amazons."

All shuddered then, thinking of ships. Of the woe left by those that had come to Themiskyra two years ago. Yet when Antiope went on, "He thinks to hurt and humiliate me, and so salve that swollen pride of his." They laughed.

"You will show him, Queen! What a pity you cannot turn him over your knee, as these man-owned women do their children. He is all bark, that Cretan puppydog, and he should be made all howl."

Antiope laughed too, but at that night's banquet she refused all wine, saying she must keep her head clear. Actually, she feared drugs that might slow her wits and her speed.

Next morning she walked out into the palace courtyard, naked save for a linen loincloth, her body oiled to make it slippery as any eel's. Similarly prepared, Asterion came, and all there wondered at the lithe grace and beauty of their bodies. Together they greeted the king and queen. Hukkana beamed upon them both, but Kadussi's eyes were downcast. Then Antiope's Amazons were led away, to seats at the back of the improvised ring. Seeing that, Antiope stiffened angrily, then saw what was worse. The Hittite officers had front seats, but all of them, even Mariyas himself, looked bleary-eyed and half-asleep. Never would he have let them drink too much last night! They must be drugged. . . . Her eyes flew back to the royal pair. Around Kadussi's throat gleamed a new necklace, gorgeous, golden, and of strange workmanship . . . Cretan? Swift as lightning, devastating as lightning, understanding came.

That is her price for telling the Great King whatever story they want her to tell him. I am betrayed! She felt a sudden longing for her iron girdle, that fairness had demanded she take off, then set her teeth. Tricks or no tricks, she would pay this Cretan viper out. She swung to face him, careful not to lose sight of the king's hand, that would give them the signal to begin.

And then—while Hukkana's hand still lay idle in his lap— Asterion sprang. Before Antiope could leap aside, both his hands gripped her right arm. His body bent like a bow, and hers sailed over it. Even as she hit the ground he was upon her. His knees crashed into her belly like clubs; one savage jerk tore away her loincloth. He seized both her wrists.

Sick and winded, agony filling her belly, Antiope still played the first trick an Amazon was taught. Her thigh muscles bulged and stiffened, braced themselves, iron-hard, to keep out the hot hard thing that rammed at her, greedy for her maidenhead. Through her retching gasps she heard the war-cry of her people: "HIP-POL-Y-TE! HIP-PO-OL-Y-TE-E!" Heard sounds of fighting too, and bewildered cries from the half-awakened Hittites. Black fear stabbed her; the King of Azzi had the right to kill any who broke into the wrestling ring. No Hittite would die unless by accident, but her girls—

Still fighting for breath, she managed to get out one cry: "Stop, girls! We two must—fight this—out—alone—"

All cries stopped; she had thrown away her only hope of rescue. Asterion laughed and spat in her face.

Again and again he rammed at her. Viciously he twisted one of her arms, then the other, hissing like a snake. "Open! Before I break them both!" The pain was unspeakable. More than once consciousness almost left her, but she hung on to it doggedly, blood oozing from her bitten lips. If she fainted, if her thigh muscles relaxed . . . When would she hear a bone snap? Whenever he tired of this savage play. He wanted to break her will, he would love to hear her scream, but those pleasures he would never get. . . .

Time passed. The strain made a lady of Azzi titter; another gave a shrill, nickering laugh. Either would have been horrified at sight of a woman of her own race fighting rape. But Amazons never married and they gave themselves to strange men; they were only whores anyhow. Queen Kadussi thought miserably: *What difference could it have made to her? And it means so much to my lord—such wealth!* And then, in sudden terror, *Which of us will my brother believe—her or me?* If Antiope were to be really hurt—

The Hittites sat grim-faced, awake now, but bound by her cry. Blood also ran from the bitten lips of the Amazons. The King of Azzi and his men were all one many-faced, fixed stare. He thought, *Subbiluliuma threatened me with death for incest—he thought I wanted the girl myself. But at least with Asterion it will not be incest. O Gods, let him not maim her!* His nails dug into his palms. The gold that had dazzled him no longer glittered. . . .

At last a scream came, but from Asterion, mad with rage. Why would she not break? He wanted into her too—into the softness of her. Her breasts, so upright and delicately delicious beneath him, enraged him. His head shot down like a striking snake's. His teeth tore through the fine, soft skin of one of those rounded breasts. . . .

But that fierce joy broke his concentration; his weight shifted, his hold loosened, by ever so little. Antiope saw her chance at last. With one mighty heave she managed to roll over, dragging his shorter body with her. Her knee shot up into his groin, and he screamed again—not with rage, this time. Antiope tore herself free and rolled away. One foot shot back, swift and savage, to kick the place where her knee had been. Asterion's howl did not sound as if it came from a human throat.

To rise without using her tortured arms was not easy, but she made it. Sweat poured from her, her arms hung limp like pieces of rope, but she stood straight. Like a bell her voice rang through the cries of joy, through the cries of fear.

"She spoke truly, that Isle-Queen whom the first Minos murdered! She who said as she died, 'No true human son will ever spring from your loins, only scorpions and all vermin that crawls and stings!' And his is not the only race so cursed!"

Her blazing eyes met the King of Azzi's, but they would not meet hers. Gray-faced he sat, Kadussi cowering like a frightened child beside him. Only Asterion, writhing on the ground, answered Antiope. Through lips smeared with her blood came his voice, shaking with pain and fury.

"By the Bull of Crete, woman, you shall pay for this! His horns shall gore you! Or else He will make your own beloved horses trample you beneath their hoofs! You, or flesh of your flesh—"

But then her Amazons closed around her, laughing and crying like other women, and she saw and heard nothing else.

For a few days the Amazons feared that Marpe might lose the sight of one eye. A man of Azzi had gouged it as she fought to reach her queen. Yet she chuckled when she heard how many attempts Asterion had made to lie with a slave girl before he had finally succeeded. "He was lucky to get away from you able to lie with any woman again, Queen!"

"He would not have," said Antiope grimly, "if I had had time to kick straight."

Not until Marpe opened her eye and saw would Antiope speak with the King of Azzi. He fawned on her like a puppy then, he swore great oaths to keep all his young men at home, and never again in any way to aid the Kaska. Antiope said only: "Since this peace will be good for the Amazons, we will keep it as long as you do, King. But if you break it we will be ready for you." He pretended to take those words as a friendly joke, but his laugh rang hollow.

Then the Amazons fared homeward, toward their own mountains. There they parted with the Hittites. Captain Mariyas said:

"May the Sun Goddess of Arinna guard you, Princess, now and always." Antiope smiled, not angry because he had not called her Queen; he knew no better, this faithful man of her father's. "And the Storm God be with you, Mariyas!"

He looked after her long. *Any other woman would have made a great fuss about all this. It is a pity she was not one of the king's boys. None of them could have put up a better fight.*

But the Amazons rode on, up out of the summer heat and the stinging flies, into the cool, pleasant high places. All Antiope wanted now was to get home, to the things she had known always. To the green pastures of Themiskyra, and the horses that fed there; to all the girls and women she had left behind. To Molpadia too. *O Goddess, Mother of us all, how good it is to own oneself!* Restlessness seemed gone forever.

The watchwomen in the mountains welcomed her, sent messengers ahead to warn Themiskyra of her coming. When she rode down into the sweet plain all the Amazons poured forth to meet her, even as swarming bees pour forth from a hive, but in gladness. Even Molpadia's fierce eyes softened when she saw the tall girl on the tall horse. Antiope slipped down into her aunt's arms.

"Child, you have been hurt. There is a scar on your left breast!"

"It is nothing, mother's sister. Oh, it is good to be home!"

When the War-Queen had heard all she said: "You have suffered much and risked far more, for nothing. Peace with Azzi will always be worth nothing. Well, I will let you learn its worthlessness. Let that treacherous whining cur Hukkana think he has us all fooled."

Antiope smiled. . . .

Winter whitened the world. The Amazons sat at home like other women; they spun and wove and told tales around their fires. This was their quiet time, when no foe would come.

But when the snows were deep a beggar woman came. She had traveled far; even her boots were all holes, her feet bloody. Her hair was white, yet her face still held the ghosts of beauty and power. The Amazons took her into the House of the Maidens, they fed her and gave her warm water and bear grease for her feet, then asked her name. She said: "It is lost, like all else that was ever mine. No kin will remember me where I go, but I would die where

I was born. Under the snowy peaks of Kaukasos, that westerners call the World's End."

"Did slavers carry you off?" one girl asked. To Amazons that was the worst of all fates.

"Pirates from the far West. I bore their captain children until he took a wealthy bride, younger than I. Then I was cast out."

"He kept your children?" Marpe's face was full of pity.

"I lost them." The dead eyes slid away.

"And did nothing?" Molpadia's lip curled.

"I did what a woman must. I found a new master. A better man, though I never loved him. Had he obeyed his Gods, I might have had another son."

Molpadia turned away then, but the girls stayed, curious. One said, "How did he disobey his Gods, this man of yours?"

"His people swear by the words of the God of Delphi, and that God bade him sleep with no woman until he got home. To me that meant—I was the woman he would have found there! *Ai! Ai!*" She rocked back and forth, moaning softly.

"Get more wine, girls," said Antiope.

"Thank you, Lady. Let it be hot—hot! The cold is still in my bones." She drank greedily, then huddled still closer to the fire, her thin bent body shivering.

"Bring another blanket, girls. Guest, be silent and sleep. You do not have to buy our hospitality."

"Thank you again, Lady. But soon I shall have a long time to sleep and be silent." Plainly the guest enjoyed listeners; probably they were the only folk who paid her any heed now. She went on: "The God had spoken in riddles, as Gods often do. Or as their priests do. So my man was puzzled, and went to seek further counsel in the little land once called Oraia. There a stranger-God from Egypt once was worshiped: Oros, as they call the Son of the woeful and wandering Mother. And there still dwells a king blessed with the ancient wisdom: one who sometimes can see what will be."

She straightened. Her voice was old and thin no longer, but rich and full. The hall became a goblet that it filled with golden wine. "He saw then, that king. I who have knowledge know something of what he said within himself. 'A new age comes. What has been ends; that which never has been shall be. Two men will bring those changes, two who never shall meet. Soon a King of the East will say to his people: "The Gods are not many, but One, and that One loves all peoples. Not ours alone." ' "

Antiope said, startled: "Pharaoh Akhnaton is saying something like that now." Then she remembered that the beggar woman might have heard that, somewhere on her long road.

Again the golden voice filled the room. " 'And in the West a king will be born who will say to his people: "God is in every man. Kings have only the power of the sword, and claim a blessing that is not theirs. No man should bow before another." And he will lay aside his crown and teach his people a new way to live. One that in ages to come many people in many lands will follow, though they will think his name and deeds only an old tale, and doubt that he ever lived.' "

She stopped, and the girls murmured in wonder. When she spoke again her voice was only a bitter, broken old woman's. "He was clever too, that wise king. He had a daughter, a girl fair as the morning. He got my man to lie with her. So she bore the fated son, the king that will be. My womb—my arms—were left empty. I— I who have been called the wisest of women, and the most cunning —surely I could have taught him better than any other how to meet and overcome the mighty perils that still lie before him! I was cheated—cheated!" She wept.

"So you were cast out again?" one girl asked.

"No." Fire flashed in the dead eyes. "By Earth and Sun, my lord had sworn that his house should shelter me always, and he knew better than to bring another woman there to rule over me!"

So flame might have flared, hot and crimson, above the snowy peak of a volcano still for ages. But even as the watchers stared it passed; the fierce eyes dulled.

"But *he* came—the boy! After killing all those who terrorized the great trade road that his father had grown too old to guard. The two Phaias first—the Holy Queen and her Holy Sow. For ages they had reigned in Krommyon, one spirit in two bodies, until men drove them out. But when the queen came back she had grown cruel; hating the new ways, she fed the Sow upon the flesh of men. My lord's son slew her, then butchered the Sow and all her piglets to make a feast for the men of Krommyon, who hailed him as king and deliverer. But he foolishly bade them appoint a council to rule them, and went on. *I* never would have taught him that—why should any man give up power? That part of the foreseeing must have been wrong."

The faces of the Amazons had hardened; they did not like to hear of a queen's defeat. The stranger went on: "Next he slew Skiron, that man who of all men most wanted to be a king. Because he could get only ruins to rule over, the fool proved his might and majesty by sitting on a cliff above the sea and making all travelers who could not pay his toll wash his feet like slaves. Then he would laugh and kick them into the sea. My lord's son threw him over his own cliff. He said, 'I deal with you as you have dealt with others.'

"He said those same words to savage Kerkuon too—Kerkuon, who had been a good king once. Until he learned that his daughter Alope had borne a child out of wedlock. 'Father, Father—it was no man! It was Poseidon!' So men say she cried at the last, cowering before his huge, uplifted fist. On those shores all sons of unwed princesses are called sons of Poseidon." She laughed, an ugly spiteful cackle. Antiope started. Poseidon—a son of Poseidon!

"But after he had slain his own child and exposed hers, madness came upon Kerkuon. He ruled in Eleusis, the Holy City of the Mother and the Maid, but he turned blasphemer—swore that being female, They must be foul. He made all poor men who came as pilgrims wrestle with him. My lord's son was still calling himself a son of Poseidon then, so Kerkuon, raging, vowed to break his back—and got his own broken! But then a boy came running up and called my lord's son brother—Kerkuon's grandson, whom peasants had hidden and reared. *He* was still young enough to believe in Poseidon's Fatherhood—if indeed the whole story was not a lie!" Again that ugly, spiteful cackle. "And that fool who had just won a crown said, 'I will not deprive my brother of his heritage'—and went on! Gave up Eleusis, that is a rich prize; the pilgrims bring wealth to any king with sense."

Now the faces of the Amazons were kind; their eyes shone. "He must be a great fighter, this son of your man," said Antiope. "He must also have a great heart."

"A few fools do, Lady—very few. No clever man ever has. But this fool of my lord's begetting went on to meet Prokrustes the Maimer. Prokrustes, the most hospitable of men!" She laughed shrilly. "He always gave tall guests a short bed—and then cut off one end of them to make them fit. To short guests he gave a long bed—stretching them out to fit must have been more trouble, but he managed it. Until my lord's son put him to sleep on one of his own beds."

"The dog got what he deserved." Antiope's lip curled with distaste.

"To get what one deserves—that can be a hard lot to bear, Lady." Suddenly the old voice was tired and dreary. "Then the victor came to his father's city. To the house where for years I had been mistress. *Ai—ai!*" The weird wail rose, quivered, and sank. "At first he did not tell us who he was; the young are playful. But I knew—by my arts I knew! And I could not bear to lose the home of my age as I had lost every home I had had in youth—"

"Did you kill him then? As once you killed the children born of you?"

Spear-straight Molpadia stood there, her eyes burning like coals. And as if hot coals had burned her flesh the stranger screamed and shrank back, hiding her face in her black, ragged cloak.

Molpadia said: "See, girls, how a woman ends who lusts after men. There stands Medea, daughter of sun-born Aietes, the hot-loined fool who fled with Jason the Greek."

All stared. All knew how fierce-hearted Aietes, called Son of the Sun, had once reigned in Kolchis, the land at the eastern end of their sea. How he would have slain his guests, the Argonauts, if Medea, his witch daughter, had not saved them for love of Jason their captain.

"She betrayed her own people." Molpadia's voice lashed the black, silent shape. "She slew her brother, who followed when she fled. Then when Jason threw her away like an old shoe—as she might have known he would, once he no longer needed her—she slew the children she had borne him. Her own flesh."

Medea's cloak fell; her face was like a corpse's face. "My brother would have dragged me back to my father—to die a hard death. And my children were boys. Since when have you Amazons loved your brothers? *Your* sons?"

Her eyes seemed to pierce her tormentor's, to look through them as through an open door. And now Molpadia shrank back, amazing all. Then Medea seemed to forget her; her face grew strange, as if she listened to sounds unheard by others. Suddenly she threw back her head and laughed: wild, bitter laughter that was like a blow in the other woman's face. "So, Amazon? We have both killed what we loved most. But I have blundered for the last time; my deeds are all done. And in the end I failed—I did not kill Theseus, son of my lord Aegeus. Someday you may wish I had."

Like a wolf Molpadia sprang for her, but Antiope leaped between. "Aunt, she is a guest in this house!" Again Molpadia turned and left, and again the stranger hid her face in her cloak. Still as a statue she stood there in the red firelight. Antiope spoke quiet, reassuring words to that black figure, but could not bring herself to touch it. The outcast made no answer; none there ever saw her face again.

In the morning she was gone; while the night was still at its blackest the gatekeepers had let her out, glad to see her go. Molpadia said: "It is well. May the Vulture-headed Women tear her heart and bowels forever, that woman who could lawfully have reared her children, yet chose to slay them!"

Antiope said, "How did you learn of that slaying?"

And Molpadia answered: "Traders from Troy came while you were yet in Azzi. Most news reaches Troy at last; even traders have their uses."

They never knew whether Medea lived to reach Kolchis. She must have had gold and silver when she left Athens, but one can buy little when crossing mountains in the snow. She may have died alone, like a worn-out old dog, on some steep mountainside. Or she may have stopped in some mountain village and become its wise woman, glad at the last to chant spells and incantations to get a bowl of stew.

But all winter, while the winds howled around the log walls of the Amazons, Antiope heard them cry one name: "Theseus!" There might well be many redheaded "sons of Poseidon" in the far West; the little land called Oraia need not be Troizen. Yet those deeds had been great deeds, and she could see him doing them— his fiery head held high, his tawny eyes flashing. She crushed back

those visions; she was not proud of him—how could she be? To
kill him—that would give her a proper and understandable pride
and joy. And if ever again he came into her sea she would do it.

Yet she could not help wondering: How had he escaped Medea's
murdering guile?

Over Athens too the winds howled that winter. Cold and grim
they beat upon the high Akropolis, but old Aegeus was warm and
happy. He had a son at last—and what a son! One who single-
handed had done what all the sons of Pallas together had not dared
to go forth and do, though if they had their success would surely
have toppled him from his throne. "But he who did the deeds
sprang from my loins—*mine!*"

Theseus was not so happy. The glow had soon gone out of his
glory; too many hard facts had come to dim it. For the first time
in his life he dreaded the coming of spring. It would bring death,
not life, to Athens—the ships of Minos swooping down like
hawks to seize their prey. On his last night in Troizen he had
talked wildly of building ships to meet them—how young he had
been! Pittheus had warned him that it took time and treasure to
build ships; also secrecy. And even if he had the first two, there
was no secrecy to be had in Attica. The sons of Pallas had eyes
everywhere. All the young men of Athens seemed to idolize Theseus for his victories, and at first he had happily believed that they
did. Then one day he had scorned a warning, and almost lost his
life. Certainly most of that hero worship was sincere, but now
there would always be the doubt. The sons of Pallas too—those
men closest to him in blood, many of whom looked like him—had
they all been in the plot? If not, how many of them had? Lykophron and he were more alike than most brothers, yet even if Lykophron were to offer him friendship, he never could dare to trust
him. He could only hope, heartsick, that Lykophron, at least, had
not been in the plot. Hard indeed to have your heart go out to a
man, yet have to wonder, *Has he poison for my belly? A knife for my back?*
In little Troizen a man could trust his friends and kin. But here—

Even you, my father, even you! You set the Bull of Marathon on me.

Never would Theseus forget the first black shock of that knowledge. He knew now how Medea had played on the old man's fears,
egged him on. "The people honor him like a God, this young man

who has killed so many mighty men. What if he wants to be king?" When Aegeus had answered, "They were all evildoers," she had said, "Will he not call you the murderer of your guest?" Theseus knew now that his father had always thought—or hoped —that the Bull was truly the instrument of God's justice, and would kill no innocent man. But with what bitterness in his heart he had gone out to meet it! Later, at his hard-won victory feast— that killing had taken more skill and strength than all the others —he had drawn the Serpent King's short sword to cut meat with. His only thought had been, *Now see what you have done, old man—and what you have lost! For never will I stay here now.* With grim pleasure he had seen the old king start and quiver when the golden snakes on that blade flashed. He had seemed about to faint. But when Theseus reached for his winecup the old man had suddenly come to life again—had come running, stumbling toward him. To knock the cup from his hand and fling both arms around his neck.

"Oh, my son—my son!" The old lips quivered, the old eyes were full of tears.

In that appalling breath's space Theseus had realized two things: that that cup had been poisoned, poisoned with his father's knowledge—and yet that he himself was powerless to throw off the clasp of those weak, trembling arms. He had gathered the old man close.

Then over his father's white head he had seen the woman. Still sword-straight and slim in her crimson skirt, her faded face bright with paint, gold in her black-dyed hair. But her eyes were blacker than those deeps that are said to lie as far beneath the halls of Hades as Hades lies beneath the earth. Very quietly she had said: "I wanted you to know my pain, Aegeus. You who swore me shelter—you gave me courage to slay my children. All these years I have hated you for that. Today I had hoped to repay you—to make you kill your own son."

Wet-eyed old Aegeus' roar had not daunted her. Unflinching she had stood there, waiting for his blow, or for the order he might shout to others. She had been brave, and Theseus had said wearily, "Father, let her go." And Aegeus, sobbing, had turned from her, to lay his head on his son's breast. . . .

Pity had come before love, and that love was more like a father's than a son's, Theseus thought, since it was given to weakness. The

THE SWORD IS FORGED

old man was happy now, happy as a child at its birthday feast, forgetting what he had tried to do to his own son, what he surely had brought upon the sons of other fathers. For those Cretan ships would come. . . .

Gamelion came first, the midwinter Marriage Moon. The time for the sons and daughters of Athens to wed, and conceive children; for that outpouring of life that would help to bring the spring. That winter many who were very young married; sick at heart, Theseus knew why. Minos could claim only the unmarried. . . . Yet he was startled when Aegeus came to him and begged him to marry. "Child, I am old. Let me hold grandsons on my knee before I die. I missed your childhood."

Theseus answered: "She who will bear my sons is already chosen. She waits for me elsewhere."

"In Troizen? Your mother and grandfather must have chosen wisely. I would not oppose their will. Yet"—he sighed—"Athens would have rejoiced to have a true queen again at last. One who, in the words of the ancient Holy Marriage, 'could see what only a woman born in Athens may see, hear what only a woman born in Athens may hear.' "

"My mother was not born in Athens."

"True. And no woman ever served Athens better!" The old man chuckled gleefully, then sobered. "Yet a highborn Athenian bride would have served you well now. Mighty as you are, you are but one, and the sons of Pallas are many. And more of them are always growing up. Someday—as sure as the sun sets—they will strike."

"My sword will be ready for them." Theseus' voice was as cold and hard as his sword blade, the blade that once had belonged to Kekrops the Serpent King. But his heart felt sore and weary. The sons of Pallas he could deal with, but not the ships of Minos. Also, Antiope was not in Troizen. He said, "I do not want to take a wife this year, Father."

The old king's face went ashen. "Child, child, this is the year of the Ninth Horai! And what man's son would Minos want as he would want mine?"

Sudden anger flared in Theseus, anger born of horror that was also complete understanding. "How could I make merry with a bride while you sent other young Athenians away to die in my place?"

Aegeus' face went gray with a pain whose bitterness seemed to wither it. To look at it hurt Theseus. He turned his eyes away, and laid a gentle hand on his father's arm. His mind raced, and more than his mind. He had always wondered why his grandfather, who did not like the bull games, had had him taught such skill in them. The fight with the Bull of Marathon had seemed to explain that. But what if old Pittheus' strange foresight had gone even farther?

"Maybe it is my fate to go to Crete, Father. To kill the Bull of Minos even as I killed the Bull of Marathon. Then all this will be over—the sons and daughters of Athens will be safe, freed from the tribute forever."

"No! No!" Aegeus' hands trembled, but both clung desperately to his son. "No, child—no. I forbid you to go. You are all I have —my only son! And the sin was not yours—you are guiltless."

"If I am to be King of Athens, I must protect the people of Athens."

"Child, you would die for nothing! Even if you conquered all the other bulls, and met *the* Bull! This Minos is not like the first Minos—not like him who made a covenant with the God his Father and brought back the sun! I have looked into his eyes and heard his voice—I know. If he feared you might conquer his Bull of bulls, you would go drugged and helpless before that God-Beast. You would die! And other young Athenians would go on dying as if you had never been—" Aegeus sobbed; his head fell forward on his son's shoulder.

The glow went out of Theseus. His father was right. Tyrants always found a way out of keeping their promises. Skylla's destroyer never would let him escape—he would indeed be the most precious prize of all! Shipbuilding was Athens' only hope. He, Theseus, must go back to his first plan and wait—for how long must he wait? For his people's sake, would he not have to give up his other purpose, that to most men would have seemed only a dream or a hope? Take a wife he did not want?

"Child"—Aegeus' voice, cunning now, coaxing, that of a man trying to bribe a little boy—"I have a ship. Most mainland kings have one hidden away somewhere, in spite of Delphi. Take it and sail away for this summer."

For a breath's space Theseus' face shone like sunrise—then dulled again. "Father, I cannot leave you to face this alone."

Aegeus smiled; that smile made him a man again. The man who had withstood Minos, the man who, long ago, had fought against great odds to kill usurping Metion and win back his own father's crown. "Child, I still have strength enough to face this Ninth Horai alone. The sons of Pallas will not rise against me, knowing that you will soon come home. Take the ship and go where you will —only do not go near Crete!"

He spoke out of the sorry wisdom of his time. That any young man should have a ship, yet not play pirate, was unthinkable. Of old that fact had caused much woe and bloodshed; it was the main reason why Delphi's ban against shipbuilding had roused no rebellion. And for himself it was not the sons of Pallas that Aegeus feared, but the gloating, accusing eyes of Minos that he might have to meet again, and still more—far more—the faces of those parents who would have to give up their children. . . . But he did not expect or want his son to think of those intangible ordeals.

And Theseus did not. His eyes were shining again; they glowed like molten gold. "Gladly will I promise you that, Father. I will not go near Crete. But I will take the ship!"

CHAPTER 3.
THE ISLE OF THE BLACK STONE

THE NIGHTS were still frosty when the ship sailed. Euneos and Thoas had come north again for that sailing, and this time Hermos and young Solois were with them. All their hearts sang like birds, but Solois' heart outsang all others. *I am going with him. With Theseus!*

Theseus thought, *Well, he will be only one cub more.* He was not too happy about his crew. During Gamelion all wellborn Athenian fathers had married off all sons who were marriageable; and a bridegroom's place was at home. Yet in a way his crew's youth served him well; they were still used to doing as they were told. They did not ask awkward questions as to why they must sail northward, ever northward, past islands that looked well worth looting.

Theseus had no wish to play pirate; Pittheus had taught him respect for other men's rights to what they earned and made. And for a while the cold sea wind was all he wanted; it seemed cleansing, it washed away black memories and the ugly new need to suspect all who sought his friendship—all those who might really be spies for the sons of Pallas. He was glad of his newborn respect for his father: in the first pain of his hurt he had doubtless been unjust. After all, no man could wholly trust even himself.

You taught me that, Prokrustes.

Skiron and the two Phaias would never haunt him. And in the shining-eyed, almost worshiping boy, Kerkuon's grandson, he had seen himself—that young self that had believed Poseidon his only father, and the warm, generous tenderness that had flooded him was still good to remember. But after he had left Eleusis had come the victory that had also been defeat. Prokrustes and those two beds of his! The Maimer had hammered out short men to make them fit the long bed; he had cut off the feet of tall men to make them fit the short one. But his eyes had been far worse than his beds. No lust to kill had been in them—to him a victim's death had meant only the end of his pleasure—but an awful, outrageous desire to give pain. A vile sickness that could pass from one man to another. For he himself had joyed in Prokrustes' screams . . . until the red madness had broken and he had looked down with unbelieving horror upon the groaning wreckage that had been the Maimer. Many had praised that deed; folk still chuckled over how the Chopper of Men had been chopped up with his own ax. But Pittheus' grandson wanted only to forget it. His own proud slogan, with which he had so gaily marched north, "I will deal with you, dogs, as you have dealt with others," had betrayed him. Some punishments no decent man can soil himself by inflicting, however well deserved they may be.

Well, a man must learn, and it was good that he had not learned on somebody worth more than Prokrustes. A mad dog should be killed but with one clean blow. A man's blow. In future he would always remember that he was a man—and soon now he would know the highest joys of manhood! Fire-hot that knowledge surged through his blood; made him drive his ship on, through winds that grew ever colder, while his luckless comrades shivered. He forgot the Cretan ships that by now must have reached Athens, the misery that his father faced alone. Nothing mattered but his quest.

Now was the time—now! Soon the Amazons would be outside their walls, on their journey to and from their seven-day spring festival upon the Isle of the Black Stone. He could still hear Antiope's voice describing that.

"I told you of that Stone that once was a burning star—how we saw it fall from heaven. Later we found it again, huge and blackened, upon a little isle where the bird-host rests on its northward flight. Every spring we too go there. On the first and seventh days all go, to cut the throats of horses. But on the five days between only women go—to lie with the men we have captured, then burn them before the Black Stone. Sometimes"—for a breath's space her voice had faltered—"the wind carries the screams to us maids who wait on shore. And the smoke . . . Mother said we need no more captives, now we could lie with the Hittites. But Molpadia says old ways are best."

Antiope! She would be waiting for him, there in that camp of virgins by the shore. Not knowing that she waited . . . Older now, her dainty breasts fuller, her long thighs round and sweetly curving. Never should all that fineness be laid down beneath doomed, frantically squirming men on that unholy Holy Isle! Never should Hittite captains enjoy her in greedy delight in their also unholy Holy Groves. Nothing could have been clearer than his conscience; he would be saving her honor even while he himself took it.

"While I live—and I will live!—no other man shall have you!" It was night, and he spoke to her as if she lay there beside him; then prayed again to Her whom Athenians called Eldest of the Fates, and the most terrible. "Mistress, Lady of Love, deliver her into my hands!"

And perhaps, in still far-off Themiskyra, Antiope stirred in her sleep. Perhaps those walls that housed only women felt the approach of man the menace, man the master of the world.

Spring had come late that year to the cold Unfriendly Sea. Through bitter winds the Amazons rode to the Isle of the Black Stone. Cunning pitfalls guarded the gates of Themiskyra; the pick of the herds had been driven inside the walls, into deep, wide-mouthed caves dug for them. Only old women and young children had stayed behind; all who could ride must make that pilgrimage.

Antiope loved those long spring rides; loved to feel Chrysippe's smooth speed beneath her, and the wind blowing in her face. After the long winter shut up in smoky houses, such freedom was like wine. With sudden pity she thought of those women who were not Amazons; those women who were shut up in the smelly darkness of houses forever.

Put the swift winds on your feet as shoes. Never had the Hittite poet's words sung so sweetly in her blood as now.

What she never told herself was that the joy of those rides helped her to keep the doors of her mind shut, to forget what was coming. How the horses would be led before the Black Stone, the proud young horses with their high-held heads, and their shiny, blowing manes. As a little girl she had wept when she had first seen the sacrifice, but Molpadia had said sternly, "The Goddess wills it." Her teeth and eyes had shone with a queer cruel hunger that was not for the flesh later to be roasted and eaten.

No sane person could deny that Amazon ways were better than all other ways. And yet—*Can You who made that beautiful winged strength really want it destroyed, Lady?* Antiope's mind always asked that question whenever its doors slid open.

In the green pastures at home the Goddess watched over the foals and their mothers, and loved to see the foals grow. And it was said that in the old days, beside the Maiotis, only bloodless offerings had been made to Her, such as fruit and cakes.

But blood is precious, blood is strength, and now She too must have it, as do the Man-Gods. To give Her strength to keep us strong. And we Amazons have nothing so precious as our horses except our children. We should be thankful that She, being kind, does not ask for the children.

That was what everybody had believed, even Mother. Yet to Antiope it seemed strange that an Immortal should be dependent upon mortals. Surely She should be able to make Her own strength. . . .

Well, maybe when I am older, the Goddess will speak with me and I can ask Her about it, Antiope told herself. Meanwhile there was nothing to be done.

"Child, I must speak with you."

The Deathsinger drew up her horse beside the Childbearer's. Antiope waited, her eyes fixed on the other. Molpadia said: "Last night I dreamed a dream. I saw no picture, as I always have before. The Goddess spoke to me; I heard Her voice. She said: 'It is time for the Childbearer to bear. She who is the last of the blood of My beloved, of her who led My people across the Great Mountains.' "

"But I am not yet twenty, Aunt! I will not be for years yet. The Law—" Antiope stared, dumbfounded.

"She who makes can unmake. We two alone are left of the ancient blood, and only in war can I serve it. You must bear a daughter. Soon."

Antiope's heart lurched sickeningly. The captives! Like all girls, she had heard whispers of those matings before the Stone. Of men frenziedly serving woman after woman, clutching, ramming, mad to keep off death a little while longer. Of the miserable few whose comrades laughed at them because in their fear they could get up no erection at all, only cower before the faggots and the torch. *O Goddess, the mate in Your grove at Arinna! Where men and women laugh together.*

Aloud she said, her lips stiff: "Who is to father my firstborn, Aunt? Did the Goddess tell you?"

"Niece, you know that we have captured not only Kaska, but a chief of the Kaska. Surely it is fitting that you lie with him before the Black Stone."

"With Harush? That fat old man who has always tortured and raped every Amazon he could get his hands on?" Antiope's face was sick with disgust.

"Child, he is in his prime—a strong man, well able to beget. What else matters? Better if you get no pleasure from him anyway; only his seed."

"I do not want his seed. I will not carry it."

"The Goddess wills it. Also"—Molpadia's voice softened—"the babe will bring you peace. With her in your arms you never again will want to wander away from us, as you did last year."

"Not that man, Aunt. Some other—not he." Antiope's voice was low, half-choked.

Pity came into Molpadia's eyes. "Child, it will soon be over. And this man cannot laugh at you as that accursed Cretan would have done. He will die."

"He is not fit to father Amazons."

"No man is, child. Men are all alike. Always cunning, always greedy, always plotting to get their own way . . ."

Sick with dread as she was, Antiope laughed. "Aunt, that is exactly what men say about women. I learned that among the Hittites."

"The Hittites!" Molpadia's voice spat venom, like a snake's. "Once I tried to warn your sister against them, those worms who gnaw at our vitals."

"But the Goddess bade Mother make a treaty with them!" Again Antiope stared.

"So your sister said, so your mother believed, but the Goddess never spoke those words. Some evil spirit of the Hittites did, to entrap us."

Antiope said slowly: "Aunt, such words rock the world. You must know that, who are older than I."

"Better to rock it than to let it be overturned. Amazons can trust only Amazons."

"Aunt, I am young, but I have learned this much. Times change, as do all things else. We are a small free people, and small free peoples grow few. We need friends and allies. Peace."

Molpadia snorted. "Men will never give us any peace but death!"

"Then we must die alone, for someday even the Kaska will be tamed, and there will be no wilderness to protect us. I had rather we kept on living alone."

"Your mouth speaks those words, but Subbiluliuma put them into your head. Even as tales of his bravery fascinated your mother and opened her mind to that evil spirit who must have been one of the Hittites' Thousand Gods! The poison came then, and it works—oh, it works!"

Antiope looked into the familiar face, and with startled horror saw another. One older and ravaged by unspeakable torments, but still burning with implacable determination, implacable hate. Almost she cried "Lysippe!" and then realized that Lysippe was long gone. But she had left behind her a Thing shaped by her will, fed by her fires. A Thing strengthened, made greater, by the will and the fires of every Amazon who had come after her. In sick awe the girl thought, *Molpadia must be right, if the Hive-Spirit speaks through her!* But then doubt came again. Was the Hive-Spirit using Molpadia, or was Molpadia using the Hive-Spirit? Or were they using each other, blindly and furiously, toward ends neither foresaw?

She said quietly: "If I cannot believe the words the Goddess spoke to my mother, how can I believe those that you think She spoke to you?"

For a breath's space she braced herself to meet attack, such madness blazed in the strange face. But it went out like a torch in the wind; Molpadia spoke in her own voice.

"Then hear, girl—hear what will come." She laid a hand on the place where her right breast had been. Her face worked as if the wound were still raw, but was again her own face. "Once I bore a child. You know that?"

"I have heard it, Mother's sister." Antiope's voice was suddenly gentle.

"Then hear more. I loved his father—it was as if I had never lived, only drowsed between sleep and waking, until we met. Until I saw him and felt him. . . . The child was worthless, being male, but because he was like his father I loved him. And somehow, using the sly craftiness of men, the man sent me a secret message. 'If you have borne a daughter, I know these words will be useless. But if we have a son, come with him and be my wife. The king loves me; he will look the other way; and so will your sister, who loves you.'" She laughed harshly. "His wife! More likely he would have made me a slave in his kitchen. Yet what is a wife but a slave who wears better clothes than the kitchen maids? Well, no matter. I was strong; I kept our Law. But someday, if we do not break with these accursed Hittites, some girl will listen to him who beguiles her—and begin the ending of our race."

Pity wrung Antiope. Since the night of Molpadia's clash with Medea she had feared that what the old woman said was true— that Molpadia had weaned her boy too soon. But she had not done it out of hate, but because she feared to keep him any longer. Feared too her love for the man, his father. What could it be like, this love-madness that swept over a woman like fire or flood, that could even make her leave all else she ever had known or loved? Curiosity and wonder stirred in her, even through her shocked pity.

Molpadia spoke again. "So now you see why it will be better if you get no pleasure from the man, only his seed. Do your duty to our people, girl, and be thankful that your burden is no heavier."

Antiope drew a deep breath. "You have always taught me never to put off the doing of an unpleasant deed, and always I have believed you wise in that. But I will put off this deed. I will not lie with Harush until the seventh day."

"So be it, niece. Lie with Marpe tonight; let her comfort you. She has loved you long, and there is no love so good and sweet and true as that between women. I never could learn its full sweetness, I who had been corrupted by that Hittite in Arinna. But you are young; you can still learn it."

But all night Antiope lay sleepless and alone. *How can I open my legs for that fat, stinking old man? For him who is vile within and without? When a deed seems so wrong, how can it be right? I am young and clean—he that begets my child should be young and clean!*

Her flesh cried out for its own integrity; her mind churned in bewilderment and pain. She raised her arms and prayed aloud: "Speak to me also, Goddess! I am young, but I too am the Hippolyte. Let me be sure what I should do, Lady—let me be sure. If You cannot make me see or hear You, send me a sign—send me a sign!"

But all she heard was a bird crying in the night, all she saw was the pale moonlight, as cold as silver and as hard.

On their second morning before the Isle of the Black Stone, Antiope the Queen worked with her age-mates to mend the wooden stockade that guarded that camp-city of virgins. Her trouble still burned like a flame within her. Her heart cried ceaselessly, less in prayer now than in demand—was not some kind of answer her right? *Send me a sign, Lady! Send me a sign!*

There had been fog, but it was lifting. The watchwoman who looked out to sea cried, "A ship! A ship!"

Days before the Athenians had sailed through the narrow straits of Helle, that were like a throat leading down into the maw of the dark Unfriendly Sea. Down into the gray gloom that was like a giant, ghostly mouth.

The bleak, cloudy sky looked dark and heavy. As the day wore, mists rose and thickened around them. And then, when they could see nothing, they heard it—a noise that was indeed like the grinding of teeth in a giant's mouth. When Theseus bade his men row away from that noise they obeyed gladly, put all the strength they had into that rowing. But their bodies were tense, and their eyes and ears strained ceaselessly. Theseus tried to cheer them; he said: "Whatever we are hearing, it will not hurt us unless we are fools enough to go straight at it. Even the Argonauts' clashing rocks only gave them a scare, and Herakles had no trouble with them at all. I know; I was with him." He did not add that Herakles had never seen them.

But that noise was dreadful to hear. One of the youngest boys cried, half sobbing: "But Herakles is the son of Zeus! And the Cretans say that Zeus is their God. Maybe He has sent the rocks after us because we ran away from Him, fearing to be chosen!"

Panic is bad anywhere. It is bad indeed for a sea captain who knows that his ship is in danger. For a breath's space Theseus took thought; then he laughed. His voice soared out, gay as ever, above the whispers and mutterings that had risen in the wake of that frightened cry.

"Men, these rocks are not rocks. They are only ice—great, clumsy lumps of ice. Hill-big, maybe, but ice. They will melt when the sun comes out."

He hoped those words would help. Ice, that melts, is not terrible like rock, that remains hard through the ages. But though for a breath's space silence fell, the muttering soon began again. One boy, whose elder brother was a friend to some of the sons of Pallas, dared to ask: "How do you know that?" And others clearly thought that, as the comrades of Herakles had, long ago. One shuddered and said, "Listen! Could ice ever sound like that?"

The crashes rang grimly through the mist. Crashes that could have been made by the falling walls of houses, by stones rolling in an avalanche. They seemed no farther away, although the backs of the whole crew already ached from rowing.

Theseus' jaw set. His mouth became a red slash across his face. "I will show you that they are ice. I will swim out and knock a piece off one of them."

He stripped to his loincloth. With a strip of leather he made a great ax fast to his waist. He walked to the boat's side, stopped, and said: "I will not ask you to wait for me. But when you hear my voice calling from the water, stop at once, and have ropes and furs ready. I may be too cold to get aboard again easily."

The cold water by itself would be foe enough, he knew. He would think of other perils when they came. But the others thought of nothing else; they never expected to see him alive again. All were silent but the boy whose brother was a friend to the sons of Pallas. He whispered, very low, "Those floating rocks will grind his bones to powder for his daring." He thought, *The House of Aegeus respects nothing. Neither guests, nor the immortal Gods.*

Euneos and Thoas and Hermos fidgeted, but did not speak or leave their places. They would have followed Theseus against lions or a host of men, but the thought of those unseen titanic shapes that were battling in the mist froze their blood. No man could fight cliffs that lived and moved like men.

But Solois came running to the man he loved. "I will go with you, Theseus! You know I am a good swimmer, and two will be better than one."

Warm as sunlight, Theseus' smile flashed; he patted the boy's arm. "Lad, you are a man."

Hermos rose then, gray-faced. "Take me instead, Theseus. He is very young." Before he had finished Euneos and Thoas were on their feet too, the same words in their mouths. But Solois caught Theseus' arm and cried, "I spoke first! It is my right to go. I am a man now—Theseus' man!"

Theseus, who never had had any intention of taking him, thought, *I cannot shame the boy now.* It was good that Solois did not weigh much; he could be carried if need be. He said: "Solois is right. But Hermos shall come with us—three will be better than two. Euneos, you and Thoas will keep watch here—see that all is ready for us when we come back."

For the first time since his sailing suspicion was stirring in him again, rearing a snakelike head. *Is there one of those here—one of my own crew—who would be glad if I did not come back?* Better to leave the two brothers in charge; they were older than any of the wellborn Athenians aboard, and they had been his friends longer. Yet even they—with a quickly smothered stab of pain he remembered that none of the three friends of his childhood had volunteered for his sake. Only for Solois'.

Ice-cold, the waves closed over the three of them. They shuddered, and then shuddered less. They swam straight toward the tumult that now, down there in the water, sounded like Zeus' thunder. The waves grew higher—sloshed over their heads and struck at them, tried to beat them back. The crashing grew louder; would it deafen them?

Then they saw—saw two vast shapes rolling in the gray dimness. Hill-high they seemed, huge bluish cliffs that moved—*moved,* and without land beneath them! After that, Solois remembered little. He knew that he bit his lips to keep from screaming; bit them until they bled. He looked only at Theseus' red head, flamelike against the dark waves and the gray mists. It moved steadily forward, and he moved steadily behind it. Hermos tried to help him, but he slid away—Hermos, though a good friend, would never be his lover. His head was splitting, but he swam on.

Then he did scream, because a blackness almost like night's covered them. But that darkness was only a shadow. Massive, mountain-high, one of the cliffs loomed over them. Beside it they were like beetles, ants. No, not even ant-big. Yet Theseus was attacking it with his ax. Could he make it feel? What if he made it angry? What would happen if he did?

Then the waves sloshed over Solois' head again, and he knew the darkness and agony of drowning. When he first saw Theseus' soaked red head beside him, he wondered if they were both dead. Then he knew that Theseus and Hermos were carrying him between them, and that now the waves were with them, not against them. They seemed to be pushing all three of them forward— toward the ship! Sight of it made him cry out with joy. Then his pride woke, and he tried to swim again, but his friends told him, somewhat roughly, to be still.

He was lying in the bottom of the ship, wrapped up as tightly as Egyptian mummies were said to be wrapped. Hot wine was burning his stomach, and Hermos was trying to make him drink more. But his eyes sought Theseus, whom he had heard laughing. Theseus squatted there, two heavy cloaks around him, but his eyes shone. He was holding something over the little brazier on which they must have heated the wine, and water was dripping from it, but it was not a pitcher. It was as big as a man's head and dully bluish. Then he understood and gasped in joyous understanding. "Theseus! You did get a piece of the rock, and it is melting."

"Yes. Because it is ice!" Theseus threw back his head and laughed again, joyously, triumphantly. Solois thought, *When he has finished he will look at me. He will recall that it was I who first offered to go with him. At last he will know how much I love him, and he will love me.*

In a happiness almost trancelike he waited. He was in no hurry; he was very tired. It was enough to lie there and know that joy was coming. . . .

Theseus had stopped laughing. He spoke softly, even gently, and Solois' heart leaped. *Now—now—though he will not say much until we are alone. . . .*

Theseus said: "The princess spoke truth; the floating isles are only ice. Many like to fool strangers and make sport of them, but she did not do that. She did not mock me."

That meant much to him, who had had to learn to distrust so many. But it went through Solois' heart like a spear. Because there was tenderness in it, and that tenderness was not for him.

"What princess, Theseus?" His voice was thin and shaky; even as he asked, he knew that the answer did not matter. Whoever she was, Theseus wanted her. Not him.

Theseus' eyes shone golden as the amber that traders brought from the far North. As dark spring water carried in a golden vessel beneath the morning sun.

"She is Antiope, Queen of the Amazons." His voice made the name ring like golden bells. "The Great King's daughter. And the most glorious mother for sons in all the world. She shall bear mine."

CHAPTER 4.
___TWO MEET AGAIN

L IKE ONE girl the Amazons raced for the shore, but before them all ran Antiope. Her heart sang within her, *Thank You! O Goddess, I thank you!* The others ran mainly because they were young and human, and so glad of a chance to stop work and see new things. If another, more primal urge moved in them, they did not yet know it.

Only Marpe, close behind her queen, whispered, "Be careful, Lady—be careful!"

But nothing is so easily heard as a whisper, and another girl laughed. "A traders' ship carries only thirty men. Shall fifty times that number of Amazons fear thirty men?"

Marpe retorted, "Men are cunning. They lay traps for women."

Then suddenly all stopped and stood where they were, staring. For the ship was turning, rounding the little headland that hid one strip of white beach from the Isle of the Black Stone. Their eyes, the keen eyes archers need, could see the men on the nearer end of it. Young men . . .

No young woman who has never had a man meets a good-looking young stranger without wondering, however deeply buried the thought may lie: *Is this the one? He that will be my lover, the father of my child?* That is a fact as inevitable and sweet as sunrise; and to Amazons lovers did not bring new homes and strangeness and all-overturning change. They came and went, leaving behind them only the tribe's greatest need—children.

Then as suddenly these girls remembered that they were all under twenty; all bound to virginity by the Law.

"They seem handsome," one girl said wistfully. "Straight and well made." She looked at them harder than ever. She could do that much, at least.

"He is handsome," said Antiope. She did not have to say which man she meant. All of them were looking hard, but hardest of all at him who stood Godlike in the prow. A helmet of boars' tusks, finely wrought, hid his hair—the red hair Antiope would have remembered. Its cheekpieces cut across his face, half-masking him. But his lithe straight young body, and the way he held his head and shoulders, were like a song: beauty and strength made one.

"They called themselves traders who slew your sister." Marpe's voice sounded almost like Molpadia's own. "Remember that, Queen!"

Antiope said slowly: "They did not mean to slay her. I see that now, since I have seen more of men and of war. That dog who seized me—he was to blame for all. He had seen Molpadia our host, and was afraid. He wanted to kill us before we could kill him and his people. Such things often happen when strangers meet."

Marpe gasped. "Queen, would you defend them? The murderers of your sister!"

Antiope laughed grimly. "No. Whatever their purpose was, they did kill her. And if ever I meet one of them again I will chop his head off and smash his skull to bits—none shall drink from the cup of his accursed head! Yet it is better to understand what makes things happen, to remember that one fool can wreck the plans of many wise heads."

So she spoke, but her eyes never left the man who was drawing nearer and nearer. Why did he hide his head with that silly helmet? It must be as good as the rest of him; and all of him looked beautiful. Better, she thought, than any other man she had ever seen. . . . Then her eyes narrowed, she spoke quickly, all queen again:

"They are almost here! If all of us meet them, we will look like a war party. Let twelve go, while the rest keep watch, their bows ready. You, and you, and you—" She named the twelve, Marpe among them. Together they went forward, leisurely, toward the shore.

By the time they reached it the ship had too. He who must be its captain came ashore with nine of his men. Antiope thought approvingly: *He has sense. He brings even fewer warriors than I have brought. He too knows better than to risk starting a fight over nothing.* That was good; she had a strong suspicion that two capable parents were more likely to make a capable child.

Then their eyes met, and all thinking stopped. Theseus knew her, and his heart cried: "Antiope! Antiope!" She was all he had dreamed of or hoped for, and more. She was better than all his hopes, for no dream, however great its beauty, ever has the wine-strong, warm sweetness of flesh and blood. He longed to cry her name aloud, but knew he must not. If she recognized him, some of his men would die; not all of them could hope to escape. Yet deep within him something mad and foolish wanted her to remember. To know him.

And for a breath's space Antiope did think: *Those eyes . . . like amber, like light on brown water . . . have I seen him before? When—and where?* Recollection hovered over her like one of those screaming birds that flew above them, longing to land on the Isle; hovered, and then was gone. What matter? This was he whom the Goddess had sent, and he was beautiful—beautiful as she had always thought the golden images of Telepinu, the young Hittite God of Spring, ought to be, and never were.

With great effort she kept her voice cool and queenlike; said, in the royal tongue of Kanesh: "Welcome, stranger. Who are you, and what brings you here? I am Antiope, Queen of the Amazons, and behind me are my people."

Theseus threw back his head and laughed. He felt as if he had had real wine, and too much of it. "Lady, you could be no other! You are more beautiful than all the soft women of the South put together. Even as your arms are stronger than theirs, so your beauty makes theirs weak and pale and faded!"

"Our arms have warlike skills too, stranger. Not only strength." She was frowning slightly, and Theseus saw that he had been too bombastic. He must not throw his luck away; it had been good, so far.

He said smoothly, "Lady, I am Pyrrhos, son of a man of Ereb, and I have goods to sell. Fine things from far away." She could not know that in Greek Pyrrhos meant "Redhead," though she might know that Ereb, itself an eastern word, meant "the West." Some said that the name of moon-bright Europa, mother of Minos, had sprung from the same root.

Antiope said: "Then bring your goods ashore, Pyrrhos, and lay them out where we can all come and look at them."

Theseus smiled—the most beaming of smiles. "Lady, I cannot hide it from you that my men are wary of you Amazons. Because of what happens on yonder isle." He jerked his head toward the distant smoke that curled above the headland. "As we came we smelled that smoke. They do not want to meet a great many of you at once."

Two or three girls looked offended, and two more gave small, angry snorts, but Antiope smiled. "Well, it is foolish to trust strangers, though not everybody is so honest about it. But if twenty of your men dare come ashore, I will meet them here tonight with as many girls. And with meat that can be roasting over a fire while we look at your goods. Another twenty of us will come tomorrow night, and another twenty the night after that. Or do you fear the fires the meat must roast over?" Her grin was a challenge.

Had she seen the look that came over Theseus' face then, it would have startled her. But her girls were startled too, and she felt their feelings as always. Even as she spoke she turned to meet their eyes, that were as big and round as moons. In their own tongue she said swiftly, "Soon you will understand," and they smiled and were at ease again. All was well; somehow they had misunderstood her.

But for Theseus the sky had fallen. Through a red mist he heard her voice speaking more words, words out of long ago: "You men will bring ashore only the knives you cut meat with . . . we Amazons will bring only ours." Yet he managed to hide sick fury, to smile. "Queen, we will do all you ask, and more. To this feast we will bring wine—rare wine from our own islands of the West, not the least precious of the goods we had meant to sell."

So thick was the red mist that he scarcely heard her answer, or saw her go. She knew—she could not help but know—what must happen at that feast tonight. For all her fine talk, her precious Law of the Amazons, she and her so-called virgins were as easy as the whores who met sailors in every port. Easier—they asked no pay.

All these years he had been dreaming of a whore! How many other men had already had her—*how many?*

He longed to leave: to sail to the World's End and over it. To be nothing, black nothingness, and forget. But his men—they had worked hard on this voyage, they deserved some pleasure at last. Besides, he had to have her—she was in his blood, she had been there too long. But never now would she be Queen of Athens. She would be his slave, the bitch who followed at his heels. Let her pay for her proud lies.

Back in camp, Antiope called all the girls together and spoke to them. She told of how the Goddess had spoken to Molpadia, what man Molpadia had chosen for her to lie with, and of her own prayer. They listened in wonder, awed yet glad. One girl said softly, marveling: "She has sent this ship then—the Lady Herself."

"To save you from lying with that worst of the accursed Kaska, Queen—that most abominable of men!"

Another said reverently: "Truly we owe Her thanks. Should we make Her an offering?"

Marpe cried out then, she whose lips had not opened since before that meeting on the shore. "Let us seize the strangers and offer them to Her! Tonight in the darkness we can swim out and board their ship while Antiope lies with their captain. Then they will have no way to flee!"

For a breath's space then there was silence. All the girls had felt that there was something lovely, kindly, about the coming of that Goddess-sent ship. And yet those aboard it were men. . . .

Antiope said quickly: "No. I have welcomed them, offered them food. I have given them guest-rights!"

All sighed with relief then, save only Marpe. She said heavily: "That cannot be broken. Yet I fear for you, Queen; a shadow that is not of the night is on me. How can you go to this man, except alone and unguarded? For none of us can go with you—the Goddess has not spoken to free us from the Law!"

Silence again; a shivering, aghast silence. Antiope drew a deep breath; she had known that this must come. She said, her voice ringing bell-clear, warm and golden through that chilled quiet: "To free me yet keep the rest of you bound would be unfair of Her who cannot be unfair. We Amazons have always shared alike;

never has a queen lain softer or fed on richer food than her people. She Who made us must mean for you to do as I do."

In her young faith she believed that. Yet a part of her that was still cool and shrewd knew also that though Molpadia might punish a few offenders, had they been all, she would not dare to punish many; the Amazons never had had enough warriors. She said again: "I trust in Her Who made us all, and if there is sin, let the punishment fall upon my head. Whatever comes, I will not lie with that old dog of a Kaska!"

A deafening cry answered her. "You shall not, Queen—you shall not! We will go with you!"

"Then let those of you who are nineteen years old each bring me a white pebble. Upon nineteen of them I will make red marks, then put them all in a dish together. She who, blindfolded, draws one with a red mark shall go with me tonight. So you who are chosen will be the Goddess' own choice, not mine."

Such lot-drawing was an ancient custom, held by many peoples to be a sure way to learn the will of the Gods. All the girls of nineteen stooped to gather up pebbles from the ground at their feet—they who, every one of them, had already killed her man, and next year would have been bound to go to the Holy Grove. Yet Marpe made one more effort.

"Should we do so great a deed without first sending messengers to the Isle? Taking counsel with the mothers, and the grandmothers?"

All eyes swung to her, but none were friendly. The look on many young faces was that of a dog who sees his bone being threatened by a bigger dog. One girl cried sharply: "You know what would happen then! The old women would take all these new men for themselves!"

"And kill some of them in the getting! *Waste* them!"

Clamor was about to break out, but again Antiope's voice cut through it like a golden bell. "Shall I refuse the Goddess' offered bounty? Take counsel with any about accepting the gifts of Her Who has answered my prayer? No!"

But before they parted she called Marpe to her. "Sister, we two have always ridden side by side. I cannot take you with me tonight —you, like me, have only sixteen winters, and I will keep as closely to the Law as I can. But there is none I trust as much as you, and I will leave you in command of the camp while I am gone."

The other girl smiled wistfully. "You are kind, Antiope. You would not leave me feeling that you are angry with me. But my heart will be cold with dread until the morning comes, and you ride back to us. Forgive me, but that is so."

Antiope said, "Wish me a daughter," kissed her, and left her. But as she went, suddenly cold fear took her, made her shiver as if she stood naked in a wet, icy wind. *We are breaking the Law!* Into what was she leading them, these girls who trusted her? Had not Molpadia said that the first, least breaking of it would set all crumbling? Be the beginning of the end? But Molpadia herself had willed the first breaking; had bidden her, Antiope, open her legs for that fat old Kaska. *And has not the Goddess answered my prayer?* To doubt now was impious weakness. She was doing right; even though she was also doing what she wanted to do. . . .

The west blazed fire-red when the twenty Amazons rode down to the shore. The twenty Greeks met them, freshly bathed and grinning, grand in gay cloaks and tunics that were also fresh, having spent the whole voyage in their sea-chests. The Amazons too had bathed, after hunting and killing the deer they carried with them. They had done nothing else; in their busy lives comfort and durability had always been all that could be asked of clothes. Now, looking at the young men, they suddenly wished that they were dressed differently. Even Antiope, who had prided herself on developing luxurious tastes at the Hittite court, was suddenly glad that at least she had her father's iron dagger. Subbiluliuma had had it made as a gift for Pharaoh, but she had admired it, and at their parting he had given it to her. Iron daggers were great treasures, most weapons still being made of bronze. It did not occur to her that they were not the kind of ornaments usually worn by women to impress men.

She was disappointed because Pyrrhos was still wearing his helmet, but soon forgot it when he stepped up beside her. To-gether men and girls built a fire, and hung up the deer to roast. All that time he was with her, keeping close to her. He said little, but the nearness of him warmed her more than the fire. He was a

splendid man, taller even than she, though most of his men were
of a height with her girls. Two or three were a little shorter.

My daughter will be Goddesslike, she thought, and smiled up at him,
happily and proudly. He did not smile back, but he reached out
and caught her arm, and that touch was like no other touch she
had ever felt. It seemed to burn her flesh like fire, yet did not hurt.
And though he still did not smile, he laughed and drew her away
from the others, toward the goods that lay, still unlooked-at, on
the sands. "Take your pick, Lady. To lie with a queen should be
worth a great treasure, whether she is virgin or not."

Antiope stiffened. He did not know the Law of the Amazons;
how could he? Yet he seemed to be mocking her. She did not like
either his voice or the cold, hard look in his eyes.

She said with dignity: "All of us here ashore are virgins. The
mothers and grandmothers lie with those they burn before the
Black Stone."

He did smile then, broadly. "Lady, I have heard all the pompous
tales about you sworn virgins who wait here ashore, while your
elders have their sport on the Holy Isle. But we young folk are all
alike; while the old folks' backs are turned, we will have our fun."

For a breath's space Antiope stared at him, stunned. Then her
eyes flashed. "Amazons do not deceive Amazons! We know nothing of the cheap foul ways of you who are all born of slaves—you
whose mothers, whether they were called whores or not, have all
been slaves to your fathers!"

For half a breath's space he looked startled; then his smile became a grin. "Then why are you not on the Isle too, Lady? Piously
opening your legs for the captives there?"

"I am supposed to go there! To lie with a Kaska chief, who is
old and fat and wicked—who also smells!" She checked herself.
"I can see why you thought what you did—we cannot be expecting to go back to camp virgins, my girls and I. But I am the last
of my race—I must have a daughter as soon as I can. The Goddess
has spoken to the War-Queen, my mother's sister, and told her
so."

"Well, that is a good excuse." He was still grinning, though his
grin seemed to have stiffened a little.

"You still think I lie?" Her eyes blazed. "That I would break the

Law of my people for my own pleasure, and lie and sneak like one of your own cowed, filthy, man-ruled sluts? And I prayed to the Goddess to send me another father for my daughter—I felt as if I could not stand that fat, smelly old Kaska! Well, She did the best She could, I suppose, having so little time. But you are no bargain, either!"

She stopped, her eyes still black flames. She was only demeaning herself uselessly. He could never understand; he was only a man, although she had thought him so fine.

But Theseus threw back his head and laughed. Laughed as if a weight a thousand times heavier than the stone that once had covered the sword and sandals of Aegeus had just been rolled off his own heart.

"Lady, purest of maids, I will show you that I am a good bargain! Better than any fat, smelly old man!"

His arms shot out and caught her. Antiope just managed to make a signal with one hand, so stopping her girls as they would have sprung upon him. Then she was crushed against him, she felt the push of his hard maleness—so different from Asterion's—even as he felt the round firmness of her thighs and breasts. His mouth found her mouth, and that kiss was like sunrise. To both of them it opened a new world, one in which all light was fire and all colors pulsed with marvelous, unknown beauty. She did not know when she began to kiss him back, or when his arms loosened enough to let hers rise and go around his neck. Her Amazons stared dumbfounded, their hands slowly falling from their half-drawn knives. His young men, who had noticed where the girls' hands were, grinned with relief.

All but Solois. His face was strained and sick.

Then Theseus' arms loosened; he felt ashamed. Others should not have seen this; a man did not make love to his wife before other men. But for a little while the world had been only Theseus and Antiope; he had forgotten that these watchers lived. Recovering himself, he barked orders to two young men, who went swiftly back to the ship. The deer went on roasting, and the fire went on burning, but now its flames seemed to have all the colors of the rainbow, to laugh like the young people around it. All was gaiety; these forty who could not talk to each other had no more need of words than those other couples had had, on that night long ago, when strong Herakles had sat beside dark Melanippe. And Theseus and Antiope, who could have talked together, were the two who needed words least of all. . . .

The two young men who had been sent to the ship came back with meal and honey and sesamun, such as were used in the cakes at Athenian wedding feasts. Theseus tried to show his men how to mix dough, but had not much idea how to do it himself. Antiope and her girls took the job over. The young men sat down and beamed happily; this was the way things should be done. Cooking was women's business. The girls thought, *Every man has ten thumbs. It is a wonder that any man can ever learn to handle weapons properly.* Yet they felt an immense kindness for these clumsy, conceited creatures who were too stupid to know their own weakness. Who needed them. . . .

Night was coming now; softly, almost stealthily, Her black wings rising from the east. The far west still glowed faintly rose and gold, and when Antiope came back to Theseus and sat down beside him, the sweetly colored light seemed to cover and fill them. They held each other's hands, and between them, for that time at least, flowed a peace as happy and life-giving as the flowing of the sap through the trees. Spring was all around them, and spring was in them.

The honey cakes were ready before the deer was. The young men, knowing their ritual significance, hurried to bring them to Theseus, who gave the biggest and most golden to Antiope.

She said, "Thank you," and then, with her mouth full, "This is good." To her, cake was only cake; she had no idea that she was being married.

"Better than you know, my queen." His eyes laughed into hers, tender, mischievous, more golden than either the cake or the sunset. She was *his* queen now, Queen of Athens. . . . He took the cake from her and took a bite himself; that too was ritual. For a breath's space Antiope stared, not quite pleased, then smiled again. This was lovers' play. But she took the cake back from him and took another bite herself; they might as well keep on with the game. This time Theseus was disconcerted. What kind of omen was this? Would a man be master in his own house, if his wife got the lion's share of the wedding cake? He took the cake back again, and the same thing happened all over again; Antiope got the last bite.

By then the meat was ready, and it too was merrily eaten, amid considerable wine-drinking. Theseus had hoped to make the Amazons drunk, and so be able to carry off Antiope without much of a fight. But her girls got no merrier than his young men did. As a matter of fact, the Amazons had good heads for liquor. Molpadia had thought strong mead made from mares' milk good training for girls; someday designing men might try to make them drunk.

The moon was high when the feasters rose and went off hand in hand, or with their arms around each other—to make their beds on the white sand.

The night wore; the moon moved westward. In the black shadow of the rocks Solois crouched, sleepless. Long since the girl he was to have lain with had eased her insulted disappointment by strolling off and lying down with another couple, the male half of which was feeling especially virile. The other Amazon was sharing him with sisterly generosity.

But Solois' eyes strained through the silvery dusk toward the dark place where two other lovers lay. His eyes were riveted to its impenetrable blackness, his ears too were strained—for sounds that, whenever they came, tore him like knives. He kept imagining those two bodies entwined, pressed close, Theseus' glorious manhood entrapped in her soft, womanly flesh. Theseus—Antiope! Antiope—Theseus. Sometimes he hardly knew which of them he loved, and which he hated. What was it, this Mystery—greater, surely, than any of those held at holy Eleusis—which could make a man turn from his friends, from all he knew and loved, to lie locked in the arms of a stranger? An enemy. . . .

What was it?

CHAPTER 5.

THE RAPE OF A QUEEN

AWN CAME, Homer's Eos, tender and rosy-fingered. Antiope woke and saw Theseus beside her. Saw his red-gold hair, no longer moon-blanched, and for a breath's space, shock stiffened her; the horrors of that woeful night years ago came rushing back. Then she heard his steady, soft breathing, and remembered last night. Smiling, she turned her head and gently kissed his cheek. Many men of the West must have hair of that color; there were some in the East . . . and it was beautiful. She ran her fingers through it, and he stirred. The gold-brown eyes opened, saw her and glowed.

"Antiope—"

"Pyrrhos!" They came together again, holding each other joyously, eagerly; last night's joy was repeated. But only for a little while; soon Antiope pulled away. "The sun is rising. I must go."

"Why?" He pulled her down to him again. The warm coaxing sweetness in both voice and smile almost undid her; her mouth curved to meet his mouth. But then her jaw set; gently but firmly she pulled away again. "Beloved, I must wake the others. We must go. Before those back in camp begin to fear treachery." Before Marpe did, she meant; the rest would have trusted unquestioningly in the Goddess' sending.

"But you will come back before sunset? Not make me wait for you as long as I did yesterday?" His voice still coaxed her, and longing tore her—bitter, stabbing longing. Yesterday getting to him had been all that mattered; she had never thought how parting would feel. Why should she have? A woman coupled with a man, then both went their ways, satisfied. That was the best way for Amazons, and a way that usually suited men.

155

"Beloved, I cannot come again." She fought back the awful pain of that knowledge, looked gravely and steadily into his eyes. "Last night we made our daughter. Tonight must be my girls' turn. Many of them are not going to get lovers before your ship sails, as it is."

For one shocked breath's space there was silence, there in the reddening dawn. Then he said roughly: "What do you think I am? A jug of wine for you to pass around? I am a free man—no bought slave. No captive, to perform before your Black Stone!"

He did care—as she did! Her heart leaped, but her voice was quiet. "Beloved, it is not that I do not want to come. For me no night will ever equal last night. When my hair is white, and my bones ache with both old age and old wounds, I will remember it and feel young again. But my girls have been faithful, risking the War-Queen's wrath to help me to my desire. I cannot cheat them."

"What do I care for your girls? If I cannot have you again, no other Amazon will get any seed out of me! Or out of any of my men. We will sail today!"

Fear sickened her; he must not go! But her voice was still quiet: "I did not mean to treat you as if you were not free; everybody should be free. But you should understand, you who are a leader yourself. Stay, and make my girls happy, and then sail to Themiskyra this summer. We can lie together again then. Be happy."

She had made it, the proposal she knew she should not make. If only he could come to Themiskyra every summer, be her only man, as her father had been her mother's! But she knew how Molpadia had both feared and hated her parents' long love. The Deathsinger had not dared to harm the Great King, but what would she do to an ordinary trader, if she thought her niece loved him? Yet surely it would be safe for Pyrrhos to come once . . . just once. . . .

He laughed. His tawny eyes were smiling down into hers again. "Lady, I accept that invitation gladly. But I want you tonight. Not some other night, in some other place. Let us make a bargain. I will let my men laugh at me—say I am tired, worn out by last night's joys, and make myself one of the five men who stay aboard the ship tonight. Five only, for I will do what no good captain should do—leave my ship ill guarded—if you will promise to swim out to it tonight. To lie with me while twenty-five—not twenty—of my men lie with as many of your girls."

Antiope stared; to go aboard his ship would be to defy everything she had ever been taught: all she knew of wisdom and caution. And yet—this was the man the Goddess had sent her. He loved and wanted her as she loved and wanted him; he could not betray her. And he was offering her a good bargain—five more men for her girls—

She laughed too. She threw her arms around his neck and kissed him. "It is not really fair. None of your men can be half as good as you are. But since my girls have never had you, they will not know the difference. I will come!"

The day passed, golden with sunlight, the loveliest of spring days. Summer seemed much nearer; had their loving last night given it strength, as some of those people among whom men and women lived together claimed that lovemaking in the fields made the crops grow? Yet never before had a day ever seemed so long to Antiope; and when evening came at last, it seemed ten times longer. She must not go to her tent too early; she must not do anything that would seem different from what she usually did. Never before had she been a deceiver; to act like one galled her. Yet she dared not let her people know what she meant to do. They would all be terrified; Marpe might even swim out to the Holy Isle to warn Molpadia.

It seemed to her that she would never get to her tent, and when she finally did get there she still had to wait. To be sure that the whole camp had settled down, that all the fires were out, and that black Night would indeed cover her going.

But at last she did go. Quietly, stealthily, hiding from the moon and slinking through the thickest, blackest shadows. To avoid the sentries she had to climb over the stockade, her heart in her mouth lest they hear her. The climb was easier than she had expected; something would have to be done about that before next year.

You sent this man, Goddess. You surely will keep us safe until the mothers and grandmothers get back.

She had to avoid the shore itself as much as she could, for there fires burned and girls and men made merry, as last night she had.

. . . If only Pyrrhos had beached his ship, as the traders who came to Themiskyra did! Still, one could not blame men for feeling uneasy near the Isle of the Black Stone. But its black shadow, stretching across the sands, would have given her shelter as she crept toward it. . . .

It was very near the shore. It looked tall and black above the dark waters, blacker than Night's self. It had a look of quietly waiting menace, of grim power, that she had never noticed by day.

I am being foolish. This is what sneaking does to women. The kind of women he has always known before me. . . .

She wore a fine, supple leather tunic belted with bronze that shone like gold. Amazon armor, for Amazons never fought on foot unless ambushed, and horses could not go fast if heavily loaded. Foolish, weighty metal corselets that made one clumsy were for men.

She ran across the moon-silvered sands and plunged into the sea. The leather tunic, well padded to protect her vitals, had hardly begun to feel wet when she reached the ship's side. When her hands closed on the rope that, expectedly, hung there.

"Pyrrhos," she called softly. "Pyrrhos."

Blacker even than the ship, a tall cloaked form loomed above her. The tawny eyes, flame-eager, burned red through the darkness that masked the face. But his voice came out of the darkness, warm and known and dear: "Antiope!"

She had no chance to climb. He hauled her overside, seized and lifted her, heedless again of the one grinning stare that was all four of the men with him. In the torchlight she saw his face again, that beautiful, reckless face, and his eyes glowed as red-gold as his hair. Triumphant as those of the hunter who at last holds his prey.

"My golden bird!" he said. "Oh, my golden bird!" And he kissed her mouth so hard he bruised it.

"You look like a hungry cat," said Antiope, a little wonderingly. "Sometimes cats' eyes are red at night." She was not afraid; she trusted him, and her trust, once given, was complete. Yet there was something here that she did not understand, and it made her laugh a little uneasy. "You had better not try to eat me, my lover. I would not like that."

He laughed too, and kissed her again, hard and exultantly. "I can think of much better things than that to do with you, my queen!"

And he did them, waiting only to carry her into the dark half-tent, half-cabin, that all day he and his men had worked to put up in place of the little platform aft. The few ships he knew had neither decks nor cabins; such luxuries were only for the ships of Minos. But the bed that almost filled this new-made bridal chamber was covered with a coverlet of priceless Tyrian scarlet; until today it had been in his sea-chest, waiting for this night. He laid her down on it, then flung himself upon her. Yet he did not take her roughly, but with blissful tenderness. Their loving was even sweeter than it had been the night before, when their bodies had been strangers to each other.

When at last they lay still, deeply content, she reached out a hand to stroke his cheek, then his hair. "I wish it were not quite so dark in here. I would like to see your hair."

"Do you like red hair?" He had been wondering what she had thought of it; she had certainly seen it that morning.

"I used to hate it."

"Did you always hate it?" He could not help asking that.

"No. I did not, but then something happened—an ugly thing; we will not spoil tonight with talk of it. But I love red hair now. I hope my daughter will have it. Carry the sun on her head, as you do."

You shall have a son, thought Theseus. He chuckled softly, rubbed his face against hers, then sat up sharply. "I forgot. There is hot wine outside, by the brazier."

Antiope drank the steaming cup he brought her. The wine had a queer taste, but his care for her, though needless, touched her, and she praised it—then wished she had not, for he refilled the cup. That second draft made her sleepy, and she did not want to go to sleep yet. She wanted to see and touch and feel all of him she could, as long as she could. For she could not let him come to Themiskyra; she knew now that she never could hide her love from Molpadia. But one did have to have some time for sleep . . . even lovers had to sleep. . . .

"HIP-POL-Y-TE-E! HIP-PO-OL-Y-TE!" Spear-sharp, those cries pierced the warm, heavy darkness that held her. Out of habit her hands groped for the weapons that were not there. Even her dagger was gone. She reeled to her feet—only to feel the earth roll

beneath her. No, not the earth: she was still aboard Pyrrhos' ship
—*and it was moving!* She heard a wild swishing that must be the oars.
But high above it rang the war-cries of her people—and the shouting of men!

Somehow the Amazons had found out where she was. They
thought her a captive aboard the ship, and were attacking it. But
why had not Pyrrhos awakened her? Had he been killed? Sick
with fear, she tore away the hanging blanket that kept her from
seeing what was happening. Saw the red morning above her, and
men all around her. Each with one hand on what must be a long,
heavy wooden oar, and in the other a long sharp spear. Had some
of her girls already been killed? Her frantic eyes searched for
Pyrrhos and found him—standing in the prow, spear in hand. And
on that spear was blood. . . .

She knew then. Yet for a breath's space she could not believe
what she knew—that he with whom she had shared so much, felt
so much, had betrayed her. But he had; Molpadia had been right!
Almost she sprang upon him then. Instead she leaped for the mast.
If she could climb high enough to leap clear of the rowers—

Some sight that was not that of his bodily eyes warned Theseus.
Even as she sprang, he sprang. He caught her, and they rolled in
the hull of the ship together, his arms tight around her, pinning
her arms fast. She tried to knee his groin, but could not; her legs
too were pinned.

She spat in his face. "Slaver! Slaver! You drugged that wine—
you stole my knife while I slept!"

He talked to her then: reasonably, reassuringly, even tenderly.
"Do not be afraid, *philtate*—best-beloved. You will not be a slave,
you will still be a queen, for in my own country I am a king, the
son of a king. You will be my honored wife, we will share one bed
together always—and you know how happy we two can be in one
bed—"

She did not answer. She only squirmed and twisted, savagely,
ceaselessly trying to break his hold—and could not break it. Sweat
soon stood on both their bodies; their muscles bulged and cracked.
Theseus wished bitterly that he had bound her while she slept. He
had thought of it, but she had looked so beautiful, lying there. To
bind those lithe, lovely limbs had seemed like sacrilege.

He still tried to reason with her. "I did not want this fight, Lady. I knew you would hate for your people to be killed, even as I hate for mine to be. So I took you by cunning—I meant to sail away at dawn, as soon as my men came aboard. But before they could get away your Amazons rode down upon them, shrieking—"

Marpe. Marpe's fears drew her to my tent—she must even have listened for my breathing. Antiope thought that, but did not say it. Words were useless now. She might as well have tried to talk with a wolf that was at her throat. She went on struggling, and Theseus went on talking.

"You will be my lawful wife, my queen—by Poseidon Earth-shaker, the God I love most, I swear it! The wife of Theseus, son of Aegeus—"

"Theseus!" Her cry made the name a curse. "Theseus—*you!* You helped to murder my sister!"

His start made his hold loosen a little. With the strength born of frenzy she tore herself free and leaped for the mast again. But Theseus' spring, quick as hers, headed her off. She turned and struck at one of the rowers—a skilled deadly blow. Over his body she could leap into the sea, if his comrades' spears did not catch her. But Theseus' fist struck her jaw before she could strike the rower, and as she fell black Night rose up to meet her.

When Antiope woke again she lay bound in the bottom of the boat. Six more Amazons lay bound beside her. Near them lay two wounded men, groaning.

In their own tongue the other girls told her what had happened. "Last night a dream came to Marpe, Queen—it told her that the strangers, like all men, plotted treachery. So she watched outside your tent, but the silence within was too silent—and when she looked in toward dawn, you were not there. So she roused us all and sent a messenger to the Holy Isle. The rest of us sped down to the shore, hoping to capture the men there and hold them as hostages. But they were already up and armed—though we killed a few, most escaped and swam out to their ship, and we swam after them—"

"And so were taken," Antiope said bitterly. "But Marpe—do you know what happened to her?"

"She was wounded while still on shore, Lady. A man threw a stone at her and it struck her on the head and she fell from her horse. But it is likely that she lives—these accursed dogs struck us on the heads with their oars and dragged us from our horses, and *we* live!"

"If she does, she will not be a slave. She is one friend I have not brought to ruin." The bitterness in Antiope's voice was savage now.

But they were quick to comfort her. "Not you, Queen—never you. They did it all, these vile slavers—these magicians who somehow managed to steal you away in the night. May the Eagle-headed Women pluck out their eyes, and rip the flesh from their bones—"

"And from mine also. For I betrayed you. Like a fool, I walked into the trap this man set."

She told them all, but still they would not blame her, only cursed Theseus, and that made her blame herself the more. In her heart, that felt as if it were all one great wound, she prayed: *Let me die, Goddess. But save them somehow—somehow. Let them live and get home!* But then the black question came: *You—You Who have let both Molpadia and me put words into Your mouth—are You anywhere to be prayed to?"*

It did not seem likely. She lay there and looked up into the blue sky at whose vastness she had always marveled, and saw the birds flying through that blueness—free. *Free!* Would she or any of these six girls who had tried to help her ever again be free? Since death must be nothingness it could not be freedom, though it would be escape. Well, they would escape; Amazons could not be tamed, and they died well. *But how much will we have to bear first, O You Who are not—how much?*

And then suddenly, blessedly, hope came to her. These men who lived in ships could have no idea of the speed of horses—they would be careful one night, perhaps two, but then they would land to enjoy their captives. And then Molpadia would ride down upon them; they would die, and though probably some of their captives would die with them, that would be deliverance from slavery.

Again she looked up at the sky, thankfully now. *Forgive me, who have sinned again, denying You.* And then saw what killed the hope blossoming within her. Now in the spring the birds were flying north—up out of Egypt, and the hot desert lands of the South, toward the great cool steppes beyond the sea—that land where the Amazons had lived before their men, like all men, betrayed them. *And this ship was moving north!* Theseus meant to put the whole width of the sea between his captives and all help. Horses could never swim that far. . . .

In her hatred of him she found her courage again; she ground her teeth. She and her Amazons could gnaw each other's bonds— be free again to kill and be killed. She thought of doing it that night, then decided, for her girls' sake, to wait until they reached shore. Maybe one or two of them could finally get home—at worst they would not long outlive the joy of hope.

Theseus' men had not liked the change of course either. "Nights at sea are always uncomfortable. And now of all times, when we have women to sleep with—"

"There are not enough of them to go around," Theseus had said dryly.

"We can take turns!"

"And wake up in the middle of the night with their whole pack of she-wolves swarming over us?" Theseus' mind had moved along much the same lines as Antiope's. "You have seen these women ride. And though they would be in a great hurry to catch us, they might not be in any great hurry to kill us."

Some of them shuddered then, and all saw that his plan was good. Theseus himself hoped it was: he had no idea how wide this sea was. But the ship was well provisioned, and in need surely his Father Poseidon would send them rain. . . .

But the Amazons lay in grim silence, and the sun was black before their eyes. Friends, sisters, mothers—all who had tended and taught them when they were little—all who had played with them and learned with them—these were gone forever. All they had ever known was gone.

Themiskyra—*home!*

Afternoon came, and the wind rose. Soon the girls, unused to sailing, lay retching in their own vomit. With all their hearts they longed for the terrible sea that was carrying them away from home to rise up and swallow them. The men thought sourly that Amazons were not so tough after all. Theseus himself tended Antiope, but she would neither speak to him nor look at him.

Night came; all was black without as well as within. But the wind fell and the waves grew still; the girls felt a little better. One whispered: "Let us roll over onto the wounded men. Maybe we can hurt them—even smother them to death—before their comrades wake." But Antiope said firmly, "No. The men might kill some of us in revenge."

"Would not that be a good thing?"

"Not yet. Our foremothers came from the other side of this sea, long ago. The trip back will be long and hard, but we can make it—if we kill enough of these men first. Not two miserable wounded ones."

She herself no longer mattered, but for her girls there was— there still must be—hope.

Dawn came, glorious and majestic. The east flamed with rose and gold. The captives lifted up weak voices and called on Her who again seemed real:

> *"Sun-Goddess in Heaven, Shepherdess of all Folk:*
> *You see all that happens, all that is.*
> *You see all things, deal out justice to all:*
> *To women in their fields and houses,*
> *To the beasts in field and forest.*
> *There is nothing Your eyes do not see,*
> *Nothing Your arm cannot reach,*
> *O Lady, Queen of Heaven."*

For a brief space all of them but Antiope felt hopeful and comforted. But soon the glory faded, and the dark sea still stretched on all sides of them, bleak and endless. From the high, far-off sky the golden sun looked down, indifferent, unhelping. Soon the wind rose, and the retching began again.

One girl moaned in anguish that made her forget her queen's: "She is angry—the Goddess. Because we have broken the Law— lain with men. We have sinned, and must die."

For a breath's space Antiope's retching sounded like a sob; Theseus heard it, and it hurt him. She would come around; women who had been carried off always did. But this was hard for her. Amazons were unlike other women, yet in one way maybe their fierce beings were softer. They did not grow up expecting to leave the homes of their childhood, to follow husbands and live among strangers. So now they were like little girls who had lost their mothers.

Yet he was doing what was best for Antiope. He had saved her honor; he would make her happy again as soon as she would let him. Nothing could have been clearer than his conscience. He turned away. . . .

Days passed, and nights, in a sick jumble. The Amazons hoped the wounded men would die, and one did, but the other grew better. Between bouts of retching the girls, too weak to run away now if they had had the chance, watched the birds above them, free in the free sky. Antiope, hopeless now too, gave what she thought would be her last order. "Starving is a slow death, but sure. We must not eat again."

That made no real difference; they had not been keeping anything down. But it worried Theseus, and whatever he said, Antiope answered only: "No Amazon may live in slavery. We will die as we have lived, choosing our own road."

His tawny eyes finally flashed. The hardness of the City-Sackers rose in him, warring with the teaching of wise Pittheus. "Lady, I have been patient with you; far more patient than most men would have been. With you yourself I will still be patient—for a while. But when you hear your girls scream with pain maybe you will change your mind and eat."

Antiope's face went whiter than her seasickness had ever made it. But she said only, "What we must bear we will bear."

Again Theseus turned away.

But he was afraid now. By this road she might escape him. He had been a fool, he knew. He had always understood his golden bird well enough to know that if her wings were broken she would die; that was one of her charms for him. He decided to try bargaining with her.

"We must be near land now." He devoutly hoped they were; there was little drinking water left. "Swear to me, Lady, by your Goddess and by the Thousand Gods of the Hittites, that for seven days and seven nights you will eat as you should and not try to run away—and for that long we will camp ashore. In a comfortable, pleasant place."

"And all that time you men would lie with us whenever you

pleased—and keep us bound between times!" Her sick eyes flashed.

He took a deep breath, and made the gamble he knew he must make. "Lady, swear the oath that I have asked, and I swear by my God—by Poseidon Earthshaker, who begot me through King Aegeus' lions—that for all that time you and your girls will be left unbound."

Antiope thought: *It is a chance.* Hope woke within her, and she said: "Then by my Goddess, by Her Who is in both Earth and Heaven—and the Thousand Gods of the Hittites too, though nobody can ever keep track of Them—I swear that for seven days and seven nights we Amazons will eat well and will not try to run away. If we are left unbound."

In her heart she laughed. The fool had not made her swear that no Amazon would harm her captors. And who need run away from the dead?

Next day they sighted land at last. Dark, wooded shores and small, wooded isles, all at the mouth of a great muddy river. Theseus' eyes shone. "This must be the great river down which traders bring amber from the far North," he told Antiope. "I am glad of this chance to see it."

Amber. The color of his own eyes. Suddenly she wondered how those eyes would look glazed in death. Well, they soon would be. . . .

That night the Amazons slept alone, with campfires between them and the young men, who were not pleased. But Theseus said: "Give them one night to get their strength back. They will be more fun then. Also they are my queen's handmaids, some of them perhaps her kin; they must be kindly used."

Tomorrow night there would be no need for rape. The Amazons doubtless meant treachery, but they would think friendliness the best way to get the men off guard. *But when Antiope has her strength back, I can make her love me again!*

In the morning the girls woke in comfort, with solid ground beneath them again at last. They were hungry, and breakfast tasted good. They ate, they stretched, they walked and ran, joying in their bodies, that were light and lithe and strong again. They had not yet seen the men, whose axes they could hear in the forest, but felt no fear of them. Enemies could be fought. To long for death had been foolishness, the weakness of the sick.

Antiope walked alone. She needed to think, to plan. But the morning was green and gold, the many scents of spring were sweet. She crushed down her longing to enjoy them, began to look for Theseus. Better to know where he was, her enemy; he must never take her by surprise again. She knew what she was likely to hasten by finding him, but that was bound to happen soon anyway. Also, since there was no Goddess, she might not yet have conceived. She must make sure of her daughter, of getting something out of all this pain. . . .

He and his men were felling trees. His brown body, naked to the waist, was beautiful. Memories stabbed her. If only he had been honorable! Had not wanted to marry her. . . .

He saw her and grinned. "Joy be with you, wife! Tonight we shall have a proper bridal chamber at last."

A hut to themselves—how easy! She could strike him in his sleep, with a stone. Maybe only stun him, let him wake up bound —as she had. Enjoy him even, her captive, while her girls stood watch over his disarmed men. As now he was planning to enjoy her. . . . Dreams. All the men must be killed as soon as possible, except two—neither of whom would be him. Two men, carefully crippled so as to be neither too dangerous nor too sick to sail the ship back across the sea. For only on the ship could she hope to get all her girls home alive. . . .

The tree Theseus was chopping fell. He mopped his forehead and grunted; the sun was hot. He looked at her again, and golden fires danced and glowed in his eyes.

"It may be cool where the trees are thicker. Come!"

She stiffened, angry because he dared command her. Well, he could—for now. When his hand shot out and caught her arm, her flesh was still stiff. She dreaded the brutal mockery of love, but to her, as to a man, honor lay in what she did, not in what was done to her. No use to resist now; better, maybe, to pretend. . . .

She went with him, yet looked back once over her shoulder, feeling watched. The handsome boy who had been working beside Theseus was the watcher; he stared even harder at her than at his lord. With a resentful, yet fascinated curiosity.

Then the trees closed around Theseus and her, and both utterly forgot Solois, whose name she did not yet know.

CHAPTER 6.

___A BEGINNING—AND AN END

E VENING FOUND them still lying in each other's arms. Upon the mosses, drowsy with a rich content. At times, as the day wore, they had slept, then waked only to love again.

"It has been good," Theseus said at last. "It has been good."

"It has been as it ought to be," said Antiope. And knew, in a sudden sweet flooding of her whole being, that this was true. Their love was right: too right for their parting not to be wrong.

He laughed and squeezed her against him, his lips nuzzling her throat. The light waned; they still lay there, warm and close. Until at last they heard voices calling them. Men shouted, "The-SEUS! The-SEUS!" Women cried: "Anti-O-PE! An-TI-O-PE!"

"It must be time to eat," said Theseus. "We must go." But instead he pressed his cheek against hers and kissed her again.

"We will," said Antiope, kissing him back. Still neither moved.

Through the clear evening stillness the calling came again, louder: "THE-SEUS! AN-TI-O-PE!"

"Soon they will be thinking you have stabbed me in my sleep and run off." Theseus' eyes twinkled wickedly.

"My girls know I never would desert them!" But Theseus' men might not; that thought cut through the drowsiness of delight. Cat-quick, Antiope leaped to her feet.

They went back to camp together, Theseus happy and triumphant. She had come around. . . .

In the morning, Theseus' men wanted to go hunting; the girls looked eager at first, then downcast. Antiope looked at Theseus, and he brought out the chest in which the captured weapons had been locked. He gave back everything, including Antiope's own iron dagger.

168

Night and morning, morning and night, and between them always the golden day. Antiope's Amazons began to think it a pity that they would have to kill these men in the end. After all, once the capture was safely made, they had not behaved too badly. They were not cruel slavers, such as the old tales told of. They had only wanted women to make love to, and lovemaking was no hardship. Spending seven days and nights with them—of course, it could be no longer—would not be too bad. Some girls made up their minds to kill certain men as quickly and mercifully as they could when the time came. But they who felt such qualms would have been ashamed to admit to each other, let alone Antiope.

Two or three times she and Theseus went back to that green, quiet place which had been their true marriage bed. The last time he said: "I will build a shrine to Bridal Aphrodite in this place." His eyes held true thankfulness, even reverence. "She has been kind to me here."

"I thought I had been. Who is Aphrodite?"

"In Athens we fear and revere Her as the Eldest of the Fates, Whose fires can make men mad. But in Cyprus, the great island of the East, folk joy in Her gifts and call Her the Rose-Crowned Lady of Love. And they are right; She made you kind." He stretched his big brown body luxuriously and grinned at her; had he been a cat he would have been purring. "Your Goddess is the One we call Artemis. The Bow-bearer, the cold Huntress Who hates love. Once as a boy I was Her priest, but no more. And I will soon teach you to forget Her; you are learning well."

Antiope laughed. "She does not hate love, foolish one! Only marriage, that enslaves women."

"We are married." His eyes twinkled.

"I keep forgetting that. But it does not matter. If I am your slave, you are mine. It is worth it." She kissed him, and he kissed her back, then frowned thoughtfully. "Artemis does help women in childbirth. Which is hard to understand, since she is love's foe."

"She is not. She is Aphrodite too. All Goddesses are one—one Form with many names!" She laughed again.

He said slowly: "I have heard my grandfather, wise Pittheus, say something like that. Yet Artemis and Aphrodite hate each other."

"They only seem to, because we mortals put our own silly words into Their mouths. The Lady is One—One only—but here in the great cities of the East you men call Her Ishtar and Astarte and make a whore of Her. And your Greeks seem to be as foolish. Only in the forest can She still show herself as She truly is—as we Amazons know Her. Clean and free, and the Mother of all things."

"She kills," Theseus said grimly. "Her arrows bring death everywhere. Should a mother kill her children?"

Antiope laughed again and hugged him. "Beloved, the Mother of all knows that all must die. It would be too bad if we did not —we who grow old! Her arrows give us new life and youth—they shoot the mystic fire of life, which is also spirit, into the mother's womb and make the young swell there. It is a great pity that your people have forgotten that—think Her arrows deal only death."

"But the young die too—"

"Only because of our human foolishness that brings want and war and death. She is life!"

"But only Aphrodite sends love. Love like this!"

He was upon her, his mouth silencing hers, all of him eagerly seeking all of her. But before delight drowned all else Antiope thought, *She does. You men keep your Aphrodite too busy in bed to be much of a mother. She has to leave that to the Artemis side of her.* But he could not understand such things—any more than he could understand what pain he had caused her and her Amazons. Big and dear and wonderful as Theseus was, in many ways he was still a child—and not an overly bright one, at that. Bed and the battlefield were the only things he really understood yet—but he could make bed a wonderful place to be! Her arms tightened around him.

On the seventh day Antiope called her Amazons together and spoke with them alone. She said, "Girls, I am not going home. But I will make Theseus let you go." Both her voice and her eyes were grave and steady.

The words were not the world-shattering shock they would have been half a moon ago. Already Themiskyra seemed far away in time, as well as in space. Yet ever since their strength came back all the other girls had been sure they would get home again— somehow, someday. They stared long and hard at Antiope. Finally one said: "But what will our people do, Queen? Without you to bear more queens?"

"Any Amazon who has fought and ridden and worked beside her sister Amazons is good enough to bear a queen. As fit as I ever was, or any other of the blood of Lysippe."

They sat awhile, trying to digest that. Then one girl said wistfully, "Lady, are you sure? It will be terrible never to see Themiskyra again."

"Always my eyes will long to see Themiskyra. Always my ears will long to hear the voices of my own people, speaking my own tongue. But I am sure."

Silence; chilling, bewildered silence. At last one girl whispered: "What if, when your time comes to mount the hill, the mothers cast you out, Lady? Drive your ghost away into the darkness, to be homeless forever? Because your delight in this man was greater than your love for your people?"

Antiope drew a deep breath. "I think that anything so strong and sweet as this must come from the Goddess. It could not be, save by Her will." That was true, she thought, if there was a Goddess. And how could she be sure there was not, she who was sure of nothing now, except that she and Theseus belonged together?

She groped for words to make them understand. "I do find delight in Theseus. Such delight as I never dreamed could be. But I could forgo delight: I could bear to lose him. One can bear to lose an arm or a leg. But I could not bear his pain at losing me."

No, they could never understand it—that time beneath the trees when his weakness had come to bind what his strength had won. *He was so glad because I seemed to love him again—because I did not seem angry anymore. Relieved, like a little boy who has been afraid. I knew then that I did love him—that I could not leave him.* Those memories were Theseus' and her own forever. Though he too could not understand, but thought he had conquered her.

Yet her girls—they who were like sisters of her own flesh—if they condemned her she could bear it, but to do so would be very hard. With all her heart she wished that she could still pray.

But in the puzzled eyes of the Amazons there was no condemnation; the Hive-Spirit made them half-feel her feelings, half-understand. One said, puzzled, "We like all his men now, but we do not like any of them that much."

Another said, surprising herself: "Well, it will be a relief not to have to kill the men. We would have done it anytime you told us to, Queen, but—we have stopped wanting to."

All laughed then, and then suddenly, painfully, all thought of the sweet plain of Themiskyra, full of flowers now. Of their own horses whinnying in their own pastures, of their mothers and their sisters. Of all the places and faces they would never see again. But still more they loved Antiope, their comrade and their queen.

All spoke like one woman: "Queen, we will never leave you. Wherever you go, we will go."

And Antiope's face shone, though her eyes were wet. "Girls, I thank you."

They would still be with her, she would have them in that new land that would be a long time becoming home. She knew the Hive-Spirit had helped her, and was glad it had not been able to tell them too much. For she knew now, in the cold, sober part of her mind, what two or three times in Hattusas had been a frightful, stabbing fear—a fear she had savagely thrust away and made herself forget. The Amazons were doomed. There was too much against them; they were too small to last many more lifetimes in a world in which small city-states were constantly being absorbed into big states. She hoped that they could die to the last woman, defending Themiskyra—surely most of them would—but they could not escape black fate. *If I could have saved them, I would have had to go back. But I cannot; no one can.* Bitter, bitter knowledge; it was a good thing she could bear the burden of it alone. . . .

Well, all things that began must end. The death-bringing, life-giving arrows at least were real. She must think of the future—of her life with Theseus. She shivered suddenly, as if feeling a queer cold breeze. Deep within her something not unlike fear stirred; as presently the child would stir in her womb. Everything in the West would be so different, unlike anything she had ever known. What would the women of Theseus' people be like?

On the ship sailed. Westward, toward the Straits of the Cow, but nobody was in any hurry to get there. The sun shone every day now, or almost every day, and the winds were gentle. Every day was good, and every night was too. All aboard were young, and enjoyed their youth together; those of them who lived to grow

old would remember that voyage as a blessed, happy time, one
almost beyond the troubles and problems of the world mortals
know.

There was only one scare. They spent many whole days ashore,
and late one day they found the tracks of a lion, and were eager
to hunt it. But Theseus told Antiope that such sport was too
dangerous for women. That started an argument.

"I have killed lions before! And bears! Do you not remember—"

"I remember, best-beloved. But I do not want to have to worry
about you." Theseus smiled coaxingly, but was firm.

"Then it certainly would be unfair to make me worry about
you!"

Woman's place was to wait for her man and worry. But Antiope
did not know her place, and any attempt to teach it to her would
upset her. Theseus realized that, and shrugged his shoulders; like
his father, Aegeus, he was an easygoing man and liked peace.

"Well, what is one lion? We will sail in the morning; we have
spent too much time here."

But that night he made the most ardent love to Antiope, while
his men did the same by her girls. Drink was pressed upon the
Amazons too, though Theseus always swore that there was no
poppy juice in it that time. But in the gray dawn the men sneaked
off quietly, chuckling over how surprised the girls would be when
they woke up alone. But they had trouble finding the lion's tracks;
it was almost as if something had brushed them away. The sun
was high when suddenly they heard a mighty roaring ahead of
them, and the now familiar cry of "HIP-PO-OL-Y-TE!" Theseus,
rushing up with his heart in his mouth, came up just in time to
see Antiope deal the lion its deathblow.

Then her eyes met his, and her Amazons stopped dancing and
cheering. For a breath's space much hung poised upon the terrible
scales of the white-robed Fates. Until suddenly Theseus threw
back his head and laughed. And Antiope, being a queen trained
in statecraft, did not say, "I told you so," but only, "We took a
short cut."

Theseus too was a statesman. He grinned and said, "Also you
poured out much of last night's wine, and feigned sleep when we
men rose. But be kind to me, best-beloved, and kill no more lions,
good as you are at it. For you are precious to me, who fear for you

as I never would for myself." In his heart he vowed that she would never get a chance at another lion. That would be easily managed, once he had her safe inside the high walls of Athens.

Antiope was silent, marveling at him. He had seen her kill that lion, yet still believed the deed too dangerous for her.

Well, he was only a man; his thinking was not clear and logical like a woman's. No—that was prejudice of her own speaking. All that ailed his thinking was his queer, almost superstitious prejudices. She would get him out of them, bit by bit. Theseus also thought that he would change her ways gradually, and meanwhile they had a very good time together.

The ship did come at last to the Straits of the Cow. It sailed on, through the straits that the Greeks had named for drowned Helle, and then out into the sea they knew, into the warm, wine-dark Aegean. And still all aboard were friends and lovers, though Theseus and Antiope were the only two who always shared one bed.

All were happy but the boy Solois, and he was unhappy enough for several.

Antiope! Antiope, Queen of the Amazons!

He had hoped that she would kill herself or escape. He had hoped that her seasickness would keep her ugly, and that Theseus would tire of her. He had hated her for daring to be angry with Theseus. What right had she—this barbarian woman, this savage —to resent her incredible good luck?

But she was not angry with Theseus anymore. And she was neither sick nor ugly.

Solois had always believed that no woman's body could compare with a man's in beauty. Its weakness was bound to make it soft and sickening; the much-bragged-of curves were only a kind of crookedness, put to shame by the straight clean lines of a man's body. He began looking at Antiope's body in order to find fault with it, to show himself what a poor mean thing she was, how little chance she could have of holding Theseus long. But to his horror, the longer he looked at her the better she got. The very shapes he had always despised because they were so different from a man's became, through that very difference, intriguing. Even curves could not spoil her; in fact, hers had a horrid trick of twisting his eyes around them so that he could not look away....

She was not weak. She was strong. Powerful muscles rippled

smoothly and gracefully under a skin even smoother. To touch it would be like touching a sun-warmed flower. And beneath it would be, not nauseating softness, but her flesh, firm and warm . . . firm as his own, yet how different from his!

One day he woke to find that he was jealous of the wrong person. He no longer dreamed torturingly of Theseus in her arms, but equally torturingly of her in Theseus'. . . . But Theseus was his beloved! No other ever had been, or ever would be. This awful, blasphemous fantasy could not be true.

But it was.

He grew very thin. He grew white beneath his tan, and his eyes could have filled two faces. His brothers and Hermos thought he must be suffering from disappointed love for Theseus.

"He has always wanted anything too much if he wanted it at all," said Euneos. "And he is not used to not getting it. Mother always let him have it because he was the youngest."

"I would like to let him have it too," grumbled worried Thoas. "With the palm of my hand, and in the right place!"

It was Hermos—Hermos, who always had thought Solois as beautiful as Solois wanted to be thought by Theseus—who finally wormed the truth out of the boy.

"I must kill myself," said Solois, weeping. "For I love Theseus, and I cannot live without his wife."

"Without *who?* The Amazon!" Hermos' jaw dropped.

"Yes. Theseus was right to love her. Theseus is always right!"

"Try some of the other Amazons," urged Hermos. "One or two of them are almost as good-looking as Antiope."

"They are not!" said Solois, outraged.

But he did try them, and they were kind to him, though they had long since decided that he was too young to be any good. Nobody was satisfied, and the thought of death grew sweeter. His brothers would grieve for him then, they who nagged him now. Theseus himself would grieve for him, never knowing what a loyal and noble friend he had lost. This way he, Solois, had all the grief; that way he could leave it all to them. He talked more and more about death to Hermos, whom he enjoyed impressing. Hermos grew desperate.

"Let me go to Antiope. Tell her your trouble."

"No. Never will I betray Theseus!"

"Lad, she is not his true wife. Never can she be Queen in Athens —'hear that which only an Athenian woman may hear, see that which only an Athenian woman may see.' If women had any brains, one would think that the Athenian women had tricked their men into making that law—to keep the queenship for themselves."

"But Medea was Aegeus' queen—"

"Never did even she dare enter the God's secret shrine. Be the Holy Bride in the Holy Marriage."

"Theseus will make them let Antiope do it!"

"Perhaps he thinks so, in his strength, but never will the proud Athenians accept her. Nor should they. All Amazons are wantons."

"She is not! She is fine—proud—"

"She is like all the rest. Did she not lie with Theseus willingly, before he carried her off? Would I risk my life—and yours, that is still dearer to me—by telling her of your love, if I thought her chaste?"

Dizziness took Solois. If she would—if she would! At last he whispered, "Go to her. . . ."

But Hermos had to wait and watch for his chance. By night the ship sneaked past Troy, as once the ships of strong Herakles had done. It lay another night at lovely Lesbos, later the home of Sappho, most famed for song of all women. It passed Chios, where Homer may have sung his first songs, unless, indeed, he was born in one of the four other birthplaces given him by the tongues of men. East of Chios, like a big tongue licking at the sea, lies the grim promontory now called Karaburna. Between it and the Lydian mainland the ship sailed, and there was another great river, and behind it a mighty wall of blue mountains, piercing the sunlit sky.

"Up there is Mount Sipylos," Theseus told Antiope, shining-eyed. "There my grandfather's grandfather King Tantalos had his seat until the earth rose and swallowed him up."

"So that is why you wanted to come here."

"Yes. Yonder town was his port, but men say it was first founded by an Amazon. By Queen Smyrna, terrible in war. That should interest you."

"My people never came this far south, but of old many tribes were led by women. Tell me more of Smyrna."

"I know no more." Theseus thought comfortably, *Such times will never come again.*

But the town was small and poor now. He had hoped to find kin of his still ruling there, men who might be friendly, become his allies against Minos. He needed allies badly. But the townsmen shook their heads. They knew the name of Tantalos, but had thought all his kin with him at the bottom of the blue lake.

"For long after the Great Noise and the Great Darkness this land lay desolate. Until our forefathers came and built this town. The Hittites hold Mount Sipylos now, newcomers who serve the Great King, the Sun. Some say that he will open up trade again, bring boats down the river, and ships up from the sea. But we do not know; we let the Hittites alone. All men should be wary of the mighty, who are often quick to wrath."

Men like these would be small forever; they could be of no help to anybody, even themselves. Theseus thought of visiting Mount Sipylos, then grew cautious himself. What if some Hittite captain should recognize Antiope, and think she needed rescuing? But he camped awhile beside that river where his forefathers had been lords of old. Its waters were cool and clear, and around it nested many swans and other birds. One day he and Antiope hunted there alone, killed, and bathed after they had killed. Then Theseus took the birds back to camp, but Antiope chose to stay where she was awhile longer. It was good there, with the sweet clean air in her face, and deep grass tickling her arms when she moved. Also she did not have her usual keen appetite for supper; even to think of it was not good.

Can this be my daughter? she wondered. *I cannot be getting seasick here on land.* And thought, with a sudden, sick pang, of Themiskyra, where this child should have reigned. Of her people and Molpadia. How miserable they must all be now, thinking she suffered blows and rape and slavery! For the last of her line would have to wait long for death, watch long for a chance to escape and get back to her people. *Yet to know the truth—that I want to stay with the man, the stranger—that is what would hurt you worst of all, my sisters and my mothers. And you, Molpadia—how could you bear it?*

She heard a step, and thought gladly, *Theseus is coming back!* But it was not Theseus; it was Hermos. Although disappointed, she smiled up at him frankly and naturally, as a boy would have done. This was her man's man.

"Joy be with you, man of Troizen."

"Joy be with you, Lady. May I speak with you of a grave matter?"

"Of course. How grave is it?" She tensed: did some danger threaten Theseus?

"Lady, it is the gravest of matters. Will you swear, by your Goddess, never to tell any other what I am about to tell you?" He thought smugly, *Woman's curiosity will make her swear now.*

"I will not," said Antiope. "Nobody with any sense buys a horse without seeing it." Her eyes were suddenly as keen as the Great King's own.

Hermos as suddenly wished that he had said nothing at all. He wished that he need say nothing more, but then her woman's curiosity might well make her mention the matter to Theseus, who might think he had been after her himself. Miserably he cleared his throat.

"Lady, young Solois will lose his life if he goes on grieving as he grieves now. But he will lose it anyhow if Theseus ever learns the cause of his grief."

Antiope's eyes softened a little. "I suppose you mean this boy has broken one of your laws, and you want me to ask Theseus to show mercy. If I think Solois deserves it I will ask, but first I must know what he has done." She was still wary; Theseus' men were his business, as her girls were hers.

"Lady," said Hermos, still more miserably, "it is not something he has done. It is something he wants to do."

"Then he had better not do it," said Antiope. She looked somewhat disgusted.

"But he will die if he does not!" Hermos licked his lips, then plunged as a diver plunges. "Lady, he loves you."

Antiope stared; her jaw dropped. Hermos said quickly, "Lady, have pity! You have seen him. You know that he is too young and beautiful to die."

"I am sorry for him," said Antiope. "But nobody has a right to make himself sick and threaten to die because he cannot sleep with another person. It is not fair to the other person."

"Lady, think of his great love, his need—"

"Nobody need let himself sprout that great a need. I do not see why Theseus should blame Solois for liking me—he likes me himself. Yet since you are afraid I will tell him nothing. I will do no more for either you or Solois."

Hermos bore that word back to Solois, who at first could not believe it. By now he had dreamed hope into certainty. He said stubbornly, through quivering lips: "But she was not angry—she said she would not tell. Go back to her, Hermos, beg her to love me. She is only being coy—women like to be coy—"

"She is not being coy," said Hermos grimly. "She was sorry for you, as one man might be for another. But she wants only Theseus."

"Theseus!" cried Solois. "Theseus!"

He saw then to what depths he had fallen. He had betrayed his friend for a woman, and to that woman he was nothing. He wanted to scream at Hermos, his own betrayer. Hermos had led him on, lured him into this unspeakable guilt, and then disappointed all his hopes. Yet Hermos loved him—had only been trying to help him. Even while the beaks and claws of great birds seemed to be tearing at his vitals, the man into whom Solois might have grown could not forget that.

With a strangled cry he turned and ran for the water meadows, where the swans lived. Hermos ran after him, but the boy whirled around again to face him, cried: "Go back! Let me go, or I will scream out the truth before all men! And then Theseus will kill us both!"

Heavy-hearted, Hermos went back to the campfires. Men laughed at him, asking if he had quarreled with his sweetheart, and he growled them into silence. All night he wondered what he should or could have done, and what Solois was doing. . . .

And all night Solois roamed the marshes, his heart heavier than the stone that damned Sisyphos is said to roll up the hills of hell forever. A white-hot stone, a searing, burning agony within him. The man he loved, the woman he loved—neither of them wanted him. Neither ever had, or ever would. They were together, loving each other. . . . His mind drew more pictures. Theseus' hand on her breast, her body pressing against his, her supple, sun-gilded young body, longing to be entered . . . whatever they were doing, they had forgotten him. As he wished that he could forget himself.

The moon was setting; the night was very black and still. And the river was before him, its waters like a darkness out of the fears of childhood, more awful than death. But this would be only death. . . .

He shivered. He said, "I will swim as long as I can," and went down into those waters. They took him, and the stars above shone on faintly, cold and far away.

CHAPTER 7
RED SET, THE DESTROYER

"WHY DID he do it? Why?" Euneos asked that, wet eyes savage above his quivering lips.

"It is my doing," Theseus said. "He loved me, and I was happy and forgot him." His mouth trembled. "Get cloaks to cover him, Hermos, and something to carry him on. It is not decent to let him lie here like this."

Silently Hermos obeyed, and the dead boy's weeping brothers helped him. Only Theseus stayed by Solois, and Solois, who once would have been so glad to have him there, did not know.

That brief time seemed long, for it was bitter. The young heir of Athens was not yet used to the deaths of people he knew well. He had killed enemies and strangers, but until now none he loved had died. And Solois had not even fallen in battle, winning glory! Theseus was aghast before the greatness of the boy's loss—of all the years that would never now be lived, and all the richness of those years. This black waste of youth seemed like an evil omen, too, for the life that was just beginning. For that morning Antiope had lost her breakfast, and though she was not yet sure that she was pregnant, Theseus was. And then into his first joy, when his heart was tender, the father-thought new and warm within him, had burst this black news of death. Fishermen had come to say that they had found a young man's body, caught in their nets. Neither fish nor the darker dwellers of the deep had yet eaten of his flesh. Yet that undamaged flesh was useless, emptied of its treasure. Solois was gone.

Kneeling there, Theseus remembered how bravely the boy had swum beside him through the freezing waves of the Unfriendly Sea, toward that monster that had turned out to be only a huge

181

lump of ice. He thought of that day when he had walked beside the Mere of Artemis, and that crazy old woman had cried out against him: "He is red Set—Set who slew his brother!" And a nameless fear struck through his pain, cold as the sea that had swallowed up Solois. Cold as the boy's own lonely misery must have been while he watched his friend's happiness, feeling himself left out, unimportant, worthless to the man he loved above all others. *I did not think! I did not think! And now I have killed my friend!*

Then the others came back, with a goatskin rug to use as a litter. They bore Solois back to camp, and there Theseus went for comfort to the woman whom he was making a mother, even as once he would have gone to Aithra, his own mother. He held her close, and wept.

"He had the makings of a man in him—and I have let him throw them all away!"

"The deed was his. No other's."

"No—mine! I never should have let him come with me! Not when he loved me, and I was on my way to you!"

Antiope was beginning to know her man. She thought: *Yet you let him come because he wanted to so badly.* She said, "You meant to be kind."

"But I was not kind! Not to him. To myself, maybe, because his pain hurt me—whenever I had time to notice it! Truly I have the red hair of destroying Set!"

"That is foolishness. People with hair of the same color are often quite unlike in other ways."

"Yet we who carry such fire upon our heads are said to have matching fires in our blood. And not for nothing. Wise Pittheus, my grandfather, used to say: 'Curb yourself, child of my daughter. A man must be master of his passions; else they may carry him away as maddened horses do an unskilled charioteer. Bear him whither he would not go.' Can there be a curse upon me, Antiope? Must I hurt all I love?"

"No. That is more foolishness. What is inside a man may bring a curse upon him, but what is on top of his head never will."

"I have already killed Solois, who loved me!"

Anger took Antiope. What right had Solois to hurt Theseus so? She said bluntly: "No. He jumped into that river because I would not sleep with him. Not because you would not."

Theseus stared, as stunned as if she had struck him. "No! Solois never would have betrayed me—he loved me!"

"He loved me too. Or so one said who came to me."

"Who?" Theseus seized her arms, his fingers sinking deep into them. *"Who?"*

Too late Antiope saw her mistake. "One who would not have lied about him. Ask me no more, Theseus."

"Who? Was it one of his brothers? Euneos? Thoas? Was it Hermos?" Her face, still as the blue sky above them, told him nothing, and his painful grasp tightened. "Which of them, woman? Which?"

She did not wince. "I made a promise. To break it would be no deed for a queen, king's son." Her level eyes met his.

Shame took Theseus. She had been true to him, his Antiope. Amazon though she was, she had proved herself a faithful wife. Now, in her high honor, she was set on keeping a promise that must have been tricked out of her.

He let her go, then took her in his arms again. He kissed her and said: "I understand. He loved you—how could anything shaped like a man help but love you? And I had him where he had to see you day after day, close enough to touch you—as no man in Athens ever sees his friend's wife—"

And then Antiope spoiled it all. She said, her eyes troubled and full of pity: "If I had known his death would hurt you so much, I would have lain with him."

Theseus stared, then glared at her, black outrage in his face. "Woman," he said between his teeth, "woman, have you no shame?"

Antiope stared back at him, too surprised to glare. Then she said quietly: "You are too worked up to have any sense. First you grieve because your friend slew himself when I would not sleep with him; then, when I say that to spare you pain I would have done it, you turn on me like a biting dog."

For a breath's space a door swung open in Theseus' mind. She would have done the deed because she loved him. Then his fury surged back.

"We will let the dead rest, and speak of him no more. Only tell me his name—the name of that dog who bore the accursed message. Of him who dared ask you to soil my bed!"

"Then I would be dishonored, having broken my word." Her eyes were still level.

"Loyalty to me—that is your honor now. And by the Dog, you must learn that!" His voice was like the growl of a beast. "I have a debt that I must pay. I must kill for my honor, that you regret not having soiled."

Their eyes clashed like swords, and neither fell. Then unholy joy leaped in Theseus; he had remembered a threat that had scared her once before. "Speak, woman! Or I will have your Amazons put to the torture, to find out what man has spoken with you when I was not there."

Antiope saw the danger. Felt it, like a knifepoint at her throat. Not only her girls' danger, but her own. His too. If she yielded now she would be truly his slave girl, sunk in a bondage that must wear out love. Yet what could she do? Answering fury would only feed his fury; so would fear.

Then suddenly she heard her own voice, cool and steady: "Theseus, do you think you can hurt my girls, yet keep me? Not for long. We Amazons love life, but we know when to die."

Before the stone-calm, set purpose in her voice and eyes his rage fell back, as a great wave falls back before the immovable calm strength of a cliff. With a great sob he caught her in his arms again, pulled her down onto the skin-covered pile of sweet-scented grasses that was their bed.

"Antiope, Antiope, tell me you did not mean it! You never could have lain with Solois!"

She put her arms around him then and said what he wanted her to say. She forgave him because he was her darling, but not her equal. It did not occur to her that her love itself was bondage.

It did occur to her that she had better point out something he did not seem to realize: her own equality. She said gravely: "I understand now. Married people must lie only with each other. If you ever catch me lying with another man you may kill me—I will not object. And if ever I catch you lying with another woman I will kill you. Both of you."

Theseus opened his mouth to protest, then shut it again. A husband's right to philander was as natural as sunrise and sunset, yet somehow unexplainable. Civilized women often made a fuss about it. And Antiope was by birth a barbarian; how could he ever

hope to shake her childlike, innocent belief that what was sauce
for the goose was sauce for the gander? To him too, marriage
began to disclose the possibility of bonds.

Well, he thought, kissing her, *she is worth a hundred other women. And
she is my woman—mine! All of her, wholly and forever!* He kissed her
harder; his arms tightened. . . .

Outside the tent men were washing and laying out the gray,
stiffened thing that had been Solois. But the two inside, whose
bodies glowed with life as his had only yesterday, had already
forgotten him.

That night Antiope dreamed a dream. Her body still lay beside
Theseus' body, but she herself walked beside the dark river. A tall
Shape bathed there, a woman's shape. Her flesh shone with a light
that made the waters around Her golden as morning.

Antiope knew Her; her hands rose in worship. "Oh, Lady, You
are, You are! I was afraid we Amazons had only dreamed You, but
You are real!"

The Goddess smiled and answered: "Child, I am. Also I am
everywhere; I have many shapes and many names, for no bond
binds Me, not even that of sex."

Antiope's mind reeled before the incomprehensible, clung to
what was knowable and dear. "Then You did send my mother that
dream of the Great King? But Molpadia"—darker memories came
—"surely she does not always hear Your voice? Only words put
together by her own hopes and fears?" Her own voice faltered; she
was not brave enough to ask what she most wanted to ask: *Is it your
will that I go with Theseus?*

But again the Goddess smiled and answered: "Would I who give
love thwart it? The Amazons love freedom; they could have seen
Me more clearly than any other people ever has. But hate and fear
bind them fast; they cannot bear the torch I would put into your
hands."

A pang tore Antiope. "Lady, can You not free them?"

"All must free themselves. A mother's well-cared-for children,
shielded by her strength—how can they be any more free than the
oppressed slaves of a master? For the Amazons I have done all I
can; through your mother I sowed seeds, but Molpadia has
blighted most of them."

Antiope's lips quivered, but she steadied herself: "This torch I am to carry: What is it?"

"Child, your Theseus is fated to bring men such freedom as men trapped in cities never before have known. Women should share that freedom. Human beings are born with two eyes each; never can they truly prosper so long as they bind one eye and say, 'Only this other has the right to see.' "

Light burst upon Antiope; brightness that seemed blinding; brightness that yet only made her sight clearer. "Then all this is Your doing, Lady? You sent Theseus to me! So that together we two might beget a new race—show the world how to live!"

"That is My hope, child, and the work you two were born to do. But I can promise you nothing."

"How can that be? Surely You know all things—rule all things, O Lady who made us all!"

"I know what great things must come, but not when or how they will come. For I have given life, the holy fire, into the hands of you who think yourselves mortals. Through bitter ages of mis-shaping yourselves and all else you must learn how to use it rightly. So only can you gain strength to know yourselves for immortals, true children of Me who bore you."

Again Antiope's mind reeled. "Lady—Lady! Is there no counsel You can give me? However hard it is, I will follow it; I will bear all that must be borne. Never again will I deny You!"

This time the Goddess' smile had a new loveliness; its tenderness enfolded her like arms. "Try to keep your mind and heart clean that I may reach and guide you. Child, that is all the Gods can do for those they love."

Antiope's face shone like the morning. Again she held up her arms. "Lady, I will not fail you!"

Still the tenderness enfolded her. "Child, you will not. Whether the work succeeds or fails."

Antiope woke beside Theseus, and there was no light, no Lady, only darkness. But in that darkness she felt the warm, now familiar bulk of him and snuggled against it. *We will do our work, beloved, whether you know we are doing it or not.* Then her troublesome mind began asking questions. *Was all this only me myself, weaving my own justification?* She did not want to learn to deceive herself, like Molpadia. But then once more the rightness of it all sang through her. Her vision had been true! She would do the work the Goddess had given her!

Day came, but without gladness. Sadly his comrades buried Solois, paying him all the honors that Greeks were wont to pay their dead. But through it all Theseus stalked in a red darkness, his face grim. Euneos, Thoas, and Hermos soon saw that his eyes avoided them. Before night fell Hermos told the brothers all; they were shocked, but did not reproach him. He had tried to help Solois, and he too was a man of Troizen. Theseus suddenly seemed removed from them, only a man of Athens now.

The three began to watch him, and covertly he watched them. Until that night when he said brusquely, "We have been here long enough. Tomorrow we sail for Athens." Most men were surprised, but thought they understood; this place held unhappy memories now. Only the three from Troizen kept close together around one campfire, though the night was warm. There Theseus came to them. He looked into their eyes at last, and his own were bright as fire. "Let us go down to the river. There we can talk alone."

Silently they followed him. The darkness hid his bright hair, and his cloaked figure, striding silently before them, looked tall and black enough to be that of Death, Sleep's brother. They had known him all their lives, yet now he was a stranger whom they feared. As a boy he had been quick to wrath, also quick to forgive; but then his wrong had been a boy's wrong. Between him and them now lay a wrong such as few men forgive.

Beside the river he stopped, faceless and black against the moon-silvered water. They could not see his face, but knew that he could see theirs and shivered. And then his voice leaped out of him, swift and savage as a pouncing beast.

"Which of you did it? Which?"

All three started, but no jaws dropped, no face showed honest surprise or bewilderment. Theseus saw that, and felt a sick grinding pain within him. *They all knew! They have all betrayed me. . . .*

Euneos spoke at last, quietly: "Son of Aithra, we four have grown up together. Two of us stood beside you when you stood beside the terrible bed of man-maiming Prokrustes. When you faced Skiron, and bone-breaking Kerkuon. You know that Her-

mos would have been there if he could. Can you believe any of
us are your enemies?"

"One of you is—that I know! And now the other two shield
him." Theseus' voice was a tortured, savage cry. His eyes blazed
with that red fire that long after the poet Bakchylides was to liken
to the volcanic fires of Lemnos.

None answered. Against the blank wall of their silence he felt
helpless, numbed. He broke through that numbness, roared as a
lion roars. "You are all against me—all! Two of you did not do the
deed, but you know well who did! Who stole in secret to my wife
and sought to defile my bed!"

"He who did that ill deed"—Euneos still spoke quietly—"did
not seek your wife for himself. He risked his own life to save
another's."

"Maybe the rest of you did not dare! Maybe you only waited
—you whom I trusted!—hoping he would bring back the good
news all of you longed for. That of my wife's whoredom!"

"No!" cried Hermos. "No! When the deed was done only two
men knew of it. Solois—and the man who tried to help him."

"Two of us would have had more sense," growled Thoas.

"No! Two of you were cowards, and all three are traitors!"

"To know a loved one's life is at stake—that is hard for the most
honorable of men." Euneos' eyes met his squarely. "Solois was not
your brother, nor your beloved. Can you not let the many days we
have been together—days when all of us were faithful—wipe out
that bad day when one was not?"

Silence fell. In it Theseus' eyes darted from one face to another,
searching, savage, yet pleading. He said at last, heavily: "Solois is
dead. But the rest of you still live—and until I know who did the
deed I can trust none of you. Tell me, and I will take no vengeance.
By Poseidon Earthshaker, I swear it! Maybe then, when I know—
when I can stop wondering, suspecting which of you it was—I can
even forgive!"

Again none answered. Hermos swallowed hard, but in the black
night Theseus could not see the muscles of his throat move. To
him all three faces were like sculptured masks, hard and unyield-
ing.

His fists clenched; he cried in fury: "Then stay here, all of you!
Come never again to Troizen or Athens—never again seek to see

the faces of your fathers and your mothers, or of any whom you love! For if ever you see my face again—any of you—that day will be the day of your death!"

He strode away through the night, his cloak billowing about him as though blown by a great wind. The three he had left stood stunned, sunk in a blackness deeper than the night's. To a Greek exile was worse than death. Yet when Hermos moved as if to follow Theseus, Euneos caught his arm.

"No. The poison has worked too deep. He would never wholly believe you now. We can never trust him now, either."

"But I cannot let you two suffer for what I did—"

"What is done is done, and you did it for love of Solois, our brother. Now let us all three stand together like brothers, who henceforth must be strangers in a strange land. Do you not agree, Thoas?"

Thoas did, somewhat glumly, yet that bargain seems to have been well kept. Years later men on Greek shores heard how the king of little Smyrna had given his three daughters to three strangers, under whose guidance the town had prospered. It was growing great again when one died, and the other two renamed that seaward-flowing river for him: the Hermos. For more than a thousand years it was to bear that name.

But in black wrath Theseus left Smyrna. Not until the ship had sailed did Antiope know what had happened. She was shocked; never would Amazons have abandoned other Amazons. "Turn back, Theseus! Two of those men have gone through great perils with you, and all three have been your friends ever since you can remember. Also their kin must be old friends of your mother's kin."

Theseus answered through set teeth: "One of them betrayed me, and so long as the others shield him, they too are traitors. Speak no more of this, woman—unless your mind changes, and you choose to tell me the dog's name!"

He left her in anger. But that night when he came to bed he was very friendly, and Antiope could see that he was relieved because she was. She had not been sure she would be. She had not liked being given orders—he would have to learn better—but in this matter she was not sure of her ground. She would not have liked him to interfere between her and her girls. And marriage was something about which men seemed peculiarly touchy; by his own standards Theseus might be justified.

And have not I, too, deserted my people? That knowledge was colder than the night winds, that now began to taste of winter. It always would be, despite that bright vision beside the dark river.

Theseus' heart was heavy. He had lost his dearest friends, and whenever he thought of wise Pittheus he dreaded meeting the old man's eyes. Aithra's too; the mothers of the exiles had been friends of her girlhood. Theseus never had much liked Hermos' mother: a fussy woman, always afraid her darling would get hurt in one of the lively princeling's wild ventures. But the mother of Euneos, Thoas, and Solois had always been friendly; often, when the boys were playing outside her house, she had called them in to give them warm, freshly baked honey cakes. And now, through him, she had lost all three of her sons. . . .

But they were all traitors, all! Stubbornly, passionately, he told himself that he had been right.

Antiope, however, was still worried; rash rages were a weakness, especially in a king. With a new subtlety she set about teaching him his business. Tales of the Great King, her father, always fascinated him, and he might learn from them. While her advice—a woman's—might still hurt his silly male pride.

She said once: "When the Great King was young and first took the kingship, his kingdom was like a smashed dish. He had to work long and hard to put it together again, yet now it is greater than ever it was before. He has conquered many cities, many men, who used to raid Hittite lands. But he never seeks revenge. Always, even at the last, he has offered such cities peace. They may keep their old laws, their old lords—but never again must their men go to war save as part of the Great King's host."

"But he can never trust them! Men who have once been free kings will always hate being called another man's men. Someday, when he is busy elsewhere, or ill or very old—then they will rise against him!"

Once Antiope herself had thought that. But now that she had come out into the great wild world of men her father's ways seemed to her to be the best arrangement that could be devised. Amazons, with their Hive-spirit, could live like sisters, but could

men ever live together like brothers? There were too many of
them, and some even seemed to take pride in being quarrelsome.

She said: "Some will, but not many, my father thinks. He also
says"—here she smiled—"that trust is a luxury no king can afford.
'Smile on all, use them when you can, but watch them all. Have
eyes in your back always.' He says that is the only rule for a king
who would live long and prosper."

Theseus shot her a keen glance. He did not altogether like this
talk of trust, but he himself had used the word first; she might
mean nothing by it. He said only, "That does not sound easy."

"Can greatness ever be easy? But when people prosper and live
in peace, they hate to risk losing all that. It is not easy for a small
king to make them rise against his overlord. Also, Subbululiuma
never pushes the kings too far; he thinks it best to let them keep
most of their pride."

Theseus frowned. "Are you sure of all this? I have always heard
that whenever the Great Kings of the East said 'Come,' or 'Go,' all
men came and went. Like dogs."

"That is the way of the kings of Babylon and Assyria. Of many
Pharaohs. Fatheaded, fat-bellied fools who call themselves Gods.
No Hittite king is ever called a God until he mounts the hill."

"Until he dies?" Theseus nodded, pleased. Old hate, old disgust
still rose up in him whenever he thought of Minos the God-King.
Of that treacherous murderer whom men called the Just.

Then he frowned again. "But your father makes many wars. Are
not the underkings' men always being called away from their
homes to fight for his gain? Not for their own people's?"

"No. Of old"—now Antiope looked troubled—"those little cities were always warring against each other. That is the vice of
small free peoples. Now, in spite of the Great King's wars, people
get to stay at home in their fields and shops more than they ever
did before. Trade flourishes between city and city."

Trade—that was what made Mycenae and Messene rich! Yet to
most Greek kings war still meant loot, and was the surest way to
wealth. War against Crete was Theseus' own dream. But on the
mainland—suddenly, stabbingly, Theseus thought of his own Attica. Every summer some part of it was torn, either by old enemies
or by hungry strangers. Men had to flee to the nearest city—to the
fortified hilltop that was its Akropolis. To leave their fields and

home and cattle to be the prey of despoilers who were seldom strong enough to keep what they took, but always strong enough to destroy. But if all twelve kings fought side by side, whenever one was attacked, like Subbiluliuma and his underkings—well, they never would. All twelve were never attacked at once, and each always hoped that this year he and his would escape.

Then like lightning a thought slashed through Theseus. *If all twelve had stood together against Minos—if those eleven other kings had helped my father! Then we could have driven him back into the sea—Minos, the Son and Friend of God!* He trembled, he ached, thinking of all that glory that might have been, that salvation of many. It could have been done—it could have been—if only those eleven others had helped! Instead they had all stood aside, watching while men of their own blood died. Some of them had even sold supplies to Minos. His jaw set. *Never again shall that happen. All those sluggards, those false friends, shall be my men, shall obey me as the kings of the East obey Subbiluliuma.*

He heard himself talking to Antiope, telling her what he had never told her before. Of Athens' defeat and shame, and the cruel tribute Minos had laid upon the conquered. She listened in indignant horror. "Did not one of all those other kings help your father? Had he no friends, no kin to stand beside him?"

"Two kings were his brothers. One was loyal to him and died for it, betrayed by his own daughter. Minos beguiled her and used her, then slew her. Else Pallas, my other uncle, might have joined him, hoping to be rewarded with my father's crown."

When Antiope had heard all her lip curled. "He is not worth spitting on, this Minos. He has lost all the shrewdness with which that queen-killing dog, his ancestor, won a kingdom. That one would have loaded this Skylla with gold and then carried her off to Crete, where he could have done whatever he liked with her without any mainlander's ever knowing."

To hear Minos so calmly and casually belittled thrilled Theseus. Had any Greek man or woman ever had such blasphemous thoughts, they never could have been spoken aloud save in some lonely desert place, far from the ears of men. His heart sang, then sank again. The difficulties of his new plan seemed to pounce on him from everywhere, like swarming wasps.

"If I conquer those other kings of Attica they will never forgive me—they will always hate me. We of the West are not used to bearing yokes, like your conquered eastern kings."

"This Mycenae you speak of—is not its king the overlord of lesser kings?"

"No. He taxes only the roads he builds between their cities. He lays neither taxes nor commands upon other kings."

"Who must know that he can tighten his fist and squeeze them if he chooses. . . . But what you need is allies in war."

"Allies! If only they could be that—not men shamed by having been conquered. . . . Well, when I have conquered Crete maybe they will seek my friendship. Certainly they will fear to be foes." Suddenly Theseus' fists clenched. "If ever again I let Minos take that tribute may I bring shame and woe on the mother who bore me—may I lose the son you will bear me!"

"Better to pay even that tribute a second time than to strike too soon and fail." Antiope remembered what the Amazons never had had a chance to forget—the need for caution. "Yet you are right —you must deal with Minos first. In summer, when all his own ships are away—being traders as well as fighters—only a few should be needed to take his wonderful Knossos. Maybe even his wonderful self." She laughed. "What fools men make of themselves when they call themselves Gods! Growing bloated and soft and rotten. We queens of the Amazons have been called the Mouths of the Goddess, but we never have claimed to be the rest of Her."

She laughed then, and Theseus laughed with her. In joy they went to bed together. But when they lay close and Theseus felt the soft firm belly in which his child was growing, he thought: *I do not deserve you, little son, if ever again I let the children of other Athenian parents be dragged away to a cruel, mangling death. I was young last spring—too young to understand what I left my people to bear alone. . . . Truly you are more than man, Minos, who can make men sit still and bear such horror. Less than man too—lower than anything born a beast!*

Surely there must be some way to bind the Twelve Cities of Attica together in harmony—then such woe could never again fall on any of them! There must!

·   ·   ·

On the ship sailed, westward through that wine-dark sea. Islands filled it, seeming as many as the stars that fill the night sky. The Amazons marveled, they whose own foggy sea was almost islandless. Then one morning they saw at last the western mainland, a dark, many-mountained mass. Saw high lovely Sunion, that sailors loved. Like a welcoming arm it reached out into the sea: a point of land on whose white beaches the small ships man had then could be safely beached. On three sides of it the blue sea glowed brighter than jewels, above it flowed the blue sky, cradling clouds white as the lashing foam below. Mountains reached for that glorious sky, so becoming quiet neighbors of the quiet clouds. Before all that beauty even the Amazons, used to the higher mountains of the East, caught their breath in wonder.

They landed. Theseus and his men knelt and kissed the good Greek earth, as homecoming men might kiss a mother's face. The Amazons too knelt to kiss it. Though not their native soil, it was still the breast of Earth their Mother.

Then all climbed up onto the windy heights, and a priest whose one white linen robe was now yellowed and threadbare brought an old black bull for Theseus to sacrifice to Poseidon. The shrine was a poor place now, since mainland men were forbidden to have ships. The Goddess had a smaller, older altar, and the Amazons were given a goose to sacrifice upon it. They were not pleased; one muttered to Antiope, "Lady, this is not right." She answered: "I know. The Goddess should be honored above all. But to set things right here will take time."

Then Theseus raised his arms high above his head and prayed. "O Poseidon, Lord of All! You who hold Earth the Mother in Your mighty arms and make Her fruitful. You from whom all moisture comes, the wetness of the salt sea, of lakes and rivers, and also that holy fluid which comes from the life-giving members of bulls and men. We thank You, holy Begetter, who have brought us safe home to our friends and kindred."

But the Amazons were not coming home to their friends and kindred. They were going to a strange city, full of strangers. *And there we must live until black death takes us!* Sudden and harsh as a blow, the full meaning of that came to them. They clustered around Antiope, like little girls around their mother. She smiled, trying to cheer them, reminding herself of her mission. "Girls, the Goddess wills this."

But when a chariot was brought from the city for Theseus, and she stood in it beside him, behind the horses, whose reins he held, then her hands felt queerly empty. Never before, since she was a little child, had she stood in any chariot or wagon that she had not driven. But now he was the driver, and she could not protest. His people waited to see him drive proudly home, and she, a queen, knew well the importance of prestige to any leader.

Book III
ATHENS

CHAPTER 1.
THE AMAZONS MEET LADIES

OLD KING Aegeus wept for joy when he saw his son again; and Theseus, holding him, felt the pitiful lightness and flabbiness of the old body. Last spring it had been massive. His own eyes blurred.

Then Aegeus saw the seven cloaked strangers who waited behind his son, tall and soldierlike. Antiope's proud bright head drew his eyes, though her cloak looked no richer than those of the others. "Child, is this the son of some friendly king who gave you good guesting on your travels? He is very beautiful."

Theseus smiled proudly. "Father, this is no guest, but my queen, who already carries your grandson."

Then old Aegeus laughed and laughed. "Joy be with you, my children! Get your own children as fast as you can—I cannot have too many grandsons, or too soon."

He made much of Antiope, and finally doddered off to the storerooms to look for the golden snakes that always decked every royal child born in the strong house of Erechtheus. Antiope's Amazons fidgeted; they were tired and sweaty, and longed to get to some place where they could take their clothes off and have a bath. Yet one girl giggled. "That old man acts as if you were going to have the baby tonight, Queen." But to her surprise Antiope answered softly, "I would not mind if my second were a boy." Theseus' determined belief that she carried his son always irritated her, but now she felt a sudden longing to please this old man of whom the years had made a child again. Who clearly did not have many of them left.

Soon noises came from the storeroom; Aegeus could not find the golden snakes. Theseus went to help him, and could not find them either. Presently Antiope went to help them both; she found the golden snakes.

She also found dirt and disorder such as she never had seen before in all her life. Medea, for all her magic, had not been a good housekeeper. The Amazons went to war again: a war that lasted for days. They worked the fat off lazy, long-slack servants who sadly realized that their days of ease were over. Everything movable was moved, everything scrubbable was scrubbed, all that should be polished was polished. Corners that had lain undisturbed since the death of Aegeus' last Greek wife yielded up their ugly secrets. Theseus and Aegeus beamed. Amazons were true women, after all.

The Amazons thought: *This is what comes of letting men rule.*

But a place on which one has worked hard becomes a source of pride to free women and so, in a sense, their own. The Amazons were feeling wholly at ease and mistresses of all they surveyed on that day when at last they came out between the now gleaming golden pillars that were shaped like women and called the Maids —Aegeus had had them gilded to please Medea—whose slim graceful strength upheld the south porch. They meant to have a look at this strange land that now was to be theirs. But at the great main gates of the Akropolis the gatekeeper refused to let them out.

"Lady, I dare not!" Trembling but resolute, the old man faced Antiope. "Both the kings would be wroth with me."

"Why?" asked Antiope, astonished.

"Let us kill the old fool, Queen." The words, spoken in broken Greek, were half a jest, but only half. Six hands had gone to six knives. The old gatekeeper understood and trembled harder than ever.

"Lady, ask your lord. Please ask him!"

Antiope went back to the palace and did. Theseus said coolly: "The ladies of Athens never go out on foot."

That took her breath away, but not for long. "Why not?"

"It is not done."

"Why not?"

"It is not done. It is a deed for harlots, seeking to lure strange men to their beds."

"Then give us horses. Amazons cannot live indoors, like mice in mouseholes."

Theseus said, "You can have a chariot. Ladies drive chariots. Though only in quiet, settled country," he added hastily. "Be careful, love—think of the baby."

"No chariot will hold all of us. Give us horses."

Theseus had hair-raising visions of fast, hard riding, even of races. Of a fall that would make Antiope miscarry and perhaps hurt herself badly, certainly lose his son. He said, "A wagon will hold seven women. Give me time to have one properly painted and decked out—made fit for my queen."

"Today we will use it unpainted. We need to get out into the open again. To feel the wind."

In the end she was led to a wagon piled high with rugs of finely tanned goatskin. Harnessed to it were two fat, glossy old mares— Theseus had had sense enough to know that she would never accept the usual wagon-drawing mules. Antiope took one look at those mares, then another at the grooms. "Take away these grand-mothers of many, and bring me something that can gallop."

"Lady, your lord himself chose this team—"

It was time to make a stand. Antiope knew that and made it. "I will speak with my lord later. Now show me the rest of the horses."

The grooms said they could not, but they did. Antiope finally chose two frisky, half-broken young beasts, white as milk, the last pair Theseus would have thought fit for a pregnant woman to drive. They did not equal the horses her people had bred so long and so carefully in Themiskyra, but they were real horses. Behind them she drove out of the Akropolis, heartsick to think that until Theseus had looted Crete and could afford more good horses, this must henceforth be her only way of riding. For until each of her girls could have a good horse again she herself would never strad-dle one.

But at least I am being true to you, my golden Chrysippe, so far away. Do you still miss me?

Only the king and a few high officers of his household lived on the Akropolis. Even the nobles, the Eupatridai, and the still more proud priestly castes of the Butadai and the Eteobutadai, his own kin, had their houses in the unwalled lower town. The Ama-zons drove between white houses whose high windows and deep porches loomed black against their whiteness. The golden afternoon was very still; perhaps all within slept. Here, by Amazon standards, the heat was still great, though by now autumn winds might be cooling far-off Themiskyra. Yet to the strangers all these windows seemed like black, watching eyes. Here too was a hive, thought Antiope; one vastly different from her own, yet as rigidly, perhaps even as fiercely, set in its ways. Women, however dwarfed and stunted by the way of life forced upon them. All the women who must have longed to get their own daughters into Theseus' bed, all the daughters who must have longed to get there. And she had snatched the prize from them, she a foreign woman, a stranger. *Goddess, Lady, help me to keep them from hating me! That hate would slow Your work.* But none came to look out of their windows and smile, as folk in Hattusas would have come to see a new queen riding by. Curiosity there must be, but no welcome showed. For all their courage, the Amazons were wild things; they found it hard to keep from looking back over their shoulders into that empty golden silence, into those black pits of shadow. . . .

They breathed easier when the houses were left behind. They went fast then, as fast as they could go, joying in even this poor measure of speed, laughing as the wagon bumped and jolted beneath them. Until now they had not known how much they had missed speed. They felt no fear for their unborn babes; children, once rooted in the strong, agile bodies of young Amazons, were not easily displaced. They were sad indeed when they realized that they must turn back. Time had gone faster than the horses; soon the evening meal would be served in the strong house of Erechtheus.

On the way back they did finally see one Athenian woman, a lady on a balcony, wasp-waisted, her big, bell-shaped skirts reaching her feet, her tight jacket baring the gilded nipples of her breasts. Antiope smiled and waved, but the lady only turned and went back inside, her head held high. The Amazons heard the door slam behind her, and one whistled. "She acts as if we smelled." But Antiope, looking around, suddenly understood. Until now she had not noticed a sight so ordinary. Her girls were standing in the wagon, and a wind had risen; it was blowing their short tunics straddle-high, showing all their long, bare brown legs—even sometimes the dainty, perky patches of fuzz that rim a woman's most useful woman parts. To a white-skinned lady used to Cretan fashions, that showed no leg at all, such a sight must have been shocking indeed. She tried to explain, but her girls could not understand.

"Why hide any part of oneself unless there is something wrong with it? And why should it be any worse to go naked at one end than at the other? She was showing both breasts—we never show but one—and her whole front down almost to her belly!"

"Leg-hiding is her way, and the way of her mothers. People always think their own way is right, and other people's wrong. I have seen this same kind of silliness among Hittite women."

"Well, our way is right, and theirs is wrong!"

But then all fell silent, some of them wondering whether it would be nice to have gilded, shiny nipples like that lady's. Antiope wondered too, but not about gilding her nipples. To shame her man before his people seemed wrong, yet compromise, that grim necessity, could be carried too far. She and her Amazons were not built for ladylike clothes; they were not wasp-waisted now, and soon pregnancy would make their waists much bigger. Instinct warned her that to make oneself look any worse than one had to would be like throwing one's arms down before a charging enemy. How glad these foolish, hostile woman would be to make Theseus' eye stray! This must be the time for her to begin making those changes she was fated to make.

When she reached home Theseus met her as if nothing had happened, and she was not long in guessing why. The grooms had not dared to tell him what she had done, fearing he might think they should have stopped her. But once she was in bed with him she told him herself, firmly but calmly, and again Theseus foresaw storms and backed down. She would be more reasonable after the baby was born, he told himself; babies settled women down. Besides, he could not help feeling a little sympathy for her; he too loved speed and open spaces.

But he did warn her again. "Be careful, best-beloved. Think of him you carry." And Antiope answered: "Amazons are never careless." (She believed this to be the truth.) "From childhood we Amazons are taught the value of daughters to our people. And besides, I want our baby—I want her!" She threw her arms around him, and for that night they forgot all strange, differing customs, and all else that troubles the world of men.

During the next half-moon the Amazons learned much about Attica. They picnicked in the green oak woods of nightingale-haunted Kolonos, where later Theseus was to welcome the wandering, blinded Oedipus, him to whom no other Greek king ever dared give shelter because of the curse that lay upon him. They climbed the steep slopes of Lykabettos, that squatted dark and huge above the Akropolis, a pyramid not reared by men; also the purple slopes of Hymettos, famed for honey, and heard the singing of its bees. They were surprised to hear the beekeepers call the queen bee "he" and "king," then remembered that such folly was natural in a race that thought all rulers must be men. They saw high Penteli, later to be famed for golden-white marble, and pine-covered Parnes. They saw the little, low hills around Athens: the Pnyx and the Areopagos, the Hill of the Nymphs and the Hill of the Muses.

They also learned how many places they could not go to and how many things they could not do, being women. They could not join the young men in their lovely games and races. They could not go to the Agora, the marketplaces, and look at or buy any of the many things there. Modest women never went to the Agora; merchants who had things fit for the ladies of the palace would bring them there. And when men came to see Aegeus and his son, to make petitions or take counsel about public matters, then the young queen and her "handmaids" could only bring in cakes and wine for their refreshment. No woman might stay and listen, let alone share in the talk.

Antiope realized that she had won freedom to amuse herself: no more. Housework and ladylike play—these were the only things women could do. She felt bound and gagged; she felt like a sword rusting on the wall.

"Amazons may be overworked," she told Theseus, "but being underworked is worse. Is there nothing that women here can do outside a house but ride around and look at things? Nothing that matters?"

"Yes," said Theseus. "They can do the washing. All the women of Athens, rich or poor, take their washing down to the River Ilissos."

Antiope opened her mouth, then shut it again. Washing did

matter, though not in the way she had meant. Also it would be a way to meet the women of Athens and talk with them. . . .

But then she heard that the Thesmophoria was near, the Festival of the First Sowing, since midsummer was the Athenian New Year. For three days and three nights even the greatest ladies of Athens would camp outdoors, allowing no man to come near them. The Amazons were delighted. This was one time when even these women followed the old ways, shutting out their men and doing the sacred things by themselves, to make the grain grow. Even old Alexandra was going, the aged wife of one of those few high officials, old like Aegeus, who lived on the Akropolis. They had thought her too feeble to go anywhere, or to take much interest in anything—certainly she had shown little in them. But now they made another attempt to be friendly.

"Let us go with you, Lady," said Antiope. "The crops of our new home concern us too."

The old lady hesitated, but not for long. She could say she had been afraid, that the wild women had forced themselves upon her, but also she could show them off. Most women were curious about them. But she said firmly: "You must wear long skirts. Dress modestly, so as not to offend the Two Queens, the Mother and the Maid, who rule all growth."

Antiope did not think the Goddesses would be offended, but she decided—to Theseus' great relief—that she and her girls would wear long loose robes such as priests wore. Religious taboos must be respected.

"But be careful," he warned her yet again. "At the Thesmophoria women change—a change that is almost like madness. Of old, men who spied on their rites died."

Antiope smiled. Nowadays they surely could not be such tigresses, these weak, silly not-women. . . .

The first day of the Thesmophoria was called the Day of the Down-going and of the Rising-up. In the gray dawn all women silently crept from their houses. Many welcomed old Alexandra, but not the Amazons, who silently fell into step around her litter. They came to the sacred precinct of the Two Queens, and all litters had to be left. From there on kinswomen and slave women helped the feeble; the Amazons helped Alexandra.

Flame-bright the sun rose, yet three women lit three torches and planted them in a trench before the dismal cleft that was said to lead down into the Underworld chambers of the Two Queens. Crowned with the Mother's own crown Her priestess came, glowing in bright scarlet, rich as newly shed blood. To her came three ladies, each bearing a fat young pig too full of poppy juice to squirm or squeal. To one she gave the sacrificial knife, made of flint—these rites dated back to a time before the use of metals. The lady swung her pig out over the trench, then cut its throat. But the cut had not been deep enough; the pig, aroused, struggled and cried pitifully. After two more cuts it died, blood spattering the lady's dress.

"An Amazon could have killed it the first time," one muttered. "Without making any such mess or fuss."

"We are used to killing our own meat," Antiope said fairly. "Probably this is the only day of the year when any of these ladies ever kill anything bigger than a bug."

Then, with a covered basket in one hand and her pig's dripping carcass dangling from the other, the lady went down into the dark cleft and vanished. Women moaned with awe, seeing her go. A second pig-bearer received the sacrificial knife. She raised it and all moaned again, differently this time, with a soft, ecstatic moaning: *"Ai—ai!"* Too many of their eyes shone with a red eagerness.

The second pig bled and died, then the third, both killed clumsily and too slowly. Two more ladies vanished into the darkness of the cleft. Others followed them with baskets of cakes, but soon came back up again. The pig-bearers did not reappear. "What are they doing?" one of Antiope's girls whispered, but Antiope could only sign to her to be silent. A hush had fallen; soon it became that deep golden hush, too bright, too still, that through the ages has made men in lonely places fear the Midday Demon.

Then suddenly the crowd opened; everywhere there was a sudden, sharp sucking-in of breath. Four young girls skipped out onto the barren heath before the great trench. Their huge skirts dazzled the eye like great golden bells, the thin, fine spangles sparkling as they moved. They too carried baskets; each kept stooping, then rising again as they circled, the rising right hand always curled carefully around nothing—a nothingness she exclaimed over ad-

miringly, then pretended to drop into her basket. Old Alexandra
chuckled, then explained to the wondering Amazons.

"They are the Maid and Her maidens, come to gather flowers,
as they did on that day when Death first came into the world.
When the Dark Lord seized Her, He who conquers all kings."

"Which one is the Maid?" asked Antiope.

Again that eerie, gloating chuckle. "The priestess knows. None
of the girls does. Each wonders—yes, she wonders."

The Amazons stiffened. One said to Antiope, very low, "Surely
they will not offer another *woman* to the Goddess?"

"I am afraid they will. Theseus spoke of this, but I hoped he was
wrong. Men always believe wild tales of what women do in their
secret rites."

"But how can He come—Death—if no man is allowed here?"

Horses neighed suddenly and sharply, answering her. The four
girls dropped their flower baskets and screamed. The crowd
wailed. "Aidoneus! Aidoneus! He comes—the Unseen One. *Ai—
ai!* Woe to the Maid!"

In the tumult it seemed that a chariot big as a hill was rolling
down upon them. They could hear the cracking of whips, the
cumbrous rolling of huge wheels, the pain-maddened horses. The
Amazons realized that whips were being cracked, huge plates of
metal pounded, and that women must have been trained to make
horselike noises, but how all the sounds were made they never
knew.

This way and that the four girls fled, their shining skirts like
lightning flashes. They turned and twisted, they doubled like
hares, frantic for some way of escape. Sometimes one seemed to
open, but always the fleeing girl would find a wall of massed
bodies between her and freedom. Shrieking wails still rose, more
in glee than in dread now: "Aidoneus! Aidoneus! *Ai—ai!*"

At last one girl was allowed to get through. She vanished, and
in due time a second followed, then a third. The fourth and last
girl, finding herself alone, squealed like one of the butchered pigs,
then began to sob as she ran. . . .

Then, with one great exultant howl that seemed to come from
all throats, the living walls closed in. Swift as hunting dogs they
seemed, despite the long skirts that hampered them. Their cries

were dog-eager, dog-cruel. The Amazons ran with the rest, but took good care not to shoulder their way into the front rows, not to be among those who caught up with the living quarry. They knew only that the girl was finally thrown or driven down into the cleft. Shriek after shriek rose from its depths, agonized screams of pain and fear. Until pain killed even fear, and then died itself.

In the red twilight the three pig-bearers came stumbling up out of the cleft, gray-faced, with sunken eyes. One staggered, fell to her knees, and vomited. Women came running to embrace and comfort them. Some took the heavy baskets they carried, and others brought them hot soup and wine.

"What have they been doing, down there all that time?" an Amazon asked in wonder.

"Cutting up the pigs. And the girl." Antiope's voice was grim. "Opening up the *pithoi* too, those tall jars that hold last year's dead. Ladling out the stinking rottenness inside to make room for fresh, bloody flesh. Every farmer sends part of his seed corn here to be mixed with last year's kill, so that its holiness—that of the Maid's own flesh—may make his fields more fertile."

"What have the pigs got to do with it?"

"Pigs are sacred to Her. Their flesh is Her flesh."

The Amazon made a face. "Down there in those dark caves the smell must have nearly choked those she-butchers. Why not use the fresh meat on the fields?"

"It is not their way. And those three take great risks, or think they do. The guardians of the caves, great snakes who come out at the smell of fresh blood, would tear the meat from them if those baskets of cakes did not hold them off awhile."

"And we thought these housebound women soft!"

"Sh-h-h!" Antiope glanced at old Alexandra, who was dozing now, exhausted. Better not to talk too freely, she thought, even in a tongue the old lady could not understand.

She added presently: "It is not their own daughters whom they use so, but slave girls who have stolen from their mistresses. They think that after this the three who survive will be very good, and never steal again."

"Why should not slaves steal?" An Amazon snorted. "They have been stolen from themselves."

Antiope said: "They are all slaves together. The so-called mistresses have had masters all their lives. They must be full of bottled-up rage and hurt, however hard they try to hide their feelings from themselves. When, for a little while, they do get power, they go mad."

"But why hurt the wrong people? Women should not hurt women. They could get hold of a man somehow—buy a slave, and smuggle him in." The speaker was deeply shocked. Amazons had a great respect for all womb-bearing creatures: for all who seemed to them to be shaped like the Goddess.

"Who can expect the sick to reason?" They were all sick, Antiope told herself, blinded and warped by ages of slavery. They must be taught to see clearly again.

Night fell; fires were kindled, and food cooked. The Lady Alexandra woke and ate as heartily as if she had done a hard day's work. "Eat well, girls—fill yourselves full. Tomorrow is the Nesteia, the Day of Fasting, when we mourn with the Mother." Soon she slept again, hugging her many blankets close about her. All warmth had gone with the sun, and few of the sheltered women of Athens were comfortable that night. But the Amazons, used to hardship, had a merry time around that fire that reminded them of campfires of old. Though Antiope did think, before she fell asleep: *When Theseus has conquered Minos he will be the greatest king these western lands have ever known. All men will honor him like a God—he will be able to make many changes. And besides setting women free he must put a stop to things like this—I will see to that!* But her sleep was dreamless; she could not grieve for a strange girl as she had grieved for the horses who died before the Black Stone. She had known and loved those horses. . . .

Morning came, gray and bleak, a true beginning for the cheerless Nesteia. With empty bellies, with parched lips, the richest women in Athens crouched on the cold ground, even as once She Who was Mistress of Earth and Sea had crouched upon a bare rock at Eleusis. The Mother, grieving for the Maid, as any mortal mother grieves for her lost child. All day long Her worshipers mourned for Her grief. That night no fires might be lit, and cold hungry bodies were stretched out on cold hard earth.

But next morning there were fires and food again. This was the third day, the Day of Good Birthing, of gladness and new beginnings. All were like children, long shut up in a dark place, but let out to play in the sun again at last. Neighbor kissed neighbor, rejoicing. Several women came to greet old Alexandra, and some even showed a little friendliness to the Amazons. All of them, Antiope soon realized, wanted to find out all they could about her. Questions were eagerly fired at old Alexandra, who reveled in her new importance. Nobody ever seemed to think that the barbarian woman, the outlandish stranger, might know enough Greek to know that she was being talked about.

Until Alexandra's sister Theodora, wife of Lykidas of the priestly Butadai, came and smiled at her shrewdly. "You bear yourself well, girl. You know a good deal of what is being said about you, yet you show no anger. Although you have good reason to feel some."

Antiope's face shone bright as the morning. Truly this was a beginning! Perhaps this woman was to be her friend.

"By showing my feelings I could only frighten your country-women, Lady. Not change theirs."

The old lady chuckled. "Well, girl, it would be strange if we loved you. All dogs—even bitches—have little use for the dog who runs away with the biggest bone."

"I did not take Theseus from any other woman."

"You did—you took him from many. Every mother in Athens —unless her daughter is harelipped or cross-eyed—believes now that if you had not got him her girl would have."

"Lady, have you no daughters?"

"None. Five tall sons, thanks be to Artemis who helps us in childbirth! And three of them with boys of their own now."

"You are fortunate," said Antiope politely. She thought, *How can the woman think so? Not even one daughter!*

But old Theodora quickly made a magical sign to ward off the Evil Eye. "Never say so, child! The Gods smite the proud. But you yourself, if you give Theseus a fine boy, and keep up this quiet, ladylike behavior, may yet win honor. Even though you never can be his lawful queen."

Antiope flinched. So the old lady had called her "girl" in con-tempt, not with the kindliness of an older woman speaking to a younger. Sheer surprise—not fear—made her say: "But why can

I not be Theseus' queen? He says I am. And I thought that here men ruled all."

Another chuckle. "They do, girl, they do! As the Gods meant them to do. But only a woman born in Athens may be Queen of Athens. Queenship is one honor the Gods keep for us women of Athens, great though Their wrath against us once was."

"Why should the Gods be wroth with the women of Athens?"

A shadow seemed to settle on old Theodora. She said heavily: "Of old the women here sat in council with the men. And of that came great woe. Today men fling it in our faces even as they flung it in the faces of our grandmothers' grandmothers. As they will fling it in those of our granddaughters' granddaughters. To our shame and reproach forever."

"But what happened?" Antiope stared, dumbfounded.

"Kekrops came. The Teacher King from Crete, the Serpent King. He found us living like the beasts of the field—any woman lying with any man, whenever lust took them, no child knowing its father. He joined us together in holy wedlock, one man with one woman. He showed us how to build the high walls of the Akropolis to shelter us from cruel raiders. He said then, 'Now you have a city. Choose a Spirit to guard it.' And the men all chose Poseidon, Earthshaker and Earthholder. But we women chose the Goddess Athene, who had taught us how to plant and spin and weave. Who had given us the olive, that great source of food and oil. And since we outnumbered the men by one, we prevailed."

"By one accursed woman's vote—one only! *Ai—ai!*" In a fearful wail the words burst from old Alexandra. Somehow, through all her busy chatter, she had heard and understood, she who was too old for the hardships and fierceness of the Thesmophoria. And now she rocked back and forth, weeping like a scared and miserable child. Theodora ran to her, caught her in her arms. Women closed in around them, glared suspiciously at Antiope. Like a beast roused from deep sleep the savagery that had seemed utterly spent woke and stirred, to blacken the bright morning.

CHAPTER 2.
___MEN AND WOMEN

"LADY, I do not understand." Antiope stood her ground, ignored all but Theodora. "Your foremothers voted for their Goddess, as was their right, and so Her name was sealed unchangeably upon your city. What was wrong with that?"

"It brought down the God's wrath upon us!" A woman's shrill cry rose in answer. "He sent his floods to destroy us—our crops and our herds and many of our folk!"

Theodora, still holding her sister, said sadly: "And to those who yet lived, King Kekrops said: 'Never again may women sit in council with men, they whose mad folly is proven. Never again shall children be known by the names of their mothers, but only by the names of their fathers.' So it is and shall be, forever."

"But did your foremothers not appeal to the Goddess?"

"The Goddess Herself was wroth with us, who had not done Her Father's will!"

Yet another voice leaped at Antiope, savage and bitter. "She knew Her duty! She said, 'Look not to Me for pity. I am all for the Father.' Those were Her own words!"

"They were not!" Outraged wrath outweighed all caution in Antiope. "Lying men put those words into Her mouth! Never could the Goddess have so basely forsaken those who honored Her." She checked herself, tried reason. "Think! Such a flood must have ravaged other shores, hurt other folk. Would a just God have made them suffer for what you of Athens had done? Can Gods be Gods, and not be just? Never could Poseidon have acted so, He who is one of Theseus' fathers!" She was not really sure what she thought of Poseidon, but she saw the need for tact.

"He sent the flood!"

"King Kekrops said He did—earth-shaking Poseidon!"

"Kekrops, the wisest, most pious of mortal kings! Dare you say he lied, barbarian woman?"

"She blasphemes, this spawn of the man-butchering Amazons!"

Antiope knew the savage voice of the pack, realized that she herself was likely to be butchered. But she was young; it seemed to her that truth, once clearly spoken, could not be denied.

"I said, think!" Her voice soared out above the wild-dog barking. "In mortals injustice is evil. How can it be otherwise in Gods? You used your vote as you thought right—the best that anyone can ever do, man or woman—and that king tricked you out of it! We must get it back. Tonight I will speak to my man; the rest of you must speak to yours. Let us make this a true Day of Good Birthing—a day to be remembered forever as the rebirth of freedom and honor for the women of Athens!"

Silence then; a silence like a gasp. Deep in a very few minds something may have stirred: wonder, bewilderment, questions. Then again venom was spat forth.

"Kill her, the witch! Already she has bewitched the young king. Now she would bring down God's wrath upon us again—lure us into our sin of old. Kill her! Kill her!"

Some stooped, began to pick up stones. Antiope saw that no reason could pierce that beast-madness. Not only her own life was at stake, but her girls' lives, and the lives within their wombs and hers. She called out coolly, clearly, "Joy be with you, women of Athens. I leave you in peace. In what you think peace," and turned her back upon them. She must walk neither too fast, nor too slowly—she knew that. If one stone flew, so would a host of others. One step, two—her Amazons closed in around her, and she felt sick fear for their backs, as they had for hers. Three, four—never had she dreamed that steps could seem to take so long. Five, six, seven—she knew then that no stones were coming. Knew also the bitterness of defeat.

Old Aegeus was afraid. If the wrath of the mighty dead fell upon his son's wife, his grandson would never be born. Theseus soothed him. "Surely Kekrops loved Athens too well to harm its kings—he who taught us kingship. Let alone an innocent babe!" So far, old Pittheus' teachings had guided him; then he added cleverly: "Nor do I believe that my wife ever said half the things these foolish women are saying she did." He was anything but sure of that, for he knew Antiope; but the foolishness of women was always a good line to take—one always agreed on by all men everywhere.

Aegeus promptly brightened up. Of course she had not—she was a good girl, Antiope, a fine woman who would bear a fine boy! "Yet we must offer a holocaust before the tomb of Kekrops—even if he has heard the slanders, the blood of a hundred bulls will surely stay his wrath."

That night when Theseus went to his wife he said only: "I am glad you got home safely. You must see now the uselessness of trying to change the women of Athens." She was pregnant; if she had not been he might not have had sense enough to keep from telling her that he hoped that now she had learned her lesson— something which, in fact, he did hope. Antiope had her draw- backs, although the rest of her far outweighed them. All of her seemed to fit together, somehow, like the petals of a flower. She needed to be changed, but could she be, without letting out too much of the life and glow and bloom of her?

Antiope wished that he could understand; not being able to speak with him of matters so near her heart made her feel lonely. Yet his very lack of understanding made his lack of reproaches wonderfully kind. And she felt guilty because of those rich offer- ings that must be made at the tomb of the Serpent King. Theseus so needed to hoard all of Athens' slender resources for his war against Crete—and now, because of her, he must squander them. She herself would have been glad to face the ghost of Kekrops— she felt sure that she could have sent him scuttering back to Hell with his tail between his legs.

To her girls she said only: "I ran when I should have crawled. Next time I will do better."

But the truth was that she did not know what to do next, or where to start. Would it be better to wait awhile, until after her baby was born? Give these crazy women time to cool off? Her own head might be clearer then too.

Lady, I must not fail You a second time!

Like dawn it came then, the memory of the blue, gentle Ilissos.

She said to her Amazons: "Let us take our washing down to the river. We have left that to the slaves too long."

She did not expect to meet the great ladies there. They would send their daughters to do the washing—young arms and backs were stronger. Also the young were more flexible, less set in their ways . . . and she would woo them.

Very politely the Amazons asked the bright-eyed, wary young daughters of Athens to show them the best washing places. "For we are strangers here, and ignorant of this river." They were charmingly eager to make friends, and to ask other people's advice and then loudly admire its excellence has always been one of the best ways in the world to do that. With wonder the girls remembered what their mothers had been saying about these pleasant, friendly strangers. It must have been wrong: a discovery that was not world-shaking. The young always know that their elders can make mistakes.

Besides, they were curious about these other girls who were young too, and whom they had heard so much about.

Amazons and Athenians worked together, and finally sat down to eat together. These picnics beside the river were one of the greatest treats the shut-in Athenian girls knew. After eating they played ball, and asked the Amazons to play too. They played well; Antiope's eyes shone. *I can make real women of these girls!*

She said, "Let us show you some of the games we played at home." They were curious, and her Amazons fetched out bows and arrows, set up a target, and shot at it. Soon the Athenian girls were squealing joyously whenever the target was hit, and groaning whenever it was missed. (Had the Amazons been alone it never would have been missed, but Antiope was wily.) Then she offered them bows too. Some hung back, but more reached for the new playthings, with giggles and shining eyes. At first they invariably missed the mark, but the Amazons were patient and encouraging, and by evening several thought themselves fair markswomen. Antiope did not, but she praised them. Happily she drove back to the Akropolis, her heart soaring high as any bird.

But the Athenian girls got home late, and their mothers wanted to know why. They were evasive and took their scoldings in silence—the young also know how to keep secrets from their elders. But then one sharp-eared mother overheard her two girls delightedly whispering together, and the truth came out. All the mothers were shocked; so were all the grandmothers, aunts, and married sisters. The tale grew in the telling; it took as many shapes as fabled Periklymenos, Prince of Messene.

"Have you heard? That wild woman has been teaching our girls to use bows and arrows! She has been trying to make them kill each other!"

"Those fierce Amazons came upon our girls washing by the river, and shot at them—drove them away!"

Soon many of the girls were said to have been killed, but nobody ever knew precisely which ones.

"No—she did not kill them, that wild woman. She tried to corrupt them. Make Amazons of them! Our daughters!"

"She tried to arm them—lead them against the palace!"

"I am not surprised. That vicious bitch has no gratitude. Never has she been thankful to Theseus for bringing her among civilized people—pampering her like a lawful wife!"

Soon the Amazon herself was dead. Theseus had had to kill her in self-defense. When he heard that Theseus laughed loud and long. So did Aegeus. Not since the dread Cretan ships had sailed away with their awful tribute had there been such a to-do in Athens, and this time, thanks be to all the Gods, none could say that it was any of his doing.

With great contentment Theseus thought that this time Antiope surely must have learned her lesson.

Antiope herself stormed: "How can they say such things? They are mad! Nothing in all the world can be as foolish as your Athenian women!"

"That is what I have been trying to tell you, best-beloved," said Theseus, playing with her shining hair. "Let them alone; they are happy as they are."

"They are not, and I will not!" Antiope tossed her head with such force that she jerked her hair away from him and pulled it. "Those girls have good eyes and good hearts and good hands! They are fine girls—they can be taught!"

Theseus and Aegeus exchanged glances. Best to humor a pregnant woman. She would soon find out for herself that she never again could do anything for or with those girls.

She did. When next she went down to the river all the girls there told her sorrowfully that they could not have anything more to do with her.

"Our mothers would beat us if we did. They say too that if we learn your wild ways we will never get husbands. No men will marry us."

When Antiope did not look impressed by this most terrible of threats, they added: "Our fathers are angry too. They say that bows and arrows are too dangerous for us to play with—that we might hurt ourselves. We are not the daughters of War-God Ares, like you Amazons."

"Bows and arrows do not hurt your brothers. Even a kitchen knife can be dangerous unless one knows how to use it."

"That is different. Our brothers are men."

There was no more to be said. Antiope was learning how hard it was to fight women who did not carry arms.

No doubt the mothers of Athens did truly fear for both the minds and bodies of their daughters. Fathers may have been afraid too; not so much of clumsiness with weapons, but because the girls might get ideas. Exactly what ideas they did not know, but the fewer ideas women had, the better. Antiope could have told them. Women who could use men's weapons would soon share men's responsibilities and demand men's privileges.

Yet some, at least, of those girls who were never again to bear arms must have remembered all their lives that one golden day beside the blue Ilissos. Have told big-eyed grandchildren, their own old eyes shining, of how once they had stood shoulder to shoulder with the fierce Amazons, had joined in those dread games, and used the warrior women's own bows.

Winter whitened the world: a long dull winter for Antiope. Once she tried to reach Theseus' buried intelligence. "You are losing half your fighting power. If ever again your city is besieged —and cities often are—it could fall just because all these long-skirted idiots do not know how to use their own arms and hands! Even to defend their homes and children!" But Theseus laughed comfortably. "We men of Athens can always defend the women of Athens." She knew that if she said more he would only tell her again that fretting was bad for the baby.

Her daughter! A girl like oneself would be lonely here. *I have Theseus, my lover, but he will be only her father. Better if you do not come to enter my womb, Melanippe, as once I longed for you to do. But maybe your spirit could never cross these vast waters.*

Back at home, in Themiskyra, there would have been so much joy in her unborn baby, so much laughter and hope. But here the ladies of Athens would be glad indeed for her to miscarry; gladder still if she died in childbirth. She had not only beguiled their young lord, and tried to teach their daughters evil ways. She was guilty of that crime which, always and everywhere, has disturbed people most: she was "different." They despised what they called her sunburn, her ungainly height, her big waist that was constantly growing bigger, but most of all the brazen way she showed her legs. They were being used to kick her with—her own legs! Once even Theseus said, "Now that it is winter you would be warmer if you wore some kind of skirt," and she wondered who, or how many, had been at him. She answered, "I am not used to them, and I will not stumble on these stairs of yours, and lose our baby." That silenced him, but she knew—the slave women let her know—how many tongues still buzzed like stinging bees. "The young king will soon tire of such a great gross creature!" All the ladies said that hopefully, especially the mothers of marriageable daughters.

Yet they knew what she did not: how often their men's eyes followed her and dwelt upon those long, lovely legs. How a few foolish girls were whispering: "What use is it to squeeze ourselves into these terrible, tight Cretan girdles when Theseus himself loves a woman who does not wear one?" Some women grew worried; a few even took action. They bribed two of the palace slaves to poison Antiope.

But the better-natured slaves there had come to like their new queen; she never beat them, and she and her Amazons worked hard alongside those they made work. They took the bribe, but warned Antiope. She did not tell Theseus; if he lost his head again, as he had at Smyrna, he might make things worse. But her girls knew, and henceforth watched over her like lynxes.

Gamelion came, the coldest moon of all, yet also the Marriage Moon, when the weddings of men helped to put new life into Earth the Mother. Winds howled round the Akropolis, fierce as the tongues of the women below, and the noble lords of the Butadai and the Eteobutadai came to speak with Theseus.

"Lord, your father is old, and you are his only son. It is time, and more than time, that you took a wife."

He said: "I have a wife. The daughter of the Great King, of the Sun the Hittites. Of him whose arm is as mighty as Pharaoh's own. And my son waxes big within her."

All stared, as if surprised. "You mean that spear-won slave you sleep with? The Amazon? Amazons lie with many men: none could know her father."

Theseus' eyes flashed. "Antiope, Queen of the Amazons, came virgin to my marriage bed! And no man but the Great King ever lay with the queen her mother."

"So she says, but what does he say? What dowry did you get with her?"

Theseus' hands clenched hard on the ivory-inlaid arms of his great chair. "I took her by force, as well you know. But her sons will make their grandfather my friend. A mighty ally for Athens."

"A far-off one. And the woman never can be anything but your spear-won slave. She who is Queen of Athens must see what only a woman born in Athens may see, hear what only a woman born in Athens may hear. When we had such queens we prospered; Minos, the Son and Friend of God, was our friend then, not our foe."

Theseus' hands clenched yet harder. His very effort at self-control betrayed him into the weakness of excuses. "My father was beguiled by an evil woman. Like many other men before him."

"Too many, truly. A true queen keeps foreign witches away."

The ivory-inlaid chair arms cracked; Theseus roared like a lion. "My queen is no witch, and I will keep her! Go back to your cackling geese and tell them that!"

They went, those noble fathers of the city, wrathful but beaten, and Theseus paced the floor and ground his teeth. How dared they —how dared they—those worn-out old ganders fit only for the pot! Running their wives' errands like little boys. For they never could have had the sly malice to think of those insults that had come so smoothly from their mouths. . . . Could the women of

Athens really have more power and influence than they were supposed to have? No—this was only the folly of senile old men who had let spiteful hags put words into their mouths! How blessed—here he somewhat anticipated the later words of golden-tongued Homer—was that man who could share his heart and mind with his wife as well as his bed. Who had a wife he could talk to! But he would not talk to Antiope of this: the feud between her and the women of Athens was already great enough.

But that night when he went to bed her calm voice came out of the darkness. "Theseus, what is it that only a woman born in Athens may see? That only a woman born in Athens may hear?"

His growl was like a prodded lion's. "So the slaves heard and carried tales to you! The dogs!"

"They told me what is being said of me. No more. Except how you stood up for me." She hugged him. He had done no more than he should have done, but he had not had to do it.

"But why vex yourself with slaves' tattle?"

"Here in your city—in all the cities of men, I suppose—listening to slaves' tattle is the only way a woman can know what is going on."

"What need have you to know, now that you have me to shield you from all harm? Besides, none can trust slaves—fawning dogs who will say anything to get a reward. Well, if they do it again I will reward them by taking the hide off their backs!"

"Who can ever fully trust what another says? It is always bound to be colored by what that person thinks and feels. Kings and queens must learn to winnow wheat from chaff." How, she wondered, could men ever trust slaves? Amazons would have been afraid to sleep in the same house with folk they had robbed of that most priceless of all possessions: freedom. Though Theseus was no hard master; his worry for her spoke now.

She went on: "Slaves must use their wits, having no other weapon: and what they hear goes from house to house, like dust. I could tell you most of the words each lady used to make her man come here today—and how many nights it took her to work him up to it."

Theseus cursed and groaned. Antiope said: "Some said more than their men dared repeat. Told them that when my girls and

I drive out beyond the city we stop and lie with any comely young man we see along the road."

Rage nearly choked him, then pity outweighed it. "Antiope, all the time since you heard that foulness—have you sat wondering whether I would believe it?"

"Had I been afraid of that, the tale would have reached you from my mouth first."

"As it has."

"But only because I knew that sometime you must hear it. Theseus"—for once her voice was not quite steady, words meant to be a flat statement were almost a plea—"Theseus, we Amazons must ride free. Not be utterly hedged around and shut in—"

"But you must have guards now! If they can lie like this—my own people!—a trap may be set for you—"

"Guards would only make people sure you did not trust me—cause much sniggering. And we would feel as if their nearness were taking the breath out of our lungs. Amazons are used to danger; we live and die in it. Once I swam into a trap—remember?—but on land I have always been able to take care of myself. As Cretan Asterion learned, when he would have raped me in Azzi—"

"When he *what?*" roared Theseus.

She had to tell him all about Asterion then, and his wrath could have been no greater had he himself wooed her with all propriety.

"By the Dog! But I will make that Star set. I will cut off his balls and make him eat them! I will—"

Antiope started, then began to laugh. "Stop it, Theseus! You are getting the baby worked up too."

She took his hand, laid it on her belly. He too felt it—the quick hard thrust against the smooth wall of her flesh. For a breath's space he stared in wonder, then let out a great laugh of pride and joy. Then he spoke sternly to his wife's belly: "Young man, it is not respectful to kick your father."

"I got the worst of it," said Antiope. "She has the kick of a mule."

Theseus fondled her breasts, felt the scar that marred the lovely, rounded delicacy of one. "And I thought you got this in battle!"

"Amazons are seldom that clumsy." She laughed, and then he

laughed and they clung together, loving each other and the child who would be born to them.

Far away, across the wine-dark sea, on their high bed in the famed palace at Knossos, Queen Pasiphae said to King Minos, "Lord and brother, I carry your child again at last. Now you can leave me in peace."

Minos laughed for joy. "Make it a son, wife. A fine boy, to put Asterion's nose out of joint."

She stiffened. "Asterion was born of us, brother. He is your seed, nourished in my womb. Do not kill him unless you must."

The king laughed again, grimly this time and without joy. "Never tell me you love Asterion, woman. You never have loved any son of mine."

"You are wrong." Her body quivered, but she kept her voice steady. "Androgeos was easy to love until you took him from me and taught him to despise me as now all men despise all women, even the mothers who bore them. Nobody can love Asterion, yet he is still our flesh."

"You never loved either of them—my sons. You do love that pup Daidalos who got on you while I was away warring on that other accursed mainland dog, his kinsman! You did that, woman —you lay with a dog of the same foul breed as him who killed Androgeos, our son! How could you do it—even you!" Talonlike, his fingers curved to tear her, then fell, remembering the precious load she carried.

"No! no! Naukrate bore him—secretly, here in the palace. And when I found out I freed her and sent them both to Daidalos. He is her son—not mine!"

The man smiled, pleased by her fear. "That is why you go so often to Daidalos' house to fondle the boy. But you are never in one room with Daidalos; my watchers see to that. I would hate to lose him; he is a great craftsman. And so long as only your defiled womb can bear another Minos I would hate to lose you, wife and sister."

"Yes, you need my womb! That, but only that!" Bitterness brought back spirit, fire blazed in her face. "I am the only daughter of our mother. And though now the throne passes from father to son, still only the queen's blood gives any man's son the right to rule. The blood of all of us, mothers and daughters—queens here in Knossos through the ages! The chosen vessels of the Goddess, whom sometimes Her spirit fills. . . ." Her voice trailed away; she lay in a kind of ecstasy, then suddenly the fire leaped up again. Light-quick, she sat up to face him, laughed mockingly. "If the son of Daidalos were my son—if I told the people so—they would think him as fit to be king as any son of Minos. Without my womb your seed counts for nothing!"

She expected him to strike her then, her body was braced for the blow, but he only smiled. "Yet the Goddess has fallen, woman. Only the God rules now."

"Only as Her Son! The Bull of His Mother!"

"Because Her insolence had grown beyond all bearing, He smote Her. Night came at noon, the sea rose up to heaven. With fire and smoke and scalding ash He seared Her breast—"

"The breast that had nursed Him!"

"The world would have ended then had not the first Minos offered Him sacrifice upon the mountaintop. Begged forgiveness of Him who alone can give life."

"Give life—*He?*" She spat the words. "With His floods and fires He can take it, but never make it. His precious seed would be nothing without wombs to grow in. The people of Crete know well that without me beside you, no grain would grow in their fields, no tree in their orchards bear fruit!"

"Yet the power is His. He can destroy all Her womb brings forth, and She cannot stop Him. Remember that, foolish woman. One queen already has died beneath the hands of an avenging Minos."

" 'Avenging!' " Her lip curled. "In the dark he slew her—he, her sworn servant! In the dark of that night that came at noon and lasted many days. Then he took her throne and her daughter. As ever since every murdering Minos has taken us—us, the rightful queens and rulers!" She glared at him, her hate fierce as his. But he still smiled.

"Sister, is not Earth the Mother beneath all men's feet? They know that now, they all walk on Her and own Her. Presently the queen will be only the king's wife, and that will be good. In more ways than one, for though two as close akin as you and I may be fruitful, I think our fruit is scarcer and less sound than that that grows on other trees."

"Ariadne will be queen after me! You cannot prevent that!" She trembled, but not for herself now.

"So she will—that bitch-pup whom you love, even though she is of my get. But the son of this son you carry may not need her daughter."

"If I thought that, I would kill him unborn!"

"Then I would kill you. And slowly. And Ariadne would bear my son; soon she will be old enough."

Sick with fear and horror, she yet managed one last flare of defiance. "No, for then even Asterion would pretend pious grief and avenge me, his mother! To make himself Minos."

"But you would still be dead. And Asterion might die before you. Let us sleep now, wife. The welfare of him you carry means much to both of us."

They lay with their backs to each other. He prayed: *Make it a son, O my God and my Father. Make it one, You who somehow are me—*

Why could he so seldom feel the Godhood, the true power flowing through him? Many feared him, many fawned on him, but few loved him. Androgeos had loved him, but Androgeos was dead, slain by that mainland dog whom unbelievably, outrageously, his father had been unable to reach. And Asterion waited, ceaselessly watching for a chance to kill his father, he who had sought to slay his brother. *But I do have power, I am Minos!* They should learn that, all of them! Once Asterion had a brother, he would die. Soon her bastard too would die, before the father's eyes. *Also before I have them chopped off, those wonderful, skillful hands of his!* Which loss would hurt Daidalos most? To find out would be interesting, interesting enough even to compensate for the loss of his skill. . . .

Pasiphae lay staring at the moon-washed walls of the nearby light-well. Many starred this palace that now was called the Palace of Minos. Lit their depths, that made her feel as if she were at the bottom of a well. Down here no winter wind could reach her; little of the fragrant breath of spring ever would either. *But for me there will be no more springs. There never was but one, and it was short. . . . Oh, Daidalos, Daidalos, we had so little time together!* She pressed her hands against her face and wept silently, for all she had ever known of tenderness, man's tenderness. Daidalos had loved her; to him her body had been more than a way to get sons. Their Ikaros had been made in joy. She would never dare hold him in her arms or on her lap again, but he was safe. He was surely safe! He was with his father, and Daidalos was clever. . . .

But Ariadne—the only child she had ever been able to keep and enjoy. To know. Whether Ariadne had to lie with her brother or her father, her lot would be cruel. And she might have to lie with both. The new child too—if it was a girl, how her father would hate her! *O Goddess, help them both if that must be! Whether it is or not, help Ariadne—help her! If You have any power left to help. . . .*

On the mainland, in the strong house of Erechtheus, Antiope stirred beside Theseus. Said drowsily: "What is it that only a woman born in Athens may see? Or hear? You never did tell me."

He laughed. "How should I know? I am no woman, and I was not born in Athens."

She laughed too, nuzzling her cheek against his. "You are no woman—that I know well! But what is this Mystery?"

"I am not sure. It happens on the Night of the Opening of the New Wine. All that night"—he grinned—"we kings are kept busy, opening—and sampling—the wine. The queen is alone in the God's House with the God. With Dionysos of the Marshes. Him who gives us wine—and other things."

"Must the king drink all night long? Never join her there?"

"He must. But inside the innermost shrine is said to be a wooden image of the God. One with the horned head of a bull, and between its legs a third horn."

Antiope made a face. "Well, I am glad I was not born in Athens! Such lovemaking would not be pleasant. But what does the queen hear?"

"Who knows?" Theseus rubbed his face against hers. "Queens should have their little secrets. Besides"—his face sobered, grew grim—"I think the whole thing was a compromise made with Crete long ago. That the Queens of Athens might not have to sleep with a visiting Minos or his emissary as the Isle-Queens often do. We Kings of Athens like to get our own sons! As I do!"

"I know that too." They both laughed, he feeling no irreverence. That wooden bridegroom was not Poseidon. He was the God of Crete, and should have stayed there. Athens needed no Cretan Gods. Yet to get rid of Him might be even harder than getting rid of Minos, Theseus thought suddenly. Once people got used to a God He was harder to conquer than any king. . . .

Yet before Antiope slept she thought: *I was in a hurry, and foolish. I forgot how little time means to You, Lady. My daughter will not be lonely, for my girls too will have daughters—and keep on having them. Soon there will be a new kind of woman in Athens. They will be greatly outnumbered, but they will be strong.*

But Theseus lay awake, and his hands itched for Asterion's throat. He should have gone to Troizen long ago; but his old father had needed him—had clung to him like a child. Also—he had not wanted to admit to himself that he had hated to face Pittheus and Aithra. But as soon as warm weather came he must go; his ship-building must be put off no longer. Ships—ships with which to fight Minos!

CHAPTER 3.
___BIRTH

G AMELION CAME and went, the Marriage Moon. Anthesterion came, the Moon of Flowers, when the murdered Son of the Maid first stirs in His sleep below. When the first flowers of spring push their way up through the hard black earth, sometimes even through the whiteness of lingering snow. The precious lump inside Antiope grew bigger and bigger, it stuck farther and farther out in front of her, and one day Theseus said uneasily, "You will need women with you at the birth."

"I will have my Amazons."

"They would not know how to help you. They have never had babies themselves."

"They are all going to have them now; your men have seen to that. We will learn by helping each other."

"No. I want experienced women with you. Besides, the noble ladies of Athens are supposed to see every future king of Athens born. They did not see my birth—they must see my son's." She was queen enough to see the point of that last argument, he knew, little as she might care for her own danger.

She did see it. She said, "Well, let them come and watch, then, but only my girls must touch me. They want me to keep on living." She told him of the poison plot then, though she did not name the murderous ladies; he could only have made himself unpopular by punishing them. He listened in horror. He wanted skilled care for her, and surely most of the noble ladies could be trusted, but which ones?

He was still wondering what to do when one of the Amazons was brought to bed. Her unskilled comrades, scared as they never would have been in battle, managed to save both her and her baby, a girl. She was apologetic—surely her queen should have been the first to give birth—but Antiope praised her for having gone ahead on scout duty, so to speak. "The rest of us will profit greatly by what we have learned on you."

Two days later they needed that learning. In the cold red beauty of dawn Antiope woke sharply, dreaming that a spear had pierced her in battle. But there was no battlefield, she saw no foes. Only Theseus, sleeping peacefully beside her. Nobody could have got at her with a spear. And then again it tore her—that deep, savage thrust of pain. She understood then and smiled proudly; this was no enemy who came. But her face was gray and wet with the sweat of pain when Theseus finally yawned and woke. He took one look at her and started, paling beneath his tan. "The baby—is he coming?"

"I will not get her out before noon. Let my girls have their sleep out."

But Theseus sprang up shouting, and the Amazons woke, hands darting weaponward as of old. To face again this new kind of night attack against which weapons were useless.

Antiope made no more fuss than she would have on any other battlefield. In silence she bore the savage onslaught; but to bear one spearthrust is hard, let alone many, and the pains kept on and on, relentlessly. Noon brought no birth; all day the cruel attacks kept up. Her girls hung over her in helpless fear, while the noble ladies of the Butadai and the Eteobutadai sat in sour silence, offended. They had no desire to tend this outrageous outland woman, but they were insulted because they were not allowed to. They made worried servants bring them cakes and wine, and were very bored.

Only when the sky flamed red with sunset did Antiope have a brief, blessed respite, and she dozed, exhausted. But all night she had none, nor did her Amazons. They searched every inch of the house for magical knots, such as spiteful women weave to hinder birth. They climbed up into the rafters and finally out onto the roof itself, vainly trying to find what they were sure the ladies must have managed to hide. They shot grim glances at those haughty, indifferent matrons of the Butadai and the Eteobutadai. And still Antiope's fruitless agony went on.

Theseus too paced up and down, in agony himself. By nightfall he would gladly have given up his longed-for son if he could have been sure of keeping his wife. When the second dawn was near he made a decision and set his jaw. Even if Antiope's would-be murderesses were here, they would hardly dare play tricks under the eyes of the others, and she must have skilled help—she must!

"Girls," he said, "you have tried hard, but you are young, and know little of these things. Leave your queen now to those who have been mothers of many."

Sullenly the ladies moved forward, not glad of their triumph. Many thought, *How dare he—how dare he!—bid us, the chaste and highborn, to tend his spear-won slave.*

The Amazons glared like mother animals fearing for their young. But Antiope said wearily, "Let them come. Maybe they do know something we do not." If they did they would not use it to help her—she was sure of that—but there must be no strife between Theseus and her girls. That was all that mattered now; she had done all she could, and she was very tired. . . .

So her Amazons drew back, they who would have died for her. They even felt a sneaking relief. After all, this was business for older women; back in Themiskyra the mothers and the grandmothers would have handled it.

Old Lysidike, the most skilled midwife there, said to Theseus: "Go, Lord; this is no place for men. These girls must go too; their ignorance has done harm enough already."

Six hands flew to six knives, suspicion reborn. The Hive-Spirit warned Antiope; told her what they felt. Her voice rang clear as of old. "My girls must stay! They are my friends—my sisters—" But it was not of her own need she thought.

Lysidike said sternly: "Be still, woman. We know what is best for you."

Antiope ignored her. "Theseus, my girls must stay! Or I—will —fight these women." Her pain-hazed eyes did not see the grim spark that briefly lit Lysidike's.

In the end only Theseus left, heartsick and afraid, but sure he had done the best he could. The Amazons had sworn by their Goddess, and by the Gods of Athens, not to move, to do nothing unless the ladies bade them do it. Miserably they waited in the far end of the outer room, like children put in a corner.

The ladies stood over Antiope. She was in their power now, laid low by the pain that makes all women helpless. A few gloated, in some pity stirred. After all, by helping her could they not show her their own strength, this proud, insolent Amazon? If with one word, one look, she had asked for help—but she did not. The two old sisters, Alexandra and Theodora, were the only Athenian ladies who were not utter strangers to her, and they were not there. Because of their age they had not been summoned, and before these others she lay silent, pride stiffening her face into a mask, though nothing could keep her body from writhing in the pain of its unavailing battle.

Lysidike said, "We must stretch her."

Many shrank—especially those few who themselves had been stretched and had survived. One said, "That may kill her."

"To save the child is our duty."

All agreed. That was true; the unborn might be a man-child and the mother was only a woman.

Two ladies took Antiope by the right arm, two by the left. Four more seized her legs—those long legs she had displayed with such brazen wantonness. Others grasped her around the middle. With all their strength they pulled and hauled, as if to tear her already pain-racked body in two, to rip it apart. Gasping, Antiope came up out of unbelievable agony, blood from her bitten lips running down her chin. To hear a voice say "One!" and then to lie quivering, knowing nothing except that this new torture was over.

But then it came back—like hungry beasts they pounced upon her, tearing her. . . .

"Two." She heard the counting voice and knew it for a lady's; thought she understood. Theseus and her girls were gone, cleverly got rid of, and would never know that she had been tortured to death. Well, these monsters shaped like women should not have the joy of hearing her scream. . . . Then once more agony blotted out all else, but her training held. More blood ran down her chin.

"Three."

"Four."

This was what these Greeks called the *sparagmos,* the tearing in pieces of the holy victim. She was back at the Thesmophoria, and this time she herself was the captured quarry. Bits of her would rot in those great jars, down in the dark. But there would be no screams. This time they had caught an Amazon.

"Five."

A lady, looking down at the sick convulsed young face, said uneasily, "She can never bear it ten times."

Antiope heard and understood. To be stretched ten times was the last desperate measure taken to make a Greek woman give birth. She had heard of it, but only as the fearful way used to start forced labor. Now it was being used to torment her to death—and Theseus thought that these so-called women were trying to help her. Even her girls—if she cried for help, might they not think she was only screaming in the pains of childbirth? Like these weakling not-women who were not Amazons?

For the sixth time it came—that rending agony which was unbearable yet which somehow she must bear—and this time she did scream. But her cry was the war-cry of her people: "HIP-PO-OL-Y-TE-E-E! To me, Amazons!"

And her Amazons came. They sprang upon the ladies, they seized and shook them as dogs shake rats. Their hard fingers sank claw-deep into soft, pampered flesh. Their eyes rejoiced in the sight of terrified, purpling faces, their ears in half-strangled gasps and moans. But before they could kill, Antiope's voice came; she was thinking again. "Stop, girls! Do not—hurt them. Throw—them—out."

Most Amazons had ladies by the throat, and by the throat they dragged them. Others dragged their prey by a foot, or by the hair. They opened the door that gave upon the stairway; they hurled their captives out and down. . . .

The noble ladies of the Butadai and the Eteobutadai rolled downstairs. Their backs and bottoms smacked hard against the hard steps; with great bumps they landed on the stone floor below. A cry rose from the men there. Theseus raced upstairs, but the Amazons slammed the door in his face and barred it, ready to hold their betrayed queen's quarters like a fort.

Theseus pounded on the door and yelled. He ordered them to open the door and let in women who knew what they were doing. "Would you kill your queen, you mad bitches? Slay those who alone can save her? Open! Or all of you shall die!"

The Amazons paid no heed. Through that palace built by men, for men, rang again the battle cry of the free north: "HIP-pol-y-TE-E-E. HIP-PO-OL-Y-TE!" When a log meant for firewood came crashing against the door, they ran to seize furniture and pile it up as a barricade. Theseus bellowed more threats.

They roused Antiope from her swoon. She staggered up, pushing away the girls who bent over her, and tottered to the door. Through the tumult her trained voice rang, bell-clear again: "Theseus, stop! Girls—my man. Be still—both of you—"

She fell against the door then. There, in a last rending spasm of agony, her baby was born. The newcomer, being a strong child and already much disturbed, managed to let out an angry, gasping cry; it soon did better. Outside the log dropped. While Theseus hammered the door with both fists, his frantic demands to be let in mingling with his offspring's outraged yells, the Amazons somehow managed to get the birth cord cut and Antiope back to bed, her howling baby beside her. Father and child together were making as much noise as Antiope's warrior training had kept her from making. But when at last the Amazons did let Theseus in, he hugged them all and they hugged him, all wrath forgotten; and from her bed Antiope smiled weakly upon all. Then old Aegeus came, eagerly asking the question that Theseus had forgotten to ask. Neither parent yet knew the answer, and most of the Amazons had been too busy to notice. But when one did answer the grandfather, somewhat ruefully, he beamed like the full moon. His son had a son!

Antiope's long-dreamed-of daughter was only a dream. But now that she had him in her arms her boy seemed as good as any girl, and exactly what she wanted because he was exactly himself. But when Theseus gingerly reached out to touch the brownish fuzz that one day would be the color of her own hair, she feebly tried to make a face. "If he had been a girl he would have had sense enough to be redheaded." But Theseus grinned and said proudly: "Wife, you make a fuss about nothing. He is fine—he could not be better!"

In the strong house of Erechtheus all was joy and good will. But the ladies of the Butadai and the Eteobutadai limped home forgotten, but not forgetting. Theseus' newborn son had already lost any chance he had ever had of being acknowledged as heir of Athens. Their hearts were not softened when later the young father sent them rich gifts. He still believed that they had done their best to help Antiope, and that her frightened, loyal Amazons had misunderstood their good intentions. Antiope did not try to disillusion him; it was only good kingcraft to try to appease these wives of his greatest nobles. What if the gifts were wasted? In her happy pride she felt sure that her son's greatness would sweep all before it, whoever plotted against him.

In the darkness of their first night together she hugged her baby and whispered: "It is you who will set women free, little king. Give them the wide world, and air and wind enough to blow away all this spite and meanness that come of being kept small. The work will be far easier for a man. Why could I not see that? Oh, Goddess, how wise You were!" Suddenly, for the first time, she understood the meaning of those words spoken beside the dark river. "No bond binds Me, not even sex." Like a great light it burst upon her. "You are our Mother, Virgin who bore all. But men too came forth from You, so manhood must be a part of You . . . You are Lord as well as Lady, and more. You are a Mystery beyond human understanding."

Next day the young parents spoke of a name for their child. Antiope said: "Why not call him Anthos, or Anthas? He was born in Anthesterion, the Moon of Flowers."

Theseus said thoughtfully, "My mother had an uncle called Anthas—"

"And think what befell him!" old Aegeus cried in fear. "They always come to bad ends, these young Flower Princes. Their lives are short, even now when most men have grown too civilized to offer up their own sons to angry Gods. Death or exile is their lot."

"But the son of Mother's mother's mother was not driven out of Troizen, father. He left in peace, many other young men with him, to found a new town far away, because our people had grown too many for our own sweet plain. He died king of that town, old and prosperous and honored like a God."

"Yet in exile—far from the land of his birth!" What seemed an inspiration came to Aegeus—one that should lay the wrath of the Serpent King forever, if any yet lingered in that stern ghost. "Name your boy Kekrops, my children—no man ever has done as much for Athens as he did, that greatest of teachers!"

Antiope stiffened; her eyes flashed. Her mouth began to open, and Theseus needed no Hive-Spirit to tell him what was going to come out of it: "Name my child for that enslaver of women—that slimy, shameless teacher of lies and iniquity!" He spoke hastily, before she could, yet with what to him too seemed inspiration. "Let us honor the mother of my son, Father—her who has given us this good gift. His name shall be Hippolytos: Horse-Looser— He of the Galloping Horses! That is a good name for a king."

He meant well; to object would be ungracious. Yet deep within Antiope the memory of old times twisted like a knife—Horse-Looser should be a queen's name, not a king's. *Is that too to be taken from us?* Then she smiled her thanks to Theseus.

All of them forgot that in the Greek tongue "Horse-Looser" meant also "Horse-Loosened"—the one torn to pieces by horses.

That was a fair, smiling spring. During its sweet warmth Theseus sailed across the little blue Sea of Saron to visit Troizen. He knew that he should have gone long ago, to see his kin, and now he wanted to show off his wife and son; also he had other plans. And all went as he had hoped. Pittheus and Aithra gave their guests a great welcome, and said nothing to Theseus of what was over and past, of those sons he had not brought home to their parents. Yet somehow, that first night in Troizen, while Antiope and the baby slept peacefully beside him, Theseus kept seeing those four bereaved faces in the darkness. *How would I feel if through somebody's haste and anger I lost him—my little Hippolytos?*

But what was done was done; his shipbuilding was what mattered now, and that depended on the young men of Troizen. The mountains of Attica were wooded too, but here there were no spying sons of Pallas. . . . And his old comrades hailed him with delight—he was their pride and their darling, the slayer of many tyrants, the captain who had sailed farther, to stranger places, than any man born south of the Isthmus. At first a few of them were stand-offish, remembering Euneos and Hermos and Thoas, who had been their friends too, but his glory and his friendliness soon melted them. Soon all agreed to cut down Troizen's lofty green pines and build ships—all for a share in the glory and the golden loot he had not yet won. At first the greatness of his plans took their breaths away, but, after all, the Godlike glory of Minos had faded a little since for all his huge fierce host he had failed to breach the walls of Athens. Why should not their great Theseus be able to overwhelm mighty Crete, he who had already done so much? And if they helped him do it, they too would be heroes.

That visit was the first of many happy, friendly times. Since no Amazon ever had been married before, Antiope had heard no evil tales of mothers-in-law. Only a fine woman, she thought, could have borne her Theseus, and Aithra was equally ready to like this lovely, boylike girl who was making her son happy . . . who, the wise, ageing eyes saw, was not altogether happy herself. Unmarried and a queen in her own right, Aithra knew that she too would have found little friendship among the ladies of Athens. Between the two women love and respect flowered swiftly.

Antiope also liked the simple ways of little Troizen. What if the young women did ape the silly fashions of Crete and the great cities? Surely they would grow up to be like their mothers, shrewd, capable housewives who ruled in their own homes. To be able to leave the fields to men was not a bad thing, and most of these men of Troizen did not seem to be overbearing. Troizen, though not perfect, was still a good place. Her man's kin and the folk they ruled were good people.

"Women are women here," she said once. "Not ladies." She meant that as a compliment, and Aithra, after one startled stare, understood and smiled. . . .

It would be good, Antiope thought, if Hippolytos did a good deal of his growing up here in Troizen. She would never see a city of free women again, but he would—he would make one! And through ages yet to come women of the West would praise and bless his name as their deliverer's. . . . He would need a wife to help him. But the royal alliances that Theseus would foolishly plan for him would never do. He should marry a daughter of one of her Amazons, though perhaps a girl of Troizen would do. And then lightninglike the thought flashed through her—what if he were to take a royal Cretan wife? In Crete women must still remember their old freedom, secretly long for it, and also such a marriage would make him seem Crete's rightful king, not only the son of its conqueror. What a pity that Ariadne, the daughter of Minos, was several years older than he!

She talked of that idea with both Aithra and Pittheus, who told her that Queen Pasiphae was with child again. Her heart leaped then—surely it would be a girl; this was another wise plan of the Goddess. . . .

Old Pittheus puzzled her at first. He was wise, but not in the same way that Subbiluliuma, her father, was wise. His was a kind of wisdom she had never seen before. She rejoiced when he told her that no true God or Goddess ever craved blood, though lesser and lower Powers often thirsted for it, and masked themselves as Gods, beguiling men and women.

"Then I was right to hate the slaying of horses before the Black Stone. The Goddess Herself does not want it!"

"Child, the Gods are whole and need nothing. They give, but never take."

She breathed deeply, feeling old bonds fall away from her. "That is good to know, Grandfather. I will teach it to my son."

"If you teach him all you plan to teach him you will make him a greater conqueror than your father is, or than his own ever will be. Peace too has its battlefields, child; sometimes they can seem as hard as those of war."

She said suddenly and gravely: "Grandfather of Theseus, why did not you, who are so wise, teach him more? Then there would not have been so much for Hippolytos to do."

Wise Pittheus sighed. "Child, all of us climb a stairway, and it is high, and the climbing slow. Each stair brings the climber closer to the light, yet from it he can see only so much. I thought I knew on which stair Theseus must stand. I taught him more of pity and justice than any other king's son on this shore knows—all I thought he could use. But no man can know much for certain; no man is yet a God."

"I see. Well, the next step on those stairs is for Theseus' son to take—for my son, whom I will teach! To his Cretan princess he will be such a lover as his father is to me, but he will also understand how she feels."

Theseus would never fully understand her, she knew that now. But here in Troizen she could go everywhere with him, share his work and plans as she never could in Athens. Day after day they rode out together in his chariot, which now she was used to not driving. Sun-bronzed young shoulder pressing against sun-bronzed young shoulder, they watched the great trees fall and his ships begin to rise. Often they helped with the work; the men of Troizen were used to building only fishing boats, so new designing was needed, new shaping and planning. Theseus and Antiope would help carry logs down to the shore and try to think how to place them. "This should go here—that should go there—no, back here again!" They would scramble among the doubtfully placed timbers, thinking gleefully how one day these clumsy wooden skeletons would be monsters far more huge and terrible than lions —monsters to eat up the crushing power of Minos the God-King! It had a heady, winelike loveliness, that shared scheming and dreaming, their young minds afire with hope, their young bodies often ending by being afire with the loveliness of each other. In bed they would whisper long into the night, their arms about each other, until whispers turned to kisses. Until he found the now familiar but unfailingly rapturous way between her thighs. Then, when love was over, they would sink together into the soft depths of strength-renewing sleep.

Antiope knew nothing of shipbuilding, but she knew that conquest is not an end, that peace must be not only won but held, and Theseus learned all she had ever known of Subbiluliuma's ways in both war and peace. She was widening his horizon, even as he had narrowed hers. More and more the thought of all those leagued cities enthralled him; but the conquest of Crete must come first.

"Can Minos really be fool enough to leave that gold-packed isle of his unguarded all summer? With the terrible pirates of the Lukka so near? They *are* near—my grandfather has maps."

Antiope laughed. "Minos holds the seaports of the Lukka lands —those terrible pirates are his own men."

Theseus frowned. "It is said that the first Minos quarreled with his brother Sarpedon, who fled from Crete to found a kingdom among the Lukka. But he was his brother's foe, not his brother's man."

"That tale is ill told. And for reasons it is easy to guess. The Cretans do not want you Westerners to know how much they too suffered during the first years after the Great Darkness. Their ash-poisoned fields grew few crops, so Minos was glad to give his brother men and ships to seize lands elsewhere. Yet I do not know"—now Antiope frowned—"how he had ships to spare then. All Crete's great fleet must have been lost in the Great Darkness."

Theseus laughed harshly. "No. Your Hittites are an inland folk, but all seafaring men of the East say that the open sea was far safer

than any harbor. That my grandfather has told me. All ships in
port were destroyed, but since the Great Darkness came in midsummer no Cretan ships were so caught."

"I see. The weight of white-hot ash that fell upon them must
have sunk many, but not all."

"Always the sea helps Crete!" Theseus ground his teeth. "In
summer, Boreas, God of the North Wind, guards her from all
northern foes. Makes their sails useless—makes men row hard
against His might. But when my ships are ready my Father Poseidon will send me the wind I need! Then Minos will learn who is
master—he and that Asterion who would have ravished you! Then
those bulls that have gored Athenian children will be roasted and
butchered. They will fill Athenian bellies!"

Who was Poseidon? Antiope wondered. Probably one of those
lesser, lower Powers of whom wise Pittheus had spoken. Nothing
she had heard of Him sounded like any aspect of the Goddess. But
Theseus' faith in this extra father of his was a thing precious to
him; it must not be disturbed.

She said gravely: "Kill Minos and Asterion, but not too many
other Cretans. My father will starve Mitanni into submission, but
once it submits he will send wagons of grain into the city to feed
the people. And many of them will be so glad to get something
to eat that they will be grateful to him who starved them, blaming
only their own lords for their woe. Few love the defeated."

"That last is surely so! My father would not have lived long if
many Athenians had not feared the sons of Pallas."

He meant Aegeus this time, Antiope thought. She said: "Remember too how great Crete's queens were of old. It would be a
good thing for Hippolytos to marry a Cretan princess. It might
even help him in Athens, where people dislike me."

Theseus laughed. "Once I have conquered Crete, none will dare
to dislike anything that is mine! Yet"—his eyes narrowed—"in
Crete such a marriage might serve us well."

Her arrow had gone home. Antiope knew that and was content.
Yet she was also his woman, and now she laughed aloud in joy and
pride. "You have not one whole ship yet, and Minos has hundreds,
yet already you see yourself as his conqueror. There is no other
man on earth like you."

Her face was shining; she held out her arms without even knowing that she did so. Answering flame leaped in his eyes. Then and
there, on that white beach, he took her. Love was the one vent for
the high bright fire that surged through both of them, and neither
would forget that hour as long as either lived.

That evening Theseus talked with Aithra. "Mother, we must go
back to Athens soon. Will you come with us? Just for a little while
—I know you cannot leave Troizen long. I know Father would be
glad to see you, Mother."

But Aithra shook her head. "I am middle-aged now, and your
father has grown old. I am not the young girl he remembers, nor
is he the great splendid man who came to Troizen long ago. Better
that we two remember what we had."

"But many couples comfort each other in old age, Mother."
After that afternoon Theseus felt sorry for his father.

"Child, the years that might have bound your father and me
together we have spent apart. Nor could it have been otherwise.
I am queen in Troizen, he is king in Athens."

How good, Theseus thought, that that old way of life that still
bound her had been trampled underfoot by most men of today!
He thanked all the Gods that he had carried Antiope off; she was
happy, she had no regrets.

"Greet your father for me. And do not stay away so long again,
child. Your grandfather is old, and I grow no younger."

"I will come, Mother. I must see to my ships."

She smiled somewhat wryly. "Yes, child. I need not have asked.
You will come to see your ships."

Summer had left the mainland, the leaves were fire-red, when
in Crete a child was born to Queen Pasiphae. Her name was
Phaidra, "Bright One," but her coming brightened few. Her
brother, Asterion, did smile broadly, but King Minos, their father,
drove all men from him. Flame-fierce, he paced up and down,
alone in his splendid, many-columned Hall of the Double Axes.
In the nearby Queen's Megaron, Pasiphae the Queen lay gray-
lipped and weary, among her scared, whispering women. When
the young Ariadne came to see her little sister, she too had to
whisper; no sign of joy in the newcomer must reach the king's ears.

The queen was too weak to nurse her babe, but it throve at the breasts of a healthy slave woman, who loved it like her own flesh, yet also revered it as the Goddess'.

Soon Minos set himself grimly, doggedly, to the getting of another son. But no living child was ever born again to Queen Pasiphae.

CHAPTER 4.

GROWTH AND WAITING

I N THE new moon of the next Thargelion, Antiope woke sharply in the strong house of Erechtheus. Deep night covered all; full of mothers and babes as the big outer room was, she could hear nothing anywhere but the soft, quiet breathing of the sleepers. Yet she had been wakened from sleep as deep, and by something grim and ominous as any bell of warning. How and why? All her girls and their babies were safe outside, and Theseus slept beside her. She knew the sound of his breathing now, as well as she did that of his voice. She knew her son's too, where he slept in his well-made little bed in the doorway between the rooms.

All must be well, and yet—

Through the varied darknesses of that familiar room that night always made mysterious, the thick blacknesses of walls and furniture loomed up grimly. Through the thinner darkness of Night's self, her eyes searched until they found the moonlit window.

Something half-blocked that window: a massive, rounded shape, squatting there monstrously between her and the light. For one breath's space her heart did not seem to beat, but pounded against the chest that held it, like the futile, frightened leap of a trapped animal.

Then she saw that the Thing was only an owl. Huge enough, but shaped like other owls; no monster. She half smiled, both relieved and ashamed. "I am getting as silly as the Women." For so she and her Amazons, using the Greek word, now not unnaturally called all the women of Athens, including the highborn ladies who would, they knew, have been annoyed by it. Again she stared through the darkness, weak enough to want to make the creature seem wholly of earth. Great red eyes burned savagely in the night-blackened head, above the mighty, cruel beak, and her heart jerked painfully, then steadied again. Those eyes were not meeting hers; they glared at the whole bed, at the two bodies lying on it together, as if they found that sight an outrage. They flamed with unspeakable hate. . . .

She thought dizzily, *I must be dreaming,* and tried to open her eyes, but they were already open. She tried to move, but could not; the horror of those hating eyes held her fast. She could only lie there, staring at the Thing that stared, not at her, but at the two of them —Theseus and herself—together. . . .

And then Hippolytos screamed.

Shrieks that shattered the silence, the dread majesty of night. Wholly human, they beat against the darkness, a child's awful, mind-consuming screams of utter fear. Normally the first would have made Antiope leap out of bed, but now she lay where she was, and the owl sat where it was, and neither moved.

It was Theseus who started up, wrenched out of his sleep, and went to his son. Through her entranced stillness Antiope heard his half-growling, yet soothing murmur, heard the screams sink into low, broken sobs that could not stop yet, although now the child felt safe. Theseus carried him back to the big bed, then froze as he saw the Thing in the window. "By the Dog! Was that it?"

All in one swift movement he stooped, laid the child down beside her, snatched up a sandal, and threw it at that black, still shape. There was no startled squawk, such as would have burst from any true bird. The Thing seemed to waver, then vanished, as soundlessly as mist-shapes vanish when touched.

Antiope, freed, rolled over and put her arm around her small son. Theseus lay down beside them, and both tried to comfort their boy. They thought sight of that great black shape in the window must have frightened him—it had been a sight to bring fear—but he only clung to them and sobbed: "Dark! All dark. 'Pol't couldn't see. . . ." All the babies were crying now; sleepy, bewildered Amazons were hushing them. When at last all was quiet again, Hippolytos slept, but with his back still pressed hard against Antiope's warm breast and belly, and a small hand clutching as much as it could of one of Theseus' big hands.

"I wonder why he did not say 'bird,' " Theseus mused. "He knows the word. I have heard him use it."

"Our bed is higher than his," said Antiope. "Perhaps he could not see it, only felt that all light was cut off from him." In spite of herself she shuddered, and Theseus felt her do it, and chuckled.

"So you were scared too, my warrior wife? Well, I am glad that wise Pittheus taught me not to fear such things—see omens in them. That was the biggest owl I ever saw. I wish that sandal had hit it; I would not like for it to come back . . . better if the boy did not see it."

Antiope hoped with all her heart that the owl had not seen Hippolytos. Theseus soon slept again, but she lay awake, staring into the shining emptiness of the window. That had been no true owl, hatched in an earthly nest. Those eyes had held human, or more than human, hate. She shuddered again, remembering old tales of Amazon wise women who had left their sleeping bodies and gone wandering, in the forms of beast or bird. They had used that power to spy out enemies in their people's path, or to find needed food or water, sometimes even someone who was lost. . . . Molpadia! *Could you have won such power, Mother's sister? Grieving for me who am lost to you—longing to find and save me. Willing yourself to win it, you whose will is so strong?*

No—that could not be, thank the Goddess! Active women never had that power; only those who were crippled, or too old to ride to war. Few even of them ever had it, only one or two in a generation. Yet Molpadia's will was very strong. . . . Did not many people believe that witches gained great power by sacrificing their nearest and dearest? Molpadia and Lysippe—each had brought death to a child born of her. And Lysippe had had such power. . . . Could it have been the nearness of Molpadia's hate, not the pitlike darkness that she hoped had hidden him, that had made Hippolytos scream?

O Goddess, do not let her have seen him!

A fool's prayer. Either that had already happened or it had not. Had the terrible burning eyes been fixed on the bed alone, or had their gaze been wide enough to see what Theseus carried? Had the Thing heard as well as seen?

And if Molpadia had come tonight, did she now believe her

niece a victim or a traitress? A willing slave, or one who bore degradation quietly, still hoping for freedom, even as Lysippe had before her? Either way, what could Molpadia do? Could a bird's eyes choose landmarks, map out a road from sea to sea, all the long way from Themiskyra to Athens? A road bound to be full of foes. *Whether you love me or hate me now, Molpadia, you still love our people. You will not lead our whole race to death and destruction for my sake.*

No, never would Molpadia do that!

Nor could the Deathsinger herself take vengeance, however great her wrath. The beaks and talons of such phantom shapes were not strong enough to tear living flesh. At least no old tale gave them such might.

Yet for many nights thereafter Antiope slept uneasily, when she slept at all. Often she lay awake, stiff and tense, eyes fixed on that moon-silvered window that grew brighter and brighter as the moon grew full, dimmer and dimmer as the moon waned. But neither in brightness nor in dimness did that grim black shape ever squat there again. Gradually her fears dimmed too and grew dreamlike. Nothing would happen; nothing could happen.

The heat of summer passed. The trees blazed like torches, lighting the Maid's way down to Her terrible Lord in the darkness. The grim winter winds came, and the white snow; then once more the green gentleness of spring. And in all that time only two things of importance happened: Theseus' ships rose, putting on hulls and keels and masts; and his son grew. The baby did a great many other things, often too many; only sleep could keep him still. But in his doting grandfather's eyes he could do no wrong; in fact, he could not do much in anybody's. By now every Amazon had her own baby, and most had two, yet the big soldier-girls came near fighting over him. He was their queen's baby, and as beautiful as morning. Whenever Theseus said they spoiled him Antiope answered: "They know better than to let him have whatever he wants whenever he wants it, as your father always does. As you generally do." Which was true.

He needs a brother, Theseus sometimes thought, yet was not really sorry that the boy remained his only son. His wife's first childbed had scared him badly. Also Antiope's innocent belief that what was sauce for the goose was sauce for the gander had inconvenienced him. By his own choice he had not lain with her during

the last heavy moons of her pregnancy, but he had not enjoyed
his celibacy. Of course she neither would nor could kill him if she
caught him lying with another woman; that had been all talk. But
what if she should take it into her head that such action on his part
left her free to lie with another man?

That last spring Antiope did think, as she had the one before:
*We could start a little sister for Hippolytos now. But it is hard on Theseus—
and I will not give any of those poisoning bitches a chance at him!* After all,
she had already given him his longed-for son and heir. She did not
know that nobody outside the palace looked upon her son as the
heir of Athens. Theseus had not dared to take his boy to the
Apaturia, that yearly feast at which all new-made Athenian fathers displayed their sons to their clan brothers. By then he had
known that his clansmen would not accept his son, and why. If
Antiope had known, he thought grimly, she might have stopped
talking about how much power women needed. Certainly the
women of Athens already had too much.

*But all will be different when I have conquered Minos. Then none will dare
to deny my son his birthright.* So he told himself, his eyes flashing, his
jaw set.

So far, Hippolytos himself was aware of only one lack in his life:
size. There were so many things a boy could not do until he was
bigger. So many things that could not be climbed or handled, used
or investigated, because they might hurt him, or he might hurt
them. He had many good times playing with the other little half-
Amazons, but there was so much else to do, so much other fun to
be had, if only one were not little. He longed for the lovely, shiny,
sharp things that Father and the Amazons played with. Sometimes
they pretended to let him play too; but always their hands were
around his hands or over them; they were not really letting him
do anything. Father was worst of all about that, Father who in all
other ways was the most splendid playmate in the world. When
Mother would not let Hippolytos do something she simply said so;
she knew how he hated to be fooled. There were plenty of things
that, like all grown-ups, she did not understand and had no sense
about, but she did understand that. Sometimes Mother was very
nice.

Best of all, better than anything else in the world, were the times
when Mother took him driving in her chariot (Antiope had one

now, as well as the wagon). Their wild, all but winged swiftness
was joy as far above all joys as the stars were high above his head.
He did not mind the bumps. He did not even mind keeping still,
as for once a good deal of him had to do, because Antiope, having
to have both hands free, had devised a kind of comfortably padded
leather harness that hung from her shoulder and held him. It
brought his small hands high enough to grasp the chariot's front,
and so gave him a little illusion of doing something, sharing in her
activity. He never tried to wriggle out of the harness; he fully
understood that staying in it was the price of his joy. In the hard
world of the Amazons such understandings between mother and
child had always had to be established early, so early as to be
perhaps half telepathic. Besides, one did not need to move when
the great, glorious white horses were moving so wonderfully.
They made Hippolytos feel as if he and Mother were birds, lifted
up above the world and skimming over it. Going faster than anything down on earth could go. . . .

A child does not remember when it first becomes aware of
summer and winter. But Hippolytos already knew that he hated
winter because it meant less driving. He was very glad when
spring came, but somehow that spring was different. Father said
they were going to Troizen, and Grandfather said they did not
usually go there so early. He seemed surprised and troubled. Hippolytos thought that that was only because Grandfather would
miss him.

He himself was glad to go; he liked Troizen better than Athens.
Grandfather was never there, but Grandmother and Great-Grandfather were, and besides, people in Troizen were very friendly.
Whenever he and Mother went driving there, everybody they
passed waved and called greetings to them, and they waved and
called back. Here at home nobody paid them any attention when
they went, and they paid none to anybody. In Troizen too, whenever visitors came Grandmother brought him to them and showed
him off proudly. While in the strong house of Erechtheus, even if
he and Father were in the middle of an exciting game, the coming
of guests always meant that it would be stopped and he would be
carried off to the rooms that belonged especially to Mother and her
Amazons. He did not know that this was done because Theseus
could not bear for him to be slighted or treated with condescen-

sion; but he did know, vaguely, that the people of Athens did not
like him.

But this spring Troizen was strange and different. People were
busy and in a hurry; they seemed to be too busy thinking about
something else to think much about him. When they first saw him
they made the usual fuss over him, but it seldom lasted as long as
usual. Once he heard that some young men were coming from
Athens, and was surprised and pleased. That had never happened
before, but it probably would mean a feast, and a lot of good
things to eat. He asked when the young men were coming, but
nobody knew; they would have to "be careful." Hippolytos, who
knew so well how tiresome it was to be careful, was glad that for
once it was not he who had to be. But he would have been still
gladder if everything had been the way it always had been before.

Then one morning Mother took him out driving. All was wonderful again, with only him and her and the beautiful, beautifully
moving horses. But they stopped too soon: on the white shore,
beside the blue water. Antiope would have let him down to play
in the sand, but he clung to the rim of the chariot. "No! 'Pol't 'tay
wiv hors-es!"

Antiope was surprised. She had supposed he would like having
room to wiggle; as a rule, he never could get enough. But then,
during these last few days, he had not seen as much of the horses
as usual. She looked at him thoughtfully. "We have been thinking
so much about your future, little king, perhaps we have not
thought enough about you as you are now."

She was thinking only of him, and liking him; Hippolytos understood that much, and chirped agreement in the birdlike, sexless
tongue that seems peculiar to very young children. But then understanding left Antiope again; she picked her son up and held
him high. Out toward the tall new ships that were heavier in the
water now than they had been a few days ago—heavy with the
food and water that would be needed on the way to Crete. . . .

"See, little king. Your father's ships."

Hippolytos felt no interest. Ships were no good unless you were
actually on board one, and could scramble all over it, and see
everything on it. But to humor her he looked at them. At those
queer, big, black shapes, from which black shadows were stream-
ing across the blue water . . . Suddenly he did not like them. Not

only did they keep most uninterestingly still; they made him think of the dreaded, mysterious blackness of night.

Antiope too felt a sudden clutch at her heart: a most un-Amazonlike sick feeling. Soon now those ships would move—they would carry Theseus into battle and leave her behind! Yet she, trained to be a queen, knew that there were good reasons for her to stay behind; much better reasons than her man's foolish belief that women ought not to fight. All the men Theseus trusted, or hoped he could trust, were young men and would be sailing with him. Only she would be left to guard their son and old Aegeus. He would come back—surely neither her Goddess nor his God would let harm befall him! But he might well be gone longer than he expected; conquered territories could not be set in order in a day. She could not make him understand that as she did, she who was Subbiluliuma's daughter. And already the sons of Pallas must know of his planned going—that much must have leaked out. She thanked the Goddess that those young men who were coming did not yet know where they were going, only that they were to follow Theseus into a glorious new adventure.

How easily she could have held Athens for him if his people had trusted her! She would have joyed in it, in using her own wits and strength and courage again, however great the danger. But in matters of importance no man in Athens would ever trust her because she was a woman, and the Women would never trust her because she was herself, not one of them. . . .

She spoke again, thrusting away her bitterness and her half-formed fears.

"Child, those ships will make your father a great king. One who will free many people from fear and pain. But he will not free all. It is you who must do that, a long, long time from now, when you are king. You will free all slaves—even those who are not called slave. You will make men and women friends, little king."

Her little king put his thumb in his mouth. If both he and the lovely swift horses must keep still, he needed some refreshment. Antiope noticed the thumb and took it out. "You must not do that. Your hands are dirty. Why can I never keep them clean?"

Hippolytos ignored her, and looked longingly at the horses. If only she would make them go again! But once more Antiope spoke to the man who was not yet there.

"Your father and mine are alike. In each of them there is a power
—something like a great wind, or a great, flooding river. Something
that can never stop, or be stopped. Yet they are different, too. The
Great King is always cool. Nothing ever carries him away, neither
love nor hate, fear nor wrath. Fear will never carry your father away
—the Goddess knows that! But the other things . . ." She paused,
frowning.

Hippolytos looked at her expectantly. Would she make the
horses go again now? It was surely time!

Antiope said, still frowning: "Your father feels more and thinks
less. But he is the one the poets will sing about. They will make
so many songs about him that maybe, when he is long dead,
foolish learned men will even try to say that he never really lived.
Was only a hero of songs. Is that because he is like the poets, who
sometimes must let themselves be carried away?"

Hippolytos was leaning forward over the front of the chariot;
he had had enough. But Antiope, intent on her thoughts now,
noticed only that he had changed position. She went on: "But I am
afraid it is not right for kings and queens to be. You must never
let yourself be carried away, little king. You must always be cool,
like your Hittite grandfather. Always able to master yourself, as
you will your horses—"

Hippolytos had got hold of the nearer horse's tail. He pulled it,
at first experimentally, then with vigor. Being spirited and unused
to pain, like all horses who were allowed to associate with Antiope, the stallion neighed and reared. His startled teammate joined
in. Antiope gasped, caught her son firmly in the crook of one arm,
and tried to quiet her team. But Hippolytos too was startled. He
yelled and squirmed, and his yells inflamed the already excited
horses. They plunged and reared; the chariot seemed bound to
overturn. Antiope had her hands full; with one hand few men on
either side of that sea could have mastered that rearing, raging
team. When the struggle was finally over and she could put down
her son, she looked sternly at him.

"Your father chose well," she said, almost between her teeth.
"You are rightly named Horse-Looser—"

The future King of Crete and Athens whimpered. He had been
badly scared and shaken up, and now his mother was angry with
him. Antiope stooped and with her free hand tilted up his chin,

so that their eyes met, although she still kept one hand and one eye for the horses.

"Listen," she said, her voice low but stern. "It hurts horses to have their tails pulled. It hurts them. You must never—*never*—pull a horse's tail again."

She was still angry; Hippolytos understood that, although his fear blurred her words. To escape her anger he burrowed into the comfortable, warm softness of her. Burrowing, he was irresistible; Antiope hugged him.

"You would be yelling now if your mother were a lady. Not a hard, fierce warrior woman."

The Amazons had been inexpressibly shocked the first time they had seen an Athenian woman spank her baby's bottom. Theirs was a simple code still reflected in many cultures that show traces of the matriarchal: Violence was for enemies. Foes should be killed as fast and as cheerfully as flies are swatted, but never should one's hands be lifted against one's own.

Hippolytos snuggled against her and relaxed. He was still loved —his brief doubt of that had appalled this small center of his own universe. But he had done something that he had better not do again; although he was not quite sure what it was. His eyes moved longingly back to the horses. To those fascinating tails whose possibilities he had only just discovered. . . . Antiope saw that look and sighed.

"I see that I am going to have to watch you all the time. Without ever stopping. Until you are old enough to have some sense." A conclusion reached by most mothers, whatever their methods. Hippolytos smiled up at her and once more made soft, birdlike noises of agreement; all was well.

But already the Horse-Looser had almost become the Horse-Loosened. And down the years the wilder, more westerly reaches of that same white shore of Troizen waited, their huge, gray rocks grim against the sun. . . .

When they came back to the deep-porched house of Pittheus, Antiope heard that strangers had come. Whether messengers or mere traders, they were few, so she felt small interest. They could not be those young men who were eagerly waiting to drop their tools in their fathers' fields—Thargelion was the Greek harvest moon, a bad time for men to leave home—and come at Theseus' call. And very soon that call would come. He was wild to get his ships provisioned. He had said: "Then I will set sail! Then Poseidon will send me my wind!"

Can you be quite sure of that, Theseus? Cool Hittite Subbiluliuma's part in her could not help asking that. Yet surely it would come; both his God and her Goddess must will it.

But she was tense, unhappy, like all Troizen. The cream of Athens' young manhood would sail, but so would all the young men of Troizen. Already their weapons were burnished and shining, their eyes shone brighter still. Eager, unshadowed, as if all of them would come home. Would *he* come home?

This is foolishness. I am getting as jittery as the Women. There will always be war, and never can all the warriors come home. . . . If only I were going with him!

She went to bed early, hoping that Theseus would soon come to her. Tonight was theirs, but tomorrow night, who knew? He could not sail that soon, but he might be too fiercely busy to come. . . .

The moon rose high, and still he had not. Why? Did he not want her as she wanted him? She began to grow angry, and told herself that that was folly. She must not spoil what time they had left together. No—that had an an unlucky sound. What time there still was before he went away. He would come back—he must, to do the deeds his grandfather had foretold for him. But how could she have thought, this morning, that she could have joyed in holding Athens for him, while he was far away from her and in danger?

Foolishness, more foolishness. This was what came of being shut inside a house. This morning she had been outdoors, tonight she was shut inside, helpless and deedless as the Women. Acting and thinking like them. Fiercely she ordered herself to be sensible, and go to sleep, but could not. There was a darkness on her spirit, as if she felt the approach of some evil thing.

The moon was near to setting when Theseus came at last, quietly, so as not to disturb his wife and boy. But out of the darkness came Antiope's voice, asking the timeless wifely question: "What kept you so long?"

He yawned; she could not see that that yawn was as false as her casualness. "Traders came from the North, from Thessaly. There is fighting there."

"Who is fighting whom?"

"I do not know. I do not think the traders do. I only wanted to make sure that the fighting was too far off to trouble Athens." He yawned again, and she took the hint, and said no more, thinking him sleepy. But when he got into bed his arms closed round her fiercely, and hers round him. For that night, at least, they were still together. . . . From his arms she sank at last, content, into the arms of Sleep, Death's brother. But Theseus lay beside her and felt as if he were caught fast in nightmare as well as darkness, and could not wake.

He had asked them question after question, those traders who were not true traders, but his spies, sent north when he had first heard those wild rumors. Always hoping that each question would bring an answer that would break the black illusion, let him wake. He had let them sleep, then questioned them again, and then he had paced alone in the black night, that to him had seemed moonless and starless.

There was often trouble in the North. Landless younger sons were always dreaming of the golden cities of the South, of Mycenae and Messene. Whenever enough of them came south, by way of the Isthmus, Athens was in for trouble. That had been all he had feared at first, and that would have been bad enough, the Gods knew. This moon, this Thargelion, was his last chance. Unless the whole order of nature were reversed—and he could not expect his Father Poseidon to do that much for him—no south wind would blow again until the beginning of winter. Until Crete's own ships had come home.

And Minos must not collect that tribute again next year—he must not! Father Poseidon, help me! Let me sail!

This year, of all years, when at last his ships were ready—how could he bear not to sail? It must be only raiders—it must! Athens had weathered their storms before, and could again, bad as it would be to leave her. But if—

A whole horde was driving south, they said. A demon horde, in which several men rode in one chariot, and the women were monsters like the fabled Centaurs, half horse, half human. They rode like the wind, screaming like the wind, and killed all they could catch and cut down. They cut off the heads of those they had slain, and drank from the skulls. They were monsters of bloodlust, as well as in shape.

It could not be true. It was mad, lying rumor, growing bigger on every tongue that retold it. Northern women often rode in wagons with their men, and fought beside them; but if the women came, so did the whole tribe, the children and the old. But all swore that in this whole horde there were only killers, mad to kill. . . . Lies, mad, wild rumors spawning madder, wilder lies, but he knew what Antiope would think, if she heard of those women.

The Amazons!

It could not be. They could never have come so far. When that happened a south wind could blow in midsummer.

Yet the Hittites did ride three to a chariot. . . . He had hoped to win the Great King for an ally, had told his people so. Subbiluli- uma had no ships, but he could hire them. Could both his men and the Amazons be coming? Could any of the Thousand Gods of the Hittites have been cunning and wicked enough to devise such a horror, and to laugh at it?

Savagely and silently he prayed, stretching his arms upward in the darkness. "O Father Poseidon, let them come swiftly! Let my heart be eased of this one fear, that is surely a fool's fear. No— that does not matter. I cannot ask You to set aside the laws that all You Gods together must have made to order the world and the seasons, but somehow—somehow—let me sail!"

CHAPTER 5.
THE COMING OF THE HORDE

H E WOKE in the corpse-gray dawn, suddenly and fully alert, though he had heard no sound. He left his wife and boy and went downstairs quietly. In the *megaron* big-eyed servants met him, "Lord, Lord—" Their faces were white with fear.

In the deep porch where long ago he had mistaken Herakles' lion skin for a living lion, he found three gaunt, exhausted men, their faces grayer than the ghostly light, his spies.

"King, you must get home as fast as you can! The foe cannot be many days behind us!"

"They are coming to Athens? You are sure?" To them Theseus' voice sounded quick and firm; to himself it seemed to come from a long way off.

"They come, Lord, they come! They have captives now who can speak Greek, and always these ask, 'Where is Athens?' To him who can tell them the way, they give good gifts—and that most precious gift of all, his own life!"

Theseus felt as if the great rock that once he had lifted to gain his father's sword had fallen upon his own heart. This—just when he was ready to sail for Crete!

"Who are they?" Again, his own voice seemed far away.

"None knows, Lord." One of the men shivered.

I know. His heart cried that, though his mind still rejected the unbelievable. He said, "What is their war-cry? Many must have heard it."

Now all the men shuddered. "Yes, Lord, many. Like the wind the women come, astride horses—faster than the men in their

chariots. And as they come they cry, 'HIP-PO-OL-Y-TE-E-E!'
They cry that as they slay."

The silence that followed was as loud as any cry. Until Antiope's voice broke it. "My people have come for me." Theseus
turned to see her standing in the doorway, her face as rigid as
the golden masks the men of Mycenae put on the faces of dead
kings.

"You heard?" He looked at her.

What she saw in his face made her close her eyes in pain. For
a breath's space only; she was not one to hide from what must
be faced. She opened them again and said, in the royal tongue of
Kanesh: "I am sorry. It will wreck all for you, this war for me."

Against her will, her eyes asked: *Do you regret having taken me?* She
had forgotten that in the beginning he had given her no choice.
But the grandson of Pittheus remembered, as no true Achaian
City-Sacker would have done, and pity burned through his self-
pity. He gave a sudden great laugh, strode to her, and caught her
in his arms.

"It is all your fault, wife, for being so beautiful that I could not
do without you! Let them come—Hittites and Amazons, with all
their Thousand Gods and your Goddess too. All of them put
together shall never take you from me!"

Yet what moved in him then was less the desire of man for
woman—that terrible, man-maddening Eldest Fate whom later
men were to call the Rose-Crowned Lady of Desire—than that
tenderness which is perhaps the noblest gift of the Mighty
Mother, that which She, the Unchanging yet Ever-Changing,
weaves between those who have lived and loved and worked
together. For a breath's space Antiope gave herself up to it, joyed
in it as those dying of thirst joy in fresh water—then she drew
back and looked straight into his eyes.

"Love, since the Hittites too are coming, you will have hard
work to save Athens. But you can buy peace with me, and you
must. Make both Hittites and Amazons swear to take no vengeance if my girls and I are given up whole."

Theseus stared, his face blank with unbelief. "Have you gone
mad?"

"No. We are a king and a queen, you and I; bred to know where our duty lies. You will save Athens, and have it and Hippolytos, and soon Crete too. I will save what is left of my people."

And how many of them would that be? she wondered bitterly. Molpadia must still believe what she wanted to believe: be thinking of her niece both as a miserable slave and as the irreplaceable Childbearer, worth any sacrifice. She must have abandoned Themiskyra itself. Worse even than that, she must have abandoned all who were either too old or too young to make this long, fearful ride. Have left them to the mercy of the Kaska. *O Lady, Whose hopes must all lie shattered as all my joy in life is—how could You let her do it?* Truly the Gods must be bound by Their own laws to let humans do as they would; no matter how many the blasting of one would save from death and slavery. . . .

Like one of the precious eggshell-thin cups made by Cretan potters of old—like such a cup hurled to the ground and shattered —so then her thoughts were shattered. By Theseus' raging voice, Theseus' raging face.

"You want me to give you up? You want to go to those accursed and unholy Holy Groves—to wallow there with the Hittites! Or do you think you need not wait for the groves—that all the way home you can squirm beneath your father's men—!"

This too was like him; this as well as the other. She steadied herself, her eyes seeking his. "All my life my heart will be an aching wound within me. Always I will long for you—and for Hippolytos—"

"Will you? You never wanted him! You wanted a daughter, and maybe you think you will get one now! Even if it takes a thousand thrusting, squirting Hittites to get her into you—as many of them as they have Gods—"

"Theseus, spare us both this nonsense!" Sword-hard, her voice cut through his. "You do not want Athenians to die because of me. Any more than I want Amazons to die."

Theseus trembled. The sky outside was red now, and his eyes shone as red. "Woman, I swear by Poseidon Earthshaker—by Him Who begot me, by Earth the Mother, and by the all-seeing Sun— by Them all I swear that I will never let you go. That if you flee from me I will follow you with all the men who will follow me —alone, if need be—and either bring you back, or die!"

"Theseus—"

"Silence, woman! Else may my old father die, his gray hairs red with blood, and our little son too, foully murdered in his innocence. Never will I shame my city and my people and myself by selling my wife into harlotry. Never again could they respect me if I did, either as king or man—"

Only her long training in self-control kept Antiope from bursting into wild laughter. How could he have chosen such words to justify himself to himself? All Athens thought of her as his spear-won slave—would think no peace ever more cheaply bought. And how the Women would rejoice! To keep back that laughter she pressed her hands hard against her face. Theseus thought she wept, and caught her to him again, held her close.

"Antiope, Antiope! I did not mean those ugly words—I know you love me! But to think of losing you—of all those other men having you—it drove me mad!"

She said very quietly: "Many will die because of your oath, Theseus. Many, both of your people and mine. I am ashamed because part of me is weak enough to be glad you have taken it."

He joyed in that confession; such weakness was proper and womanly. He laughed with triumph, and kissed her fiercely.

In haste they returned to Athens, and Theseus was not surprised to find three sons of Pallas there before him.

"Joy be with you, kinsman," Lykos, the eldest, said easily. "Now that you are here to defend the city and our uncle we can go home to defend our father and Pallene."

How glad they would have been, Theseus thought, if the horde had come before he did—if they had been the only war leaders the men of Athens had had to look to! Well, at least they had courage, these men who were his kinsmen, nearest to him in blood of all men. . . .

He said harshly: "Why should Pallene need help? If the enemy should learn of our kinship, they will surely also learn that Pallas is not his brother's friend."

"Who knows who these mad barbarians will spare?" The second brother's eyes flashed. "You have brought great danger on all Attica, Theseus. You deserve no friends—and you will soon learn you have none!"

Theseus said between his teeth: "Go! Before I forget that we are of one blood."

They went, Lykos somewhat alarmed now and hurrying the other two, but at the door Lykophron, the youngest, stopped. His face, so like Theseus' own, was troubled. "No man may forsake father and brothers, kinsman. Yet I wish you well."

He bit his lip then, sure he had incurred his brothers' wrath for nothing. Theseus would only laugh at him. But Theseus' face flushed with gladness. This was the kinsman he had always felt should have been his friend. He smiled as only he could smile. "Joy be with you, Lykophron! To you alone of all my kin I can say that truly."

But when they were gone, great loneliness fell upon Theseus. Truly he had no friends. He had brought danger on all the eleven other kings of Attica, and not one was likely to see that in unity lay their best chance to save themselves. All his father's kin except Lykophron wanted his heritage, and great Herakles had survived the Twelve Labors only to die in agony, of a brew his jealous second wife had thought a love potion, sure to bind him to her. A mean end for the man no other man ever could have conquered. . . . No man needed forty-nine brothers, but how good it would have been to have had one—to talk to and plan with, as well as to fight beside him! He had Antiope. He could talk to her, plan with her—she had as much sense as any man, and all the Gods knew she would be willing to fight beside him if he would have let her! No, she would not—not against Amazons. She was no longer wholly his, if she ever had been. She loved his enemies. . . . And in many homes in Athens tonight people must be whispering: "Aegeus brought war and death upon us by taking a foreign woman's evil counsel. And now his son brings them upon us again by lusting after another foreign woman. Why could not our daughters have been good enough for him? The daughters of Athens?"

Like a drenched dog coming up out of deep water Theseus shook himself. A man must not whine, he must face his foes and kill them, or be killed.

But, oh, my people, what have I done to you? Next year your children will go to Crete again, to die. And how many of their fathers and brothers must die now?

He buried his head in his hands, knowing that what they would reproach him with was true.

Before dawn he went down to help the farmers. They were swarming in with their families and beasts and—by great good fortune—their crops, just harvested. A besieged city must have food. The children would need milk, and at worst the beasts could be eaten. The people from the lower city were coming in too, and all must be housed. Soon every house, even the strong house of Erechtheus, was packed with as many people as it could hold. The ladies of the Butadai and the Eteobutadai settled in the palace, where they would do their best to annoy Antiope. But for many folk porches had to be built along the inner sides of the walls. Fences had to be built too, to hold in the worried, restless animals. Main gates and postern and the towers that guarded them had to be strengthened. Provisions had to be stored. Even stones had to be piled up, that later they might be hurled upon the besiegers. No man, no woman, child or beast, would have much room to turn around in. It was a time of hard, bitter work, of harder planning. And in the midst of all Antiope came to Theseus. "You must block up the outer entrance to what you call the Cave of Aglauros."

"Why? The men of Minos paid no heed either to it or to the little wooden Stair of the Arrephoroi, which I have blocked up." He had, so grieving the two child-priestesses who used that stair in their yearly rites, and shocking their elders, who had said, "Trust in the Gods—let the little maids serve them." But Theseus meant to take care of those little girls. And when war came, not even the Long Rocks, the formidable, clifflike northwestern slopes of the Akropolis, would be any place for children.

Antiope answered: "Minos the sea king is a hawk used to swooping down on island villages. But I think the Hittites, used to sieges, would soon find those entrances you think inaccessible. I know my people would."

Your precious people, the Gods curse them! What is there they cannot do?— so long as they should not do it! He wanted to yell that at her, but did not. She was trying to help him.

He went down from the Akropolis and looked up, saw that black hole that opened into the Cave of Aglauros staring down at him like a jeering eye. He had it blocked up, and promptly. For the

Holy Cave could not only be used as a way to enter the Akropolis:
into it opened the long, more than night-black passage that led
down and down, by terrible, tortuous ways, to the deeply buried
well that, in time of siege, was Athens' only source of water.
Cretan craftsmen might have been able to build a staircase leading
down into those frightful depths, but for any man born of woman
the task would have been fearful. There even the good limestone
that crowned the Akropolis was made treacherous by the softer,
more earthlike stone below. Mighty as they were, the huge rocks
continually cracked and crumbled. In places great logs, split in
half, served as ramps, in others the water-bearers used ladders.
Into the well itself big jugs and pitchers had to be let down by
ropes, through blackness no torches could fully pierce. If the
enemy found their way into those Underworld-like depths, set
guards between the people and that precious water that was their
very life—!

He thanked Antiope, and was surprised when her face did not
light up. *Anything I do to help him hurts my people, who think I love them.
As I do. Yet how can I not warn him against pitfalls? He is my man.*

Useless as he feared it was, Theseus sent heralds to all the
neighboring cities. He even sent them south into Apia. Eurystheus,
Herakles' unworthy kinsman, was also his; and little as kinship
mattered to Eurystheus, the greatest king was a fool to let a king
from overseas conquer the least city-state on his side of it. What
if the Hittites should decide to stay in Attica, establish a foothold
in the West? But the herald brought back only courteous good
wishes from Eurystheus; his northern kin could take care of themselves.

Only two kings did any better. The boy Hippothoon, his
brother in Poseidon, wanted to help Theseus. But he was young;
he needed time to prevail over his council, the cautious elders of
Eleusis. Yet if they delayed him too long he would set out alone
—and surely many of his young men would not let him get far
alone! "I do not forget who made me king, Theseus my brother."
And King Elephenor of Chalkis said that while his Euboians felt
unwisely safe on their island, many disliked the thought of men
from a great empire of the East settling so near. In time he would
get them to Athens, but probably not before the summer heat
broke. Meanwhile carrier pigeons could pass between him and

Theseus, and if supplies were needed, he would try to smuggle them in. Even such qualified promises warmed Theseus' heart. Only the greatest and richest of kings dared go wholly against their people's will, and neither Elephenor nor Hippothoon was such a king. But he believed in their goodwill, and that was pleasant when so many were reproaching him; the rash youngster whose desire to sleep with a barbarian woman was bringing ruin upon them all. He would have allies if he could hold out long enough. But how long would he have to fight alone? And how hard? How much of his might had Subbiluliuma been able or willing to send overseas? He himself could not have come; that would not have been fair to his own people. Antiope was sure of nothing else.

The day came at last when the men of Athens saw pillars of smoke rising in the north, and knew what must be feeding the fires that smoke rose from—Greek homes, and Greek bodies. Athenians were not dying—not yet—but their neighbors were, men who spoke the same tongue. They had lived near the mountain passes by which invaders usually entered Attica, and which the twelve kings would never unite to defend. Theseus thought of that, with the old exasperated bitterness, but with a deeper pain. *Great bride-gifts do I make people of my own blood pay for you, Antiope, my darling.*

And soon his own people would be paying them.

Then, lightning-swift, lightning-bright, a thought darted through him. He had sent out many heralds; why not send one more—himself? He put on a helmet that would hide his red hair, though not the fine boars'-tusk one the Amazons might remember. He called the young men he trusted most, and had them ready their chariots, and his own. To his father he said, "I am going to find out the cause of those fires to the north," and old Aegeus said, "Be careful, my son. Though Minos cannot be coming that way —he would come by sea." The preparations for the siege had been a great shock to the old man; he seemed to be reliving old days, thinking that the enemy was still Minos.

To Antiope, now in the unpleasantly crowded Queen's Megaron, Theseus sent word that he might be gone overnight; he did not tell her where he was going, or why. She would worry, but not as much as if she knew the truth. He and his men rode forth.

The sun set, with fires redder and more vast than any upon earth. And then, in the first gray dusk of evening, the Athenians saw from afar the enemy campfires, shining as if all the stars of heaven had fallen and the night sky would be left black and empty. Never before had such a host come against any Greek city. The embassy shuddered; was Athens so hopelessly outnumbered? Even Theseus shuddered, yet the wild hope that had brought him there leaped yet higher. He began to call aloud, his voice ringing bell-like through the clear air of evening: "Heralds! Heralds from Athens!"

His heart cried: *O Poseidon Earthshaker, Father, let it be the men who come!* To all men heralds were sacred; otherwise there could be no intercourse between peoples; their tongues might as well be without language, like those of the beasts. But the Amazons were not men; until Antiope's mother had made that treaty with the Great King they had truly lived like beasts, always slaying, always being slain. But the Hittites must far outnumber them, and if once they realized that their king's daughter was still a queen, would they want to drag her back and let these crazy women make a whore of her? He could offer them all the wealth of Crete for her dowry —if they would help him get it.

And then suddenly shapes were all around him! They were rising out of the night-blackened earth as silently and grimly as ghosts or shadows. The fading light glinted as grimly on spear-points. A voice said quietly: "You seek the Great King's men, man of Athens?" All the Athenians let out great sighs of relief, and Theseus said proudly: "I do. Take us to him who leads you."

The voice said again: "Then get down from your chariots and follow me. Your horses will be well cared for." Words that could mean more than one thing. Theseus had brought most of his best horses, anxious to make a good appearance before the Great King's captains. But there was nothing to do but obey. . . .

He stepped down from his chariot lightly and proudly, and his men stepped down from theirs. They could see little of their guide but his cloak and helmet, and as little of his men, who closed in around them, shadow-silent. They walked toward the many campfires, and soon Theseus' heart rose within him again. Sun-bright visions danced before his eyes: the Palace of Minos in flames, and the dread bulls of Minos roasting on spits above fires like these. Those God-Bulls goring no more young Athenians, but filling Hittite and Athenian bellies . . . why not? Surely such a hope was reasonable. The Great King must love his daughter dearly to have sent so many men after her; he could not want her to live like an Amazon, risking her sweet body in battle, wantonly lying with many men. *He will be glad to have her well married, and soon he will be proud of me, his son-in-law. Me, the conqueror of Crete!* The Amazons would still be angry; nothing would ever satisfy them but Antiope herself. But what did that matter? They must be hopelessly outnumbered. Hittite shrewdness, Hittite good sense, would prevail. The good sense of men. . . .

They were threading their way among the campfires now; they came at last to a campfire beside which sat a stocky, broad-shouldered man. The crimson cloak of a leader covered his powerful body; his eyes were cool and hard, like bright stones. A man to be reckoned with; Theseus' heart leaped at the challenge of meeting and dealing with such a one. And then he saw that beside the man sat a woman, tall as he and still handsome, her cloak blood-red as his. Like a blow the sight of her smote Theseus—a heavy, sickening blow. There was something terrible about this distorted image of his beloved: this ageing, fierce Antiope. Then he saw her eyes, and all likeness vanished.

She spoke, not the man. "You come from Athens, dogface?"

Theseus did his best to turn his back on her and still face the man; that required no mean contortion of his lithe body. "I come from Aegeus and his son Theseus, Kings of Athens, to speak with him who speaks for the Great King, the Sun of the Hittites."

The man answered, his voice cool as his eyes: "I am Tarkun, the Great King's man. He has sent me to help Molpadia, War-Queen of the Amazons. Until her niece Antiope returns to their people she is sole queen. Speak to her."

Both voice and eyes were as feelingless as stone, and like a stone Theseus' heart sank. But his face showed nothing; he squared his shoulders and faced both of them.

"My lords ask: 'What quarrel have you with Athens? Antiope, once Queen of the Amazons, is now Theseus' queen, and the happy mother of his son, the grandson of her father, the Great King. Let an embassy of her father's officers and also of Queen

Molpadia's women come to Athens. To see with their own eyes
what state she lives in, and to hear from her own mouth that she
is well content."

He went on: "Theseus asks no dowry, since he took his bride
by force, but he will lay out great wealth to show the honor in
which he holds both his lady and her mighty father." He could
afford to offer great bride-gifts—he could pay them if he had a
chance to conquer Crete.

But the eyes of Tarkun the Hittite did not change; he sat as he
had from the beginning. And for a breath's space longer Molpadia
sat as silent, but with clenched fists, her face growing ever more
purple and distorted, seeming more than ever to disfigure Antiope's own face. Then her voice came at last, harsh as the hiss of
a snake:

"Aye, we know how he has honored her, dog of a dog—with
rape and slavery! He is scared now, he whines like the cur he is.
He offers to buy her—this sneaking thief who stole her—*buy* her!
Like a horse or a cow."

"Lady, you are wrong! Come and speak with the queen your
niece—"

"And let her be beaten—though by now she must be used to
that!—or tortured in other ways to make her speak the words your
vile master would put into her mouth? Though never would she
speak them! Tell him this—that dog of dogs! Until she stands
before me a free woman, never will I speak with my niece Antiope,
Queen of the Amazons!"

Theseus swung to Tarkun. "Lord, will you let this madwoman
make you throw away your men's lives for nothing?"

The Hittite rose. Like flowing blood his cloak fell around him,
and the firelight gleamed on the hilt of his sword. "Go back to your
masters, men. Bid them give up Antiope the Queen whole and
unharmed, and with her the wealth you have promised. Then we
men of the Great King her father will be content; that much I
swear by the Thousand Gods of the Hittites. But for Molpadia the
War-Queen I cannot speak."

Molpadia cried: "And by the Goddess our Lady I swear that if
she is not given up—and also the other six Amazons who were
taken with her—your walls shall be razed, and your city ground

into the dust! Every woman, child, and man in it shall die! And he that enslaved Antiope—let him not think to take vengeance on her beforehand, or he will die the worst death of all! His pain will last as long as we can make it last—many times he will be tortured until he prays for death, then brought back to life that he may suffer again. And yet again!"

"And if my lords say no? As they surely will?" Theseus ignored her now, his eyes on Tarkun.

The Hittite answered, his voice like an icy wind: "Up then, and let the Storm God, my Lord, decide between us! Soon your city shall be laid waste, and its site made accursed. Serri and Hurri, the twin Bulls of Day and Night, shall trample it into nothingness forever. And if any harm is done to Antiope the Queen, all that Molpadia, the Deathsinger, the War-Queen, has threatened shall be done to your people and to their kings. And more besides. Now go."

And Theseus and his men turned and went.

Their chariots were given back to them, but before the moon set they heard others rumbling after them. Heard, too, the sound of hoofs, and the dread war-cry of the Amazons, "HIP-POL-Y-TE-E-E-E! HIP-PO-OL-Y-TE-E!" Molpadia in her wrath had been unable to wait for morning, and her allies were with her.

In a dawn gray as ashes, gray and dead as Theseus' hopes, he and all the other watchers on the Akropolis shuddered to see the huge, heavy Hittite war chariots roll up, three-man chariots far more formidable than the light, two-man cars they knew. And all too soon the Hittite foot soldiers came marching up, unhurried, implacable, in steady, disciplined menace equally unknown to the youthful West. But first of all had come the shrieking Amazons, swarming up like ants over the grim gray Areopagos, that stony hill second in size only to the Akropolis itself, and too near the latter's great gates.

The Hittite captains took over the vacated houses of the Butadai and the Eupatridai, and their men camped around them. Systematically they set about rolling away stones, and all that would make the land below the hills hard going for their famous chariots.

When the besieged came out they would indeed be thrusting themselves, not only their heads, into the lion's mouth.

"Madness! This is madness!" Theseus raged, when he and Antiope were alone at last. "How could your father do it—put his men under that madwoman's rule?"

"He has not. But he is the ally of the Amazons, not their overlord. If I had not been his daughter he never would have sent men to help her—that is all. This war is hers." She wanted to say: "If only you had told me what you meant to do—let me prevent this folly that has enraged Molpadia yet more." But their unity—hers and Theseus'—must be preserved at all costs now. There was soon going to be strife enough all around them.

"But your father cannot want you to lie with many men—to be a whore! Surely he would be glad to know that you are an honored wife—that he has a fine grandson by you! Can you not appeal to Tarkun in your own name?"

"I can, true. I write the royal tongue of Kanesh, although not as well as I speak it. But many moons will pass before Tarkun can get word to my father and receive his reply. Even then Subbiluliuma may feel himself bound by the treaty. I have broken the Law of the Amazons, beloved, and if Molpadia killed me for it, Subbiluliuma would have no right to interfere."

Theseus thought that both his wife and her mighty father must be mad, but did not say so; he too saw the advantages of unity. He merely urged her to write to Tarkun at once, and she did, though for one unused to writing the task was not easy. Black night came before she finished, and when she woke in the golden morning only her girls were with her, all round-eyed.

"Queen, Queen, our people! They are building real walls on the Areopagos—as if they meant to stay here forever! All who can get up on the roofs are there, watching them. Even the Women, much as they hate climbing ladders!"

The big outer room, that upper Queen's Megaron built to please Medea, did indeed seem queerly quiet and at peace, with only wary slave girls there, carefully keeping their charges away from the half-Amazon children, who played alone. For the Women openly regarded the outland brood as vicious wild beast cubs, dangerous to their own civilized offspring; and Hippolytos, wary now too, had precociously appointed himself his comrades'

leader. It was a siege within a siege, one of which Theseus did
not dream. *What could he do about it if he did?* Antiope had thought
bitterly.

Already her six girls had drawn lots to decide which two of them
must stay behind to guard their babies. She and the rest were
climbing up onto the roofs that sheltered the ordinary refugees.
The highborn ladies, already there, drew back to make way for
Antiope, yet contrived to look as if they did it because she and her
Amazons smelled. When first they had come up into the Akropolis
she had tried to welcome them, knowing such courtesy to be
useless, yet a queen's duty, and had been soundly snubbed. But
today she and her Amazons cared as little for this rudeness as they
always had pretended to do. All eyes, they peered out and down,
through the crystal-clear air.

To the west, a hundred feet below, walls were truly rising.
Women were building them—women were hauling and sawing
great logs, and putting them into place. Smearing them with clay
to make them proof against fire arrows.

"Queen, Queen, they are here!" Star-eyed, a girl beside Antiope
babbled that, "Our people—*ours!*"

"Look, Lady, look! That is Xanthippe, my own sister—I would
know her crest anywhere!"

"We should be down there with them, Queen—*you* should be!
Leading them, not letting Molpadia do it all!"

Antiope looked. Felt her heart become all one ache of longing,
as memories rushed upon her and over her. The thrill of headlong
charges, of seeing raiding Kaska drop their spoil and run. Long
days of working and riding in the open, beneath the sun.
Campfires beneath the moon, the talk around them, and comradeship warmer than the fires . . . the freedom, friendliness and the
sharing . . . Her head spun, her heart cried: *There is my place! Down
there with them—my people!* Up here, among all these unfriendly people who did not want her, there was no way, no place for her.
Never could she belong. . . .

But then again her heart cried, out of depths as great: *Theseus.
Hippolytos. My man—my baby!* Her boy baby, whom the Law of the
Amazons would never let her keep. . . . She looked up at the blue
mountains, up higher yet, into the brighter blueness, the vast, pure
vault of the sky. She tried to fill herself with air, with space. To

find her own smallness, and in it strength and sanctuary. What was done was done. There could be no way back into childhood and girlhood for her, no escape. . . .

She said quietly: "Never again will I ride with the Amazons. But I must make peace; somehow, I must make peace."

CHAPTER 6.
___WAR

B UT WHEN she went back to the palace, Theseus met her, grim-faced, with grim news. The herald who bore her letter had been turned back; no more heralds would be received, unless she herself went out with them, to be given up. "Your aunt is clever," Theseus said heavily.

"Yet tonight"—his jaw set—"I will be still cleverer. I know the house in which Tarkun is lodged, and the chamber he is most likely to be using. With two or three men I think I can manage to sneak into it. He will read your letter then—with my sword at his throat, while they guard the door."

Fear stabbed Antiope like a sword. "No, beloved—no! You do not know how well a Hittite camp is guarded—you never could get into the quarters of a Hittite leader unseen. You cannot dream of half their hard-learned skills—" She stopped, biting her lip. How could she make him understand? In experience he was a child beside the Hittites, who outnumbered his men, even if her Amazons had not been with them. But because he was marvelously quick and brave, and had killed a few bandits who had been foolish enough to let him meet them man to man, he thought himself a great warrior. And his pride was so tender—much more tender than Hippolytos' baby skin—

He laughed shortly. "Maybe I know more of the game of war than you think, my wife. I am not afraid to match myself against both your Hittites and your Amazons."

She said simply: "I was born of both peoples, Theseus, but I love you. I did not speak in pride—as a Hittite, and one of your foes. Only as one who has known them and their ways much longer than you have."

He sobered, but said bitterly: "Well, how are we to deliver your letter then? Make many copies of it, and shoot them, tied to as many arrows, into the Hittite camp? Will he pick one up and read it—he who has refused to receive my heralds?"

She stiffened. "There are other ways. I know one—if I have the power to use it, as my mothers had. It will come to me—it must."

"How long will it take?" He was not altogether pleased, yet knew she might be right.

"Give me tonight and tomorrow night. I think it will take only tonight."

He agreed, and she questioned him closely about the window of the room he thought Tarkun would have. It had a balcony, and some kind of flowering tree growing in a tub on that balcony. She made him send for the old Butad lord whose room it rightfully was, and made him explain—although he looked as if he thought her mad—exactly what kind of tree it was, and all he could remember of how it looked. Glad that she had once seen it herself, she went back to her room then. Mainland Greeks bought little of the costly Egyptian papyrus generally used for letters, but her best tunic was made of mist-fine Egyptian linen, the kind through which the legs of Pharaoh's favorite ladies showed as through water. She and her Amazons tore it up, and though it was less easy to write on than the well-tanned hide she had used before, she finally managed to rewrite her letter on it, and to fold this up into a tiny, tiny roll such as the original never could have made. Then she drank a little wine and rested a little while, carefully keeping her mind blank.

After that she rose and went alone to the dovecote. She fed and stroked a little hen who was one of Theseus' best carrier pigeons; she held her long, sometimes talking to her and sometimes silent. From of old there had been friendship between birds and Amazons. Save for that, the Amazons never could have made their springtime visits to the Isle of the Black Stone. The host of migrating birds would have pecked out the eyes of any others who had dared to land there then, on their chosen resting place. But always they made room for those women who were, in a way, their kindred: also two-legged creatures mercilessly hunted by men. Amazons never ate the flesh of birds.

Now this bird stared into the eyes of Antiope the Queen, even as birds stare into the hypnotizing eyes of snakes who will devour them. And she stared back.

It is a hard task I set you, little one. Harder—far harder—than the simple command the mothers and grandmothers of my people lay upon your kind in that far-off isle in the Dark Sea. But you must do it—you must. See Tarkun—see Tarkun . . .

In her mind she was making a picture of Tarkun, she was dredging up every detail of his face and form, fitting them together. In Hattusas she had known him; he had been a comrade of her father's youth. She became eyes that stared at Tarkun; she became a pipe through which that remembered image poured as water pours. Straight into the tiny brain of the bird she poured it. *Seek Tarkun. Seek Tarkun. Fly in through his window that is like this. . . .* Through the pipe that was herself such an image of that window as she could give poured also, but what mattered most was Tarkun, Tarkun himself. *Cry out to him, flutter your wings about his head. He must see this message.* She bound it to the bird, went back to her picture-making, her pouring. Strength seemed to be pouring out of her like water. She was straining as hard as ever she had strained to get out Hippolytos—

Then suddenly the bird left her hand. Up it flew, straight as any arrow that ever had left her bow, and headed for the walls of the Akropolis. Night had come, and the shadows around them were black and heavy, but it flew through these as through the brightest sunlight. She reeled and pressed her hands against the wall to steady herself. She had done what only a few of the Childbearers had done before her—when there had been great need to send detailed messages to an absent War-Queen.

The bird would find Tarkun—and he would know that it could be no ordinary message that an ensorceled bird had brought him, there in the darkness of his own chamber. He would know. . . .

Through the morning she lay white and waxen, like a lifeless image of herself, and it was one of her girls who found that the bird had returned to the dovecote, and without any message. Knowing what her queen had been doing, she showed the bird to Theseus and told him all. He was both awed and elated, yet somewhat disappointed because Tarkun had sent no reply. Well, perhaps that had been too much to hope for—until word came from Subbiluliuma nothing could be changed.

He made a great fuss over Antiope when she finally awoke, but she ate lightly and soon slept again. A full day and night of sleep, her girls told Theseus, would probably be needed for her healing.

She did not get them. That night, when all the people of Athens slept, or tried to sleep, cries of warning from the towers suddenly rang through the sultry blackness. Soon battering rams were crashing against all three gates, the postern as well as the double-doored main entrance. The ram-bearers came under heavy canopies made of shields. These shelters would soon have been broken by the stones hailed down from the towers by Theseus and his men, but to hurl stones the Athenians had to show something of themselves. Arrows promptly whizzed up from the bows of the Amazons riding close behind the ram-bearers. Two men of Athens fell, writhing in agony. Neither had been struck in a vital part; yet too plainly the arrows were poisoned. Their victims died, and Theseus decided that to sally out and seize the ram at the main gates—with the ram-bearers between his men and the deadly bows—would be safer than mere defense. He did, and after a short, knife-sharp skirmish, got the ram inside, and slammed the gates again on both Hittites and Amazons. But when he tried to capture the ram before the postern the Hittites were ready for him. They charged in, ram and all, with the Amazons close behind, and there was a fearful struggle in the twenty-foot-long, black passage that was the postern itself. To drive them out again was hard, though mercifully the Amazons could not see to use their arrows. Panting and exhausted, Theseus finally returned to the palace; and then, for the first time in her life, Antiope shrank from the sight of a bloodstained sword.

Blood, perhaps, of an Amazon. Of one of her own people.

Yet sickening as that thought was, she was overwhelmingly glad to see him. She washed and salved his hurts thankfully. All the time he had been gone, she had been feeling, as if it were her own flesh, every part of him that could be hurt, pierced by either blade or arrow. *They are braver than I thought, the Women. They who must sit through every battle, feeling like this, wondering about their men—*

But her girls were thinking only of the blood on Theseus' sword. Each knew it might be mother's, sister's, or friend's. Ever since the night of Hippolytos' birth there had been great friendship between them and Theseus; they had been like the sisters he had never had. But now he saw their hard, quickly averted glances and was hurt. Suspicion stabbed him too; enemies in his own house would be dangerous indeed. But because Antiope loved him they would be loyal to him—surely they would be! Yet he began to steal hard, uneasy glances at them, as they at him. Antiope saw both sets of glances, and they made her sick heart sicker. Strife between her girls and Theseus—that was one thing she could not bear.

He said only, "Your letter—if he ever read it—does not seem to have made Tarkun less eager for war."

She said wearily, "His orders are unchanged. Also if Molpadia attacked alone she would probably use fire arrows, and my father would not like that, fearing for me."

"But she would do it? She who claims to hold you so dear!"

"She would think any death better for me than slavery. And in that she would be right."

They went to bed then; Theseus fell asleep promptly, for once too tired for love, though it was good to have Antiope beside him, to feel the loving warmth of her. But she lay awake and thought, *Am I a slave, after all? I can never turn against you, Theseus—you are part of me. Yet whenever your sword pierces an Amazon, it will be as if it tore my own flesh.*

They had come so far to help her, her people—they had striven so hard and sacrificed so much.

The days dragged on, hot, baking summer days that yet seemed dark. Sometimes the nights would pass quietly, then for two or three, Hittites and Amazons between them would give nobody in Athens any chance to sleep. That dreadful pounding on the gates seemed to keep on ringing through heart and brain even after it had stopped. Sometimes Theseus spent most of the day overseeing the repairing of the battered gates. He had a complete new pair built inside the old ones at the main entrance.

He also made several sallies through the postern—the besieged were supposed to go out and fight the besiegers, not crouch inside like holed-up rats. But always the poisoned arrows of the Amazons drove him back; they were good watchwomen, and their eyes never seemed to leave the postern. Only once did he reach the base of the Akropolis, and then the terrible Hittite chariots rumbled down upon him and his band. Too many of his men merely leaped aside, and in so doing made their backs fine targets for the fearful arrows. But Theseus himself leaped straight up onto the chariot that came at him, his sword driving into the charioteer's belly with all the force of that leap behind it. The shieldbearer had to grab the reins then and do his best to bring the frightened horses under control, while Theseus fought with the swordsman. He killed that man too before he leaped from the chariot, but his pride in having proved that the supposedly invincible Hittite chariots could be met and conquered did not change the hard facts. He had gained nothing else and lost too many men.

After that, he decided that it was better to play the rat and stay inside his walls awhile, except when sallying out to capture battering rams. He had devised a way for shields to be held over the men in the tower windows, so that arrows did not often pierce them while they were hurling down their missiles. And fierce as they were, the Amazons never again succeeded in getting through the outer postern gate and fighting the Athenians in the passage.

Yet both sides still lost men; Amazons fell too. What was worse was the fate of the wounded. Too often defenders had to rush back inside and slam their gates, leaving fallen men who later would move and groan. But any who tried to rush out and drag them back inside would be picked off by the arrows of Amazons or Hittites who waited just beyond reach of the hail of stones from the slitlike tower windows. And the enemies who fell before the gates or halfway down the steep sides of the Akropolis fared no better. Those who tried to rush to their rescue would also be felled by arrows or a hail of stones. Sometimes the wounded would lie groaning all day, until the heat and the flies finished them.

Once a fallen Amazon's moaning lasted well into the night, and a couple of grim pranksters among the besieged had their comrades let them down by ropes so that they could reach her. In the rosy tenderness of early morning, when Antiope and her girls went out for a breath of fresh air—something it was hard for them to get now—they met a merry band, each of whom carried some part of the woman. They had cut her up like a butchered calf, and the man who had the head grinned and waved it at Antiope. All the men jeered and laughed at the furious, heartsick girls, and it took the sternest commands Antiope had ever given to keep her

Amazons from drawing their knives and springing upon the murderers. When he who held the head gouged out an eye and threw it in her face she nearly failed.

She took the eye and showed it to Theseus; he heard her out in silence and then said heavily: "I will get you the head at least, to be buried according to your own rites. But for their own sakes, Antiope, your girls must be disarmed."

She stared at him, stunned and unbelieving. "But why? I was able to hold them—"

"What if one of them had grabbed one of you? Anything could have happened. Then all of you could have been killed—you yourself could have been."

Her lip curled. "Do you still know nothing of Amazons, Theseus? That pack of dogs was a small pack, and we could have handled it."

"No, for the noise would have brought everybody within reach running to help their countrymen against you. You would have been down before I could have got out of the palace."

"Then how can you ask us to walk unarmed among such a mass of butchering hounds?"

"Because it would be hard for your slayers to say that unarmed women had started the fight. Antiope, you must see that there is no other way."

For a breath's space she stared at him again, too shocked for speech. When her voice did come, it was almost a whisper. "Theseus, you do not know how an Amazon feels, disarmed. What it means to her, the loss of all rights and all honor. If you put such shame on my girls, who have done nothing—"

He said doggedly: "It must be done. To save their lives. I have not told you this, Antiope, but some of my people whisper that it is dangerous to have the enemy walking free inside our own walls. That some fine night your girls may rise, kill the sentries, and let in their own people."

Do you yourself half-fear that? She did not ask the question aloud. She closed her eyes in such pain as she never had felt since she lay bound aboard his ship in the middle of the dark Unfriendly Sea. In worse pain than the awful agony of birth, for that had hurt only her body. . . .

She opened her eyes again. She took her father's iron dagger from her girdle and laid it on the tiny table beside her bed and Theseus. "If my girls are disarmed, so must I be, Theseus. So they will know that I am still their queen and their friend, and surely it will make your people feel safer too—"

"Put that dagger back where it belongs, Antiope. I will get you that head—I said I would—"

"We will all be glad to get the head and save it from more ill usage. I thank you for that, Theseus. But I cannot bear arms if my girls cannot."

"They cannot. Antiope, I have offered you all I can—and all the Gods know that your people are not gentle with my wounded, either, when they can manage to get hold of them."

The thought came to her then—the shining, unheard-of thought. She said very quietly: "Perhaps you are right. As you say, none can fear unarmed women. But one thing I must ask of you, Theseus." She stepped nearer to him, and he looked at her almost in fear. What was she going to ask? Such surrender was utterly unlike her.

"If ropes can let your men down from the Akropolis to deal with the wounded in their way, they can let my girls down to deal with them in ours. Those who are too badly hurt we will kill swiftly, with little pain—we have done that on many battlefields. But those who have a chance to life if tended—let us bring them back up with us and tend them."

"Bring Amazons into the Akropolis?" He stared at her in horror.

"Wounded ones, who can do no harm. We will eat less that they may be fed. We will lay them in the magazines, the crowded storerooms, that they may use no space your people are using—"

"Woman, you are mad." His voice was harsh, almost afraid. "My people would be sure then that you were betraying me—and that I was a man no longer, but only your dupe, God-maddened. They would cry for help to the sons of Pallas."

"Many still love you, Theseus." Her eyes shone as he had never seen them shine. "Show those who do not that you are still their lord. Say, 'My wife's kindred make war on us because they think her a slave in my house. But if I let her take in and tend their wounded, then all will know that she is loved and honored.' "

Being Pittheus' grandson, Theseus saw what she saw. Yet what seemed to him his sanity also saw objections in plenty. "How

could that help? Knowing the truth would not lessen Molpadia's
wrath, and Tarkun already knows—"

"He would have more proof then than a letter that might have
been written by some other hand, not mine. And though Molpadia
will never believe it—only rage and call it all a trick—those Amazons who have been here and seen me will *know*. And many will
believe them."

"And will their belief please them?"

"I do not think all of them will be angry. Theseus, I cannot say
what will come of this—nothing like it has ever been done before,
since women and men can remember. But it is worth trying because it may help. It is a good thing to do because it is good itself."

Theseus was a man who always liked new ideas, but he could
see clearly what would come of this one—his people's rage and
fear, their scorn of him, the woman-ruled, their possible turning
to the sons of Pallas. Yet the very danger was a challenge to him:
was he to bow to his own subjects out of fear?

Am I their lord or am I not?

Antiope's hand touched his cheek. "Theseus, let my people in."

In rope slings, cloth-wrapped to keep them from grinding into
already hurt, tormented bodies, Antiope's six Amazons hauled
their wounded sisters up into the Akropolis. Onto the roof where
their queen herself waited—Theseus had refused to let her go
down—with himself beside her, sword in hand. And disarmed as
they were, they knew him for their friend and loved him again.
They never knew that their weapons would have been taken from
them even if they had not been allowed to go on these undreamed-
of errands of mercy.

Theseus had to be able to swear to his people that only the
unarmed and sorely hurt had been brought inside their walls. He
also had to guard the six and their helpless burdens all the way
back to the palace, past all the angry, outraged eyes. In the cool
darkness of the magazines a few wounded Amazons died, but
more lived. There was pain to be borne, and tiring, sometimes
disgusting work to be done—often at first the sick could not control themselves, and fouled both clothes and bedding—yet also a
queer happiness bloomed there in the dark. Sometimes the rescuers found friends or kin among the rescued; often they gained

news of these. And always all whose minds were clear enough to know her rejoiced to see Antiope the Queen. They believed in her vision of the Goddess—the minds of the sick are not so closely guarded by pride and fear and custom as those of the well. They marveled, but accepted what they could not understand.

Yet much of their news hurt her cruelly. A dream had indeed told the Deathsinger where to seek her niece, and so Themiskyra had been left deserted—Themiskyra the long-cherished, the long-fought-for. Before going they had burned all their houses, poisoned all their wells. Many had burned down their fruit trees too—determined that others should not eat of their fruit—but some had not had the heart to spoil what they had planted and worked over. "We could not do it, Lady, we who had watched them grow."

"But the children? And those too old to ride far?" Antiope had to fight to make her voice loud enough to ask that question.

"We left them in our Lady's cave." The girl spoke of a sanctuary high in the mountains, one that Antiope knew well. "We dug out the big outer chambers enough for all of them to be able to sleep there—not to have to go down into the inner chambers that are damp and dripping. It may be She will care for them there."

"You left the foals and the oldest mares with them?" Antiope remembered that there was some good pastureland not far below the cave. She remembered also that at the cavern's very mouth there was a chasm—a clean, sheer drop, a fall no flesh could take and live.

Another Amazon, the mother of two small daughters, said quietly: "None who shelter in that place need fear slavery if they keep good watch. And it will be kept—you know our old women. And if the Goddess is kind, and no foe finds them this winter or next, they may be able to manage until we get back. Or until many of the little girls are old enough to fight."

But what she saw in the mother's eyes made Antiope turn her own away. They both knew how likely foes were to find those forsaken ones. . . .

The Amazons had left what provisions they could with those they had deserted, then had ridden westward to the very end of the sea they knew, killing and being killed all the way. They had found the Straits of the Cow frozen over, also buried beneath winter snow. Binding strips of hide around their horses' hoofs lest the slippery ice beneath might still betray them, they had crossed from one side of the sea to the other, then ridden southwest, as Molpadia's dream had bade them. Through sleet and snow and men more savage than either, they had battled on until, somewhere on the Thracian coast, they had met Trojan ships hired by the Great King.

"Leukippe, whom we had had to leave behind, wounded, and had not had time to kill—somehow she had reached the Hittites and told them what we were doing," one Amazon explained. "Molpadia cursed her for a traitress, but most of us think she did well. For if we had had to fight all the way to Athens, there would not have been enough of us left to help anybody. We soon knew that; maybe the Deathsinger herself did, down underneath her fury. For she finally came to terms with Tarkun the Hittite and let us board the ships he had brought for us. To do that was safe enough anyhow, because we outnumbered those lightly armed Trojan crews. Or would have, if we had not soon been too busy trying to outpuke each other to fight anybody."

Antiope and her six smiled then, remembering the beginning of their own voyage.

But for both Hittites and Amazons the whole cruise had been bad. They had been storm-tossed and seasick all the way, although the ships had always hugged the shore. And in the end the Trojans had cheated them, landing all—men, women, chariots, and horses—at a river that they had said was near Athens. "But it was not. They hate to sail in winter, those lying sea-folk, however much you pay them. We had to fight our way across all Thessaly. The Hittites really were a help, although Molpadia would not admit it. It is good to see men run away from their chariots."

Antiope could only marvel at how much her people loved her. Her father too—she had known he liked her, but never dreamed he would pay out so much gold, risk so many men for her. Or for anything but the welfare of the Hittite nation. And all this had been done and borne for love of her who did not want to be rescued—of her who, by her own choice, must live out her life among people who hated her.

Yet I am here by Your will, Goddess. If I were not, how could I bear to live, knowing all the woe I have brought upon those who love me?

Yet in spite of her pain, her hopes were rising. These women would go back to the other Amazons and bear witness to her happiness, and to her vision of the Goddess. Molpadia would do her best to smother the story, but such a thing could not be kept quiet. It would reach Tarkun, and he might well believe, he who must already be puzzled, and not only because of her letter. For Theseus had managed to make his men stop killing the Hittite ram-bearers who were left wounded outside his gates, and her Amazons had bandaged several of them, and then helped them downhill to places where their friends could find them.

There came a night when two of the wounded Amazons were well enough to be lowered from the walls. Helped downhill by Antiope's girls, they had promised to stay quietly where they were left, until their helpers had had time to get back up into the Akropolis. At dawn, Amazons coming down from the Areopagos for water would find them, the two they must have given up for dead, sitting peacefully beside the well called Klepsydra. How surprised they would be, and how glad! Antiope thought wistfully of that gladness; many had died for her and many more would, but not those two. They would tell their tale, and though one might not have been believed, it would be hard for even Molpadia to make all the rest think that both had been weak and sick enough to be deceived so long and thoroughly.

Who could tell what would happen then?

O Lady, is this the real beginning? Will I live to see men and women make friends, after all?

Dazzled by that sun-bright hope, she forgot that men must be changed as well as women. And how fearful is the strength of hate.

CHAPTER 7.
THE MEETING OF THE QUEENS

I N THE rosy dawn the two women beside the Klepsydra were
found and rejoiced over like people risen from the dead. But
when Molpadia heard their story she raged even as Antiope
had foretold. "Lies! All lies! He made her lie, fools—to save your
lives. And in your sickness you believed it—swallowed such blasphemous filth. For love of her and of the Goddess never tell such
a tale again—never dare to remember it!"

But several Amazons had already heard, and each told several
others who told several more. Soon all knew that something must
be kept secret, even those who were not sure what it was. Tarkun
heard, for although Hittites and Amazons were forbidden to speak
to each other save when ordered to do so by their chiefs, they
inevitably did. He demanded a chance to hear the two women's
story, and when Molpadia refused he said: "Then maybe they
speak truth, woman. Truth you do not wish to hear."

"They do not! They speak only lies—*his* lies."

"He has always called Antiope his wife."

"What is a wife but a slave?"

Tarkun shrugged. "Well, whatever he is up to, this sparing of
our wounded is good. I had begun to think he must be doing it on
purpose, and now I am sure of it. Henceforth my men will kill no
more of his wounded."

"I will kill all of his men that I can reach, wounded or unwounded—the vile, slaving dogs!"

"No doubt you will. But take care that all those fine poisoned
arrows of yours go over my men's heads. A few that chanced to
go too low—that would be the kind of mistake you would like to
make, Molpadia. I know you of old."

So he left her without even that small vent for her sick fury. For all men needed killing; it was more bitter than death to know that she needed this man and his men.

Yet what are they really doing for you, Antiope? How much are we doing, your own people? Only teasing these holed-up rats while we wait for them to starve—and yours will surely be the first belly to go empty! They can get no more food in, but from somewhere they are getting water. Where?

She shut herself up in her tent, and used herbs to make brews that would make her body sleep, but only her body. At night she flew low over the Akropolis, an owl again. She saw where long ago, perhaps before men ever came there, the huge cap of rock had cracked and the outer piece had broken away, sliding down a little. But its top still rested against the main mass, and the wall built by men had been reared across it. She found an opening there, like a mouth in Night's own black face, leading down into depths darker than Night's, black beyond all imagining. Down into those depths her weightless wings bore her; she searched and searched, sightless. To any human being those ways would have seemed terrible; to a creature so small as a bird they were like a whole monstrous world of eternal night. But at last she found what she sought—down there was water.

Many times she flew in and out of that cleft. She learned all the length and breadth of it, then she went back to her body and lay there long, eyes closed, mind busily translating what she had learned into terms comprehensible to human eyes and human memory. But that entrance, so vast to a bird's eyes, was small and hard to reach. Could even Amazons get inside it, without having to kill enough sentries to alert the city above?

Next night she tried. Her Amazons wriggled uphill on their bellies, snake-silent, their bows on their backs. Several crawled into the cleft unseen, but suddenly a cry rang out—one of the sentries above had seen movement below. The remaining Amazons sprang up, freed their bows, and used them; every sentry fell. But more men came rushing up, with that most hateful of all men at their head—she knew it was he, somehow she could smell him, him she hated, though at that distance and in the dark, no human eyes could have known his face. Two Amazons fell, trading arrows with the defenders, before those who had crawled into the cleft could crawl out again, shadow-still. She was sure they had not been seen, but there was nothing left to do but retreat.

From now on that way in would be too well watched. Was there no other, lower down? None where Earth the Mother's own wall was thin, and determined women, wriggling up- and downhill snake-flat, night after night, could dig their way in, unseen?

She brewed more brews. She became an otter. Inch by inch she searched that steep slope, hard work for such small legs. Her paws would have been worn to the bone, they would have bled many times, had they been made of flesh and blood. Though tireless, they were weak, and for all their strange speed, that was greater than that of any solid body, the search took time—too much time.

She learned to turn her will to force—force that could move earth and rock. And at last she found what she searched for—a place where lately men had worked, filling up an opening. Then she left the otter and in some subtle yet mortal shape—what form it had, if any, she never knew—she descended into the cave that had been blocked up. She studied that blockage most carefully— its exact depth, and the material used in it, mostly earth and loose stones. She went back into the otter, and then into her own body. Carefully she chose the women who, night after night, must indeed crawl snake-flat up that hill and dig. She chose none who were young, although the strength of youth would have been useful. Something told her not to do so, although she told herself that no Amazon could ever be a traitress. Those lying tales, that spittle that dripped from the mouth of that dog of dogs, was meant to set Amazon against Amazon, make them doubt each other. *But you shall never do that, cur. You have not corrupted her, Antiope, whatever else you have done to her. You will make none of us believe your lies—you who are so clever, smearing even the Goddess Herself with your lying filth.* She trusted every woman, every girl, in her little army, as she trusted herself. Or so she thought. Yet she did not confide in the young.

There was unrest among the Amazons. Had Antiope been forced to lie, to save the wounded captives from cruel deaths? So cautious older women said, but not all the younger ones were sure. They remembered what those freed prisoners who were now so silent had said at first—or were said to have said. How Antiope had laughed and talked with them as of old, her head high and her eyes clear. How she had stood straight, never looking back over her shoulder as if uneasy or afraid. She had been herself—her very self—unhurt and unchanged. . . . Now that Themiskyra was gone, could their whole way of life be going too? Could the Goddess really be going to make great changes, lay down new laws? No— surely that was going too far! So many told themselves, shrinking as if from doors suddenly flung wide open—too wide—letting in fresh air that was really a destroying hurricane. And yet—well, maybe these strangers had skilled witches who had distorted the memories of all who had seen the young queen. Very skilled witches indeed, for the minds and wills of Amazons were strong; wounds did not long confuse their thinking.

But one thing none of the Amazons ever doubted—that Antiope still loved them. They thought wistfully of her hands tending their wounded. If and when more of these came back, all must hear their stories—not only a few. Some could not help thinking of Antiope and the man together—that young, handsome man. He had been treacherous once; he certainly had carried her off. Yet now he was as certainly letting her help her wounded people. . . .

Wonder and dizzying uncertainty; strange new stirrings. . . . The few—the very few—Amazons who in secret had dared to take Hittite lovers felt the blossoming of strange wild hopes. *If what we are doing is not wrong, after all. If we could marry our men and sleep with them always. Never have to be afraid of the War-Queen again.* Yet marriage too would be risky; it gave men too much power, too much chance to be bullies. . . .

It was hard to be sure of anything, yet many stealthily cleaned the poison off their arrows. When some Athenians received arrow wounds yet did not die, they were surprised. There was wonder and talk in Athens too then, but most—particularly the older men —said grimly: "The Amazons must have run out of poison. Here, in country strange to them, it is taking them time to find the right herbs and brew a fresh batch. Never of their own will would they spare any man, those whoring she-butchers!" All the doubters were silenced; many ceased to doubt.

But in Theseus hope flowered; maybe Antiope's wild idea was bearing fruit. Certainly the Hittites had stopped killing wounded Athenians; even the old men admitted that. Yet he dared neglect no precaution; he strengthened the postern gates, both inner and outer; he looked long and frowningly at the great main gates, trying to think of more ways to reinforce them. Dimly in his mind moved a plan—the plan that was to become the famous Nine Gates that over a thousand years later in classical Athens Euripides and Socrates and Pericles knew.

But there was not much the besieged could do except wait, and waiting seldom makes people happy. Men muttered: "We sit here trapped; our enemies sit and wait for us to starve. When the time for the autumn sowing comes, we cannot sow it." The women said, "We cannot hold the Thesmophoria." And there was too much truth in such mutterings; Theseus could not answer them.

Too much heat, and too little space, and too many people packed together in it, all afraid. The Akropolis had become an oven, and everything in it baked. For two moons there had been no rain, only dryness and unseasonable heat, and still the blue blue sky blazed down relentlessly. The besiegers could bathe in the cool, lovely rivers below: in the blue Ilissos, and the sparkling Eridanos. But though the besieged had water to drink, they dared waste little on anything else. Unwashed, sweat-soaked bodies baked and stewed in unwashed, sweat-soaked clothes. Many families mourned for dead or dying babies. Gnat-sized grievances were nursed into bloated hugeness, and people eyed each other like surly dogs.

Ugly whispers began. Maybe those men whose ugly sport Antiope had interfered with began them. Yet anybody might have started them, for people who are miserable and afraid respond like dry wood to any spark. "Must we roast out here in the sun while those bitches who came here to kill us loll inside in the cool dark? Our enemies, pampered and cherished, faring better than our own sick children!"

Wiser voices answered: "They lie in the windowless magazines, packed in among the great *pithoi*. Like a bunch of extra pots."

"Where they can open all those big pots whenever they please! Must we count every mouthful that goes into our mouths, or our children's mouths, yet endure that? Keep on filling the bellies of these bloodthirsty whores from the East?"

Theseus had never dreamed of holding Antiope and her girls to her promise that they would eat less if he took in the wounded Amazons. But he heard those whispers and knew how dangerous they were. After all, no more food could be brought into the Akropolis; that fact was his greatest weakness, and his foes' greatest strength. . . .

There were other, even darker whispers, fear-poisoned. "Who knows how sick they really are, those murdering bitches? Who ever sees them but their own kinswomen? Theseus' own brazen whore, and her sister sluts?"

When Antiope told him that two more Amazons were well enough to leave, he said heavily: "I cannot let them go. People keep talking of how those two you did set free must be fighting against us again. Of how much they may have learned while they were inside our walls."

Antiope's hopes too had been growing. Now all of them came crashing down around her, left her sick and stunned. Must this plan fail too? She had been so sure the Goddess had sent it. But it had failed. No more hope of peace and understanding between peoples—and once more wounded Amazons must groan beneath the walls of Athens, at the mercy of heat and flies, and of the killers Theseus plainly no longer thought himself strong enough to hold back.

Well, to wallow in grief was useless. She said quietly: "If I cannot free them, what can I do with them? I will not have them slain or enslaved."

"I will try to smuggle them to Elephenor in Chalkis." Plainly he had all his plans made. "I will ask him to give them good care."

"The women of Chalkis will not want to tend those they have been taught to think of as wild beasts. Some of my girls must go with them." She still spoke quietly, but pain more bitter than death tore her heart. *If they go, will they ever come back?*

"Then they can drive the wagon, and my men can follow at a distance behind. To pick up the beasts and bring them back."

To make sure what my girls do? She nearly asked that, but bit her lip. He *was* risking something for her. To his men capture meant torture and death, while her Amazons would only be returned to their own people.

But he felt the need to defend himself against her silence, that was so different from the way a Greek woman would have taken this. "Love, for days now, whenever I left you, I have been afraid

for you. For I know you; if a mob broke in here to attack your
wounded Amazons you would die defending them."

"Who would dare to break in while you lived?"

"The leaders of that mob would not expect me to live long.
When I came rushing home to help you a man could be waiting
to stab me in the back—under cover of the clamor and the crowd.
Then you would all die: you, my father—even Hippolytos."

"Hippolytos . . ." Hot as the room was, she shivered. But when
she spoke again, her voice was as steady as ever. "I see. The sons
of Pallas. I have given them a new chance to strike at you."

That night Theseus slept soon and soundly, far more relieved
than he would have liked to admit. She was being sensible. But
Antiope, beside him, felt more alone than she ever had in all her
life days. Doubtless all six of her girls would be safer out of Athens
now; but how could she bear to give them up? She prayed long
to her Goddess: *Be with me, You who set the stars in their places. Show me
how to end all this.*

She prayed to That Which she called Mother and which men
still call Father, to That Which must be both and neither. But the
Power she prayed to did not answer her. The night was black and
still around her. She fixed her eyes upon the golden doves of the
little shrine Aegeus had given her when she first came to Athens;
it had belonged to the wife of Pandion, her who certainly had been
Theseus' grandmother, whoever his grandfather had been. Sometimes watching the moonlight shining on those golden doves had
helped to cleanse and clear her mind. But now they were only
lifeless, glittering images, unhelping as the black night.

It is not You who are far away, Goddess. It is I whose misery shuts You out.

She dozed at last, but then a head came rolling across the floor.
It leaped up onto the bed, onto her breast, and sat there, staring
at her with one eye; where the other should have been was a
bloody pit. She said, amazed: "But we buried you! We washed and
wrapped you as lovingly and reverently as if you had been mother
or sister to one of us." As perhaps it had been to one of her six.
She remembered sickeningly with what anxiety all seven of them
had scanned that dead face, both relieved and disappointed because it had been so hacked and abused that none could tell how
it had looked in life. She spoke again: "Can you not rest?" and the

head opened its gray, withered mouth and answered: *"Wife of the Athenian, I died for you."*

The face changed then, became that of a dear friend of her mother's, one on whose lap she had sat in childhood. No—it was the face of a girl with whom she had played as a child. It started to change again, and she closed her eyes, sick with fear that it might become Marpe's face. But through her closed lids she still saw it. It was the faces of all the Amazons she had ever known gathered together into one face. Into one vast reproach.

"Must we all die for you? You who lie with the chief of our slayers, and shame us by calling yourself his wife? Mock us with your poor, niggling mercies? Even they must end now—leave you no rag with which to comfort yourself!"

Her eyes started open. Theseus' hand was lying where she had felt the head. Sleeping, he had laid it on her breast. She had dreamed—or had his touch opened a door through which the angry ghost could reach her? Well, the reproach had not been unjust. *Oh, my people, who have come so far and suffered so much—given up so much for me! Forsaking those who did still need you. . . .*

Gently, she put Theseus' hand away. She rose and went to the window. She could not see the Areopagos, but she looked toward it. Up here all this hate, and down there all the love she could never have again . . . that would never satisfy her again if she could have it. She was no Goddess, like that aspect of Her these folk of the West worshiped at Kanathos in Apia, where a yearly bath in a sacred spring was said to make Her virgin again. A bath that, to mean anything, must have to wash away all memories as well as give back the fragile physical seal of maidenhood. *I cannot un-be what I have been—my man's woman and my baby's mother. Yet to Theseus too my love has brought only evil. Great evil.*

She looked out into the vast heavens, where now the moon was setting, and again a plan came to her. She hoped it came from the Goddess, but even if it did not, she could see no other. She went back to the bed and woke Theseus; she said: "Beloved, I must speak with Molpadia."

He was not pleased; he would have liked to sleep longer. He said: "Why? Besides, you cannot. She has refused to see you—unless you are given up."

"She will see me. If you threaten to send her my fingers, one by one, every day until she does."

He grimaced. "Yes, that might make her see you. But what can you say to her if she does? The truth would only make her turn on you."

"I have nothing to say to her except the truth, but I will never have more. Can we afford to leave any stone unturned, Theseus?"

In the end he yielded, and when the ugly threat against Antiope was called down from his walls through a trumpet, Molpadia gnashed her teeth, but also yielded. Terms were made; the two Queens of the Amazons were to meet at the very foot of the Akropolis, beneath the main gates. Twelve Athenians would stand thirty paces behind Antiope, and twelve Amazons thirty paces behind Molpadia; neither queen would be armed. Except that Antiope, to Theseus' horror, insisted on carrying Hippolytos with her.

"Sight of him would soften the heart of any true woman; I can see that. But the heart of that aunt of yours must have been forged by a blacksmith at his anvil—not shaped in any mother's womb!"

"I, whom she has nursed through childish illnesses, know better. Sight of him will make her angry, but it may also make her something else. I say again, can we afford to leave any stone unturned? Can you—for your people's sake?"

He yielded again. Once more Antiope donned her Amazon war tunic; it felt strange now. She took one of the all-but-man-tall shields used by many Greeks, settled her son in the curve of her arm behind it. "Be still, little king. Mouse-still. We are going to surprise someone." The child nodded, half puzzled, half interested. He knew the word "surprise"; this was some new kind of game.

Antiope walked out through the great gates, and down the ramp below them. She heard the feet of the soldiers behind her, and did not know that their captain's heart was beating almost as hard as hers. To him Theseus had said: "Watch well. If you let a hair of either head be harmed—my queen's, or my son's—never come back to Athens. For then I will cast you down from the wall with my own hands." She saw the thirteen Amazons below—her own people, waiting for her—and her eyes misted. *Oh, our Lady, be with me!* That walk seemed very long. And then one tall, crimson-cloaked figure advanced and stood before the others. Molpadia! At first she was only a figure, but soon she had a face. That well-remembered face! Antiope saw it, and knew suddenly that she was afraid, shamefully afraid—*she!* But the face beneath the helmet was afraid too: stiff with strain, and old. Much older than her niece remembered it.

Antiope herself wore no helmet, and at sight of her face, her shining, high-held head, a great cry broke from the twelve Amazons behind Molpadia. The rest of the Amazons, ranged well behind the twelve, took up that cry; the earth below rang with it until Molpadia's raised hand stilled all sound. Silence fell like a blanket, over all the sun-baked space beneath the Akropolis.

The War-Queen looked at the Childbearer, and that grim bleak face was indeed full of fear: dread of what might have come to the girl who for years had been a slave. When her voice came at last, it rang with triumph: "Child, he has not broken you! You are yourself still!"

Antiope came nearer. Each had to wink to see the other clearly. Memories came to flock around them—memories of other days and years. . . .

"Child"—now the older woman's voice shook—"child, it has been a long time."

"It has, Mother's sister."

"But you are the same—the same! Whatever you have had to bear, all your courage is in your eyes."

"I need it," Antiope said simply. She lowered the shield; showed what she held against her breast.

Molpadia's face went gray and dead as winter. She looked away, silent for a breath's space; then said, her eyes still averted, her voice flat and heavy: "When we have you back, and that man's head grins above his gates—as you must long to see it grin!— Subbiluliuma will care well for the boy, child. You know our Law."

"I know it. Once you too had a son, Molpadia."

"I gave him up. As the Law bids, girl!"

"And he died at another woman's breast, crying for your milk. Before he was many moons old. I have had my son in my arms for years now. Molpadia, my mother's sister, you who know what fear made you give your baby up too soon—the fear of loving him too much to be able to give him up—you of all women should understand. Know how hard it would be for me to give up mine now."

In the red rage that darkened Molpadia's face she looked like some Fury sprung up out of that dismal cleft in the rocks below the Areopagos. That cleft through which the avenging Goddesses of the Underworld were said once to have descended into the darkness, Their own place.

"I gave up my son, as was my duty—I kept the Law. But you —you love the man, your master. Your loins itch for him—for that slaving dog!"

Antiope stood very still. Hippolytos shrank back against her, frightened, yet too surprised to cry. Horror blanched the faces of the twelve Amazons, and the Athenian captain stirred restlessly. The woman was probably safe enough, only plotting escape. But the boy—well, Amazons were said to strangle sons at birth. And that hag looked evil. . . .

Molpadia raved on: "You have learned to crawl on your belly like the bitches men breed to pleasure their lust—*you!* You have shamed the blood that is in you—Lysippe's blood, that you alone could have carried on! And for such as you we gave up Themiskyra —left our young and our old to die!"

Antiope said quietly and clearly: "I do love the man—my son's father. That is a thing which has happened to others—that too you know. But if he had made me crawl I would not have loved him. And never, for love of anyone, would I have left helpless folk of my own blood to die. That was your deed, not mine."

Fire seemed to twist Molpadia; her body writhed as if in its red grip. "Slave—lying, whining slave! You, who alone could have carried on the blood of Lysippe—you had to be the first traitress that ever the race of the Amazons has brought forth! May the Goddess you have blasphemed against blast you—you have destroyed Her people, and left them to wander, hopeless and homeless, to their end!"

Hippolytos whimpered, really afraid now. Antiope patted him and said quickly: "It is all right, little king. Be still. . . . Mother's sister, you can choose another Childbearer. The blood of any Amazon is worthy. Can you not see that now, you who say that I have shamed our House?"

Molpadia laughed: an ugly, savage sound. "And leave you here with the man? That would suit you well. . . . Oh, would to Her who made us that I had strangled you when first your mother laid you in my arms!" Again her face twisted.

Antiope set Hippolytos on his feet, turned him gently toward the Athenians. "Go to the men, little king. Tell them I am sending you back to your father." As he started to toddle off, she turned to face her aunt again.

"You can still strangle me, Molpadia. Once he is back among his father's men, I will make no move to stop you. My death will end all this, for Theseus is too true a king to bring more woe upon his people by seeking vengeance. Nor will Tarkun waste more of my father's men, when I am past help. Kill me and go—save what is left of our people."

Silence again, utter silence. The twelve Amazons shuddered; they had not been able to hear all of Antiope's last words, but they had heard enough. The Athenian captain, though keeping one eye on Hippolytos' advance, still kept the other on the two women. They were quarreling; that much was plain, even to one who could not understand their tongue. Maybe the young one was loyal to Theseus, after all.

Antiope finally broke that silence, her voice low. "Maybe I have done some of the things you charge me with. But this I know— I have never blasphemed. Never could She, Who pities the pregnant hare, be willing for a baby to be slain, or taken from the arms of its mother. And you and Foremother Lysippe have done both —you are the true blasphemers, breaking Her true laws, and putting false, cruel ones of your own making into Her mouth."

She expected the Deathsinger's spring to come then—to feel the merciless hands around her throat. Then all would soon be over —peace, peace at last for Amazons and Athenians and Hittites alike. And for her. . . . But Molpadia made no move. Even when at last her lips moved, her hands still made none.

She said: "Queen you are no longer, Amazon you are no longer. Go back to your master, slave. Lick his feet like any other whipped bitch."

"Lady, you will always be our queen. We would tear to pieces any other who dared to call herself the Hippolyte in your place!"

So, with tears running down their cheeks, the six unwounded Amazons in the Akropolis tried to comfort dry-eyed Antiope. Who smiled and shook her head.

"Girls, in some ways Molpadia is right. I can no longer be the Hippolyte, I who no longer live like one. The Amazons need a new Childbearer, and if Molpadia chooses one I will be deeply glad. But"—she tried to laugh, then checked herself, afraid she could not keep the laugh steady—"what can I be if I am not an Amazon? What else could I be?" *Not an Athenian, surely: Theseus' people too have rejected me. . . .*

The others saw some of her pain, and one girl begged childishly: "Queen, do not let her hurt you! She is not so wise, except in war. My mother used to say that the real reason Molpadia hated men so much was that she could not see them oftener."

All laughed then, some too loudly and none with the merriment they were trying for. Antiope smiled again and said: "That may well be so. She has not had enough to love." She thought: *And I who was given to her to love often longed to escape from that love, and did at last.* What a tangle it had all been. Otrere, generous and herself too innocent to realize that her sister's wounds could never heal cleanly, giving away what she had had no right to give away. And Molpadia, who had betrayed her own motherhood, clutching too eagerly, too hard, at the gift! How clumsy human beings were with each other. Even when they tried to be kind, which they seldom did. . . .

She said: "Today she met me with love, and I gave her only the truth. Years too late. Never since she let her own child die has she been able to bear the truth."

"What truth, Queen?" All six looked puzzled; they loved her, yet not even they could understand.

She drew a deep breath, then said: "Girls, none of you has yet taken one lover, and turned away from all others. Maybe you would still be happiest as Amazons, and among Amazons I no longer have any place. Go back, Molpadia will be glad of you."

They stared, then bristled. "We have no place with Molpadia, Lady. We would like to cut her head off!"

She thanked them for their loyalty, her own eyes wet at last. Perhaps they had chosen rightly: three of them had sons too. Also she suddenly remembered the wagons that must go forth with the wounded, with drivers pledged not to desert to the enemy.

That night Antiope played with and petted her little Horse-Looser as usual. She smiled, but Theseus knew that it was with her eyes only. Yet that smile made him feel better, made her pain seem less real. She had been a fool to hope that she could do anything with that mad dog who was shaped like a woman; she had behaved madly herself, risking both her life and their boy's. But the siege was being hard on all of them. It must be hardest of all on Antiope; for the first time he realized that. . . .

He was glad that here in the palace she could not hear the wailing clearly, the wild, woeful wailing that drifted up eerily from the Akropolis, where the Amazons mourned for their young queen as for one dead. Would they keep up that screeching all night? When he went to bed with his wife, he did not make love to her, but only put his arms around her tenderly and held her close. Soon he thought her asleep, and went to sleep himself.

But Antiope lay awake, and listened to her own death dirge. Her heart could hear what her ears could not. *Exile. Outcast. There is no place left for you anywhere, nothing anywhere that you can do. You have failed again and again. You can help no one, least of all yourself.*

She looked at the quiet silver moonlight. She could not bear to look at the golden doves that belonged to the Goddess. *I should not have come back today. I should have taken a knife with me, and plunged it into my own heart when I could not get Molpadia to kill me.*

Too late now. If she died inside the walls, none outside them could be sure the deed had been hers. Molpadia, in her madness, might yet seek vengeance.

CHAPTER 8.
THE WAR GROWS WORSE

A LL THROUGH that night, and through the next night, and the next, that dirge rose, wild and weird and strangely troubling to western ears. The third night Antiope felt uneasy. Why? she wondered. Three nights of wailing were customary when a Queen of the Amazons lay dead.

That night she turned to Theseus, and sought his love fiercely. Not the warmth of comfort, but fires whose heat could burn away all else. And he took fire from her fire; they strained together as if trying to become one indeed, that primordial he-and-she being that long ago was severed to create the human race we know. She sought refuge in that oneness, in that new being, Theseus-and-Antiope, which they two had first created beside the dark Unfriendly Sea. She knew that escape would not last long—soon she would be Antiope again, as she always had been and always would be. As always before she had preferred to be. But for a while now it gave her rest. . . .

Spent, they slept in each other's arms, still one flesh, his implanted between her thighs, while the moon rose higher and higher. And on the Areopagos the Amazons still gave her deathwail. The death-wail of Antiope, Queen of the Amazons. Gradually even it grew lower. . . .

And then, thunder-sudden, the night silence was split and shattered. Again the Hittite rams crashed against all three gates.

Theseus sprang up, seized his weapons, and ran out. Hippolytos cried, and Antiope rose to comfort him. The room outside was full of children's crying, of women's frightened whispers.

Antiope did not know why she felt that this new attack was somehow different, unlike all the others. But the feeling was strong. Presently she left Hippolytos with another Amazon who had only one baby. She went down to the magazines, checked with the girls who watched over the wounded there, and bade them be watchful. She went to the palace doors, and bade the doorkeeper lock them behind her. To be sure, too, that every other entrance was made fast, and to open to none unless he was sure that he recognized Theseus' voice or hers.

Shadow-silent, she moved through the night, both eyes and ears straining for any least sight, any least sound. She could see almost nothing in the now moonless blackness, but she could hear talk among the tense, unhappy refugees. She made the circuit of the whole Akropolis, stopped a second time outside the dark, silent precinct of the Arrephoroi. Molpadia had made one attack there; what if she should make another? The first time Antiope had passed the place it had been utterly silent. Now she thought she heard faint stirring, movement. But the old priestess who instructed the two child priestesses might have come there to pray, frightened by the attacks upon the gates.

No—many people were stirring there, very stealthily. But that could not be! Even if the sentries above had been unaccountably lax, not many could have scrambled through that almost inaccessible opening in so brief a time. And then she heard flesh collide with flesh, and a brief, swiftly stifled murmur in her mother tongue.

Two Amazons had run into each other in the darkness. However they had got there, they and too many others were there! For a breath's space her head spun, her heart shrank as if from a blade imbedded in her flesh. She knew now why she had been afraid. She was still part of the Hive, of that one vast, unseen body. Now that the Amazons were near her again, not many of them could move together without her knowing it. And she must use that oneness that was in her blood and theirs to betray them, her own people! For she must warn Theseus. . . .

Lightning-swift, she turned and ran for the main gates. He was more likely to be there. And he was. He listened, then sternly bade her go up into the tower and stay there. She obeyed him, meek for once as any Athenian woman. For this time she had no desire to go with him, to fight beside him. How could she fight against Amazons?

Yet already I have betrayed them.

In the tower the crashing of the ram against the gates below sounded thunder-loud. Men told her that Theseus had sallied out and captured the first ram, but a second had already been brought up. The defenders were hurling down stones that crashed upon the stony ground below, or bounced loudly off ram or helmets, whenever they did not strike human flesh. The din was deafening, yet still Antiope's ears strained constantly for the cry she dreaded.

It came, stabbing her with many memories: "HIP-PO-OL-Y-TE-E! HIP-PO-OL-Y-TE-E-E!"

Bitter fighting raged within the walls. The Amazons broke Theseus' first charge, and themselves charged for the postern gate, doubtless led by scouts sent ahead to creep through the night and locate it. Through that gate they could have let in the Hittites. But with desperate ferocity Theseus drove them back, forced a heavy wedge of heavily armed men between them and it. Again and again the Amazons charged and were thrown back. Then, cruel as the rain of hot, searing ash that once had fallen upon all lands near the broken island of Kalliste, they turned upon the rest of the Akropolis. From the porch along the north wall came the screams of women and children—screams not only of fear. Heartsick, Antiope knew that Molpadia was breaking the ancient law that forbade wasting time upon the unarmed. Though doubtless she thought it no waste—only the surest way to get the defenders away from the postern.

And they came. Arms clashed, and the shouts of men and women mingled; Amazons too cried out in death. Back and forth the fighting surged, but still Theseus managed to keep it away from the postern. Dawn came, ghost-gray, and the Amazons turned upon the few buildings within the walls. The strong doors of the strong house of Erechtheus threw them back, but other doors were lighter and weaker. They surged into all the rest, including the house of old Alexandra and her husband Eubolos. From these houses too screams came, and men rushing to the rescue were fallen upon by Amazons who leaped upon them from either side of the doorways through which they entered.

To get the warriors out of those houses, all well provisioned, would be hard indeed; and they could not be permitted to stay there and sally forth whenever they pleased. Grimly Theseus gave the order he knew he must give: "Fire those houses."

The morning flame that filled the heavens was answered by flaming torches below. Torches that had been the homes of men.

Some Amazons died, spitted upon waiting spears, when they tried to break out of those refuges that were no longer refuges. But more cut through their attackers. They charged the postern again, and again were flung back. Some tried to scramble up through the high windows of the strong house of Erechtheus, and the women inside shrieked with fear. Theseus, sick at heart, had to abandon all attempts to keep watch upon the entrance to the underground passage that led to the all-important well in the depths. More attackers might come up through it, but he must guard the two places he knew to be mortally menaced—the postern and his father's house.

And then suddenly, unbelievably, the mighty doors of that house were flung wide. Through them charged old Aegeus, sword in hand, his faded eyes aglow with the light of battle. After him, armed too, poured those honored ancients who had taken shelter beneath his roof. "Ex-men," as the Greek tongue named them, but the men who had been his men, the battle comrades of his youth.

For a little that youth came back to them. They were still Athenians, and they fought for Athens. They fell upon the enemy, and drove them back, away from the strong house of Erechtheus. Before the Amazons could recover from the shock of that unexpected charge, Theseus and his men were there, leaping in front of the old men, pressing forward. Step by step, still fighting like true daughters of War-God Ares, the Amazons were driven back —toward the violated precinct of the Arrephoroi. Theseus saw Molpadia's hated crest and tried to reach it, felt, like an actual touch, her fierce longing to reach him. But many pressed between them, and neither leader dared be rash, risk leaving his or her forces leaderless.

In the precinct of the Arrephoroi the Amazons made their last stand. In the fiercest of hand-to-hand fighting some held the men of Athens until a line of their dreaded archers could form behind them. Then they fell back, and their foes stood like dogs that face a lion or a bear, savage but wary. They had seen too much of the kind of death brought by poisoned arrows to rush upon it. So shielded, the rest of the Amazons scrambled back down into the underground passage, back down through that dark, Underworld-like way through which they had come. The archers tried to follow, but a great volley of spears brought many of them down. At last they used their terror-bringing bows, but nothing now could stop the charging avengers. Spearlike, the Athenians followed their thrown spears. For the space of a few breaths only that terrible fight lasted, then the last archer fell, Greek blades still hacking her dead flesh.

Being Pittheus' grandson, Theseus wasted no time in such futile, ugly vengeance. His father had been wounded, not badly, but the strength had gone out of all the old men now. They stood panting, leaning heavily upon whatever they could find to lean on. Theseus told off men to support Aegeus, and to lead all the old fighters home. Then, having made sure that the gates were still holding, he took his force and plunged down into that darkness that seemed truly like the Underworld. He dared not risk letting the Amazons regroup somewhere in the underground passage; above all, he dared not risk their poisoning the well.

Again there was fighting: blind, bitter fighting, in such blackness that only by voice could friend be told from foe. The Athenians fought their way forward by ways so narrow that sometimes only two of them could go abreast. Over rocky floors that sometimes were slippery with blood; over fallen bodies that sometimes were those of their own comrades.

They fought their way at last into the Cave of Aglauros, and by the light of its reopened entrance fought again where they could see those they were fighting, know where their blows fell. They drove the Amazons out.

One Amazon's body had to be caught on a spear and fished out of the well—had she landed there by chance, or sought it out with grim purpose? But to all who drank, the water tasted the same as ever. Theseus left guards at the cave entrance, thankful that the hillside below was so steep that a few men could hold the place for some time if they kept good watch. Long enough, certainly, for one of their number to go back and fetch help. Then he and his tired army had to rush back by the way they had come. If any of the gates fell—

And for a while longer the rams did keep up their battering work. The Hittites knew that the women had failed, but knew also how hurt and worn the besieged must be. . . .

Not until noon did they stop, and what was left of the day was long and hard. The old original main gates were all but done for; Theseus set skilled carpenters to work on them at once, using what solid beams and posts could be found in the burned houses. Not one inhabitant of those houses had survived, those old, trusted officials of his father's, and their families and servants. There was much weeping among the refugees also; the Amazons had been merciless.

Theseus' second most important task was to reclose the Cave of Aglauros, fill the entrance up again with earth and stones. While there he made sure of something he had feared: two of the young men who had followed him down into that underground darkness were missing. He had hoped against hope that he might find them among the guards he had left there, but he did not. In the heat of battle had they followed the Amazons out of the cave? Followed them too far? He risked a search, but no bodies, dead or wounded, lay on the hillside. And he dared send no men down into the flatter lands below; he had already lost too many. . . .

Heavy-hearted, he went back up into the Akropolis, found the families of the lost ones and told them the grim news. Saw the fear and misery in all their faces, and heard one mother weep. Then he went back to the palace, through young men who hailed him joyously; in last night's bitter, triumphant struggle their love for him had blossomed anew.

But in the pale evening, when he led Antiope out of the palace and, before all men, thanked her for the warning that had saved them all, there was little cheering. What there was all came from young men who had been with them both in the dark Unfriendly Sea. Sullenly most of his people watched and listened, their unspoken suspicions loud. *She and the old hag planned last night's attack between them—why else did they meet? And when she was sure that enough of her accursed pack were inside to overwhelm us—then she ran, somewhat*

slowly, to warn Theseus. Oh, she is cunning—cunning and treacherous, like all
her breed.

She was an Amazon, and all Amazons now seemed awesome, unnatural foes, terrible as the dim shapes children fear in the dark. Women should not be able to fight; and women who could were monsters. Had proved themselves so.

His people's silence chilled and disappointed Theseus, but not Antiope. Traitress they thought her, and traitress she now thought herself. When she had awakened, unrefreshed, from her day-long, sodden sleep, memory had seared her like fire. Now she was truly what Molpadia had called her.

Yet what else could she have done? Theseus—Hippolytos! Two or three children younger than Hippolytos had died last night.

Passively she went back into the palace with Theseus. Free to rest at last, he sat with his wife and boy in a small courtyard that once had been bright with potted plants. All the plants were withered now, dead of thirst; they would bloom no more. But the place was quiet, and a little breeze blew through it; after the scorching heat of the day it seemed cool. Hippolytos played happily, and his father and mother watched him. Contentment could not come to them, yet slowly its gentle shadow did. . . .

And then a man came running, looked at Theseus. "Lord, Lord, at the gates—"

Sheer habit made Theseus leap up, then he stopped, puzzled. "I hear no ram—"

"It is no ram. It is one of those accursed she-devils, and she calls for you."

The Amazon had a bundle of bloodstained clothing hanging from her spear, and she laughed as she called upward and gave Theseus her message.

"Hear, man of Athens! The Deathsinger, the Hippolyte, beloved of the Goddess, sends these tokens to show that she speaks truth. Sends them by me who alone of her women speaks the royal tongue of Kanesh well." She dropped the stained clothing in the dust before the gates. "Rejoice, for those two foolish young men who pursued us last night still live; as yet, they are not even sorely hurt. Look down tonight and watch them making merry with us upon the Areopagos. In bright new clothing of the queen's own giving!"

That night the Amazons set up two stakes upon the Areopagos. To these were bound Lykias, son of Lykomedes, and Meriones, son of Alexander, their naked bodies blackened with pitch. Molpadia herself laughed up toward the Akropolis, then applied the torch. The young men screamed horribly, and for what seemed a long time. All Athens, including their own friends and families, watched them burn.

In the ash-gray dawn Theseus came at last to Antiope, his own face so gray and gaunt she hardly knew it. But she did know that now he regretted his oath, and wished that he had let her return to her people.

He looked at her once, then swiftly looked away. She thought, *Can he not even bear the sight of me?* He said heavily: "After last night, I doubt if anyone with Amazon blood can be safe inside these walls. Even you and my son."

She did not answer, and he spoke again, as if from a great distance: "Tonight a fishing boat will take you and the boy to Troizen. I will send a pigeon to tell wise Pittheus and my mother of your coming."

She spoke then, saying: "My girls, and the wounded—what of them?"

Her cool, matter-of-fact voice repelled him; he did not sense the strain beneath it. Did she despise him for sending her away? For not keeping his people in such fear of him that he could have been sure of her safety? No doubt that would have been the way of any of the kings of the East.

He said: "You need have no fear for them. They will go at once to Elephenor, and if they should be caught on the way—well, they will be with their own kin!"

The last three words leaped at her, savage with all his bitter hate, and for a breath's space she closed her eyes in pain as bitter. When she opened them again she said. "Then I must tell them to pack. I will be packing too—for myself and Hippolytos."

He winced. Any other woman would have clung to him and wept; have begged him to say he still loved her. As he did; what had happened had not been her fault—he knew better than to share his people's suspicions. Yet that accursed blood was in her; she had even poured it into his son's veins.

He said, unrealized harshness in his voice: "Is that all you have to say?"

"What can I say?" Her own pain and bitterness flashed out. "Would you have me weep and howl like one of your Athenian women?"

It was too much. He was still sick from last night's horrors. He would never forget how the mothers of Lykias and Meriones had wept and screamed while their sons burned. And now she dared mock that sorrow—*mock* it! She still loved her people, admired their never-breaking hardness; and why not? None of this was new to her. Every year, before the Black Stone, men had been burned, and she had waited on shore, knowing—

"Be silent, woman!" He ground the words between his teeth. They were as savage as a blow, and she started; her whole body jerked as if beneath that blow. Then she turned her eyes away from him, rose, and silently set about her packing. For a little while Theseus watched her, uneasy and miserable, anything but glad or proud because she was obeying him. If only she would weep—if one tear would run down that face that now was like a carven mask. But no tears came; well, she was hard. He turned on his heel, and whirled away.

The day passed, long and slow, with misery all around him, and some within him. Several times he nearly went back to her. In spite of her love for her accursed people, she had warned him of their coming that other night, that now seemed so long ago. Now she must be thinking him ungrateful and unloving; perhaps she even feared that he was sending her and Hippolytos away forever. But each time his wrath rose again. She had not spoken one word of regret or pity—she loved the burners, and was proud of the blood she shared with them! Perhaps she did not want him to come to her, but did despise him as a coward. . . .

That night the Hittite rams again pounded the gates of Athens. Tarkun was not one to spare the weary and shaken defenders; he believed in pressing every advantage. Theseus did not go back to the palace at all that night; neither did Antiope or any of her Amazons leave it. In the morning he sent a messenger to ask how his father was, but Aegeus' wound was doing well. His son was glad, and did not admit to himself that he was also disappointed, having now no excuse to go home. Neither had he admitted to himself that he had been glad when the attack had given him an excuse for staying away.

There was much work to be done. He went down into the Cave of Aglauros, and would not let the men working there stop until the blockade was much deeper than it had been before. Yet still he would have to double the guards on the northern wall tonight, and every night until the siege was over. Make sure that no more creeping Amazons came.

Long ago she had warned him what a danger the cave was. Antiope . . . and she was still here. . . .

But when he came back up into the sunlight he found that the new repairs on the gate—needed after last night's attack—had not been well made. Cursing, he made the men do the work over again, and stood over them while they did it, sweating himself. The sun was so hot—if only rain would come! He could not help thinking how good a bath would be, down in the cool Ilissos. The Hittites could bathe there . . . and the accursed Amazons. He thought of Antiope's lithe, lovely body, so white wherever the sun had not reached it. How happy they had been, he and she, when they had bathed together in that far-off eastern river. But there Solois had drowned himself—

"Lord, a pigeon just brought this message." There was a man beside him.

Never would Pittheus refuse to receive Antiope and the boy! Could this be word that either Hippothoon or Elephenor was ready to join him at last? Hurriedly Theseus opened the message, read: "From Lykophron, son of Pallas, to Theseus, son of Aegeus: Joy! I write from the camp of the Hittites, where my father has sent some of his sons—"

Well, that was no surprise. The Amazons killed every man they saw, but Tarkun never had been harsh with even the country people of Attica. Hippothoon had reported receiving friendly overtures from him, also rumors that he was dealing with Pallene. No doubt Pallas, that truest of brothers, would gladly help the Hittites all he could, with both supplies and information, for a price—the kingship of a battered, war-torn Athens! Theseus ground his teeth and read on:

"—seeking to learn whether they mean to settle here. I alone of all fifty of us can write"—that too was no surprise; most noblemen chose to leave such dull work to trained underlings—"so pigeons that rise from my quarters are spared, though now the Amazons shoot down all others they see, lest these be messengers to or from Athens. Yesterday they shot down one you would have sent to Troizen. I know that from the half-Cretan interpreter the Hittites brought from Troy; he can read, and translated your letter to the queen. She bribed him not to tell Tarkun of it, and last night she rode south with many Amazons to Troizen. The Gods guard your kin there. For what befell the two captives my heart bleeds as yours must; I too am of Athenian blood. May this letter reach you!"

Ashen-faced, Theseus dropped it. Troizen broken and in flames, the women and children fleeing from those she-butchers who had slain their husbands and fathers! Wise old Pittheus and Aithra, his lovely mother, naked and burning! Or would Molpadia devise even worse torments for them—if such could be!—when she found that Antiope was not within their walls?

This could be a trap. One set by the sons of Pallas. Strange that Lykophron should have been told what had been kept from Tarkun. Yet maybe he and the interpreter had been brought together by their shared knowledge; not all men could read and write. He need not have told how he had come by his knowledge; did not that very fact indicate his truthfulness? Or did it? Theseus' head spun. He did not want Lykophron to be a traitor—with all his heart he did not. Yet if only this message could be dismissed as a lie!

I cannot be sure. But if it is true—

All his life days Theseus would remember the time between then and nightfall as a nightmare. Faces, many faces, all startled at first; then some quivering, pitiful with fear that he was deserting them. But many were grim with wrath; the older men were all against him. "We know where your mother is. But will you desert Athens, and the father who begot you? Are you a foreigner, a man of Troizen, after all?" Of them all only Aegeus, still spent and feverish, backed him. "No man can refuse help to the mother who bore him. Not if he would still be called either king or man." And the love of the young men stood firm; Theseus was their hero, their darling, the doer of all those unheard-of deeds on the road to Athens; the captain who had sailed to the World's End, and back again.

Only at nightfall, when he and his men were creeping out through the postern, did Theseus remember that he had not seen Antiope before his going. Or left any word for her. But she would be safe, she and the boy. The people would not turn on the Amazons within their walls; not during the little time he would be gone.

What would he find in Troizen? Sick with dread, he pushed that thought away. All he could think of now was getting there. . . .

Through the hazy gloom of early night, when blackness is not yet deep, yet seems more mysterious than if it were—through that, as through a maze of traps and pitfalls, the Athenians warily picked their way. They clung to the cover of brush and trees, and of the black shadows of the rocky hills. They feared every new sight or sound; it could mean the approach of an enemy. One they had no time to deal with now.

At last they reached the shore; found fishermen to whom Theseus paid the full worth of the boats the owners feared never to see again. They sailed, and then Theseus had no way to use his wits any longer, to keep from thinking of what might happen in Troizen before he got there. *Oh, Poseidon, my Father, if ever my mother was fair in Your sight, protect her now.*

Molpadia must have ridden through Attica unopposed. The towns of the Isthmus might attack her, afraid of being attacked themselves; but if she rode past them before they could gather their forces—and the Amazons were fabulous riders—they never would pursue her. Most men preferred the sight of Amazon backs to that of Amazon faces. Unfair to blame them for that, although those towns owed much to him, Theseus; he had delivered them from the bandit kings. But that was years ago, and this was now. . . . Korinth, just south of the Isthmus, was an important town and might give Molpadia trouble. He prayed to the Gods that it had. But a puppet king ruled in Korinth now, an unwarlike man of Eurystheus'; he would be in no hurry to go out and face the Amazons. If she rode by without stopping, he would do no more than send word to Eurystheus, whose concern was always all for himself, never for his kin.

But the impassable cliffs between Epidaurus and Troizen—they would stop her. Must have stopped her. Without an interpreter she could not get a guide, and even if she did, the way around those cliffs would be long and circuitous. *I may get there in time—I may!*

All night he and his men rowed hard, needing the south wind that at this time of year they could not hope for. Dawn came and they still rowed, their salty sweat dripping down into the salt sea. Then at last Theseus had to let them stop a little while, to eat and rest. But soon he drove them on again. They could see where they were going now—all night clouds had covered the moon and hindered them, the rain clouds that they had longed for so long. Clouds that now, mockingly, were gone once more.

And then, in the golden morning light, they saw black smoke rising above the blue Bay of Methana. Smoke such as might rise from burning ships. Theseus drove himself and all others as only the cruelest of men would drive horses. Soon they saw pillars of fire beneath the pillars of smoke, and knew beyond all doubt what fuel fed them. Those flames were eating up all his hopes—all his high dreams of conquering Crete, all his long-dreamed-of precious ships!

But even that pain was one he did not yet have time to feel; he and his men rowed on. To avoid the burning ships they had to hug the opposite shores, those of sacred Kalaureia, until they could turn west and land at last on a strip of white, deserted shore. Inland too smoke was rising—from what had once been farmhouses. But Theseus raised his eyes still higher, and then cried aloud with such joy as no man can ever find words for.

No puff of smoke soiled the flaming blue of the sky above the Akropolis of Troizen. Three thousand feet high it towered above that low green plain, seemingly as peaceful as the clouds that were its neighbors.

Swiftly he led his men toward it. They passed burning houses and burning trees, trees that would bear no more good fruit, yet flamed now with a final, awful blossoming. Twice they passed the bodies of the slain, and once Theseus, seeing a face he knew, both groaned and cursed. But near the mountain itself the sun still shimmered on gray-green olive trees, in whose shade a sleek, shining herd of horses waited quietly. Unguarded, for these were the steeds of the Amazons, trained to battle to the death if any but their own warrior mistresses sought to mount them.

When Theseus saw them his eyes shone red, and he laughed and leaped at the nearest. It swerved to avoid him, but his spear gashed its foreleg. It screamed and reared, trying to strike him with its forehoofs, but the second spear thrust ripped its belly; its entrails spilled out onto the earth. Theseus laughed again—he who, before those burnings on the Areopagos, would have been sickened by the screams of a tortured horse. He leaped at another, and many of his men followed suit. The horses stampeded, and fled wildly.

Nor had their cries gone unheard. Far above, the Amazons who were lugging a huge log up toward the Akropolis dropped their crude ram. They poured back down the steep, crumbly slope. Quickly Theseus called out orders, and his men scattered, to wait in ambush under the trees.

Had the Deathsinger's head been cool, as of old, the Amazons never would have rushed into that trap. But now they came on blindly, raging like she-beasts who have heard their hurt cubs crying. None ever had a chance to aim her dreaded arrows. Some died quickly; more survived to fight for life and vengeance. Duel after duel was fought, one man against one woman: hideous parodies of love, ending, not in life-giving ecstasy, but in death. Only Theseus raged everywhere, his eyes red now as his hair and sword, glad of every Amazon who fell. Yet always he sought only Molpadia, and always the white-robed Fates kept them apart. Twice he saw her crest, and twice found only what she had left behind her—the fallen, bleeding body of a man.

None knew when the gates of Troizen opened, when the men of Troizen came pouring downhill, led into battle this once by the wise and holy Pittheus, a helmet covering his white hair, in his hand the sword of his own grandfather, Goddess-loving Tantalos.

But as he drew near a strange cry rose, a cry that seemed to come from under every tree, out of every shadow. Three times it shrilled, and every Amazon who could turned and fled. The Athenians leaped after them, but Pittheus' voice soared above the tumult, high and clean as the white eagles that flew over those waters that were the grave of Tantalos.

"Stop, child of my daughter!"

And Theseus knew that voice, one he had obeyed of old, and stopped. He and all his men stood stunned and panting, until the aged king came toward them, his hands outstretched toward the son of Aithra. Theseus ran to meet him, and for a breath's space the two stood clasped in each other's arms.

CHAPTER 9.
___FIRE ARROWS—AND A MISTAKE

THEN THOUGHT came back to Theseus, and rage with it. He drew back, crying: "Why did you stop us? They have wrought havoc here! Let us all go after them—"

"And throw more lives after those that are lost already? They will trouble Troizen no more. Listen." So Pittheus spoke, and once more they obeyed him; and in that sudden silence a weird whistling rose from the plain behind them: many eerie, birdlike sounds together that filled all with wonder. Of the young men, only Theseus knew what those sounds were: the Amazons calling their horses back to them. And indeed no steed was too far away, too weak from wounds or too mad with fear, to hear and answer that call. The men of Troizen never afterward found any of those horses save the slain.

"But they may come back!" Theseus, finding his voice, raged again.

"They will not." Wise Pittheus only smiled. "At dawn, from the tower above my gates, I spoke with the queen. I swore to her, by the Goddess, that Antiope was not here. She refused to believe me then, yet in her heart she feared I spoke the truth, and now she knows it. When I came to reinforce you, her battle-fury broke and she saw her folly—called her people together to begin the journey back to Athens."

Well, it would take her a while to get there, and once she did it would be another while before even the Amazons were ready to fight again. Also it was no use to pursue them once they had their horses back. Theseus relaxed; once more he felt the peace of Troizen flowing into him again: unchanged, strong as ever, violated though it had been.

No Athenian was unhurt, and Pittheus had food and drink and other comforts brought for those too weary to climb up to high Troizen. He had all the badly wounded carried up, Athenian and Amazon alike. That roused Theseus' rage again. "Waste no kindness on those she-wolves, Grandfather. I let Antiope and her girls bring in those who lay wounded beneath my walls—and hear how they have repaid us!" Savagely the story of the burnings poured out of him, and sadly old Pittheus listened.

"Great evil has been done, and so great evil has been sown. In you the seeds already sprout."

Theseus flinched and bit his lip, thinking of the slain horses. "What do you mean?"

"Ask yourself. You know, who are no longer a child. What you do not know is whether that other sowing, which was good, has been wasted. Seeds well sown must stay down in the darkness awhile before they flower beneath the sun. Those Antiope tended now know her love and goodness—and that you let her show them."

"Think what those she-wolves did!" Theseus' fists clenched. "And it was done after those who had recovered rejoined their vile pack—not before!"

"In war they must follow their War-Queen. Or else break and set aside all that for lifetimes has kept them free. It will take a while to change that." Pittheus sighed. "Yet it has begun. All their arrows are said to be poisoned, but several of my people were pierced by them as they fled—and over half the wounds are clean. Have you noticed nothing of that sort at Athens?"

Theseus bit his lip again and was silent.

He too was weary, but he did climb up to the city, to see his mother. And Aithra welcomed him, and made a great fuss over him, mother-wise.

"How is Antiope?" she asked, after she had tended his hurts. "These must be bitter days for her."

Theseus flushed, and Aithra's eyes suddenly shone with a keenness he remembered. "Son, have you made them still harder?"

His flush deepened. "Yes, Mother, I have."

"Child, none of this is her doing. And she loves you."

"She loves them too! Those murderesses who are butchering my people—torturing them with tortures such as no true man ever would inflict upon a foe! But they are neither men nor women, but black fiends of the night shaped like women!"

"Child, they are her people. She knew them at home, where all are human. They nursed and fed her, taught and loved her, as other women do their children. And I need not tell you that the fruit of their teaching was good; you know her."

He was silent. As of old, she looked at him and waited, and presently he said heavily: "Nobody with a heart could forget such things. I have been unjust. And when she was most miserable, having to bear the wrath and hate of her own people—mine have tormented her always—I made her bear my own wrath too."

"Her own people have turned against her?" Aithra's voice was shocked. "How did that happen?"

He told her, then said sadly: "I have brought woe upon all I love. Upon her, upon Athens, and Troizen too. I could not even spare the people among whom I was born."

"Few have died here, child. A dream warned your grandfather, and all day yesterday families were being brought up here, and beasts. Houses can be rebuilt, and fruit trees will grow again; you know that in making things grow your grandfather has skills no other man can understand. The men of Troizen will build your ships again too."

He laughed harshly. "That would be much to ask of them. They built the ships for love the first time, unpaid; and why should they love me now?"

"They will do it. All in Troizen know you were born to a great destiny. The ships will rise again."

"But not in time!" His voice rose in a sudden, bitter cry. "I thought I could save those who now must die next year—those innocents whom Minos the Just will have torn upon the horns of his bulls because of a crime with which they had nothing to do! I thought I had given up hope of saving them, but I know now I had not. Not while those ships still stood!"

"You will save many, child. You must wait a little, but age teaches us all that life is full of waiting."

"How long must I wait? How long? Until Hippolytos is old enough to prove to Athens how right I was to take his mother— even if her accursed people did come after her?" He tried to steady himself. "No, not that long, I know. But those fourteen Minos will kill next year—them I cannot help!"

He was very tired; he had had no rest since the burnings, and had borne much. He covered his face with his hands then, and behind their shield sobbed like a child. And as if he had still been a child Aithra comforted him, her hand gently stroking his fiery hair. She thought: *How much more fuss he makes over those fourteen deaths than over the many that have already died in this war—and the many more that will die! Well, that is the way of men. All men but my father.*

She said: "Let us hope there will be no more burnings. But if there are, do not make Antiope pay for them, child."

"I will not! I will make it up to her—"

"Child, we cannot put a price on the pain we cause others. Show her that you love her; that is all you can do."

"I will."

He reached Athens long before the returning Amazons did. Only later did he know their story: how Tarkun's bribed interpreter had been bribed again to get Molpadia a guide, and how to reach Troizen she had made a ride unbelievable save to Amazons, and never matched before by even them. But on their way back no such riding had been possible. They had got past Korinth safely, but the Isthmus towns, seeing that now it was safe to do so, remembered their debt to Theseus. Although even Alkathoos, husband of Nisos' elder daughter, and the man to whom Theseus had given Nisa, had let them ride southward unhindered. But on their way back the beaten, battered Amazons were spared by none. Only a sick remnant lived to reach the Areopagos, where Molpadia sat and nursed her wounds in fury, swearing that her time would come.

But in the rosy tenderness of that dawn when Theseus returned to the Akropolis, he had little thought for any Amazon save one. Eagerly, his old father and many others came out to welcome him, but as soon as he could he went into the strong house of Erechtheus and to his bed, on which Antiope sat silent. She had heard the joy made at his coming, but had not risked rebuff by going out to meet him.

Unsmiling, he looked down at her, but his eyes were soft. "Antiope, I have come home. Can I make you glad to see me?"

She opened her arms. He had suffered much, and he was still her child as well as her lover—only a man. And the sun was high before they had any more need for words. . . .

As soon as he woke he left her. He had to go to his men, and to see to many things that had been done or undone in his absence. But that night they did talk together. She said: "I am to blame for the burnings. I gambled when I went out to meet Molpadia, thinking that if I lost I would be the only one to die. And the last one."

He said in horror: "You thought she might kill you?"

"Yes. But I was sure I could keep Hippolytos safe. I could have kept her busy until your men came—and even if our two escorts had fought my people never would have harmed him. They still loved me then."

The pain in her quiet voice as she spoke those last words made him groan. "Antiope—Antiope!"

"It seemed the best thing to do—the only way to stop the war. But it did not work. I did cause the burnings, and I was afraid you could never look at me again without remembering that—and that I was the cause of all, from the beginning."

"It was not like that! If anybody inside these walls caused this war I did, and I know it. You did not carry yourself off. But I was in great pain, and I was jealous. I will never be jealous of the Amazons again, beloved—I have you, and they have not." Fiercely he crushed her against him and kissed her as fiercely.

As soon as she could move her arms she put them around his neck. "We have each other."

They did, but Theseus knew that the friends of the sons of Pallas only waited. It took all his power and prestige to keep the wounded Amazons and their nurses from being mobbed, and if Molpadia burned any more men they surely would be. On the third night after his return, two of Antiope's six, with their children and half the wounded, were smuggled out through the postern. Another two went also; they were to go to Troizen. "For although the women of Troizen will obey my mother, I know well they are not eager to nurse the wounded Amazons there," Theseus had said; Antiope understood why well enough. Both girls must be needed in Troizen, yet their going was a bitter wrench—she had hoped to keep these last two with her. Tomorrow night another pair must go to Chalkis.

The night was moonless, yet the wagon mules had to be led down with hooves cloth-wrapped for silence. Only Amazons could have been sure to keep them from braying through that journey. Theseus himself, with carefully chosen young men, carried down the body and wheels of a wagon, to be put together once they were beyond sight and sound of the enemy. Then the wounded were borne down in litters. The Amazons went back up to the postern to get their sleeping babies, whom for once they had drugged with watered wine mixed with poppy juice.

At its outer gate Antiope said goodbye. Those wounded who were weakest from their hurts wept and said, "Will we ever see you again, Lady?" But the four who had come with her from Themiskyra said nothing, only looked their sorrow. She said, "The Goddess be with you, sisters, until we meet again." But when would that meeting be? They could only hug her, hard and silently, as she did them, and go. Alone, Antiope turned back into the dark, narrow passage that was the postern. She passed the hard-eyed sentries at both gates, and walked through the crowded sweltering Akropolis, where all who were awake eyed her with sullen hate, this woman who was the cause of all their woe. In the strong house of Erechtheus the same sullen silence greeted her. If any of the house slaves still felt friendliness, none dared show it now that the palace was packed with highborn refugee women who were her foes.

She went to the magazines, where her last two Amazons tended the remaining wounded, and watched over both their own children and Hippolytos. She longed to stay there with them—wherever they were tomorrow night they would not be with her. But Theseus had said, "I want you in our bed, beloved, when I get back." And how could she refuse him? Because of her he was risking much tonight. So all too soon she had to leave these friends she was losing—her sisters in all but birth now—and carry her boy upstairs, back through that silent, festering hate.

But alone in the dark she had nothing to do but think of Theseus' danger. To wait, and think again how much harder waiting was than fighting. Why had Elephenor insisted that his friend be there to identify the women his men would bring back to Chalkis? Pittheus' boatmen had asked no such pledge. Elephenor's must be cowards, afraid of meeting any Amazons alone. *As if we were all wild beasts—*

And with cause now. Those burnings— But if Molpadia could capture Theseus, would she be content even with burning him? *O Goddess, bring him back to me!*

In the red sunrise he did come back, laughing and triumphant, like a boy who has just won an exciting game. "All is well, love! I saw them all off—two to Troizen, and the rest to Chalkis." And she hugged him even harder than he hugged her, joy in his safety making her forget the pain of all partings that had been or soon would be. Everything but him. She never knew that during his absence he had been afraid for her. Afraid that some rumor of harm to him and those with him might make his people turn on the Amazons still within their walls.

But soon full day came, hot and long and golden, Antiope's last day with her last two Amazons. Theseus let her spend the whole of it with them, turning to his father and his men. And to all three of the girls from Themiskyra it seemed very short, yet also the longest day that any of them had ever lived through. Words were too small, futile clutches at what was being borne away from them, inexorably, remorselessly, as if upon a flooding river. Sometimes they would laugh, recalling fun they had had long ago, and then suddenly the laughter would become too loud, too shrill, too determined. With every breath's space night was coming nearer— the night that must end their long comradeship.

It came. With them too she went to the postern gate. They hated to go, and one said fiercely, "Make Theseus leave the wounded at the foot of the Akropolis, where our people will find them in the morning. We cannot go. Our place is with you!"

Antiope said, "Think of your children, who are no longer safe here. Of Theseus' oath to his people; you know he had to promise to free no more of their enemies to fight them again. Go—and the Goddess be with you!" When they still hung back she spoke again, sternly: "If you still call me Queen, obey me. Go."

They understood. Their obedience was the last gift they could give her. The last obedience any Amazons would ever give her. But warriors though they were, they went weeping through the night. For they knew that the long nibbling at the gates would soon be over; soon both sides would sink their teeth deep in each other's flesh. And when that happened they would not be there, they who would have died defending her against Molpadia.

Antiope stood in the postern gate and watched them go. They were the last she had had of home, of Themiskyra. And it was life that she feared, not death.

Again dawn brought Theseus back; again all was well. Antiope was glad, yet the hot golden morning was night-black before her eyes.

That afternoon a little rain came at last. Not the heavy, soaking rain that was needed, yet it put a little water into many pots and jugs hastily thrust out into it, and sent the besieged to bed refreshed. Those chosen to be tomorrow's water-bearers hoped they might be spared one of their long grim journeys down into the dark. All were deep in the sweet arms of Sleep, Death's brother, when the catastrophe came. Shouting woke Theseus and Antiope, and through their window they saw the sinister red glare of fire. Bright and fierce it glowed, and across it small, low lightnings seemed to be darting. Both seized their clothes and ran, Hippolytos, wide-eyed in his mother's arms. He did not cry; with her there, nothing could happen to him.

Flames were shooting up from the rudely thatched roof along the northwestern wall—eating it up like savage tongues. Some of the refugess it had sheltered were still scrambling out, wild-eyed. The Amazons were shooting fire arrows into the Akropolis!

Theseus shouted for water, and for men to use it. All the precious, heaven-sent water gained the evening before was gone in a breath's space. *If only that rain had lasted long enough to soak the roofs,* he thought grimly. But it had not, and though water-carriers were already speeding down into the depths, such Underworld-like journeys took time. Soon that northwestern porch blazed like a fallen sunset; men could only fight to save the roofs around it, using cloaks and bedding to try to smother and stamp out the flames. But the whole northern roof went; Theseus had to withdraw the men he had sent there to shoot return volleys at the Amazons, whose first act had been to kill all the sentries originally posted there. And their ceaseless hail of fire, though launched blindly now, found targets enough. Two entered the cattle pen, and set the scared beasts milling, while ugly bellows rose from one in whose hide a flaming arrow had stuck. The third pierced the shoulder of a great black bull. Mad with rage, he hurled himself against the fence, that shook and strained beneath his weight. But there was a harsh sound of splitting wood—the barrier would not hold long.

Theseus dropped the pail of water he carried and snatched up a spear. He ran back toward the wall, and then forward again, toward the pen. The magnificent charge ended in a flying leap that brought him level with the top of the fence. Grasping it with one hand, he drove his spear between the great, bellowing jaws, and on into the little brain. The bull fell, and so did he, his spear lost, and his now bleeding left hand all one great bruise from the force with which it had had to clutch the rough, narrow wood.

Within a breath's space men were around him, praising him, marveling at that spearthrust. But he pushed away the hands that would have helped him up. "The God was with me. Get stuff to strengthen that fence, men—if those beasts get out—"

But Antiope took over that work, calling to the dazed, scared women to help her, and let the men get back to their firefighting. For as fast as one fire could be put out, another was springing up. She and her bewildered helpers had to pile up benches and tables against the fence, and pack whatever they could find between the legs. At first Antiope herself felt sick—what if Theseus had over-balanced and fallen inside that wall?—but soon she began to notice that some of her workers were doing well, and praised them. These common women who had to work still had worth. But only a few thanked her, warily and without warmth. Before the siege a few, whose needy families she had helped, had begun to like her. But now they too were back in their old comfortable rut, following the lead of their betters—of those fine ladies who now crouched terrified in the palace, doing nothing. A queer, mad thing, this idea of an aristocracy of birth. All Amazons had to prove their own worth, all were born equal save the royal race of the queens; they were revered for carrying the blood of Lysippe—of her who had thrown her baby into a river! That reverence too could be called a queer thing. *Goddess, forgive me! How dare I judge her, I who never have suffered what she suffered? To be raped, and by one's own son—*

She looked at Hippolytos, sitting nearby on a pile of stuff carried
out by those the fires had made homeless. He looked back at her,
bewildered and a little scared, yet trustful: she was still there. The
idea of being raped by him suddenly made her laugh; she could
not help it. A woman's narrowing eyes stopped her. Next they
would be saying, "The Amazon laughed while our homes
burned." Well, maybe a night like this could make people laugh
strangely, at strange things—

Then screams tore away all thought. A woman came running,
an arrow stuck in her thin summer cloak, that was blossoming into
an awful flower of fire. Antiope leaped for her, thinking crazily,
This will make Hippolytos cry! She tore off the cloak, burning her own
hands. Others ran to help. They had been in time, Antiope
thought—the creature was still moaning horribly, but the Women
were taught no self-control—until she saw the seared, sickening
horror that had been one side of the woman's face. . . .

She and the others went back to work, each thinking, *Next
time it may be I.* All who were mothers also thought, *Or a child born
of me.*

On and on they came, those frightful, ceaseless arrows, raining
pain and fear and destruction. Until, suddenly, they stopped.

"Thanks be to all the Gods, it is over!" Young Phorbas said that,
mopping his brow, as he and Theseus came up to Antiope. He had
been with them in the dark Unfriendly Sea and was now Theseus'
most trusted lieutenant.

"Until they get more arrows made." Theseus' voice was raw
with the bitterness born in him that summer.

Antiope thought, *They used no fire arrows until tonight, and I do not think
they will use any more,* but knew he would laugh if she said so.
Besides, she might be wrong.

She was right. On the dark slope below, Tarkun finally had
found Molpadia. Stone-hard, his eyes met hers that were hawk-
fierce. "Madwoman, the Great King's daughter is up there!"

"My sister's daughter is. Let her burn! Better that than for her
to live on as that dog's bitch."

"You Amazons count only the womb, not the seed, yet we are
here, we men of Subbiluliuma, because she sprang from his loins."
Tarkun's eyes were sharp as two knives now. "In Thrace we two

made a bargain, woman. Keep on breaking it, and you will have to fight me too."

Silence then. Silence that stretched between them, taut as any rope. Until at last Molpadia broke it, laughing bitterly, her eyes still blazing in her gaunt, gray face.

"That would be no new thing. You are both men, you and that dog whose cunning lured me to Troizen—those he hurt by doing that are only his womb-kin! Maybe both of you hoped I never would come back—all men are always the enemies of all women. But tonight I came back. The game is not yet over, Tarkun of the Hittites."

"Use no more fire arrows in it, woman."

He turned to go, but her voice stopped him. "That letter was a lie. As I should have known when it seemed that my scouts had failed to see Antiope leaving the Akropolis that night. You knew it was a lie—and you let me ride into the trap, and laughed!"

He turned again and faced her, hard and cold as any of the great figures his people carved upon the far-off Anatolian cliffs. "Woman, it was you who tricked me, bribing my interpreter to read you that letter and tell me nothing of it. An act he now regrets. Why were you so anxious to get your hands on Antiope without my knowing of it? What did you and she say that day you spoke together?"

"What we said was between Amazons. And the Goddess will show me how to reach her yet—even without fire arrows. Now go, you most accursed of all men but one!"

He went, cursing his own folly. Even though she had only just ridden in, sick and spent, his men should have had their usual orders to wake him if she did anything unusual.

I should have kept watch. I who know her.

More days dragged on, and no more fire arrows came. But there was no peace in the strong house of Erechtheus. Theseus saw little of his wife and boy during those last days of Metageitnion, when the golden, baking summer was over at last, and the nights were growing teeth. He was with his men, talking, planning. Antiope, knowing that he had finally had word from both Hippothoon and Elephenor, understood why she was left out of his councils, and was grateful. Yet, unreasonably, her exclusion hurt. Also she was afraid—both for him and for her people; the Amazons could not take much more. Of the Hittites, and their trained might, she dared not think. . . .

Hippolytos was lonely now, bereft of all his half-Amazon play-mates. Realizing how outnumbered he was, the Athenian children harried him in small ways. The Women were careful not to let big boys strike him; they feared Theseus' wrath. But he was big for his age, being also born of the Amazons, so many of his opponents were twice as old as he was. Antiope's proud little Horse-Looser went about like a small wild beast who knows the hunter's dogs are near, fierce yet wary. Several times, for all her watchfulness, blows were exchanged.

One day Theseus came in on what he chose to consider a fight, and laughed uproariously. "He will make a famous warrior! If you were just a few years older, how you would be helping Father now! Eh, child?"

He swung his son aloft, and Hippolytos delightedly crowed agreement. But the women glared and Antiope winced, glad though she was nowadays of anything that made either Theseus or their boy laugh. Later, when they were alone in the little chamber that was now their only real home and also their last refuge, she said gravely: "You would not want to fight Amazons, little king; they are Mother's people. You were born to make peace between men and women—to bring a new day. . . ."

Hippolytos laughed and agreed with her too; his spirits were still high from his father's visit. And she could not help laughing with him and at him.

Yet often sickening thoughts came to her, like black, huge birds tearing at her with their awful beaks. Theseus had seen the recent trouble as a fight between two Athenian boys, but his people had not. To Athens her son was an alien, an interloping upstart. Whatever glory Theseus won, it would be hard for the boy to make a place for himself among his father's people. And that would be bad for him, and for the Goddess' plans too. *Or did You ever really come to me, Lady, there beside that far-off river? Is Your curse on me, the sinner?*

She prayed, but only silence answered her, or rather the rasping, wearying noises that now always filled the strong house of Erech-theus. The scolding and weeping of the worried uncomfortable Women, the whining and angry crying of their cherished but now often slapped children. Antiope shrugged and thought, *Well, maybe that is all the answer my lack of faith deserves. Or is it still only the darkness within me that keeps Her out?*

The moon called Boedromion began, with cool nights and golden leaves, and one afternoon she and Hippolytos dozed. Whispering in the outer room woke her. Whispering as sinister, after all that ugly, petty noisiness, as the hissing of snakes.

"Did you hear what old Lord Habron said to King Theseus in council this morning? About *her?"* Habron was the oldest and most revered of the Butadai; the voice was a slave girl's.

"No." A young lady's voice, eager as that of one panting of thirst. "What was it?"

"He wanted the king to stop sleeping with her. He said, 'Even if she is loyal, she is a sword in the hands of the sons of Pallas. Their friends ask what will happen if our war leader is murdered in his sleep. To all of us.' "

"What did the Lord Theseus say then?" The voice that spoke whispered, but two girls squealed, half-choked, ecstatic noises.

"He said he would sleep with his wife, and not one or all fifty of the sons of Pallas had better try to stop him!"

"Oh-h!" More squeals. "Then what did the Lord Habron say?"

"He said, 'Well, take your pleasure if you must, but set guards at your door at night. With orders not to let her pass alone. And make sure she knows of those orders.' "

"That will make her behave!" Delighted giggles.

"But she really does not do anything anymore." Another voice, puzzled. "Now that the other Amazons are gone she stays quietly at home, just like a lady. Like a civilized woman. She does not seem dangerous."

"She is scared now!" Derisive giggles, a great many of them.

That last charge was too much for Antiope. Hawk-swift, she sprang up and darted out among the girls and women, who squealed and cowered before her. Her voice slashed at them. "Be still. Savage outland women sometimes kill squeaking rats!"

They fled, and she looked around the emptied room, and knew she had been a fool. Given them one more tale to tell.

"Women!" The Greek word was a sick, exasperated curse. *"Women!"* To her it meant only these who had long been her tormentors, not herself and her girls and all womankind.

The sense of eyes upon her made her turn. Her son stood there watching her, his brown eyes very big. He knew what Women were: silly, giggling slave girls and silly, spiteful ladies; by now he fully shared the Amazons' contempt for them. He also knew that for a long time something had been upsetting everybody, even Father, and making Mother unhappy. He had thought it was bad people outside the walls; people of whose names he was not sure. Could it be the Women? They often spoke in ugly voices of Amazons, and his mother and the mothers of his lost playmates were Amazons; he knew that. They did not like Amazons' little boys, either. . . .

Antiope did not quite like that wondering stare. She went back to him, smiling. "Let us go to sleep again, little king."

But something had been stamped ineffaceably upon Hippolytos' mind, the more surely because he was still very young.

Women were bad.

CHAPTER 10.
BEYOND THE WORLD'S END

W HEN THESEUS came to Antiope that night he did not set guards before their door. But the constraint in his voice went through her like a sword.

"Our allies are on their way at last. Before dawn I must rise to sacrifice before my men to Phobos. To the Power called black Fear."

In the dark he could not see her face, but he saw her eyes, and added quickly: "It is not an Amazon we will offer, beloved. Today we caught a young Hittite."

One of her father's men, the men he had sent to help her! But that sickening knowledge was not what, for a breath's space, almost stopped her heart within her. She knew what this offering to black Fear must mean. The battle—the great battle that she had hoped against hope might never be fought!

She broke her resolve to ask him no questions. She said, through stiff lips: "Then tomorrow you fight?"

"I have often fought before." He laughed and reached for her, but she pushed him away. "Not fighting such as this will be! Oh, my dearest, let me think—"

He laughed again, got into bed, and pulled her back to him. "Do not think, most beautiful! Women have much better business." His mouth found hers.

She said, "May the Goddess keep you, best-beloved!" and threw her arms around him. Soon his hands were seeking in all those secret places of her that knew and loved him, and before long, more than his hands. Man and woman, they loved each other with the wild tenderness and fierceness, the pain-sharp ecstasy of two people who know they may never love again.

But when at last he slept, she did think, staring sickly into the
darkness. He must be planning an early-morning attack, to keep
his enemies too busy to see the approach of his allies until the
newcomers were upon them. But the Athenians lacked the Hittite
discipline. They knew nothing of the planning and maneuvering
of great battles, of the deadly cunning of their foes. Quick and
keen as he was, he was young, her Theseus; could he outwit that
old fox Tarkun, wise in war?

Oh, beloved, if this is indeed the last of our nights together—! She kissed
his chest, his shoulders, his mighty arms. She let her mouth hover
over his mouth, breathe his breath. So warm, so steady—yet tomorrow night he might have no breath at all! *No! Oh, Goddess, have
pity! No!*

Her brain thrashed like a trapped animal. *I must wake him, talk with
him! Not to tell him what to do—he would not like that anyhow. But to warn
him against Tarkun's tricks—I do not know them all, but I do know some!
Against the openings he may give Tarkun.*

But how could she do all that without asking him about his
own plan of battle—and then correcting it, improving it? Plotting
against her own people?

Yet to withhold any help at all might mean his death. *She who
is upon one side cannot be upon the other. You must choose now—make up your
mind at last. For the truth is that you never have. Face that, you who are queen
of nobody and nothing now. As you should have done long ago.*

And she knew what her choice must be; she could not let him
die. . . .

Yet he was sleeping so peacefully now—quiet and satisfied,
after their love! To let him sleep a little longer would hurt nothing;
she would not be doing it to postpone her treachery to her people,
to those of her own blood who had come so far to help her. Also
when she did wake him she must be calm, able to think clearly,
choose her words carefully. She must not hurt his male pride.
. . . In the thick darkness she dozed herself, worn out. When she
woke the bed was empty beside her. . . .

In that corpse-gray, dismal dawn, the men of Athens watched
Theseus sacrifice to Phobos, to black Fear. With set face he cut the
young Hittite's throat. This was an ugly business; he knew well
what old Pittheus would call it—murder. But somehow he must
put heart into his people, them upon whom he had brought so

much woe. *Never would I have done it for myself, and never again will I let myself be caught in such a trap that I must do it.* In his heart he made that vow, and knew that if he broke it something within him would be more dead than the man who lay dead before him.

Yet this time you have done it, knowing it to be a great wrong, and for that you will surely pay. So a grim voice whispered within him, Pittheus' or his own soul's. Well, no matter. All that mattered now was to save his people, his city, his old father and his little son. To save Antiope from her beloved Amazons—from that pack of mad dogs who now howled for her blood.

Wet-eyed, old Aegeus blessed him. "May the Gods keep you, my son. Give you victory, and bring you back to me."

With half his men and all his chariots, Theseus sent young Phorbas, now his most trusted captain, out through the great gates, whose width gave speed by letting more men out at a time. With the rest he himself waited by the postern. Before Phorbas' men had more than begun to emerge he heard the hated, now familiar "Hip-PO-OL-y-TE-E! HIP-PO-OL-Y-TE-E!" Knew that the Amazons were pouring down from the Areopagos as a flooded river pours into the sea. They would be at the foot of the ramp before Phorbas was. With luck they would ride up to meet him, and so put themselves at a disadvantage—striking from below at those who struck at them from above. Then the Hittites would come to their help, and he, Theseus, could hurl himself upon them from the rear.

His plan worked. Once there would have been Amazons waiting for him below the postern, but now all who could still fight were before the main gates. Swift as hunting dogs who scent their quarry, he and his men rounded the Akropolis. Straight as thrown spears they struck the charging Hittites, sliced through the climbing foot soldiers as a knife slices through cheese. Men screamed with startled fear, and then with pain; some screamed in death. The Athenians shouted in triumph.

But then the Hittite chariots came, lumbering up with a terrible, clumsy sureness. Soon Theseus learned the truth of all Antiope's old warnings. One man, if quick and skilled, could hope to fell both riders in a Greek chariot. But these eastern chariots were different; the shieldbearer shielded both charioteer and fighter.

Theseus had thought that in his one brief brush with them he had learned to allow for that difference; laboriously, day after day, he had trained his swiftest men to meet them. But he had had no real way to make them see what he saw, no clear picture in his own mind except of pursuing chariots. And these were charging; they cut down his men and trampled them. Phorbas' chariots cut through the mounted Amazons and rushed to help them, but they were too light to meet the heavier chariots that carried half again as many men. Some, racing downhill as they were, did manage to crash into the enemy cars and overturn them, but were overturned themselves. Far more Hittite charioteers, practiced veterans of many battles, swerved aside and then turned to pursue their lighter foes, as dogs pursue deer.

Theseus yelled to Phorbas to go back, up toward the Akropolis, and to his own men to turn north. There, on the steep ground toward the Areopagos, he could make a stand. He broke through the Hittite lines, but the Amazons were after him like a swarm of stinging wasps. They had recognized him; like a single shrieking madwoman, monstrous, many-armed, they were riding down upon him, leaving the battle at the gates to their allies. Arrows were whizzing; he saw two men fall, neither with great wounds, and thought: *Once more those arrows are poisoned. The Death-singer rules.*

Behind the younger, lighter women who had outridden her, he saw her crest, and ground his teeth. He could get back to her—he could not be stopped, he felt that power within him—but killing her might take a while, woman though she was. And meanwhile those arrows would sting his men to death. He hurried them back, their shields high, their outthrust spears keeping off the foremost Amazons, who were more careful of their horses' hides than of their own. Not far away now were the great rocks—greater and more numerous even than in later days—that stood around the dark, dismal cleft through which once the Furies, those grim Goddesses older than all Gods, were said to have gone down into Earth Their Mother. *If we can get there we will be safe from the horses. We will have a chance!*

If they could hold until the help that was coming came, all might yet be well. Hippothoon and Elephenor and their men would come up behind those cursed chariots—*O Gods, let the Hittite charioteers be too startled to turn in time!* But if among the rocks he could meet Molpadia face to face at last—then, with the Deathsinger dead, the Hittites should be willing to lay down their arms and talk.

Those rocks were so near now! Yet to hold off his foes he had to fight every step of the way—fight as if he hated to yield every inch of ground that lay between him and his goal. And his men kept falling! But those in the rear were scrambling in among the rocks now. Out of the corner of his eye he saw that, and rejoiced. Hold a little longer—a little longer—until almost all of your men are in—

He reached the rocks at last. He laughed, his teeth shining white in his bronzed face. His eyes glowing like a lion's, he shook his dripping spear in the direction of Molpadia's crest. *Come on, hag—let us settle this between us! Then no more of my people need die!*

"We have him now! The slaver has finished himself!" So Molpadia exulted, laughing at Tarkun, whose chariot had clattered up over the stones behind her. "He is trapped—may the Goddess give him into our hands alive! But you—why do you not go back and crush those fools who wait up yonder, with their gates open?"

Tarkun stroked his beard. "That seems to be what they want me to try. I do not understand this. That Redhead never has been a fool before, young as he is."

"He is one now! So are you, who idle here!"

"Your head was cooler of old, Molpadia, when your loins were hotter. . . . Today that boy must have brought out every able-bodied man he has. Except for a few in the towers. Why take such a risk?"

Molpadia snorted. "You think he plans some trick? Expects friends to come and help him play it? He has no friends! Not one of all these cowardly Greek cities dares to help him!"

"Maybe not," said Tarkun dryly. "But before I send my chariots charging uphill—never a good thing to do—I will send out scouts. Make sure this boy's move does not mean what it would mean if I made it."

. . .

On the Akropolis all had heard the din of battle. All had become ears; any who had to move crept about as if afraid to make a sound —a sound that might prevent their hearing another more meaningful. The wishful few who took some war-cry to mean that son or brother, husband or father still lived were very few. Most knew all too well that in that terrible sea of sound all individual voices were lost, perhaps forever: mere drops of water—unspeakably precious water—that might even now be being swept away into black death.

But one thing was certain—the battle was not going as Theseus had hoped. Something had gone wrong.

In the little Court of the Women, for the last four moons so crowded, empty now save for her and Hippolytos, Antiope waited as all the women of Athens were waiting. Hippolytos was playing and getting himself dirty, very happily. He knew only that everything was as it should be again. He and Mother were alone. Their hateful enemies, the Women and their children, were gone.

Antiope knew where they were. The rebuilt roofs were crammed with breathless watchers; even the nursemaids and the children waited just below. She longed to be up there too, but feared to see Theseus kill an Amazon. Or—to see an Amazon kill him! If his unknown plans succeeded, if he came back, she would be too glad to see him to grieve for her broken, beaten people. She would do that later, in the long years to come. But would there be any years? They sounded triumphant, those cries of "HIP-POL-Y-TE-E-E! HIP-PO-OL-Y-TE-E!" Her war-cry. The dear sound that had come from her own throat so many times of old. Crashing against her ears now like the ending of her world. . . .

If Theseus did not come back— Her hand closed hard on her father's dagger. Under a light cloak she carried her sword. If Molpadia came for her she would fight. Not to kill Amazons—never could she do that!—but to draw her own death. *But let the Hittites come first, O Goddess—let them come first! Then my son will be safe; he will grow up a Hittite warrior.*

If the Amazons came first, she would have to kill him. He must not fall into Molpadia's hands.

Time passed; the gold of morning wore. The battle must be

farther from the city now, for the din had lessened. Surely the coming of Theseus' allies would have caused a great clamor. . . . Like icy water, fear soaked her. How awful it was to have to sit through a battle and wait! The worst fighting could be nothing beside such torture.

Then—lightning-sudden, awful as lightning—she heard startled, dismayed cries inside the Akropolis itself.

A scout Phorbas had sent out through the postern had crawled back, hurt, up the ramp that led to the main gates. The chariots that now barred that way to all able-bodied men had let him pass; the Hittites were still sparing the Athenian wounded. Two of Phorbas' men had rushed down to his rescue; Phorbas had heard his tale, then had him carried up to the strong house of Erechtheus, to tell his grim tale again.

Antiope left Hippolytos with a slave girl, one of those who had once been friendly. Only fear of the Women had changed this one. Antiope was thankfully sure of that when she saw the delight in the girl's face, the way she looked at Hippolytos. *Did we keep him to ourselves too much? Should his father's people have had more chance to know him—and he them?* No woman but an Amazon ever had been allowed to touch him; memory of that attempt to poison her had made her afraid—not for herself, but for him. Trustworthy girls might have been simple enough to trust the untrustworthy, those who had been bribed. . . . Yet what did all that—or indeed, anything else—matter now? Antiope took one last look at her boy, then ran as if the winds were truly her shoes. And as she ran, she heard the distant slamming of the great gates—knew that Phorbas and his men must all have retreated within them.

In the great *megaron* she found old Aegeus wailing and calling upon his Gods. The old men around him looked at her sourly and did not speak. But young men were there too—bending over another young man, who lay there, bloody and panting. They told her simply, "King Theseus is trapped."

She brought wine and helped them give it to the wounded man. Then, through Aegeus' wailing, her questions shot, arrow-swift, arrow-straight. "Where is he? How many men are still with him?"

"The Gods know how many. Or how few. He is in—or near—

the cleft of the Goddesses of old. He came on the Hittites from
behind—as he had meant to do. But their chariots mowed men
down like grain. But he is brave and mighty, the Lord Theseus—
he got many of them away. Toward the cleft—"

I should have warned him. But to think that was useless now, and
besides, she had warned him about the Hittite chariots. She said
swiftly: "His allies? They have not come?"

"No, Lady; they—never will. The Hittite chariots have driven
them back—they flounder in the waters of the Ilissos and the
Eridanos. They cannot get past those terrible chariots." He
stopped and she gave him more wine. But her eyes and voice, more
than the wine, brought him back. He stumbled on: "They should
have come long ago. The smoke of sacrifice above the Akropolis
—that was to be the signal. But they did not come—and they did
not come. And Phorbas sent me out—to see—if they were coming.
But it was—no use. The Hittites had stopped them—"

His head fell back. Over his limp body Antiope started fiercely
at his comrades. "Phorbas! Why does he not try to help his king?"

Until then they had surprised themselves by answering as if she
were their lord. Now their eyes grew hard; they were Phorbas'
men. "He tried, woman. But as our chariots charged out, a thrown
stone struck his head. He lies mindless and groaning now."

And no other would try. Looking into the grim eyes of the old
men, Antiope knew that. They would say that all the young men
were needed to guard the city now. To crouch here and wait for
their foes to batter in their gates and butcher them as Theseus
would already have been butchered—oh, the fools, the fools! But
words were useless now.

Deer-swift, she sprang up and ran again. She heard Aegeus'
voice behind her, calling upon all to open the gates and follow him
to his son. But she knew none would heed him; he was old, and
his power, long a shadow, today had become only a memory.

At the great gates she found only leaderless, miserable men. But
she did find her own white horses, that Phorbas himself had had
today; no chariot horses could have been spared in this battle.
Nobody had even unhitched them; nobody opposed her when she
led them away. She talked to them as she went: "Be brave, my
white ones, my fine ones. We will be together—"

She came to the postern. The guards there were young men,

each of whom limped, or had a useless arm. She cried to them, "Open! I go to my man!"

They stared dumbfounded, many jaws dropping. But one of them, like Phorbas, had been on that voyage to the dark Unfriendly Sea. He hobbled to the gate, answering a comrade's protest shortly: "Man, even if she wanted to do harm, what harm is there left for her to do? Maybe some God has come down to help Theseus through her. Only the Gods can, now." Every guard helped with the gates then; of all in Athens, the young men seem to have been the least set against Antiope.

Both outer and inner gates swung open, and she sped through, calling her thanks. Long afterward those men who had seen her go told their children and grandchildren of that last ride of the Amazon. Of how she had looked like a Goddess come down from star-high heaven, proudly straight as a young tree, her sunlit hair flying in the wind, golden bronze above the white, flying manes of her horses.

Down that steep way never meant for horses she plunged at full speed, the quiet power in her voice and hands holding her team steady. Halfway down she had to swerve to avoid a man who was plodding wearily upward. With hate-filled eyes he looked up at her. "So now you go back to your own, treacherous bitch?"

"I go to my man. Not away from him."

Under her steady eyes a dull flush burned his gray face. "Lady, I could not keep up with him. That Demon-Queen, your aunt, tried—she made her horse go where surely no horse ever went before."

"And then?" Antiope's voice was almost a whisper.

"He wounded her, and her she-wolves carried her away. But they have him penned. They are howling for his blood, and soon they will drink it."

"Then they must drink mine with it. Joy be with you!" She sped on, and for a breath's space he looked after her, then plodded on, blood seeping out sluggishly onto his stained tunic.

Over stones and around rocks her chariot careened. Hittite chariots were still massed before the main gates of the Akropolis, but she saw no other Hittites; had Tarkun not wanted to be in on the kill?

But she heard the fierce shrieking of her Amazons, before that black chasm under the stony brow of the Areopagos. And as she drew nearer the quality of that shrieking withered all hope within her. For she had hoped—had meant to call to the Amazons from a distance, offer to trade them herself for Theseus. Perhaps she had hoped against hope to do more than that—after all, the wounded Amazons had still loved her. But no human voice could ever pierce that din, that dehumanized howling.

In vain You gave us speech, O Goddess. We are still making beast-noises, killing each other because we cannot understand each other. Well, forgive me for not having served You better—and watch over Hippolytos, who may.

She had no thunder and lightning, like the big, noisy Gods men believed in. But she had her chariot. With set teeth she drove it forward, straight as a thrown spear. Straight into the now dismounted mob that milled and howled around the great stones.

Screaming with pure surprise, startled Amazons leaped to either side of it as it clattered down upon them. She cut through them like a scythe, sword in hand now. If she must, she would whip them back with it, though to do so would hurt her deeply. She saw the rocks, close and near. *Oh, Theseus, if only a few of your Athenian chariots would have followed me!* She could have saved him then. Now there was only a slim chance—a very, very slim chance—that if he and his men rushed out quickly enough, they could be well on their way to the Akropolis before the Amazons could remount and turn upon them.

Then it happened. One Amazon's backward leap was not quite quick enough. The chariot, passing over human flesh, lurched almost to overturning. Beneath her wheels, Antiope heard the death-cry of one of her own people.

Sick with horror, she looked down into all those known, loved faces, and saw all of them accuse her. Saw them all turn into one face. An aged, terrible Face, unspeakably tortured, burned and blasted, yet still aflame with quenchless hate—the Hive-Spirit's own Face. From every head she could see, that Face glared up at her. Its wearers no longer leaped away from her, but forward. Her great white stallions screamed as many blades pierced them. That was the horror that almost broke her—never before had Amazons hurt horses except when sacrificing them! Blindly she struck out to protect them, and felt her sword, whose point she had forgotten, sink deep. Another Amazon screamed, horribly. Then many hands had her, dragged her down. Were they trying to take her alive for Molpadia? Her arms and legs and body, even her hair, were held fast, but her sword was still in her hand. She squirmed and twisted, trying to prick with it. If only she could make them angry enough to kill her here and now—

A different cry rose shrill above the howling, as if in protest. Another body pushed desperately between those that held her— surely she knew that voice! It turned into an awful, gurgling groan, as the force of its own thrust spitted it on Antiope's still upraised sword. Then indeed the howling rose to high heaven, louder than she had ever dreamed any noise could be. It filled her swimming head, it seemed to fill the earth. The din had changed; new voices seemed to be ringing through it, men's voices. No, that could not be. Then a thrusting spear darted across her and again an Amazon screamed—on one head that glaring Face became only a woman's face again, twisted in pain, and pitiful. Two of the hands that grasped her hair fell away.

It was a man's voice shouting now—Antiope knew that voice, and bitter resentment surged through her. *Will he make all I have done go for nothing? Even you, my white ones, my brave ones?* She could hardly bear to think of her horses; she could not bear to think of the Amazons she had killed. And now more must die—Theseus would not go down without taking many of his foes with him.

Then Theseus himself stood over her, his sword whirling. Fresh blood was dripping from it, Amazon blood, and she closed her eyes. More cries, more blows. And then he had her—his tawny eyes, blazing down into hers, seemed to burn them open. His hands were clutching her as hard as those others had—she knew that clutch. For a wild breath's space she thought she was back again on that ship in the dark Unfriendly Sea, fighting him who had betrayed her. He was carrying her, and his men were closing in around him. Swords were clashing, and women shrieking—her Amazons. But this time they were not trying to rescue her—they hated her now.

Perhaps the pain of that knowledge made her faint—even she who had been Antiope, Queen of the Amazons. Who was still Antiope. . . . She knew nothing until the rocks closed around them. Until he laid her down, and began anxiously feeling over her for wounds. Swords were still clashing behind them—his men were holding off her Amazons, who must be trying to scramble up into the rocks after them. Who were screaming like starved beasts whose food has just been torn away from them.

He was breathing hard, the breath was hissing in his throat, but when she sat up and pushed him away from her it became a great, ragged gasp of relief.

"Antiope—"

She cried angrily: "You are back again—back in this trap I tried so hard to get you out of!"

He answered harshly, "Be still. This is no time for talk," and went back to his men.

Time became mist. But still there was fighting, shrieking. Two more Amazons screamed and died, and when the first fell Antiope half sprang up—this was one of her people and needed her help —then, sickeningly, remembered . . . *Amazon you are no more.* An Athenian fell, and was dragged into shelter, and she bandaged his hurt as best she could. But her eyes never really saw him; he was not Theseus. Her ears heard only the crying of her own people and her heart wept for their pain.

Then a great new shouting came: "The-SEUS! THE-SEUS!" Voices still far off were crying that name, and her heart leaped. Men in the towers must have seen what had happened and told those within. The men of Athens had taken heart and were coming to their king.

Like the wind that cry came, nearer, ever nearer. "The-SEUS! THE-SEUS! Anti-O-PE!" But they never would have cried her name; she had only imagined that help was coming. Disappointment came, bitter as a knife twisting in her flesh.

Yet still the cry came—it was real! Her Amazons were turning, knowing they had new foes to face, and again pain for them lanced through. And now Theseus and his men were yelling in triumph, running out of the sheltering rocks.

Oh, Theseus, what if you are killed? Oh, my people! Again her heart seemed torn in two within her. She rocked back and forth in pain terrible as that of childbirth had been.

The yells of hate, the cries of pain—they were within her now, and would be always, as long as she lived. Were her Amazons being defeated? She feared so, hoped so, then heard yet another great cry—men shouting in victory.

Theseus came running back, his whole face one blaze of joy, bright as the sun upon his hair. He seized her, dragged her out into the open. There were men around them—men everywhere. She saw Phorbas, pale, his head bandaged, but grinning proudly. Had he roused and rallied the rescuers? No matter; Theseus was safe. He was alive! Alive!

He still had her by the arms, concerned, but yelling at her. "Madwoman, are you hurt?"

She shouted back at him, herself again, "No more than you are! What do you think I am? One of your tame, house-bred Women, to sit in the house and shed tears while you shed blood?"

If he made any answer, she never heard it. More Athenians were coming up—back from chasing Amazons. Her Amazons—beaten, broken, gone like the foam from broken waves. Shadows, being swept back into shadowland; shadows now forever. . . .

They were happy, the men of Athens. They had their young king back, and he had his queen, loyal and no foe. Joyously they cried her name too—this time there could be no doubting it. "AN-TI-O-PE! THE-SEUS!"

She heard them, and her heart sang. They loved her at last, her man's people. She forgot, for that brief space, the queer agony of that battle in which her sword had seemed to be plunged into her own flesh. Theseus was yelling at her and she at him, but that did not matter. The loveliness beneath was too near the surface of their rage. There was no future, only the glorious now.

"You might have been killed!" Theseus shouted, and she answered, "So might you!" She reached up to put the disheveled hair back from her bruised face. The movement raised her arm above her head.

Swift as light, deadly as lightning, the arrow flashed between them. It pierced her armpit, where there was no armor, and went on, deep into her body. She fell across Theseus' arm. He slid to his knees with her, holding her close in his arms.

She spoke once: "Make peace with my people—if you can. I have—killed—Amazons—for you. And they—have killed me. It is just. *Chaire"*—the Greek word used for both greeting and farewell —*"chaire,* best-beloved! Joy be with you, and—with—Hip-polytos."

There was silence then, there beneath the brooding, stony

heights of the Areopagos. Until, from the place where her warriors had laid her, Molpadia the Deathsinger, the War-Queen, raised her voice in the death-wail for the young queen, whom she had slain. The voices of all Amazons still alive joined hers.

Antiope, Queen of the Amazons, had gone to a country beyond the World's End.

CHAPTER 11.

AFTERWARDS

ON THE field called in after-ages Horkomoseion, "The Swearing of the Oath," Theseus made peace with the armies of the East. The Amazons wanted only one thing now: their queen's body to be laid in the earth like those of her foremothers, and Theseus knew that she would have wished it so. He made only one condition: "So long as she lies here, in the land where her child was born." And they answered, "Not indoors, not walled up in stone, like your stranger kings. Let her lie in the open, where she fell. Under the sky that also covers Themiskyra, where she was born."

So they buried her near a shrine of Earth the Mother, Her from Whose breast all come and to which all return. Long after, indeed more than a century after Christ was born, much-traveled Pausanias was to write of how in Athens he was shown the grave of Antiope the Amazon. Evidently the Athenians had learned to be proud of the woman their forefathers had feared and hated while she lived.

But that first evening, after the day of battle, when Theseus came back to his desolate palace, he knelt beside their bed and hid his face in it; sobbed as Hippolytos might have sobbed had Hippolytos understood. Only last night she had lain there, warm and lovely and alive. How could so much life be dead?

For many days magnificent funeral games were held, all three armies honoring her who was gone. On the last day golden Chrysippe was brought out—the steed of Antiope's girlhood, led riderless all this long way in the hope that her mistress might ride her home again. The frightened mare reared and struggled, but iron hands held her and in the end Molpadia cut her throat. Theseus turned his head away, knowing how Antiope would have hated that deed.

On that same day letters finally came from far Hattusas. In silence Tarkun read them, then smiled wryly at Theseus. "A week ago this would have been good news for you, Redhead. The Great King bids me stop fighting and treat with you until I can get speech with his daughter—find out where her heart lies."

Theseus groaned. "Then if I had only waited—"

"Not many fighting men would have. And you have the makings of a great fighting man in you, lad, though you still have much to learn."

Once those last words would have cut Theseus' fiery pride. Now he said only: "I am still glad. She thought that it was too late to let her father know the truth—that his treaty with the Amazons would still have bound him to fight against her."

"He never would have given a fig for that treaty once the Amazons had turned on her." Tarkun sighed. "We have all been caught in a bitter web of mischances. Never would he have taken such risks—sent an army so far from home—had he dreamed that Antiope was not being held against her will. And how could he have doubted that, knowing the Amazons? Once we came here I myself soon had doubts, but not enough of them until I learned of that letter my interpreter had been bribed not to tell me of." For a breath's space his jaw set hard. "When he told me what was in it —eager to save some pieces of his skin—I told your cousin Lykophron. Let him send you that message. I am used to sizing up men, and I had seen that he had no great taste for his father's plots. A pity you two cannot stand together as kinsmen should."

"Many things are a pity," said Theseus bitterly. "But I thank you for that message; it may have saved my kindred in Troizen from death. . . . That bitch of a Molpadia! And all the others too. They all tried to kill Antiope while she lived—they who mourn so loudly for her now that she is dead."

"Not all. One tried to help her—Marpe, I think her name was —and died for it, by mischance spitted on your lady's own sword."

"One out of the whole host—one!"

"They had come a long way for her, lad. Giving up much and enduring much. Molpadia never could have brought them to lift a hand against her if she had not ridden against them at the last."

"To save me! She loved me—but she loved them too. Would to all the Gods that they were all dead—that my sword had pierced her accursed hag of an aunt's heart instead of only wounding her! Then Antiope would be alive—alive!" Theseus' voice broke; he covered his face with his hands.

Tarkun said quietly: "For Molpadia that death would have been best. She has dealt herself a wound that can never heal. You, who are young, will presently take another woman, though now it seems as if the sun had fallen out of the sky."

"There is no other woman like Antiope! And Molpadia—never can that iron heart of hers know grief."

"It can. She is human. She was a good lover once—do not look at me like that, Redhead; I know what I am talking about. Long ago there was a moon when she and I lay down together every night, and hated to see the morning. But then some fool called her my woman, and she turned from me. I think that never again has she lain with the same man for two nights running."

Theseus stared, remembering. "Then were you the father of that boy of hers? Of that baby she sent off to die? Then how could you bear to ride all this long way beside her? Even seem to bow your will to hers?"

Tarkun smiled wryly. "I was the only man Subbiluliuma could trust not to get into a war with her on the way. And for the task we thought we had we needed the Amazons badly—he did not want any more Hittites to die than could be helped."

"You should have strangled her with your own hands! Years ago, on your boy's grave."

"Certainly many lives would have been saved if I had. But our son is avenged. In trying to keep the Law of the Amazons she has broken all other laws, and herself too."

"An accursed law—an accursed race! Both should end."

"Soon they will. You have dealt them their deathblow, boy. Or maybe Otrere did, wise queen though she seemed to be. Change may come quietly in the beginning, like the pebble that looses an avalanche. But once truly begun, it cannot be stopped. Well, my king will grieve for his girl."

But Theseus thought that his own grief for Antiope was greater than any other grief on earth ever could be.

That night he could not rest. His solitary bed, the silent night, all seemed full of her who was not there. More clearly than when it had lain on the pillow beside him, he saw her face. The sweet mouth and strong chin, the clear eyes. All the loveliness and dearness of her who was gone forever. The fires within him always burned too hotly to let him keep still long. Late that night he rose and went to the postern, then down to the Place of the Furies, of the dread Goddesses. To the earth that covered all that beauty and bravery. Here, near what was left of her, she might seem nearer. . . .

But another already sat beside the grave. So quietly that at first he took her for only another shadow, black and still as the rocks above her. Like the heart of the night she looked as she sat there, sick and lined and old, dead as dead Antiope.

"Molpadia!" He ground the name between his teeth. His breath caught hard, in a hissing gasp.

She looked up at him, and the hate came back into her haggard face. "Be glad, man of Athens. Your sword pierced my lung that day. I cough blood, and soon I will die."

"Then I thank all Gods that the sword was mine, woman!"

"It was, O destroyer of all we Amazons have fought for and built through the ages. But I still would find strength enough to make you follow her—you whose doing all this is!—if she had borne no child. You are his father, and he will need you. Men forget easily; you will take other women, and cease to long for her —but if ever you cease to cherish him may you lose all you have on earth! May you die in shame and ruin, and your ghost sit chained in darkness and filth forever."

"You dare say that to me—*you!*" Theseus' fists clenched.

"I have said it. Remember what you owe the child, you most accursed of men. The mother died for you."

"By whose hand?" Again Theseus ground his teeth. "I know how to guard what is mine. But you—you carried her in your arms and held her on your knees when she was little, and she thought you loved her!"

"I have killed her," said Molpadia grimly, "and I still love her. Pray to all your Gods, Athenian, that you may never know such grief as that."

"How could you do it? How?"

"I did not know, until she fell, how it would seem to know that she was no longer in the world."

For a little while both were silent, Theseus glad of her grief, yet full of baffled hate. He could not kill her now; the treaty bound him. His people needed peace. Besides—and that thought was good—death might shorten her suffering.

Molpadia said at last: "She killed Marpe—Marpe, who had been her dearest friend. Together they learned to ride and shoot. I doubt if she ever even knew what she had done—she who thought only of you. . . . Truly it is terrible, a devouring flame, the love between women and men. Even if all else should change—the sun set in the east, and men cease trying to enslave women—still all who love them would be hurt when a woman and a man come together. Friends, kindred, those who bore and nourished the lovers. Such love breaks many bonds for every one it forges. And for the woman it must always forge bondage."

"How do you know what it would forge—you who denied it? You, who would make all women harlots! That fate at least I saved her from. Go—and my curse with you!"

"And mine with you," said Molpadia, "if ever you fail the babe that was born of her."

She rose then, and walked off through the night, majestic as a great king's corpse. Theseus never saw her again.

The wounded Amazons who still lived were brought back from Chalkis. A few had died there, and their graves too were shown to future generations. Antiope's own six Amazons came back and wept over her grave, and over sad, bewildered little Hippolytos. Then they took their daughters and went to the Areopagos. Their sons they left with the fathers—when they knew who these were. The rest were adopted into honorable Athenian families. Many homes in Athens lacked sons now.

"Our kin are with the host," the six told Theseus, "and the friends of our youth. And Molpadia's feet are already set upon the hill."

He hated to see them go. They too had loved Antiope; they would have reared her baby as she would have wished him reared. And in their arms he could have felt more faithful to her than in other women's. They too hated to go; although none of them would have slept with him while he belonged to their queen, not one of them but would have liked to try him now. Also all of them wept more over leaving Hippolytos than over leaving their own sons. But their hearts heard the call of their own people, from whom no Amazon might lawfully live apart. . . . And Molpadia did die before they left Greek lands. Learned Pausanias says that her grave too was shown in Athens, but certainly Theseus would have refused to let her lie near Antiope. More likely she died on the Isthmus, where Hittites and Amazons together waited for ships from Troy. There too the grave of a Queen of the Amazons is known. But where the warrior women went, after their return to the East, no man knows. They must have been too few to retake Themiskyra; some say they took Skythian husbands, and bred a warrior race called the Sauromatai, whose men and women fought side by side. Others say they kept to their old customs, but retreated into mountain fastnesses of the Kaukasos. One who called herself Penthesileia, Queen of the Amazons, did later try to help besieged Troy. But she may have led a band of homeless wanderers, who raided when and where they could, even stooping to hire out their swords to men. Before windy Troy great Achilles is said to have exterminated the whole race of the Amazons, just as Herakles was said to have done the same thing before Themiskyra, and Theseus before God-built Athens. Greek heroes seem to have made a habit of exterminating the Amazons, who were too stubborn to realize that they had been wiped out and kept on fighting. Only the shining haze of legend has finally succeeded in swallowing them up. . . .

But Theseus was left alone with his old father and his baby son, with a hurt city and a hurting heart. He had withstood power greater than ever before had been arrayed against the western world. Not until the Persian invaders came would an empire of the East menace the West again, and then many Greek city-states together would fight it, not one. Theseus had kept his city, but he had lost his wife. . . .

All through that ghost-white winter, whenever the winds screamed around the Akropolis, he heard the voices of young Athenians shrieking while the bulls of Minos gored them. It would happen; the Ninth Horai was near, and he could do nothing. His burned ships lay beneath the blue waters around Troizen; all his hopes and plans were in ashes too.

Spring came, in warm loveliness. The Maid came back to the

Mother, as Antiope never would come back to those who loved her. And northward across the wine-dark sea the Cretans came, vulturelike in their black ships, to claim their prey. The doomed were chosen, as Theseus had sworn they never again should be. Heartsick and ashamed, he sat beside bowed Aegeus, his little son on his lap, and thought of those other parents whose sons were old enough to make sport for Cretan bulls. Into his boy's shining curls he whispered low, with stubborn, indomitable fierceness, "There will be another Ninth Horai!"

Words spoken not in fear, but as a threat. . . .

He could not foresee then what was to come. Himself in the bull ring at Knossos, and a young girl's face watching him, full of love and wonder and pity. He still saw only one woman's face clearly. Many other women would be his bedfellows, some would be his wives, but he had lost the one woman who would ever be his mate.

All he longed for then, holding her little son close, was ships—more ships. His love was gone, but his foes remained.

THE STORY OF THE AMAZON, AND THE BEGINNING OF THESEUS' WARS.

___AUTHOR'S NOTE

WERE THERE real Amazons? Their existence has been much denied, but so once was the reality of Troy, and also of America, and the tradition persists. The Romans had to fight with such unusual savagery to conquer their Themiskyra that no archaeological remains are left. Could it have been a lingering residue of Amazon blood, Amazon courage, that made the defense so hard to break? Maybe the reality was simply one of those northern tribes in which women fought beside their men, if needed. In just one sentence Plutarch says that the Amazons did not enter Attica alone, but with Scythian allies. But could not a real race of women warriors have sprung from the few fugitive survivors of such a massacre of women by their own men as Joseph Campbell tells of in the first volume of his *Masks of God?* That would account for their traditional hatred of men; Plutarch's late tale of Tanais does not. To me it smells of whitewash.

Archaeology has resurrected the mighty, long-forgotten empire of the Hittites, who would have been neighbors of the Amazons. In his essay "Mursil and Myrtilos" the late distinguished H. R. Hall suggested that the Hittites were the real invaders of Attica. That seems unlikely, since they were always an inland power, but Subbiluliuma, greatest of Hittite Great Kings, did live and reign about the time Knossos fell. His organization of leagued vassal states could easily have inspired Theseus' famed federation of Attic city-states. Information that could have been gained from a half-Hittite bride.

We may never know the real truth about Theseus, but he was

deeply imbedded in the Athenian national consciousness. There was a great revival of interest in him after the Persian war, when his ghost was said to have risen to help the Athenians at Marathon. May not that tale have come from the common people, whose ancestors he was said to have helped? The nobles, whose ancestors' power he had traditionally curbed, may have remembered him less fondly. Also, as a son of Poseidon, he would have lost prestige after the triumph of Zeus worship. Brotherly love between the two gods was a late-Greek concept; Pindar's Delian ode shows a very different state of affairs.

I differ from Plutarch, his most complete biographer, in making Antiope Theseus' first wife. But fragments of Euripides' lost play about Theseus' Cretan exploits show that the child Hippolytos was a character, and he could not very well have been born before his parents met. And Euripides wrote before Plutarch.

Since the archaeological picture keeps changing I decided to be vague about some things, like the God of Delphi's name. So far neither Apollo nor Aphrodite has been named in the famed Linear B tablets—unlike Zeus, Poseidon, and Artemis—and Aphrodite I had to have. Theseus' life story has become too entangled with classical beliefs and customs for her to be left out. Also the Mycenaeans of his day must have had some name for so great a Power.

Apia (here the older name is known) cannot have been renamed the Peloponnese until after Atreus, son of Pelops, became King of Mycenae. I have also followed Robert Graves' view of Tantalos, Pelops' father, as given in his *Greek Mythology*. It seems to conform to an older stratum of ideas, and makes Tantalos a worthy grandfather for Pittheus.

Crete's use of Delphi to dominate the Greek mainland is, as far as I know, entirely my own idea. Or, rather, my own deduction.

The ancient writers contain many curious and suggestive passages, and I am one of those who think they also generally contain a germ of truth, however well buried. Below are a few of those which have most influenced me.

"On entering the city one sees a monument to Antiope the Amazon. . . . The Athenians say that when the Amazons came Antiope was shot by Molpadia, and that Theseus killed Molpadia." Pausanias, Book I.

"Their marriage law [that of the Sauromatai, believed descendants of the Amazons] forbade any girl to wed until she had slain a man in battle." Herodotus, Book V.

"I tremble at the mighty-sounding war between Zeus and Poseidon. Once with trident and thunderbolt they sent down a land . . . into Tartarus." Pindar, ode. A possible allusion to the catastrophe of Thera, earlier called Kalliste?

"[Upon] Cretans of Knossos Apollo, son of Zeus, smiled and said: 'Keep My Temple [at Delphi], and show My will to mortal men.' " Homeric hymn to Apollo.

"Kleidemos gives a somewhat strange . . . account going a long way back . . . how the Greeks had a law that *no ship might sail from any port with a crew of over five men.*" Plutarch, *Vita Thesaeus*. Italics are mine.

"In secret, Antiope sent some of the wounded Amazons to Chalkis, to be tended there." Plutarch, *Vita Thesaeus*.

"Men of Troizen . . . than whom none are louder praisers of their homeland, say that Oros was the first man born there. But to me that name sounds Egyptian." Pausanias, Book II. (Oros was the usual Greek for Horus, in Egypt the Divine Son.)

"My sister, whom I, the Sun, have given you for wife, has many [term used to designate kinswomen?]. They are now your sisters. . . . No brother may lie with his sister or female cousin. In Hattusas he who does such a deed shall die." Letter of Subbiluliuma to his brother-in-law the King of Azzi. A genuine Hittite document which gave me several ideas.

I have omitted Diodoros Siculus' very significant but rather long-winded writings about how all civilized arts, even speech, originated in Crete.